Happy Hour

JACQUIE BYRON

This edition published in 2023
First published in 2021

Allen & Unwin
83 Alexander Street
Crows Nest NSW 2065
Australia
Phone: (61 2) 8425 0100
Email: info@allenandunwin.com
Web: www.allenandunwin.com

A catalogue record for this book is available from the National Library of Australia

ISBN 978 1 76106 821 8

Set in Minion Pro by Bookhouse, Sydney
Printed in Australia by McPherson's Printing Group

10 9 8 7 6 5 4 3 2 1

The paper in this book is FSC® certified. FSC® promotes environmentally responsible, socially beneficial and economically viable management of the world's forests.

PRAISE FOR

Happy Hour

'Charming and highly intelligent example of good commercial fiction.'—*The Age/SMH*

'This is a bristling, fearless, funny look at loss.'—*Australian Women's Weekly*

'Hilarious and poignant.'—Mary Moody, bestselling author of *Au Revoir*

'High-quality general fiction that offers nuggets of wisdom and an entertaining ride for readers of all ages.'—*Books + Publishing*

'Told with humour and warmth, Happy Hour is a heartfelt story of grief, loss, true love and friendship. It's a fantastic debut from Byron that will leave you laughing and crying and wishing for more.'—*Better Reading*

'What a fabulous debut! Happy Hour caught my attention and held it right from the get-go, and I couldn't help but adore the cantankerous, loveable and ultra-fashionable main character.'—Maya Linnell, bestselling author of *Bottlebrush Creek*

'*Happy Hour* was thoroughly charming. Tears and laughter. Loved the relationships formed especially between Franny and the kids next door. Josh's storyline . . . was excellent and so beautifully done—I don't want to give any spoilers *Happy Hour* absolutely hit the spot, heartwarming, uplifting as well as exploring grief. Fantastic debut & great read.'—R.W.R McDonald, bestselling author of *The Nancy's*

'I found myself barracking for Franny all the way.'—Susan Duncan, author of bestselling *Salvation Creek*

'This is really good fun.'—Jane Harper, bestselling author of *The Dry*

JACQUIE BYRON grew up with wishing-chairs and Trixie Belden. Her love of reading morphed into a love of writing, leading her to study journalism while waitressing her way around various bars and tables in Melbourne and, for a short stint, the UK. Collecting and sharing stories has kept her busy professionally for more than twenty-five years, taking her from the Ogden Museum in New Orleans to an IDP camp in Uganda. Shocking herself as much as those around her, Jacquie has been a motoring writer, a jewellery editor, a fashion publicist and more. Today she writes for business and for pleasure. *Happy Hour* is her first novel. Whisky is her first cairn.

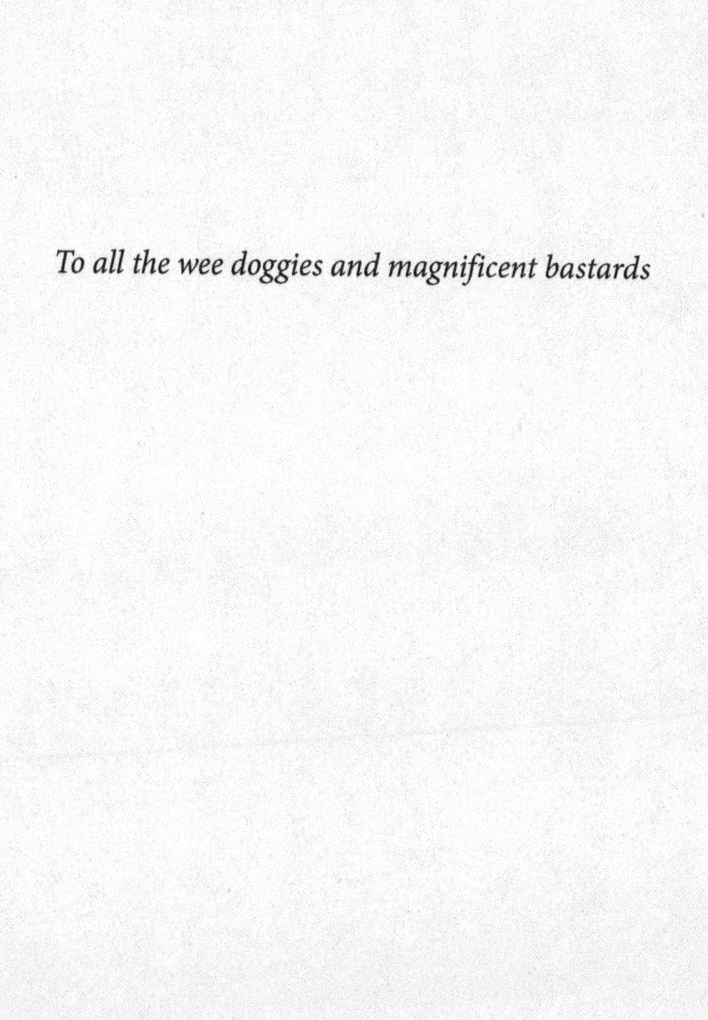

To all the wee doggies and magnificent bastards

1

Frank talking

She wrapped a third ziplock bag around the dog droppings, placed the insulated pile inside a plastic express-post envelope, sealed that and placed the whole thing neatly on the bottom shelf of her refrigerator. Though confident contamination was not an issue, Franny decided a dose of bleach throughout her Fisher & Paykel the next day would not go astray. She made a mental note to do that, but not before she had shoved the whole fragrant bundle in a post box somewhere random, away from prying eyes. And nostrils.

Now her priority was a stiff Tanqueray. Eyes shifting to the clock above the fridge, she breathed out, seeing once again she had made it to six o'clock.

'Praise the Lord and pass the mustard!' She reached for her mobile phone, switched it to silent, then stashed it inside the cutlery drawer. The last two days had been unexpectedly rough, her emotions in tumult since the arrival of a letter from The Evil Prick who had killed her Frank. Who wouldn't need a bloody gin?

Some people said the nights were the worst, but Franny disagreed. Almost daily she found herself watching the kitchen clock as it inched towards six, ready to exhale that guilty sigh.

People's thoughts turned inwards as the sun began to set. There was dinner to think of or grandkids to wrangle, night classes to pack for and mind-numbing amateur theatre to attend. Caring phone calls, sundry tender interference, would abate and Franny could crack open the gin and fire up the Netflix. Finally, and luxuriously, she could wallow in style.

'Alrighty you two, quit the carry-on. Dinner's just around the corner,' she said to her dogs, Whisky and Soda, a cairn terrier and golden retriever respectively, now both on their hind legs beside her, nails scraping against the kitchen cupboard. She sliced lemon for her drink then used her leg to heave both dogs sideways so she could reach across to place a glass tumbler beneath the ice maker in the refrigerator door. Four cubes descended with a reassuring clink.

'You know, if either of you could make a decent G and T, you'd have more sway,' she muttered to the dogs, topping up the glass with just a splash of tonic then taking a noisy, appreciative sip. 'See what I have to put up with, Frank?' she said, holding the glass up to the ceiling in a form of cheers. 'On top of everything else I have to make all the bloody drinks.'

Frank Calderwood, Franny's husband and fellow pre-prandial drinks aficionado, had been dead almost three years but Franny maintained a steady dialogue. Photos of the man populated various rooms of the largish house they once shared. Kitchen Frank, who she was chatting to now, in his frame atop the microwave, was in his thirties, armed with barbecue tongs, dressed in an apron festooned with pendulous breasts. Laundry Frank was a man in his fifties, hair thinning and brown legs stretched out on a sun lounge, his sleeping face covered by a delicately placed pair of women's underpants. Bedroom Frank was a pensive young chap. He gazed prettily through the window of a Tuscan pensione, pen in mouth, a well-thumbed travel guide on the table beside him. There was no photo-Frank in the backyard where Franny loved to potter. Out there she just chatted to the open air.

Franny refused to consider the habit odd. It wasn't as if she was expecting an otherworldly response; even the idea of that made her arm hairs stand on end. No, it was just that she'd been speaking to Frank for over forty years. Why stop now? And, as she'd tell anyone who asked, not that there really was anyone to ask, 'It's not like he always responded when he was alive.'

Frank had been knocked off his bicycle one night while riding home from the supermarket. He was sixty-five and in robust health, especially for a man who used to smoke a packet a day and still fancied a cold beer in the shower. The Evil Prick, the only way Franny ever referred to the twenty-three-year-old driver who had killed Frank, was high on ice at the time. Yesterday morning, an apology letter had arrived in the mail, forwarded through a chain of case workers and solicitors. Christopher Pavlos was deeply, deeply sorry. As part of his jail sentence he was undergoing rehab. He had ruined his own life and that of his parents. An older cousin had introduced him to drugs while he'd been depressed and unemployed. His life had hit a downward spiral. Perhaps if she knew the steps leading up to that tragic night Mrs Calderwood could forgive him, or at least have some understanding.

Franny had understood just fine. Last night Whisky had been treated to a dollop of organic strawberry ice cream after an already generous dinner, then his owner waited for the moist and reeking results. When they arrived, the terrier's contributions far outweighed Franny's requirements. She had scooped them up and shoved them in a bag, along with The Evil Prick's original letter. Her plan involved allowing the fetid little parcel to firm up for the next twenty-four hours, in readiness for its postal journey ahead. Sitting on her patio, writing out the address on the return envelope, she had sipped a glass of ice-cold Taittinger and quietly cried.

'Tatt' was Frank's favourite champagne, occasionally accessible to his widow now because of the sizeable life insurance pay-out she had received, along with a small amount from the State. 'The Crash Cash' was her name for the money. Receiving it at age sixty-two, Franny had immediately retired from the gallery where she had worked part-time selling her and others' artworks. She had given only a few days' notice to poor Darrien Bromley, the man who was not just her employer but also a longstanding collaborator and friend.

'No one cares about anything but themselves in the art world for God's sake,' she had claimed at the time. 'It's all air kissing and egos wrapped up with cheap white wine and warm cheese. They won't even notice I'm gone.'

Of course, that had not quite been the case. Indeed, Franny had been taken by surprise by the number of bouquets, telephone calls and emails that had made their way to her home, her phone and her inbox in the weeks following her departure. But, in one of his final pleading calls, when Darrien muttered something about Franny 'risking becoming irrelevant by just dropping out of the scene' she had laughed sharply then said, 'Does being irrelevant mean finally being left the hell alone?' Unsurprisingly perhaps, that was the last time the gallerist had ever called.

That night was movie night and, as she stood sipping a second gin and waiting for the dogs' dinner to warm in the microwave, Franny perused a list of film titles on her iPad. 'You know what?' she said to Breakfast Bar Frank, a photograph of her husband in his late thirties, reclining on an armchair, ginger cat asleep on his knees. 'My Cinema Decrepit seems to be expanding, not reducing. God knows how I ever had time to work.'

Cinema Decrepit and the Retirement Library were the names of two projects Franny had worked on assiduously since turning fifty. The first was a list of movies and, more recently, television shows she wanted to see before she died. That list kept growing. The second was a bookshelf of brand new, as yet unread, books. This collection was also multiplying, and two small piles had formed on the lounge-room floor. Franny would have liked a new place to store them but these days didn't know where to buy furniture that didn't require some degree of at-home construction.

'I think I'm going to take *Poldark* off this list,' she said as the microwave pinged. 'I don't think I'll ever be so old that soft porn like this holds appeal.'

While the dogs wolfed their food, Franny inspected the kitchen cupboard, looking for something to eat. The business of the letter and the dog droppings had knocked her appetite for six. She was contemplating a bag of corn chips and a jar of hot salsa when the iPad started to ring.

'Oh, bugger off,' she muttered, rushing to tap the ignore button. For some reason, while her iPhone was easily tamed, the iPad had recently turned traitor, ringing when she didn't even realise it knew how to.

'Whisky,' she said, pointing her finger at the dog, now licking his empty bowl and glancing at her sideways, 'next time dear Elouise is here you have to remind me to ask her about this. It cannot go on!'

As well as being her honest-to-goodness goddaughter, Elouise Martini also served as Franny's IT support in post-Frank life, thereby enjoying dramatically increased chances of accessing the house.

Few others made the cut and more than once the twenty-year-old had raised the possibility Franny was taking her isolationist policy a tad too far. The day she had arrived to find a new security gate installed, complete with an intercom system, ensuring visitors ignorant of the security code were now at Franny's mercy, she was particularly concerned.

'Crash Cash at work again, I assume,' Elouise had said with an air of exhaustion. 'Is this really necessary, Aunty Fran? What if there's an emergency? Like, is it even safe?'

'Now, Ellie, my dear, sweet girl,' Franny had said, handing her a scrap of paper with the security code printed on it and the words 'fire, flood and death only' added in Franny's handwriting, 'the other day two young men in suits came knocking, wondering if I'd like to read a copy of *The Watchtower. The Watchtower*, for God's sake. They wanted me to learn about Jehovah's Kingdom. I told them Old Kingdom, the Chinese on Cromwell Road, the place with the really good duck, was the only one of interest to me.'

Placing the note inside her wallet, Elouise did her best to look stern, but the upwards twitch of her lips was all the encouragement Franny needed.

'I also told them that Jehovah was make-believe, and I hoped no one was sodomising them back at the church. They didn't like it, Ellie, I won't lie. I think it's better for everyone that entry is by invitation only now. Besides, I was right in the middle of a particularly dirty martini and a great episode of *Breaking Bad*. I still cannot believe I didn't watch that show with your godfather when it first came out. He would have loved it.'

As well as Franny's strict border controls, Elouise was not overly enthusiastic about her godmother's evening communications curfew.

Early in the piece she had moaned, 'For someone who likes a lot of after-hours tech support, you'd think you could be a bit more sympathetic to other people's schedules.'

To this Franny had replied, 'I'm a grieving widow, dear. I get the sympathy.'

The look that had passed over Elouise's face at that moment was one of undisguised pain. Franny had said nothing but the next time her goddaughter popped over a department-store gift card was waiting for her.

Elouise belonged, as much as any grown child can, to Anthea Martini, Franny's oldest friend from school. Anthea had long given up trying to include Franny in lunch trips to wineries or weekends away at her hobby farm. Instead she sent Elouise, her canary in the coal mine, to keep an eye on happenings at Chateau Calderwood. The system was a fragile, delicately constructed one. As an acknowledged 'young person' Elouise was useful to Franny in terms of keeping up with the modern, digital world. She was also a serene and capable individual whom Frank had famously adored. This combination afforded her a level of privilege she was careful not to abuse. It was Elouise's phone number on the iPad just now.

'I can't answer you, darling, I don't know how to use this thing,' Franny said aloud to the tablet as she placed the device back in its spongey pouch and shoved it on the shelf beneath the coffee table. 'Tomorrow will do.'

In her conscience a tiny needle, the kind reserved for particularly delicate embroidery, delivered a fleeting prick. Elouise was well aware of her godmother's six o'clock shut-down rule but recently she had mentioned something about her mother needing a gallstone operation. Was there something wrong with Anthea?

'No, this is how they try to get me,' Franny concluded, slumping into her leather armchair and yanking the lever up so the footstool shot out. She glanced over at Lounge Room Frank, a man laughing out of a silver frame as a cairn terrier interrogated his ear with its tongue. 'Oh, don't look at me like that, Frank,' she said and turned on the TV.

2

Neighbourhood watch

Driving back from the nearest dog beach with Whisky and Soda the next day, Franny took a detour, pulling into the carpark of a bland constellation of mismatched budget retail outlets offering everything from pet supplies to tax services and manicures.

'Hang on, mutts,' she called back to the dogs, 'your mistress needs to make a deposit.'

Franny looked over each shoulder in a poor impression of an ageing spy, grabbed the excrement-heavy express-post envelope from under the passenger seat and stepped out of the car. The day was warm. She cursed herself for having left the parcel in the car while walking the dogs. After all her drying and chilling efforts, the spongy heft now left her feeling nauseous.

Franny practically jogged to the nearby post box, despite the fact no one else was parked nearby, dropped in the parcel, then returned to the car and sped off. Flying over a speed hump near the exit in third gear, she looked at the rear-view mirror just as Soda's furry blonde head came close to colliding with the car's roof.

'Sorry, old girl,' she said.

Ten minutes later, turning into Ipswich Street, Franny noticed a moving van in the driveway of the newish townhouse next door.

'What's this, new neighbours?' she said, glancing back at the bedraggled Whisky and Soda, both secured in the back seat. Their tails wagged in enthusiastic response. 'Don't go getting excited. They won't be getting to know you.'

Frank and Franny had moved to the bayside suburb of Cheltenham close to twenty-five years ago. Too far from the city for office types and too far from the beach for ladies who lunched, it was home to a mixed bag of working, and sometimes not working, Anglo Australians, many with a caravan or boat in their driveways, some with cars up on bricks. Alongside them lived Greek and Italian families who filled their large gardens with fruit trees and white-stone lions and sometimes, to Frank's delight, used their garages for salami- and wine-making days.

Back then the houses were unremarkable, old weatherboards beside yellow-brick stalwarts, all on spacious blocks with room for kids and dogs to play. Men had sheds and still mowed their own lawns, women had Hills Hoists and cleaned their own homes.

These days the suburb had changed. The definition of inner city in real-estate terms had expanded as the suburbs genuinely close to the CBD became unaffordable. Old houses were knocked down on what seemed to Franny a weekly basis, two new boxes popping up to replace them in the blink of an eye. Low-rise apartment blocks had sprung up near the train station and the highway. Cheltenham now attracted first-home buyers and renters alike, happy to find a modest townhouse they could, with careful budgeting, plywood furniture and the occasional bit of hot-bedding, only just afford.

What older houses survived were snapped up by double-income families or men with trades, those Franny considered the new suburban gods. These incomers appreciated the scruffy surf club and public golf course within a ten-minute radius, plus the fact their kids could still walk to school. To Franny, these people's driveways looked like car commercials come to life, with gunmetal-grey four-wheel drives parked close to judiciously enclosed trampolines, six-thousand-dollar road bicycles balanced on porches, and collections of basketballs and Nike sneakers stacked beside security-framed front doors.

Franny and Frank had loved the place, even loved the changes. They'd bought their house using a combination of a small inherited windfall on Frank's side and hard-earned dollars on his wife's. The couple had soon divested themselves of their mortgage, settling into a life where money had gone on travel and entertainment, leaving flash cars and continuous home extensions to the neighbours.

Frank had liked roaming the golf course at night with the dogs, sometimes seeing foxes, often disturbing teenage lovers. Franny still loved the fact the shopping strip remained largely unmolested. Florists stubbornly added baby's breath to carnations. The Vietnamese bakery still charged five dollars for a very decent salad roll.

The neighbours across the road from the Calderwoods had been there forever, at least in Franny's mind. The house with its banged-up brick-and-iron fence was occupied by an elderly woman when she and Frank had first arrived. Gradually new faces had appeared: a grown son and his wife, one baby and then one more. For a few years they had all lived together then, according to Frank, the old woman developed dementia. Soon she disappeared. The son and his wife drifted closer to middle age. The kids shuffled out each morning to school.

Today this particular neighbour was standing in his driveway, can of beer in one hand, garden hose in the other. He was watching intently as two men unpacked the removals van, his eyes darting from item to item as each was disgorged.

'Trust Tarzan to have a front-row seat,' said Franny, slowing the car to pull into the driveway.

It wasn't so much that she disliked the man, she just generally liked to steer clear of anyone who might be tempted to drop in unexpectedly or enjoy conversations about sport. She knew her husband and this bloke had sometimes talked cricket. Franny also knew the wife's name was Jane, which was enough for her to label the husband as Tarzan. He was a fan of perilously low-slung tracksuit pants and seemed to drink budget beer at a relentless pace while feigning work in his front yard. Even this wouldn't have worried Franny who, after all, considered a cold beer while weeding one of the many joys of summer. No, the real problem was she never, ever saw him play with his two children. That seemed a cardinal sin. Then there was the other small fact that once, in recent times, he had tried giving her a thumb's up when a delivery truck from one of the big bottle-shop chains had pulled up outside her house. She would like to have told him where to shove that thumb.

Right now, Franny felt rather than saw Tarzan trying to catch her eye. She glanced around, checking for cars and pedestrians, doggedly avoiding his gaze. 'No way, buddy, we're not on the same team,' she muttered.

Inside her house Franny unloaded dog balls, poo bags and a packet of treats into a bowl by the back door then went to telephone Elouise.

'You rang last night,' she said after announcing herself. 'What's up?'

'I'm sorry, Aunty Fran, I didn't realise it was six till I was already dialling. You are as predictably punctual as you are unsociable.'

'Yes, very amusing, Elouise. What can I do for you?' Franny moved closer to the window overlooking the driveway next door.

With one freckled pinkie finger, she pulled back the sheer curtain slightly to achieve a better view.

On the other end of the line she heard the younger woman let out a breath. 'I'm going away for a few weeks. I have a work placement in Darwin. It's a writing therapy program with Larrakia teens. Getting great results.'

'Oh, Ellie, haven't those poor kids got enough problems without some do-gooding, well-groomed overachiever like you leaning in?'

Elouise laughed. 'Leaning in? I know for a fact you've never read a word of Sheryl Sandberg's book so don't go referencing it now.'

'I saw her crapping on to Ellen or someone else on telly,' Franny responded. 'I know she's the kind of blow-dried superwoman your generation worships.'

Elouise sighed again but did not take the bait. 'I thought you believed in writing therapy,' she said instead. 'You're helping pay for my course for God's sake. And you and Uncle Frank used to complain bitterly about illiteracy among First Nations people.'

'Well that was before it started inconveniencing the elderly and infirm, namely me. Anyway, when will you be back?'

'Last week of April. Mum has all the details and she's here if you need anything, need to get somewhere in the car or whatever. She'd just love to see you—naturally.'

'I have a car and well you know it,' said Franny, ignoring the last statement.

'Yes, but it's not a good idea you drive it . . . is it?' Elouise's concern over Franny driving while under the influence was a well-worn topic of conversation between the pair.

'I've told you at least a hundred times, young lady, I do not drink and drive. I only drive in the mornings. And I never drink during the day anyway.' Franny was fed up with this topic. She genuinely did not drink during daylight hours, bar a few exceptions. These included Tuesdays at Bello Cielo, most weekends and, sometimes, during daylight savings. Often those summer days seemed unnecessarily long.

'Okay, okay, whatever you say. But will you be all right? I leave the day after tomorrow so speak up now if you want something done. Or call Mum, of course.'

'Ellie, you're a good girl,' said Franny, with genuine appreciation. 'Those kids up north won't know what's coming. Do you have enough money? And what about something to scare off crocodiles?'

'You know you're horrible, right? But seriously, should I come over for dinner tomorrow?'

Franny generally declined these offers and today was no different. 'No, no dear, the mutts and I will be fine. Besides, there are people moving in next door. Too many comings and goings in the first few days and they might think mine is the kind of house that welcomes visitors.'

'God forbid,' said Elouise.

'Oh bugger, oh no,' Franny suddenly moaned. 'I have to go, Ellie. Safe travels. This is really bad. Bye.' She could hear her goddaughter calling to her down the line, concern in her voice. 'I have to go, Ellie, this is bad I tell you. They've unloaded a bloody basketball thingamajig.' And with that Franny ended the call.

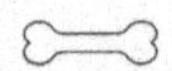

By four o'clock that afternoon Franny was in the room she used as her studio. Yes, she could see the street from there. No, she was not snooping. Her radio blared talkback from her favourite drive-time show, 'Drive with Karl'. She loved that the audience was predominantly comprised of right-wing curmudgeons and paranoid parents. They amused her no end. Franny could easily kill a very pleasant couple of hours shouting at the radio, belittling the callers and abusing the host. Occasionally, as a prank, and depending on what she had imbibed, she even phoned in.

Since Frank's death Franny had moved into the larger of her two spare rooms, transforming the original master bedroom at the front of the house to become her studio. Its floor had been stripped to bare polished boards and a wide wooden table now dominated the space. Just a stool on rollers and a bulky leather office chair lolled nearby. A large black-and-white photograph of Georgia O'Keeffe dominated one wall. The artist sat in the backseat of a car, staring through a hole in a piece of cheese. Pushed into a corner, its surface a kaleidoscope of paint splotches, stood an ancient easel, the kind you'd see in a 1960s classroom.

Franny was in the old en suite, ferreting through one of the dozen or so glass jars crowded around the sink. Most were crammed with paint brushes of different shapes and lengths; some held murky liquids in mud-like hues.

A brownish tint ringed the inside of the basin, testament to the many dyeing experiments and paintbrush-washings it had withstood. In the bathtub to the left was all of Franny's bulkier equipment, everything from tubs of paints and various chemicals to stacks of freshly washed but fatally stained towels and rags.

The studio was where Franny did all her paintings and illustrations. A small desk was shoehorned near the window so her laptop could evade the miscellaneous spills and smudges she insisted were part of her 'process'. It sat beside her digital radio, a landline telephone, one framed photograph and an overflowing tray of bills and other paperwork; filing had been Frank's domain.

Bookshelves covered two walls, built specifically to cope with lofty design and reference books. These shelves also showcased numerous awards and professional memorabilia belonging to both Franny and Frank, a mix of framed certificates and artsy glass and metal concoctions. Arguably the most surprising occupant in this collection, however, was a taxidermied ginger cat.

In death, Mr Marmalade sat in one of his favourite poses from life: two long, white-socked paws stretched out before him, head tilted coyly to one side. His mouth hung open slightly and his favourite toy mouse sat glued to the plinth beneath him.

The cat had been the first pet the newly married Calderwoods shared. He took on a legendary status in the household when his likeness became central to a series of ten wildly successful children's books, written and illustrated by Frances Calderwood. The whole thing began as a lark. Franny, honing her skills, using Mr Marmalade as her artist's model. On sunny afternoons he would lounge in beams of sunshine on the kitchen table where she worked in their small, inner-city apartment. Rather than scold the cat, Franny encouraged him to stay, entertaining him with morsels of cheese and tales of a brave ginger cat who solved crimes alongside a trusty nine-year-old sidekick called Timmy Tuggernaught.

Overhearing this cat-nattering one day, Frank suggested his wife put pen and paintbrush to paper in a more formal way, combining illustrations of Mr M with those ever-evolving stories. One thing led to another and, before she knew it, Franny was a children's author of some renown. For five years she kept the series going. The Adventures of Mr M and Timmy T eventually helped finance the house in Ipswich Street where Franny lived to this very day, plus at least three long-gone international holidays. By the time Mr Marmalade reached seventy on his cat clock, he contracted feline leukaemia and died soon thereafter. Franny would not contemplate drawing his likeness when the real cat was gone so Timmy Tuggernaught's fictional exploits expired as well. Franny had already branched out to different works and other themes but both Calderwoods were forever grateful to Mr Marmalade for the financial contribution he had made to their home and lifestyle. They felt he deserved preservation.

'He'll lie in state, like our own little Lenin or Mao Zedong,' said Frank at the time. 'You know, just without all the genocide and general tyranny.'

And so, Mr Marmalade remained, guardian of the studio, observer of their life, similar to his original self yet undeniably creepy, fundamentally wrong.

'It's done now,' said Frank with a grimace the day he picked the cat up from the taxidermist.

One look at the object in his arms and Franny started to cry. 'Frank, he looks like one of those swivelling clown heads they have at carnivals, the ones with the painted eyes and gaping mouths.'

'He doesn't look great,' her husband conceded, 'but what can we do? Surely you can work a little magic on his eyes. Paint in some sparkle?'

Franny's efforts to improve the poor cat's visage failed spectacularly. After many frustrated tears, she admitted defeat. Instead, she sewed the deceased moggy a tiny black eye patch and attached it to his rock-hard head.

'At least he looks roguish now,' she said and chucked him under the chin. This action caused the late Mr Marmalade to slide sideways down the table.

Ever supportive, Frank chimed in. 'You've done a great job, honey. He looks primed for his next adventure.'

'Stash him somewhere only we can see him?' suggested Franny.

'Most definitely,' said Frank.

Today's talkback topic was unwed teenage mothers. Franny's senses were immediately tingling.

'Get ready!' she shouted to Mr Marmalade in lieu of other company. 'Much bigotry and bullshit this way comes!'

'Um hello, Karl, it's Barry here. I wanted to say something about all those pregnant girls.' As soon as she heard the caller's plummy tones Franny's mind formed a picture of a ruddy-faced, retired magistrate.

'Yes, Barry, go ahead,' said Karl in his characteristically impatient style.

'Must they really have these children, Karl? I mean, we have the science to help them now.'

Even the host's voice betrayed a little apprehension here. 'Are you talking sterilisation, Barry?'

'No, no, no,' spluttered the caller. 'I just mean birth control is easily enough obtained. There are injections that last a year and such like. Maybe these girls should be encouraged to . . . I mean, they don't need to have these children. Especially when they're in no position to support them.'

Franny stomped out from the en suite, a delicate fan-like paintbrush in one hand. 'Right, that's it,' she said and picked up the phone. She knew the telephone number for 'Drive with Karl' by heart and keyed it in. Ten minutes later, after hold music and a quick vetting by the producer, Franny, using the nom de plume Judith, was on the air.

'Men like your earlier caller, Barry I think it was, make a lot of sense to me,' she said doing her best Dame Maggie Smith impersonation.

'Does that mean you agree these kids-having-kids need to take more responsibility, Judith? That they can't just be left to rut around like livestock and procreate willy-nilly? And we taxpayers can't be expected to pay for it all?' Karl was warming to this subject, encouraged by the sound of his own gravelly voice.

Franny turned to look out the window. She could see the driveway next door. She could see a teenage girl with short lilac hair staggering under a pyramid of assorted clothes.

'I do indeed, Karl, but I'd go further than that. I think every couple even considering having children should sign legally binding documents requiring them to remain together till the children turn twenty-one. They should also be compelled to finance those children through to university as well. No excuses.'

Karl dialled his enthusiasm back a tad now. 'That might be a bit too much to ask,' he said.

'Is it, Karl? Is it? I guess that's why your face was splashed all over *New Idea* last month because you won't pay your poor ex-wife the money you legally owe for your two little boys.'

Karl could be heard muttering, probably cursing his producer.

'Maybe you should check out the finances of that new *Neighbours* actress you're dating, quick smart, Karl,' said Franny. 'Make sure she can afford to support any of your spawn before she pops one out, hey?'

The phone line went dead. 'Drive with Karl' switched to an advertisement for funeral insurance.

Franny kissed the handset and chuckled loudly. *I deserve a bloody pinot*, she thought, just as her eyes caught movement in the driveway once more. Clearly the young girl had lost the battle with the clothing pile because she was stomping around, picking up garment after garment and grunting like a US Open competitor. Franny took a step back from the window but not before being skewered by the young girl's glare.

That night, linguine with white truffle oil was on the menu. Franny liked to cook along with Nigella Lawson now and then so her iPad was perched on the kitchen bench, the toaster acting as its support. In the old days, especially on weekends or when it came to entertaining, Frank had been the star chef, Franny his scullery maid or maître d'. Nevertheless, with a little help from her famous online friends, she liked to think she was maintaining standards.

'My romantic dinner for one,' she said to the framed version of Kitchen Frank, before touching the screen to resume the video. 'I'm not choosing an ingredient; I have a precious potion, in the form of white truffle oil,' she echoed the words of the TV chef while waving a small bottle of yellowish liquid about in the air.

On the screen, Nigella lit candles and popped an ice bucket on the table to accompany her pasta-for-one. This was where Franny drew the line.

'I'll take this as my prompt that it's time for a glass of wine, oh luscious one,' she said, opening the fridge door to grab a bottle of Arneis, 'but Ms Lawson, as my team of production assistants is currently on vacation, I might keep the set-decorating to a minimum.'

While grating parmesan into a bowl that already contained cream, egg and truffle oil, she became aware of a low, rumbling growl.

'What's wrong, Soda?'

The golden retriever was trying to fuse her nose with the glass door at the other end of the room, generating a foggy residue as a result. Whisky, who had until then been shadowing his owner around the kitchen, keen to help catch any dropped ingredients, shifted focus instantly, skidding across tiles in the rush to join his housemate. The terrier's small head tilted sideways at the sound of raised voices in the backyard next door.

'Bloody hell. I knew it,' said Franny, heading over to draw the curtains and block out the intrusion. 'Already pains in the arse and it's what?' She looked at her watch. 'All of seven hours since they moved in.'

Franny's kitchen was in the rear renovation of her 1950s yellow-brick house, the two bedrooms and the converted studio safely tucked up front, and it merged into a light, airy dining space attached to a casual sunroom-style lounge. Glass doors opened out onto the garden. All in all, it was a long, wide room and Franny had yet to light the lamps at the farthest end, focused as she had been on Nigella and her 'criminally indulgent lone linguini'.

As Franny raised her hand to close the curtains a few specific words from next door reached her ears. She shrugged her shoulders then stepped back into the shadows, quietly shushing the still-growling Soda.

'Why the hell are we stuck in this hole?' said one voice.

'Keep it down, Dakota, Joshie doesn't need to hear this,' said another.

'Joshie doesn't realise what a disaster this is yet,' said the first one and Franny immediately assigned it to the teenage girl with gaudy hair.

'This is a new start for us, honey. Why can't you see that?' The second voice, presumably Potty Mouth's mother, remained calm.

'She's a better woman than I am,' Franny whispered to the dogs.

The mother's voice continued. 'Darling, once you're settled into the new school you'll feel different. It's all just a bit scary now.'

'Scary?' said the girl, her voice rising a few more decibels. 'Scary is how deluded you are. Deluded and pathetic. If you hadn't married such a moron sixteen years ago, then stayed with him, I wouldn't be living this shitty life now.'

'If I hadn't married your father, my sweet girl, you wouldn't have been born. You wouldn't be living any life now.' The voice took on a tremulous shake.

'Nice, Mum. Maybe we'd all be a lot bloody happier then, hey?' The next sound was a slamming door, conversation clearly over.

Even without the approaching dusk, Franny couldn't see much of her neighbours' place because of the old fence that separated her driveway from their yard. Now, standing statue-still and peering through the gap beside the curtains, she released a long sigh. Through the slats in the fence a small red glow was just visible. Franny tiptoed back towards the kitchen bench, directing a whispered comment to Frank's photo along the way.

'Looks like Mum's a sneaky smoker. Can't say I blame her.'

3

Smoke signals

Thursday was Franny's cinema day, which she normally looked forward to but she had a chore to endure on this particular morning and her heart sank at the thought of it. She stood at the desk in her studio, staring at a calendar hung on the wall. A dog in a yellow mackintosh stared back at her. Each month displayed a different pitiable cairn terrier in a different jaunty outfit. She had ordered it online one night after three too many shots of fifteen-year-old Bowmore whisky.

With a moan, she moved her gaze to the framed image beside her laptop. Studio Frank was one of Franny's favourite photos but also one of the hardest to look at. When spending extended time in the room she sometimes sheepishly moved it to a bookshelf, turning the image away. Today she was immune to such sentimentality. She picked up the frame, glaring at herself and Frank on their wedding day. He was doing his best to hold her and swing her around but the strain was clear. At five-feet-eleven, the same height as her groom, Franny's long legs and arms flailed awkwardly. Her head was thrown back, mouth open colossally. Even now she remembered the intoxicating mix of joy, hilarity and fear in that moment: her long plait of glossy black hair scraped the ground and she worried her skull would soon follow.

'Your sister will be the death of me,' Franny practically spat the words at the photo. 'Why does she insist on a bloody birthday to-do the same day every bloody year? She must be a hundred. Can she not give it up?'

Today was the birthday of Frank's sister, Margaret. She was only a couple of years older than her sister-in-law. The date was circled on the cairn calendar in thick black ink, the word 'argh' scrawled beside it.

'She always wants a phone call, which always leads to an invitation to visit her in the Blue Mountains, which then leads to advice that I should be "getting out more", which then leads to her weeping and telling me how much she misses her baby brother and maybe she should come down and stay with me, and be in "Frank's space". It's too much I tell you, Frank. Too much!'

Franny put down the photograph and paced the room. Through the window she saw Whisky and Soda near the gate, fossicking in a pile of brown leaves, wrecking any neat order their mistress tried to impose. It was already eleven o'clock. In Margaret's world birthday calls only counted if they arrived in the morning. There was no more time to delay. Franny let out one long, exaggerated sigh, picked up the phone on her desk and dialled.

'Margaret, darling, happy birthday. It's me, Franny.' She looked over to Studio Frank and stuck out her tongue.

'Oh, you gorgeous thing. You never forget,' came the voice at the other end.

Franny grimaced. She had attempted 'forgetting' the first year after Frank died and had been hounded and vilified about the fact for the eleven months thereafter. Margaret's wounded and repeated declaration still made her blood boil: 'We've lost Frank. We can't lose you too.'

'So,' said Margaret, 'I'm thinking of coming down to Melbourne shortly. There's a quilting show on at that beautiful old exhibition building. What do you say?'

Franny felt her blood pressure spike. Time to panic. 'What do I say to you visiting Melbourne or what do I say to quilting?'

Margaret let out a throaty laugh. 'You've made your opinion on quilting very clear, Fran,' she said. 'I think your description of us as a herd of post-menopausal biddies with ridiculous haircuts who think tea-bagging is something to do with dyeing fabric achieved that.'

Franny felt a frisson of guilt. Margaret's sense of humour had always been her strong suit. The two women had swapped gossip and bitchy asides at countless family weddings, christenings and graduations. They'd even managed to survive a combined family holiday, renting caravans next door to each other one summer, back before Margaret got divorced and while her kids still thought bike riding and icy poles constituted fun.

'I have apologised for that, Marg. Many times, in fact,' said Franny.

'Yes, dear. I'm just teasing and, no, I am not inviting you to the quilting fair. I'm saying, what do you think to me paying a visit?'

'Next month could be tricky. A lot on. Email me the dates. We'll see what's what.'

Marg emitted a loud, exasperated sigh. The topic changed. The birthday girl went through her day's plans, detailing what her kids and grandkids were doing for her and buying for her. A few minutes of this and Franny knew it was time to ring off.

'Well I was just on my way out the door,' she said. 'I better say goodbye and let you enjoy this special day.'

'Glad to hear you're out and about,' said the other woman. 'I do worry about you not seeing enough people, Fran. You need to get back into the world. It's what Frank'—and here there was a lengthy pause—'well, it's what Frank would have wanted, dear.'

Cue the tears, thought Franny.

'We all miss him, Fran.' Sounds of tissues being scrunched, nose blown. 'I'm sorry, I'm sorry,' said Margaret, 'you don't need me blubbering on at you. But he was my little brother, Fran, my little mate. You know, when he was nine and I was twelve—'

'Marg, Marg,' interrupted Franny. 'Darling, I hate to hear you upsetting yourself, especially on your birthday. Don't reminisce on my account. I can tell it's too painful. I'll go. Speak soon.'

'Fran, no, don't hang up,' sniffed Marg. 'I was just going to say—'

'Bye bye, Marg.'

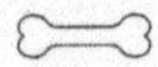

The movies were out of the question now. Fran had two cinemas she liked to patronise. One was a big corporate chain inside a shining, sprawling shopping centre, the other a charming art house called The Grand where wine was served in measures titled 'standard', 'feature' and 'epic'. More than a few of the staff members there knew her by name.

The predictable but no less infuriating phone conversation with Marg meant Franny could no longer deal with either the anonymous faces at the mall or the familiar ones at The Grand. Her mood was black, exacerbated by the knowledge that only her enforced involvement in someone else's life had made it so. She resolved to take the dogs on a two-hour beach walk before closing down the house, putting on her pyjamas, and cracking open the Margery

Allingham omnibus recently arrived in the post. Private detective Albert Campion would see her right.

It was about half past four by the time she returned with the dogs, washed and hung up their towels, nicked out to the supermarket and paid a few bills. Refilling a water bowl at the kitchen sink, Franny noticed a pot plant she had put outside the day before for some sun. As always when Franny was in the kitchen, the insatiable Whisky was by her side.

Putting down the water bowl beside the pantry door, she said to the dog, 'Okay. Pot plant back inside, heater on a little, blinds down, G and T poured, and its omnibus here I come.'

The dog tilted his head, the standard response to all conversations with his mistress.

Franny slipped her feet into the old rubber sandals by the back door and headed out, the terrier trotting behind. On the cement, Soda lounged in a meagre patch of sun, looking very much like a flokati rug that had seen better days.

'Don't bother getting up,' Franny said to the dog as she passed.

Soda closed her eyes in response.

Franny spied a little mound of dog poo beside the garden path and stooped to pick it up with one of the small bags she always had on hand. Bending down she caught a whiff of something other than canine droppings and cocked her head in a manner quite similar to Whisky's; Franny knew pot when she smelled it.

Crouched and moving stealthily, overriding the stinging pain in her knees and dodging Whisky, who assumed a game of chasey was afoot, Franny edged closer to her back fence. Pungent, unmistakable fumes scented the air and she could see a mauve head resting against the wood on the other side, a pair of denim-clad legs stretched out on the grass. Franny stood up, gamely stifling a groan.

'I wouldn't do that if I was you,' she said and put a hand on the top of the fence, straining to look over.

'What the?' came a voice from the other side. The long legs scrambled and earbuds hit the ground.

Franny found a foothold on her side of the fence and hoisted herself up a little more. She loomed over the young girl, one arm dangling on her neighbour's side, black-and-white poo bag swinging precariously from her fingertips.

'You scared the hell out of me,' said the girl. 'What are you, some kind of perve?'

'Well aren't you a little charmer?' replied Franny. 'I, my dear, am your neighbour, Mrs Frances Calderwood. And you are?'

The girl, a mix of indignation and resignation crossing her pale freckled face, looked at the joint that was burning down in her hand then looked back up at Fran. She butted out the spliff in the grass and said, 'Dee. My name is Dee.'

'Well, Dee, as I was saying, I wouldn't be smoking that thing here if I was you.'

'You're not my mother. I'll do what I want. I'll smoke dope if I want. What's it to you?'

'It's nothing to me, dear, but it's something to Senior Sergeant Shawn Dimitriades, who lives over that other fence.' Franny pointed to the house directly behind Dee's. 'He brings his work home with him, you might like to say. Fancies himself the Neighbourhood Watch.' She pointed to a large outdoor light affixed to the back wall of the Dimitriades house. 'And wait till that monstrosity comes on. You'll think you're in Stalag 13.'

'Star what?' said Dee.

Franny widened her eyes. 'Don't worry yourself, just find somewhere else to light up.' With this she unhooked her arm and let herself drop back onto her lawn. When she landed it was with an unwelcome squelch.

Behind her the girl's voice called, 'Um thanks, Mrs um Calder . . .'

Franny did not respond. Instead, just near the back door, she bent down and grabbed Whisky's ear. 'Did you have to poo right where I was going to land?' she whispered, pulling off her sandal, now coated with soft, brown matter, and throwing it, plus the original poo bag, in a bucket near the back door.

4

Message in a bottle

Red carpets were irresistible to Franny, a fact very few people knew. She adored a good awards show and watched as many as possible each and every year. She loved the outrageous vanity of it all, the clothes, the blindingly white teeth, the cloying reporters and vacuous commentaries, the celebrities acting nonchalant or, better still, sober.

Frank had indulged this peccadillo by purchasing a top-of-the-range TV recorder for his wife's sixtieth birthday. This was after he had listened to Franny moaning, one too many times, about the fact the Oscars screened in Australia in the middle of a Monday morning, completely 'killing the buzz' as she put it.

The Panasonic contraption he had bought for her meant Franny could record the show and watch it at her leisure. This she did, saving it up for a Friday night and spending the days in between trying hard to avoid news reports on the event, an almost impossible challenge that added to the ritual and entertainment.

Rubbing her hands together today, she said to Kitchen Frank, 'Ooh, honey, it's Academy Awards time. I cannot wait.' She hummed the tune to 'Hooray for Hollywood' while the coffee machine grumbled gently in the background. It was only nine in the morning but

Franny had already been out with the dogs, showered and blow-dried her hair. She always blow-dried for an awards night. 'PS: I saw Antonio and that stupid Staffie of his, Cindy, this morning. He has no control of that mutt. I took off to the other park the minute I saw them. All he ever wants to talk about is . . .' At this point Franny's words trailed off. She placed two hands on the kitchen bench and stared down at the coffee cup placed there. Clearing her throat, she said, 'Anyway, he's always asking how I am, wanting me to come for dinner with him and Nella. Pain in the arse!'

Franny and Frank had been the undisputable king and queen of the dog park a block away from their home. They handed out cards belonging to their favourite trainer if they thought owners needed help and initiated the December Christmas party, cooking sausages on the park's barbecues, and distributing home-baked dog treats in the shape of Christmas trees.

Hot summer nights often saw husband and wife sitting on folding chairs in the middle of the football oval, Whisky and Soda nuzzling tennis balls by their feet, their humans sipping champagne from plastic glasses. Deep in winter Frank carried a tiny torch that he used to illuminate a glow-in-the-dark ball. He and Whisky would tear around the park, white breath puffing out before them, while Soda and Franny sat side-by-side at the base of the playground slide, chewing over homemade dry biscuits as well as the day's events. Now Franny avoided that park as much as possible. If insomnia struck she might brave it at daybreak. She still made late-night expeditions, but only after scouting the perimeter, ensuring she would not encounter familiar faces or paws.

Their new local park was an extra ten minutes' walk away but the effort seemed worth it, especially as the reward was anonymity. No one knew who she was or what she had lost. Franny was on nodding terms with a white-haired woman with two ball-crazy, haughtily manicured poodles and she occasionally chatted to another cairn owner, a middle-aged truck driver often in a fog from shift work. Seeing Antonio there today had been an unexpected and unwelcome surprise. The next park along was half an hour's walk away. Franny prayed it wouldn't come to that.

'Anyway, can't dilly dally today.' Franny finished making her coffee and tipped her cup towards Frank and his barbecue tongs. 'Things to do,' she said and headed off to make the bed.

By afternoon a few threatening clouds were rolling in. Franny, who was repotting a recalcitrant orchid, noticed the change of light and removed her gardening gloves. 'Better hit the road,' she said to Soda, who lay wedged between a bag of potting mix and an ornate iron plant holder in the shape of a swan. 'Supplies to get in.'

For small shopping hauls, she liked to walk to the nearby supermarket, a dinky little affair patronised by slow-moving pensioners and harried working mothers grabbing stopgap supplies. Franny loved the staff there, a ragtag bunch of women, many in their late fifties, who stood around patiently, waiting for the self-serve check-out to malfunction so they could roll their eyes and commandeer the job. Today, as she walked the short route, tartan shopping jeep bouncing behind her, Franny pondered her Oscars shopping list: a good cheese, Saint Agur blue perhaps; some pâté or perhaps smoked salmon; some kind of chocolate affair; and a treat for the dogs, one that would keep them quiet. She would need to pop in and see Wayne at the bottle shop too; the Oscars demanded bubbles.

The supermarket was relatively quiet today. A couple gossiped by the fresh herbs while a toddler in a grubby tutu raced down the lolly aisle, a pregnant woman lumbering behind. Franny used the self-serve register, curtailing the need for small talk.

Directly across the car park from the supermarket was The Good Drop, creating quite the handy little precinct to Franny's way of thinking. Approaching the bottle shop she spied a now familiar purple head. Its owner stood to the side of The Good Drop's sliding doors, peeping in between the sale posters that obscured most of the glass. Taking comfort from her belief that the young never notice the old, she quickly ducked into the store, fiddling with her handbag as a way to further avoid locking eyes with Dee.

'Afternoon, Fran,' said a thin middle-aged man restocking cigarettes behind the counter. 'Looks like rain. Hope you're going to get your trusty steed home in time.' He pointed to her shopping jeep.

This was Wayne, a man Franny appreciated for specific reasons. He'd arrived in the bottle shop a year after Frank's death so he never asked about her home life or 'how she was coping'. He saw her as an entity unto herself, not the remaining half of a once fine pair.

The previous manager, Lyle, had been on great terms with her late husband. They shared a passionate disdain for craft beers and spent more than one afternoon in the store, tasting new varieties, criticising them, then tasting one or two more. Lyle had been at the funeral, much to Franny's chagrin. She hadn't done much shopping in the weeks that followed but when she finally did re-enter The Good Drop, Lyle took one look at her and his eyes misted up. A few months later, when he solemnly announced he was off to a new job with a big national chain, she stifled a grateful smile. One overly long, tobacco-scented hug and the man, his pitying looks and watery eyes, were out of her life.

Today, as always, Wayne popped out from behind the counter and joined her in front of the tall, neatly stocked fridges. Something about the symmetry and dependability of a well-organised booze fridge appealed to Franny. She liked the way the bottles stood proudly to attention, foils glimmering like military insignia, impervious to the frosty air. They reminded her of the Queen's Guard, patrolling straight-backed and straight-faced outside Buckingham Palace.

'Bubbles then?' asked Wayne. 'Special occasion?'

'It's the Academy Awards my friend. I watch them every year.'

'Um, weren't they days ago? Didn't the bloke with the big nose win for best—'

Franny held out her hand in a 'stop' motion. 'Do not say another word, pal, or I'll smash something sticky—do they still make Advocaat?—all over your nice clean floor.' She spun around theatrically, pretending to search for a bottle of the eggy liqueur. Wayne stared at her with the look of a confused toddler.

'I tape it, okay,' Franny explained. 'And then make a special occasion out of watching it.'

'I see,' said Wayne, though his expression suggested the opposite. 'So you have one of those parties?'

'Parties?' Franny crinkled her brow momentarily before realising what Wayne was on about: groups of girlfriends getting together to watch royal weddings, cliff-hangers of favourite TV shows, the Melbourne Cup and the like. Sometimes getting dressed up for the occasion.

A memory lightning-flashed across her mind: she and Frank in Manhattan at the apartment of their friends Don and Gary. It was the late 1990s, the screening of the first episode of *Sex and the City*. Don did hair and makeup on the show. Over a sumptuous coffee-table supper of caviar, shrimps, popcorn and Bollinger, he had entertained the other three with behind-the-scenes titbits, everything from halitosis and pill-popping to illicit affairs.

When the show finally ended in 2004 Gary was back living in Melbourne. Don was dead from AIDS, nursed by Gary to the end. As a tribute, and as a way of ensuring their friend did not spend the night alone, the trio had gathered once more, this time at Frank and Franny's. They drank cosmopolitans and watched the final episode, criticising every actor's hair. Their tears had rolled in tandem with the final credits. Gary used to come over and watch the Oscars each year with Franny after that, until Frank died, then she told him award shows had become passé.

'Earth to Fran,' said Wayne, waving a bottle of Mumm champagne in front of Franny's face. 'Come back, Fran. Mumm wants a word. One bottle for fifty-five dollars or two for one hundred dollars, manager's special.'

Franny plastered a grin on her face, fighting to override the lump in her throat. 'Sounds good, Wayne, but just the one. Don't want to get too overexcited.'

Wayne gave her a wink and took the bottle over to the cash register while Franny mumbled something about checking out the rieslings.

'You couldn't do me a big favour could you, Mrs Collingwood?' said a voice from behind her. 'It's just the four-packs of Vodka Cruisers are on special for fourteen dollars. I've only got eleven, but if you could buy them for me I'd drop the other three dollars to you tomorrow. It really is a pretty sweet deal.'

Franny shook her head and turned around. 'You have got to be kidding,' she said.

'Okay I could probably drop it tonight, yeah probably. But I mean, it's only three bucks,' said Dee.

Franny frowned but said nothing, prompting Dee to point at the long slim bottle currently gripped in her neighbour's hand and start babbling. 'That stuff's what, forty-five dollars? And I heard you on about the champagne. You must have a spare three bucks and I can't really buy it myself.' Suddenly the young girl looked abashed. 'I mean, please,' she added meekly. 'I'd really appreciate it.'

Franny let out a long, theatrical sigh. 'I just can't do it,' she said.

Dee would never be a champion at poker. Her cheeks flushed and her mouth straightened into a tight line. She grumbled, 'Whatever. Thanks for nothing,' and turned away.

'Hang on, little miss sunshine,' said Franny. 'I mean I will not be party to the purchase of anything called a Vodka Cruiser. Do you know what's in that stuff? No, that's because you don't work in a laboratory and don't have a list of a hundred chemicals and sugars to hand. Come with me.' She pushed Dee down another aisle, towards the vodkas. 'Now this is quite a nice place to start,' she said, pulling down a bottle of Stolichnaya. 'A good old-fashioned mix of wheat and rye grain. The Russians know about two things—vodka and assassination by poison. You can drink this straight, like an oligarch, or in a martini, James Bond-style. If you must you can have it with cranberry juice, which also makes it a remedy for cystitis. Do you suffer from cystitis?'

The young girl's mouth gaped.

'And just for the record, my name is Mrs Calderwood, not Collingwood. That's another lesson in life. If you're going to hit people up for cash or contraband, at least go to the trouble of knowing their name.'

Five minutes later, in a surprise turn of events for both parties, Franny and Dee were walking together, heading home.

'How old are you, anyway?' said Franny. 'Apparently not eighteen.' She wondered if her tone should be stern or sympathetic in this situation. What would the mummy blogs she'd read about say?

'Sixteen, actually,' said Dee with a proud flick of her head, 'but people always go on about me looking younger.'

'Looking too young. Not a problem I would complain about,' said Franny, adjusting her shopping jeep from one hand to the other while waiting for the traffic lights to change.

Dee, who had been examining the screen of her mobile phone, looked up and smiled uncertainly.

The red man turned green and the pair began crossing the road. Franny continued, 'Anyway, sixteen really is too young to be drinking, even if it is that sugary nonsense.' As she spoke, she recalled her own first encounter with booze—a sip of beer freely given by her father on her thirteenth birthday. *Still,* she thought, *things were different in those days. There wasn't a bottle shop on every corner, and I wasn't smoking pot in the backyard. And the old man was no paragon of parenting.*

Dee's protest disturbed this reverie. 'God,' she said, 'everyone my age drinks these days. Especially at my old school. It's like not a big deal or anything.'

'I see,' said Franny. 'And the dope? Does every sixteen-year-old at your old school do that too?' She kept walking but looked at her companion from the corner of her eye.

Dee had the good grace to colour a tad. 'That, that was a one-off, sort of a going away present from two kids in my class,' said Dee. 'I'm not sure there was even anything in it. I got a head spin but I don't really smoke so I get that just when I try a normal ciggie.' Suddenly the girl looked a little panicked. 'You're not going to tell my mum any of this are you?'

Franny had the uncomfortable feeling she had stumbled into some kind of midday movie.

'Well, I am glad to hear you don't smoke cigarettes and I really do think you should steer away from the pot,' she said. 'As for your mother, I hadn't planned on saying anything.' She slowed her pace and looked over pointedly at Dee. 'Unless I thought I had to. Do I have to? What was your plan with the four-pack for instance?'

Dee shook her head back and forth in protest. 'It's no big deal I promise. They were just cheap, and I thought they'd come in handy, to take to a party or something. That's all. I wasn't going to neck them all on my own.' Suddenly she pointed to Franny's shopping jeep. 'Anyway, you're the one who got a whole big bottle!'

Franny let out a shocked laugh but before she could respond Dee said, 'Not that there's anything wrong with that of course.' She was talking and walking a little faster. 'So you got champers. Are you having a party or something? Mum says champers is for special occasions.'

'Some people say that,' said Franny, stopping at another set of traffic lights, 'though Churchill drank it at breakfast and he got the Brits through the war.'

'What?'

Franny looked over at Dee who was once more absorbed in the screen of her mobile phone. 'Never mind,' she muttered. As the green man and a loud clicking noise indicated they could resume walking, she raised her voice and said, 'So Dee's an unusual name. Short for something?'

'Dakota,' said Dee, looking up, rolling her eyes. 'Can you believe it? I'm named after some American child actress who was big at the time. Sooo lame. I make everyone call me Dee.'

'Fanning?' asked Franny.

'Huh?'

'Was it Dakota Fanning? She really was a good little actress. Not sure what she's up to now.'

'Whatever,' said Dee with a shrug. 'So anyway, you having a party?'

'Kind of. I'm going to watch the Oscars.'

'You mean like the Academy Awards?' asked Dee.

'The very same. You've heard of those then?'

'Yeah they were on about it on the radio the other day. I couldn't believe that bloke with the big nose—'

'Bloody hell,' said Franny loudly. 'What's wrong with people? Don't say another word.'

Dee looked at her and grimaced.

'Sorry, it's just that I've recorded the show and everyone keeps trying to tell me who won things. I've made it through the whole week without finding out.'

'Okay,' said Dee, elongating the word to indicate she thought the older woman could well be a nutter. 'And what's the champagne got to do with it?'

'Just a bit of a ritual I've grown to like. I have pâté and all the trimmings. Makes it more fun.'

'I mainly like the red-carpet bit,' said Dee. 'You know, the outfits and everything.'

'Same here,' said Franny, 'though I like making fun of the speeches too.'

Dee looked sideways at Franny. 'I've never had champagne,' she said. 'Could I come over? You're not going to drink it all alone.'

Franny increased her pace, shopping jeep bucking like an unruly goat. Dee, unburdened by a jeep or an additional half a century on the planet, had no problem keeping up.

'What do you say, Mrs Calderwood?' she asked again, emphasising the correct surname this time.

By now they were turning into their street. Franny wanted to groan outright but suspected that would hurt the youngster's feelings. She remembered her own impatience to try new things and feel grown up at Dee's age. Though she doubted she would have harassed ageing neighbours to accelerate the process.

'What about your mother? She's not going to like that.'

'She's working late, won't be home till ten or so and my little brother's staying over at a friend's. So . . . ?'

Franny stopped walking and blatantly looked the girl up and down, taking in the hiked-up school dress and too-new shoes. How Dee ever thought she was going to get Wayne to hand over booze to her in that outfit Franny did not know. She also did not know how it would feel to be spending your first Friday night in a new house and suburb on your own. Not easy, was the conclusion.

'All right. Be over at 6 p.m. Wear something nice.' Franny keyed in the code to her front gate, leaving Dee behind.

'Mrs Calderwood, Mrs Calderwood!' she could hear the voice yelping over the high fence. 'My vodka, you've got my vodka.'

'I paid for it, dear, it's my vodka. But I might let you make a withdrawal tonight.'

5

Pop culture

Franny slipped on a sequinned floral kaftan she had purchased the summer before at a factory outlet next to her nearest Aldi supermarket. With its high neckline, wide sleeves and original five-hundred-dollar price tag, she felt like a budget Princess Margaret swanning around Mustique. The garment had already been worn five or six times by now but never beyond Franny's front door. She spritzed herself with Chanel No. 19 and glanced over at Bedroom Frank, perched on the tiny dressing table.

'God help me, sweetheart, but I've got a visitor tonight. I don't know what I was thinking. Maybe it's a mini-stroke.' The man in the photograph continued to look out his window, pen in mouth. 'I think I feel a bit sorry for her, really. Wandering around, trying to scrounge money, being forced to drink Vodka Cruisers. I don't know. I'm sure I'll regret this. I mean, she's next door. Too close for comfort in the long run. I should just cancel, but I don't have the number. I could just turn her away when she buzzes.'

Franny slipped her feet into a pair of simple leather sandals then stood up to examine her reflection in the mirror on the built-in robe. Her long white hair with its black strip was slicked back and secured at the nape of her neck, showing off the large gold hoops that hung from each earlobe. She wore a little blush on her cheeks and a lick of mascara but that was all. Normally for Oscars night she liked to apply false eyelashes and a swoosh of liquid eyeliner but, for some reason, Franny's nerve had abandoned her tonight. She and Frank had always enjoyed a bit of flamboyant dressing up but without him by her side, and remembering her own caustic teenage gaze, she had gone down the less is more path tonight.

Letting out a sigh at her cowardice, Franny bent down and touched her finger to her lips, then touched the photograph's frame. 'Anyway, darling,' she said, 'not the kind of thing you need to worry about now.' Her voice cracked.

At five past six the buzzer sounded, sparking a tirade of barking from Whisky and a low woof from Soda, who remained sprawled across a cushion on the lounge-room floor. *Prompt. I like it,* thought Franny as she quickly buzzed Dee in. She watched the young girl slouch up the path, dressed in tight, white jeans and a metallic sleeveless top. Dee's hair was scraped back with some kind of product, her eyes rimmed in thick, dark kohl. With long bony arms and her delicate collarbone exposed, Franny thought the girl looked younger and more fragile than in her school uniform.

'Here we go,' she tossed the words back to Lounge Room Frank before throwing open the front door. 'Vellcom, vellcom,' she said in a comic-book Transylvanian accent. 'Welcome to my house! Enter freely. Go safely, and leave something of the happiness you bring!'

Dee, who was holding her mobile phone and a packet of corn chips, took a step back and widened her eyes. 'Um, what?' she stammered.

Franny let out a loud squawk of laughter, doing little to reassure her visitor. 'I'm sorry, dear. That's my Dracula impression. Not a Bram Stoker fan?'

'Bram Stoker?' said Dee, trying to recover some cool. 'Was he in that old vampire movie with that Gary Oldman bloke?'

Franny raised her eyes to the ceiling. 'Something like that. I'll loan you the book. Anyway, hello, lovely to see you. Come inside. Hope you don't mind dogs.' Whisky was already jumping up to investigate the package in Dee's hands. 'Down you little guts,' said Franny. 'Sorry, Dee, he likes to snack.'

'These are for you. Mum says you should never go anywhere empty-handed.'

'Good old Mum,' said Franny, taking the pack and examining it. 'Jalapeno, my favourite. Thank you.' She wondered if she should fetch the old blue-and-white Royal Worcester bowl, an heirloom from Frank's mother, to serve the corn chips in but worried such a gesture would look ostentatious. *It's been so long since I've had a house guest apart from Elouise I'm turning into the bloody Count,* she thought.

'Come on in, grab a seat. Let me get you a drink.'

Further into the lounge room, Dee looked about her, taking in the large kitchen, the big windows, patterned lamps and rugs, the stereo with a huge stack of vinyl records beside it, the numerous artworks and neat stacks of books and magazines. She ran a finger along the art-deco chrome and glass drinks trolley standing beside the sofa.

'It's so cool,' she whispered. 'A bit like that old show *Mad Men*.'

Franny grinned. 'Well, I guess that's a compliment. I do like a bit of fifties retro, I'll admit. You didn't watch *Mad Men* though, did you? Bit adult for you I'd have thought.'

'Adult?' Dee snorted, expressing how outrageous she considered this suggestion, then said, 'More like a bit dull. Everyone smoking in the office and having affairs. I mean, who cares? Mum liked it though. Every now and then she'd let me watch with her. Anyway'—the young girl's expression turned wistful as she looked around the room—'it's just nice to be somewhere with a bit of space.'

'You used to live somewhere bigger?' said Franny, moving to the fridge and clinking ice into glasses.

'Bigger than that shithole we're in now,' said Dee, gesturing next door. Immediately she seemed aware of her language and two fingers went to her lips.

'Don't worry, Dee. I've heard worse.' Franny poured mineral water into the glasses. 'What made you move?'

Dee bent down to pat Soda, who was busy rubbing and slow-wagging against her legs. 'Mum and Dad split up. Dad's in the house.'

'Surely it would be easier if he did the moving instead of you three?'

'Dad's not into making things easier,' mumbled Dee. 'Hey, what happened to the champagne?' She looked warily at the crystal tumblers Franny was placing on the coffee table before her.

'It's always nice to have a glass of mineral water on the side, and to start off without being thirsty,' said Franny. 'You don't want to be necking three-hundred-dollar Krug just because you're parched.'

'Are we drinking three-hundred-dollar booze?' said the young girl excitedly.

'Easy tiger,' replied Franny. 'I'm just making a point. We are not drinking anything. You are having a small glass of Mumm and maybe a snifter of vodka at best. Baby steps, my dear.' She turned on the television set and punched the remote to bring up the awards coverage. 'Take a seat.'

Dee landed heavily and sulkily on the sofa and Whisky jumped up beside her. Just as Franny was about to shoo him off Dee said, 'Please don't. Our dog died a while back. What's this guy's name?'

Franny introduced both canines, who reacted enthusiastically to having a new human in the vicinity. At the same time, she picked up a white linen napkin and placed it over the top of a champagne bottle she had placed inside a black-and-silver ice bucket earlier. After gently tugging at the cork for a moment, a gentle dull thud ensued and then she was pouring sparkling liquid into two flute-shaped glasses.

'Hey, where's the pop?' complained Dee.

'The only people who "pop" are racing car drivers, TV reality stars and the royals when they launch a new boat,' said Franny. 'In real life, you're just wasting precious bubbles and spilling delicious champagne. No, dear, anyone who knows what they're on about opens champagne like this. Mark my words.'

She turned up the television as a blonde with synthetically golden skin and implausibly white teeth gripped the arm of a statuesque black woman and screeched, 'Whose earrings are you wearing?'

By the time the red-carpet phase was over and the host-cum-comedian had completed his monologue, Dee was sipping Mumm, learning terms like mousse and bead, and struggling to understand how the contents of her glass could taste like toasted bread.

'I thought it would be sweeter,' she complained, holding the tall glass against the lamp light and staring at the bubbles. 'It's kind of bitter.'

'See what I have to go through,' said Franny laughing and Dee looked at her quizzically. 'That's what my dad used to say to me when I tasted his beer and hated it. He'd pretend it was awful but he had to put up with it.'

'Well this isn't awful but it's not what I expected,' said Dee. 'Vodka Cruisers are nicer.'

Franny's eyes rolled back in disgust. 'Here, try it with this,' she said, handing over a doll-sized piece of toast topped with smoked salmon and crème fraiche.

Dee looked at the morsel dubiously. 'Really?'

'For God's sake child, there is life beyond KFC. Now try!'

Dee took a tiny, hesitant nibble, her nose twitching like a rabbit.

'Okay, now a sip of champagne,' directed Franny.

The girl did as she was told, then took a bigger mouthful of the salmon concoction.

'Not bad,' she said. 'Can I try it with the corn chips?' She reached towards the bowl on the coffee table where the bag of Jalapeno-flavoured snacks lay open. Franny made to intervene then thought better of it. Instead, she grabbed a corn chip, crunched on it then sipped her glass. Her eyes widened.

'Not bad,' she told Dee, 'not bad at all.'

Dee's face reddened a little. 'Really?'

'Bit salty, would make you too thirsty after a while but not the worse combo I've ever tried. Well done, Miss Dee. Old dog, new trick.'

She held out her glass to the young girl to toast cheers. Dee realised what was required and thwacked her glass loudly against Franny's.

'It's a shame we're not watching the live version,' said Dee, pointing to the screen. 'We could follow all their tweets.'

'What?' said Franny.

'You know, Twitter. A lot of the stars Tweet or Instagram what they're doing in the lead up to award shows, you see them getting their makeup done or choosing jewellery. Sometimes they take selfies with each other on the way up the carpet or even in their seats. Remember when Ellen nearly broke the internet.' Dee handed Franny her phone where the image showed twelve or so Hollywood A-listers crowded into one tiny screen.

'Oh, I do remember something about that,' said Franny with a laugh. 'Frank and I were going to—' She stopped mid-sentence, recalling that particular awards night may have been one of the last she watched with her husband. She took a quick gulp of champagne.

Dee said, 'What were you going to do? Who's Frank?'

Franny busied herself by smearing pâté onto a biscuit. 'Frank was my husband,' she replied.

'Divorced?' said Dee.

'Dead,' said Franny.

The young girl went silent. She sipped the last of her champagne. 'Sorry.'

'Nothing for you to be sorry about, dear. You weren't the prick driving the car that hit him.' On autopilot, Franny leaned in to top up her guest's empty glass but caught herself in time and, instead, tilted the champagne bottle into her own flute.

'What about me?' said Dee.

Franny smiled ruefully. 'I think a glass of champagne now and a snifter of vodka at "Original Song" time is more than enough for a young lady of your tender years,' she said. 'After all, this is not about me encouraging underage drinking, it's about providing some education . . . to someone who clearly requires it if the whole Vodka Cruiser debacle is anything to go by.'

Glumly, Dee eyed the half-full champagne bottle. 'All right,' she said eventually, her tone resigned, 'but I better check when Mum's getting home.' Using two thumbs she composed and sent a text message on her phone in the time it took Franny to take another sip.

Seconds later the phone pinged with a reply. *God I am old*, shot through Franny's mind.

'How long do you have?' she asked.

'Mum's home at ten.'

'Even the Oscars can't go that long, we should be fine. What does your mum—what's her name by the way—do?'

'Sallyanne,' said Dee. 'She's a nurse. Works in emergency but kind of directs things now. Don't think she does much actual nursing anymore.'

'I see,' said Fran who didn't really see at all. Hospitals and the medical fraternity generally were something she avoided. She didn't like people poking and prodding at her, one of the reasons she looked after her own hair—no need for hairdressers. When Frank died it was 'at the scene' as they say in the movies, saving Franny the turmoil of gruelling hospital visits and heart-breaking decisions. He'd taken care of her until the end was how she saw it.

'So, your brother, how old is he?'

'Josh? He's eight. In grade three.'

'Right, and he's at a friend's place tonight?'

'Yeah. Mum didn't like the idea of leaving him at home in the new house so soon. This is her first evening shift since we moved in. He's with one of Mum's friends. She doesn't have kids.'

'But you didn't have to go?' asked Franny.

'Mum tried to make me but I know what Gemma, that's the friend, is like. She and Josh will be all over her bloody piano most of the night, pretending they can sing and play. I said I wanted to set up my desk and stuff so I could get a head start on my homework this weekend. It's not like I'll be alone overnight.'

'She fell for that argument?' Franny took a sip of champagne and eyed the young girl.

Dee tried to look indignant, then giggled. 'I would have done that. Probably. If it wasn't for you.' She waved her hand to take in the room, the champagne, the food and the dogs. 'And for this.'

'Don't rope me into your web of deceit,' said Franny, then held up a hand good naturedly when Dee tried to protest. 'Anyway, your brother plays piano as well as basketball. Quite the little virtuoso.'

'What?' Dee looked genuinely confused.

'The ring. I saw it being unloaded when you moved in.'

Dee snorted. 'You call it a hoop and, clearly, you haven't met Josh yet.'

'No, when would I have?'

'Well, the hoop's mine. I played basketball at my old school. Not quite Josh's style.'

Franny, her glass topped up once again, examined Dee over its rim. 'What's that supposed to mean?' she asked.

'You'll see.' Dee took a sip of mineral water, her expression unimpressed. On the screen, the announcer was pre-empting the forthcoming Original Song award. 'Woot woot, vodka time,' she sang, fist-pumping the air.

Franny gave another theatrical eye-roll and stood up. 'Lovely to see the future generation in all its glory,' she said.

Immediately Whisky, who had snoozed happily since the canape-eating waned, was up and hurtling towards the kitchen. Ignoring the television, Dee jumped up and followed the dog, pulling up a seat at the breakfast bar while Franny took two small frosted glasses and the bottle of Stolichnaya from the freezer.

'That Frank?' asked Dee, picking up the nearby photo.

Franny nodded, carefully measuring a vodka shot then pouring it into a glass.

'He looks nice. Smiley. Cat gone too?'

'Cat gone too,' said Franny, and smiled.

It dawned on her that she liked the girl's youthful matter-of-factness. So many people were social imbeciles when it came to death. Either they pretended it did not exist or overcompensated, gushing condolences when they'd never met you or the person you'd lost.

'His name was Mr Marmalade. Here.' Franny placed one of the glasses in front of Dee but put a hand over it, signalling her to wait. 'Okay, in the movies they sling vodka back like water. Bad idea. Firstly, a lot of people gag at the immediate burn. Not a good look. Secondly, like all good booze, it should be savoured not slammed. Thirdly, and this is crucial.' Franny looked at Dee whose fingers were twitching around the base of the glass. 'You listening, girlie?'

Dee opened her eyes wide, demonstrating attention. 'Yes, I am listening,' she enunciated.

Franny put her serious face on. 'This is a drink that sneaks up on you, Dee. By the time your hand is throwing back the fourth shot your blood stream is only just registering the first one. This is how people get into trouble. You can end up very, very drunk very, very quickly and there's no going back. It can be dangerous.'

'Dangerous how?'

'Just dangerous. Now sip.'

As Whisky looked up longingly at the two humans, Dee struggled to keep her face composed. After a second or two she let out a whoosh of breath and coughed. 'Wow,' she breathed. 'It burns.'

Franny was pouring herself another shot. 'I know,' she said with a cheeky grin. 'Good huh?'

Dee's previously pale cheeks were noticeably pink. 'I'm going to go to Hollywood one day,' she said, rocking back precariously on the stool. 'I want to be a costume designer.'

'Is that so? I've known a few in my day. You should definitely visit LA then,' said Franny. 'Great town.'

'You've been?'

'Sure, a few times. The Sephora next to the Dolby Theatre is fantastic. That's where the Oscars we just watched were.'

'You know Sephora? That's a pretty cool makeup store.' Dee leaned forward on the bench, resting her head on her hands and peering more closely at Franny.

'Of course. One of my best friends was a hair and makeup artist. He put me on to it years ago in the States. It's been around since the seventies, you know. French, of course.'

'Really?' Dee looked dubious.

'Sure, but it didn't get to America till much later I think. I remember staying at Marmont for my fiftieth and Sephora was definitely around then.' Franny realised this was probably more than she'd said to any one single person in weeks, not counting the dogs and photos of Frank.

'What's Marmont?' asked Dee.

'Chateau Marmont. Look it up,' said Franny, throwing Dee a pen and a sticky-note pad she kept near the fridge. Doing this she noticed the clock on the wall. 'Nearly ten, you should go.'

From the television screen came the strains of orchestral music; someone on the Oscar's stage was getting the bum's rush.

'Mum will SMS if she gets home before me. How about one more vodka?'

The young girl's pupils were huge, her kohl eyeliner slightly smudged now. Franny noticed the dark shadows beneath each of Dee's eyes. *Tired or something else?* she wondered.

'How about you get to bed?' said Franny, moving towards the front door. 'Don't forget your phone,' she called over her shoulder.

'Oh come on, Mrs C, tell me more about LA. And what about your hair and makeup friend. Do you still see her?'

Franny grinned at this new moniker, Mrs C. *When did I become a character in* Happy Days? she wondered. Then she said, 'The friend is a him, as it happens, and this is not story hour at the local library. You came to watch the awards and try champagne. You've done both and now your carriage turns back into a pumpkin.'

Dee stuck out her bottom lip. 'I get that reference you know,' she said, her tone petulant.

'Praise the lord and pass the mustard,' said Franny, holding her hands in the air like an old-time preacher. 'Seems the Australian education system is still covering the classics. Charles Perrault can rest easy in his grave.' Before Dee could ask who the hell Charles Perrault was and, perhaps, what he had to do with things, Franny pushed her out the door. 'Night-night, Cinderella,' she said. 'See you round some time.'

6

Street life

'Okay, pooches, it's time to get back on track. Enough of this lolly-gagging around with wayward teens,' said Franny as she loaded the dogs into the car, ready to head to the beach. The weather was contrary for this time of year. One day steamy, the next day bright and clear. One evening cool enough to warrant some heating, the next one too hot to even consider a blanket. Today there was drizzle but it remained warm. Franny looked forward to a chai latte and a quick skim of the newspaper once the dogs were walked. She'd stop off at Beachcombers, a regular haunt where the banana muffins were particularly moreish and they served three-dollar 'pupcakes' that Whisky adored. Plans like this fuelled her contentment now.

She whistled the tune to 'Take Me Home, Country Roads', which had materialised in her head somewhere between morning ablutions and feeding the dogs. Franny suffered from earworms the way other women suffered from urinary tract infections. They'd pop up from nowhere and last for days. One of Frank's nastier habits had been the casual singing of 'Rudolph the Red-nosed Reindeer' when his wife annoyed him. She'd be humming that bloody carol for a week at least.

Dogs in car, car doors closed, house doors locked. Franny then made the last-minute decision to put the rubbish bins out before leaving. Her neighbourhood was cursed by Monday morning garbage collections and sometimes, after a little too much fun on the weekend, she had missed the process altogether. If she put them out on a Saturday then it didn't matter how 'tired' she felt Sunday. The job was at least half done.

'Uno momento,' she said to the dogs, opening the car windows to let in some air. 'Your pack leader has work to do.'

Franny checked under the lid of the recycling bin and saw the Mumm bottle in there. Perfect, she was up to date. About to close it again, she also noticed a pair of empty Monsigny Champagne Brut NV bottles.

In an effort to conserve funds Franny had recently taken to conducting something she called the BBEs, also known as the Budget Bubbles Experiments. Lining up at the Aldi check-out, still holding the sticky note with Monsigny scrawled across it, she remembered telling the shopper behind her, 'Any booze that costs twenty dollars and wins medals at the International Wine and Spirits Challenge deserves to be given a chance.' What she didn't remember now was polishing off two bottles of the stuff in one session. *Guess that means the experiment was a success*, she thought.

After opening the gate, Franny rolled out two rattling full-size bins at once towards the nature strip. Other houses in the street, some fairly teeming with occupants, proudly displayed the petite 'we care about the planet and produce the teeniest carbon footprint' type of bins. Franny could never understand this. She and Frank had always generated a colossal amount of waste.

'I work from home and you're only at the gallery part-time,' he'd say, 'plus, we entertain so much. It's not like we're deliberately profligate. We're just busier and more popular than our boring neighbours.'

Franny admired this interpretation but felt even more self-conscious now she lived alone. She wondered if people noticed and labelled her an ecological dinosaur, a dyed-in-the-wool Boomer. Considering her bins were often only a third full these days she knew she should get organised and contact the council. She should get the smaller versions. She should embrace the world of composting. She should stop buying deodorant and use some kind of crystal.

Bugger it, she thought, hauling her vaguely ripe-smelling cargo, *I didn't contribute to overpopulation and I've planted a bee-attracting garden. That'll have to do for now.*

Turning back towards the house, Franny saw the new woman next door coming up her own driveway, broom in hand. *Here we go,* she thought, *there's no way I can escape saying hello.* The other woman beat her to it.

'Mrs Calderwood is it? Hello.'

Bloody chirpy for first thing in the morning, thought Franny. *Bad sign.*

'Hello. Please call me Franny.' She rubbed her hands theatrically on her khaki walking trousers to indicate she wouldn't try shaking in this unsanitary state.

'Franny, of course, and I'm Sallyanne Salerno.'

Sallyanne was fortyish in Franny's estimation. She had mid-length dirty-blonde hair tied back with an elastic band and wore shorts and an oversized T-shirt. Like her daughter, there were circles under her eyes but Sallyanne's tended towards purple and were at least one size up.

'So much rubbish when you unpack isn't there?' Sallyanne said, pointing her broom towards the recycling bin in front of her house, the lid only half closed. 'This one's already full so I might as well put it out, but I'm hoping I can use this thing and squash it all down.'

Franny thought about her own half-empty bins. She knew she should offer to share some real estate but feared this could be misinterpreted as welcoming friendliness. She relented.

'As it happens there's room in mine,' she said. 'I won't have much more this weekend so you can add stuff if you need to. It's a once-off after all. But don't let anything drip or spill on the grass.' She looked back towards her immaculate nature strip, which she had personally manicured earlier that week.

'Um okay,' muttered Sallyanne, 'that's very kind of you.'

'Better than risking rubbish flying all over our street, isn't it? We run a pretty tight ship around here.' Franny's voice had taken on a slight sergeant-major gruffness. Even to her ears it sounded preposterous.

Sallyanne walked tentatively over to her yellow-topped bin and began ramming down the contents with the head of her broom. 'I'm sure we'll be fine,' she said quietly.

Franny experienced a two-pronged pang of both irritation and guilt at the woman's reaction. *Grow a spine for God's sake*, she thought, followed by, *Poor girl. She could do with a hand.*

'Hope you didn't mind Dee coming over last night,' said Franny, adding a little softener to her voice.

'And I hope she behaved herself,' said Sallyanne breathlessly. She had managed to tame the contents of the bin just enough to close it. 'And that she was good company for you.'

Franny felt heat creep up her face as if someone was playing with her thermostat. She was not 'in need of' company, good or otherwise.

'I think she learned a thing or two,' she said, gruff and sergeant-majorish again. 'Seeing it was her first night in the house alone, it seemed the right thing to do.'

Sallyanne rested her broom against the bin and opened her mouth to say something.

Franny nodded towards the dogs in the car. 'Gotta go,' she said. 'Best of luck.'

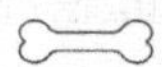

Diana Krall harrumphed onto the stage at the Newport Jazz Festival as if she'd just had a bust-up with her boyfriend backstage.

'Would it have been Elvis by that time?' Franny asked Breakfast Bar Frank. Were musicians Diana Krall and Elvis Costello already an item by the time Diana played Newport in 1999? This kind of detail used to be her husband's speciality.

Franny picked up the remote and pressed pause on Diana's opening number, then retrieved her iPad and tapped a new search into Google. According to Wikipedia, the answer was no; the pair met at the Grammys in 2002. These days, Franny could watch her Saturday night concert on the big television screen, courtesy of her too-smart television and its YouTube access. Elouise had helped set up and teach her the surprisingly straightforward system, explaining how Franny could then use her iPad to unearth interesting titbits or supplemental information.

Technically, the process was efficient. Emotionally it had the power to make her weep. Flat screens and search terms, pause buttons and websites, none of these could compare to the sound of Frank whittering on long after his wife had stopped paying attention.

Three years after his death and it was small moments like this that could still knock the wind out of Franny. On nights when it had been her turn to cook Frank would often sit at the kitchen bench and watch her. He would sip a little this or that and discuss the day's news or critique her chopping skills. In Franny's darkest moments, she sometimes envied friends saddled with unhappy marriages. Okay, maybe not the unhappy ones but definitely the ones where they had nothing much left to say to each other. If Frank had been a golfer or one of those cycling MAMILs perhaps she wouldn't miss him so much; she'd be used to the silences and even absences. The night Frank died Franny would not have lost both her husband and her best friend in one obliterating blow.

Saturday nights could be tough. Clichéd as it was, the weekends did have a particular flabbiness to them that weekdays seemed to lack. Franny had tried analysing it more than once. She no longer worked so, technically, every day should feel like the weekend. Why then did she still sense, at an almost cellular level, a soupçon of angst as the neat order of Monday to Friday slipped into Saturday's unsettling vagueness?

Sometimes the downwards slope began on Friday. Despite her best efforts there was still the chance some kind-hearted or obstinate soul would telephone to see if she'd like to 'do something on the weekend . . . maybe a movie or just a bite to eat?' These were the friends who still had jobs or retained mid-week commitments. She either ignored these calls, sending an excuse-ridden SMS a week to ten days later, or answered in a hoarse voice, feigning a 'shocking cold'. She had to be careful how often she pulled this stunt because it had backfired once or twice in earlier days. Unexpected visitors arrived at the door, weighed down by homemade chicken soup, cough mixture and boxes of tissues. If Franny answered their knock, dressed in a sarong, martini in hand, Linda Ronstadt blaring in the background, things got awkward pretty swiftly. On the upside, it did tend to put a final plug in that particular flow of invitations. Regardless, the anticipation of such intrusions and the effort of dealing with them could upset her equilibrium.

Tonight, however, Franny had reason to feel chipper. She'd been outside watering the lawn when an old school friend called regarding an imminent class reunion. The sheer bliss of dodging that conversation, avoiding the speculation over who might be dead, divorced or disfigured could not be overstated. The combination of this plus a nice cold Hendrick's martini had dampened any residual disquiet Franny might admit to since her earlier frosty encounter with the woman next door.

'I might like the "company",' she said to Breakfast Bar Frank, swinging a large knife around as she spoke. 'Can you believe the nerve of it? What a load of complete and utter bullshit. I need an evening with a teenager the way Donald Trump needs more time in the solarium. Like I say, she's got a nerve.'

A slow-cooked beef ragu, courtesy of a Jamie Oliver recipe, had been fragrantly simmering for a number of hours and Franny was slicing up the remainder of the cucumber from her martini to complete a salad. Waste not want not.

'Of course, she's a tiny thing and looks quite bedraggled.' Franny continued to harangue the portrait of her husband. 'I know you'd be over there in a heartbeat offering to move a sofa or mow a lawn but I'm nobody's knight in shining armour. As it happens, I could do with my own bloody knight . . .' At this point Franny's voice caught and her eyes filled with tears. 'Bloody onions,' she said, shoving the untouched Spanish onion on the benchtop with her knife.

Just then Whisky started barking manically from the front of the house. Franny did not call out to quieten him. Anything forceful enough to extract him from her side while she cooked deserved investigating. Ninja-like, she analysed her situation: Diana Krall remained silently frozen on the television screen and it was still light outside so there was no need to run and switch off lamps. Realistically any intruder, Franny's blanket term applying to anyone from masked gunmen to childhood friends, had no reason to think she was home. No reason except that her car was in the driveway and, oh yes, the fact that she was always at home.

Franny walked softly towards her studio where Whisky continued his carry-on, his nose plastered against the curtains closest to the driveway.

'Shh,' she said, crouching down slowly and scratching the little guy's ear. 'What's going on?' She looked towards her lovely big gate with its state-of-the-art intercom attached. 'Don't think we've been breached, matey,' she whispered. The dog dashed between the side and front windows like a demented metronome.

From the street Franny heard the sound of a car door slamming and the words 'Bye Joshie' called out as a horn tooted and the car pulled away. She often picked up street sounds in her studio because the windows were usually partially open, expelling paint and chemical fumes, not to mention any gaseous emissions from her canine studio mates.

Through the gaps in the fence palings she could see two shapes heading back towards the house next door.

'How did you go with Aunty Gem, darling? Here, give me your bag. And what's this? A teddy in a tutu?' The voice, though distant, was clearly Sallyanne's.

Franny didn't catch much of the response. A little voice mumbled something about 'ballet' and 'present'. Within moments the pair were out of sight and Franny heard their door slam.

'The famous Josh,' she said to Whisky who was now plonked at her feet, panting like a small, hirsute steam train.

Returning to her cooking, Franny set a pot boiling for tagliatelle then moved to the lounge room and switched the television from YouTube to the six o'clock news. The concert was dinnertime viewing—that was a Saturday night rule.

On-screen, one city was the site of a car bombing, another the location for a tourist bus accident while somewhere else, a 64-year-old woman had given birth to twins. Franny, who was holding a freshly poured glass of Latour pinot noir in her hand, took a large slug and briskly changed channels.

'Jesus wept,' she said to Lounge Room Frank, rubbing at a smudge on his silver frame. 'Do we really need the elderly deliberately setting out to create teenage orphans? Can they not adopt a greyhound?' At the sound of her voice the sleeping Soda lifted her head from her spot on the couch. 'Or a Golden Retriever, they could adopt a Golden Retriever.' She walked over and gave the dog a scratch.

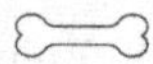

When the weather was fine Franny liked to take the dogs for a quick walk around the block after dinner to run down their engines. Admittedly the habit was risky, any one of her neighbours could be out sniffing around or she could run into a dog owner from the old park, keen to rehash good times. Still, Franny felt her self-imposed boundaries couldn't compromise her dogs' wellbeing. Plus, more often than not, she'd had a few drinks so couldn't responsibly drive further afield.

She stacked the dishes from her ragu-making in the dishwasher and grabbed the leads before heading out the door. It was after half past seven on a Saturday night and, from what Franny could see through open windows and backyard gates, most households were either temporarily unoccupied or their inhabitants were absorbed in dinner preparations.

At number twenty-four, Mr and Mrs Prozesky were heading out for the night. Mrs Prozesky, the only way the woman had ever introduced herself to Franny, was dressed in a black linen shift dress, her dyed red hair pulled back in an elegant French roll. Hermann Prozesky—Frank had once extricated a Christian name from the man while they were both in line at the supermarket deli—wore a pale-grey suit and carried a hat in his hand. Franny approved greatly of this couple. They were stylish and aloof and she never had to worry about sympathetic enquiries or unexpected neighbourly visits. Today, like any day when she encountered them, the exchange went pretty much the same.

'Good day, Mrs Calderwood,' said Hermann Prozesky, easing himself into the passenger side of their navy-blue Mercedes.

'Hello there,' said Franny.

'Lovely evening for a walk. Enjoy,' said his wife before adding a closed-mouth smile. She let herself into the driver's side and drove off. Conversation complete.

Franny looked down at Soda who was relieving herself on the Prozeskys' thick green nature strip.

'I'd be careful if I was you, doggy,' whispered Franny. 'Don't leave your DNA around this place.'

She and Frank had always suspected the Prozesky pair of being Russian spies. How could they not? The Calderwoods loved making up stories about the people around them, inventing relationships and peccadilloes for fellow restaurant diners or nearby passengers on long-haul flights. When these exotically enigmatic neighbours moved into number twenty-four some five years ago it was like a golden nugget landing in Ipswich Street.

'Did you see the giant globe they had delivered yesterday?' Franny had said to Frank in the days following the new neighbours' arrival. She had been plucking weeds from the front lawn while Frank had pruned roses.

'Yes, very promising,' he had replied. 'I'm hoping it's one of those flip-top bar thingies with all the decanters and glasses inside it. We might get an invite.'

'Or it could be the disguise for a satellite or some kind of communication device—some way of speaking to the Kremlin.' Franny nodded towards the sky.

Frank had looked at his wife enquiringly and, with a smirk, said, 'Oh, I see where this is going. You're going to burden these poor people with your old-fashioned stereotypical, arguably racist, views about Russians. They're not the Petrovs you know.'

'Really? Then how come they moved in under cover of night?' Franny had waved her small trowel in front of her to accentuate her point. 'And, anyway, I see them more as Elizabeth and Philip Jennings types.' Franny had watched the television show *The Americans* so many times she could quote entire scenes.

'They did not necessarily move in at night, dear,' Frank had reminded her. 'We went out at four o'clock in the afternoon and didn't come home till the next morning. Remember? We stayed at Carl and Linda's for Linda's sixtieth. Presumably the truck arrived moments after we left.'

'You told me yourself that Tarzan said the truck arrived at nine o'clock in the evening, darling. Nine. What does that tell you?'

'The removalists didn't have a sat nav that spoke Russian?'

Franny had guffawed. 'Exactly! Now you've got it. We have ourselves some spies, my love.'

'Thank the lord,' said Frank. 'I'm so tired of living surrounded by rich plumbers, overextended real estate agents and clean-living overseas students.'

Tonight, with the Prozeskys off on another assignment—as Franny liked to think of it—she completed her ten-minute walk and was just metres from her house when she heard chattering. In the front garden of the house next door was a small boy of about seven or eight with startling blond hair styled in a manner so precise he could have starred in a Hitler Youth poster. He was playing with various action figures and dolls including Spiderman, something resembling Dr Who, a black Barbie and another doll with pale-grey skin and long purple hair.

I can see where the sister got the idea for her purple hair from, thought Franny as she approached.

'Okay, ladies,' the little boy was saying. 'No pain no gain. Let's try those burpees again. Your butts will love you for it.' He seemed to be voicing Spiderman who was shouting at the two female figures laying prostrate on tiny strips of fabric.

Franny's dogs were at the boy before she was, straining their leashes to maximum length. As Whisky's nose appeared over the low fence separating front lawn from footpath, the small boy jumped, holding Spiderman close to his chest.

'Hello, mate,' said Franny. 'You must be Josh. I'm your neighbour, Franny, the lady next door.'

Josh looked from her to the dogs with eyes wide as saucers.

'Where are my manners?' she added, letting go of the dogs' leads. 'This is Whisky and this is Soda.'

The mention of their names was interpreted by both dogs as an invitation to jump the little fence and begin inspecting child and dolls with equal thoroughness. Unimpressed by a lack of edible treats perhaps, Whisky headed over to a small shrub and relieved himself.

'Sorry,' said Franny. By this stage Soda had plonked herself next to the boy and was receiving a gentle ear scratch while waiting to see how things played out.

'Um hello,' said the little lad, slipping the Spiderman doll behind his back.

'What's that you've got there?' asked Franny. 'I think I know him.'

Josh pulled the doll out again and looked at him forlornly. 'He's meant to be Spiderman but I call him Cameron. He's their personal trainer.'

Franny looked at the set-up and realised the fabric scraps were probably tiny towels or yoga mats and she'd interrupted a workout session.

'Got it. How much does he charge? Do you think he'd train me?'

Josh looked at her, head on one side. 'Um, I . . .' he stammered.

'Just kidding, matey. Whatcha doing out here? It's almost dark.'

'I'm allowed,' the little boy said defensively. 'Mum knows I'm here. It's our garden.'

'Of course it is, of course,' cooed Franny, sensing a rising panic in the boy. 'You're the boss.'

'Oh,' said Josh, again looking confused. 'I thought you were . . .' He put a small freckled hand to his mouth.

Franny took a seat on the low fence and Whisky sidled up and nudged her pocket for a treat. 'Want to feed him?' she said to Josh and held out a few tiny bone-shaped biscuits. Immediately Soda was also on alert.

'Okay,' said Josh. 'How many?'

'No more than two each. And make them sit.'

As the boy tentatively doled out the treats Franny said, 'What did you think I was? You were going to say something.'

Josh looked around him, a small frown creasing his perfect brow. 'The boss, I guess. Mum said you're like the boss of the street.'

'Did she now?' said Franny with a grin. 'What else have you heard?' She held out her bag of treats to the boy, nodding to indicate he could give the dogs some more. She figured she'd reduce their breakfast helpings the next day.

'I dunno. Dee said you have a cool house and nice food and she wished our house was like it. There's no dad is there?'

'No dad?' Franny didn't understand the question.

'No husband lives there? No kids, like me?'

'Oh I get you. No, none of those,' said Franny, 'but there are these.' She pointed to the dogs.

'We had a dog,' mumbled Josh, feeding Whisky another biscuit. 'She died. She was little, like this one.' His voice trembled.

'You can play with mine if you want to,' said Franny. The words were dashing across the moat before her brain had time to shut the drawbridge.

'Really? That would be great. They'll be my friends.'

'Right, I better get going,' said Franny, holding out her hand for the treat bag. 'Bed time.' She needed to cut this conversation short before kid–canine play dates were being diarised. 'You'll have new friends at school soon,' she said and grabbed both dog leads, hauling Whisky and Soda back over the fence.

'That's what Mum says but . . .'

'But what?'

'I didn't really have them at the last one so this will probably be the same. It's okay. Especially if I can play with them.' He nodded at the dogs.

Inside her head—or was it her chest—Franny felt a weight like indigestion developing. 'Mmm,' was all she could get out.

'So if you're the boss of the street, what does that mean? Are there a heap of rules?' asked Josh as Franny moved away.

At this she had to laugh. 'Only one mate: we all mind our own business.'

'Huh?' said the little boy.

'Goodnight, Josh.'

7

Deal or no deal

Franny had spent the remainder of the weekend in her studio. This was a habit developed early in her retirement, once she realised visits to stores, galleries or other attractions need no longer be made in the company of the hoi polloi. Those outings were concentrated on weekdays and nights, when the parking was ample and queues largely absent. If for some reason she did stumble into a gallery, garden or shopping centre during the peak mania of Saturday or Sunday she was genuinely taken aback. When did people start queueing for hours for everything from avocado on toast to Louis Vuitton bandanas? Had they all gone mad?

Monday was her day for heading out, especially to the botanic gardens or the city's sprawling zoo. She had two projects underway, one focusing on pen-and-ink drawings of exotic animals and the other a series of water colours of flowering plants. Both necessitated out-of-doors study of the subjects, hence her current fixation with zoos and public gardens, and both were weather dependent. She did preliminary drawings and took photographs in situ then used these as the foundations for the final works, which she created back home.

With the weather forecast to be warm and sunny Franny was keen to hit the road but first she had her weekly yoga class to attend.

Sitting on the edge of the bed, tying up her shoelaces, she said to Bedroom Frank, 'I wish you'd met Calliope, darling, you really would adore her. She's almost as good as good old Bharti, without the farts of course.'

For more than fifteen years Frank and Franny had practised Hatha yoga on and off with a woman called Bharti Brown. When, at 77, the teacher decided to pack up her yoga mat and tingsha bells and move to San Diego to be with her son, the Calderwoods were devastated.

'I cannot be downward dogging with just any old Tom, Dick or Harry,' Frank had grumbled at the time. 'I'm usually the only bloke in our class as it is. That's it, I'm officially hanging up my mat.'

Initially, Franny convinced Bharti to let them film her during one last class so she and Frank could practise using the videoed results at home. Unfortunately, by this stage the teacher's dominion over certain bodily functions was on the decline and at key points during at least two of the poses some highly audible gas leaks escaped. Frank and Franny tried turning the sound down when following along but simply knowing what was happening on-screen was enough to collapse them in giggles. The video, like Bharti herself, was retired and Franny did not seek a new teacher until after Frank died.

'I'm not sure if you'd know Calliope's studio, darling,' she continued chatting. 'I discovered it when I was over in Bentleigh at Bob's Books, opposite The Chicken Joint. It's upstairs where some dusty little accountancy firm used to be. Just imagine how much you'd love it. An hour and a half of yoga, a bit of a bookstore browse, then off for a quarter chicken and chips. That's half your day taken care of right there.' Franny grabbed her rolled-up mat and small towel from inside the wardrobe and blew a kiss at the photograph. 'Anyway, these chakras won't align themselves. Bye, darling.' She left the room.

While Franny didn't mind the ten-minute drive to class, the parking situation around Calleidoscope Yoga Studio was a genuine drawback. You had to compete with the hordes of supermarket and high-street shoppers, including inexplicably irate women in gigantic four-wheel drives, tiny geriatrics peering over the steering wheels of even tinier cars and tradesmen sporting all kinds of dangerous protuberances from their vehicle windows and trays. The battle to safely snag a spot would test the Dalai Lama's patience.

Ending up at the furthest end of the carpark from the studio but with at least ten minutes to spare, Franny felt unruffled as she pulled yoga gear and her water bottle from the back seat of the car. Suddenly she felt a tap on her shoulder. Unruffled morphed swiftly into ruffled.

'Darling, I thought it was you.'

The voice was instantly recognisable. Franny smashed her head on the roof of the car as she spun around.

'Diana, what a surprise. I thought you and Jeff were on a cruise.'

'We leave tomorrow, you silly sausage. I said that on the message I left. That's why we were inviting you to our bon voyage party last night. I must say you look surprisingly well.' The final statement was delivered with a querying rise over the last word. Diana Thompson, a small round woman with a penchant for big hair and equally big diamond earrings, had one eyebrow raised.

'Do I?' said Franny, locking the car. 'I guess that's nice to hear.'

'Well I just assumed you must be sick, darling. To not have responded to my call. You were sick, weren't you?' Diana took a step back, allowing Franny to swing her yoga mat over her shoulder and lock the car.

'When did you call, Di? My phone's been playing up.'

'Both of them? I called the landline and the mobile.' Diana was like a dog with a bone.

Franny shrugged, trying hard for an elderly, confused expression. 'You know how bad I am with technology.'

At this Diana narrowed her eyes. In the three years since Frank died this woman had invited Franny to Christmas Day celebrations, New Year's Eve parties, she had tried to throw Franny two birthday parties and had invited her to join the local wine club at least eight times. The last offer she'd hoped might at least have appealed to Franny's baser instincts. All to no avail.

'I have to dash, Di. So sorry.' Franny indicated her yoga mat. 'I'll be late for class.'

'Heading towards Bob's Books then are you?' said Diana.

Franny nodded, surprised her old friend was familiar with Calliope's location.

'Great. I'm picking up our dry-cleaning for the trip from Renee's. It's just across the road. Opens at eight. So convenient. I'll walk with you.'

'Perfect,' mumbled Fran.

'So, you missed a lovely night. The party I mean. You could have caught up with all the old crew.'

Fran could picture this particular old crew very well. Like Frank, Di's husband Jeff had been an advertising copywriter in the 1980s. Unlike Frank, Jeff moved on to his own agency, which he later sold for a motza to a big multinational. From there he'd become a political adviser, a move that proved handy when Frank eventually took to speech writing. Many lucrative contracts and commissions materialised because of Jeff's well-placed connections. In recent years the Thompsons had set up a palatial home on this side of town, only to abandon its impressive outdoor kitchen and gurgling water feature most weekends in exchange for a five-bedroom 'shack' on a vineyard they'd bought into with their eldest son.

The 'old crew' Franny pictured encompassed a potpourri of pals from Frank and Jeff's advertising heyday alongside over-tanned tennis junkies, retired political windbags and a couple of anal-retentive wine club members. Just thinking about walking into one of those soirees on her own, elbowing into a conversation, facing the solitary cab ride home and she knew a night at Ipswich Street brushing the dogs' teeth would be preferable.

'Yes, what a shame,' she said to Di. 'I bet you had a ball. Maybe we can do it all again when you get back.'

As they crossed the car park, Di moved her oversized Chanel sunglasses to the top of her head and looked at her old friend warily. She and Jeff were famous for bookmarking their trips with extravagant bon-voyage and welcome-home parties. Because the duo headed off on Pacific cruises, Tuscan wine expeditions, German market tours and Balinese cleansing breaks at least six times a year this made for a substantial number of celebrations, leading Franny to once declare she needed a holiday from all the couple's holidays. 'They're going to New York on the *Queen Mary 2* not Antarctica with Scott and co. for God's sake,' she would complain to Frank. 'Why all the palaver?'

'We might not have a soiree this time around,' Di said to Franny. 'Jeff's scheduled for surgery three days after we return so there's not really time.'

Franny's spirits plummeted. Receiving bad news before yoga was like eating lasagne before swimming. Both left you feeling sick, heavy and struggling to stay afloat. This was one of the eight thousand reasons she no longer saw people. They had too many problems and brought with them too much pain; they demanded all your sympathy and were the harbingers of too much loss. The words 'too much' flashed across her mind.

'I'm sorry to hear that, Di,' she said. And she genuinely was. Frank and Jeff had been like brothers when they were younger. Di was a hoot when not jabbering on about her backhand or the great seats they'd scored at the Australian Open. Plus, Franny had to concede, they always served amazing wine at each unnecessary party. 'I hope it's nothing serious.'

'Lung cancer, which is unfair because he gave up smoking in his twenties,' said Di, pushing the sunglasses back down over her eyes. 'Surgery first, then radiation if they find it's in something called the mediastinal lymph nodes. Apparently, it reduces the risk of it coming back.'

Franny and Di had reached the sandwich board that marked the entrance to the yoga studio.

'So how long till the surgery?' asked Franny, even though she knew this was dangerous conversational territory. Knowledge wasn't power as she saw it, if anything it was the opposite. When people are certain you have knowledge of their lives and concerns it increases their expectations in terms of your involvement and support. Knowledge diminished Fran's power.

'Five weeks,' answered Di. 'Janet had a little girl a month ago. You knew that, didn't you? We're grandparents for the first time. That's where we're going tomorrow, to Paris to see them all.' She gave a sad smile. 'It's times like these it's hard having her so far away.'

Franny vaguely remembered receiving a frothy pink birth announcement card in the post, something bearing an image of a stork landing on the Eiffel Tower. She had binned it at once. One of the benefits of never having visitors was you never had to display their useless tchotchkes.

'Right, right,' she said. 'Well won't that be lovely for you all. And lung cancer is one of the most successfully treated around now. It's the cancer to get they say.' She was panicking in her rush to end the conversation. 'Actually, maybe that's bowel cancer?' She made what she hoped was a very exaggerated, confused expression.

Di did not smile. She certainly did not laugh.

Franny looked around a little desperately, her eyes landing on a lilac-haired girl who was leaning against the side wall of The Chicken Joint, smoking a cigarette, staring intently at her phone.

'Well, gotta go,' said Fran, swooping in to give Di a peck on the cheek.

'Why don't I meet you at the end of your class?' said Di. 'It would be good to talk. I have plenty of errands to keep me busy for the next hour or so.'

The idea flustered Franny so much she dropped her water bottle and, while picking it up, once again hit her head, this time against the sandwich board. The clatter and subsequent swearing caught the attention of the nearby phone user who looked up and gave a hesitant wave. Franny's fluster faded as she was struck by a brilliant idea.

'Hi, Dee,' she called out, waving to invite the young girl over. 'What are you doing here?'

Dee was in her school uniform again, dress hitched up by the backpack on her shoulder. She stubbed out the cigarette guiltily and approached.

'Diana, this is my new neighbour, Dee. Dee, this is Diana,' said Franny.

'Hello, Dee, lovely to meet you. You waiting for the St Columbus bus?' said Di, nodding towards the sprawl of uniformed teenagers that Franny now noticed lounging and posing around a bus-stop sign on the other side of The Chicken Joint. Once again Franny marvelled at her friend's knowledge of the area.

'Um hi, yes,' said Dee. 'Hi, Mrs Calderwood.'

'Dee and I watched the Oscars the other night,' said Franny. 'Great fun, wasn't it?' She opened her eyes wide and made a nodding motion over Di's head.

Di, initially surprised to be introduced to a new person by Frances Calderwood, and a teenager no less, was now out-and-out astonished, a fact she was struggling to hide.

'Really? Nice to know you're getting out and about, Franny,' she said. 'Maybe it's just us oldies you're avoiding.'

Franny stifled a groan. 'Actually, Dee came to my place. We had champagne.' That last bit was not something Franny had meant to share. 'Just a taste,' she added quickly.

'U-huh,' said Di, her tone even.

'Anyway, Dee, I was just telling my friend here that I can't meet her for a coffee after yoga because I'm going straight home to sign for an important package for you, well for your mum really. A fridge, isn't it?' She nodded her head as she talked and even added a wink. Di was staring too intently at the teenager to notice this performance.

Dee proved a pretty good actress in return. *Might be an Oscar contender herself one day,* thought Franny.

'That's right, Mrs C. The delivery guys said they'd be there any time after eleven this morning,' she responded.

'Such a pain, isn't it?' said Franny. 'The way they'll never give a specific time. Anyway, Di, you know how it is. And with Dee's mother working full-time, I'm only too happy to help.'

At this Di turned back to her friend, surprise plastered across her face.

'Mum said to say thanks again if I ran into you.' Dee steamrollered on with the conversation. 'And thanks for offering to drive me over to Poppy's party Friday week too. It'll be great to be back with my old friends.'

'You're really pitching in,' said Di questioningly. 'I have to say, I'm surprised.'

'Mrs C has been a lifesaver, really,' said Dee. 'Mum says sometimes new neighbours can be a real pain.'

'That's what I hear,' said Franny, graceful in defeat.

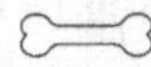

At this time of year in Melbourne, as summer handed over her reins to autumn, the light was magnificent and Franny relished the hours spent immersed in the botanic gardens. At afternoon teatime, she headed to the Terrace Café, indulging in scones with jam and cream while watching a little wooden punt glide around the ornamental lake, dodging the occasional black swan or small water bird. Not for the first time she thought, *Is it wrong that I don't miss being in the workforce one iota? I don't even know how people manage it now.* She was nearly ready to start painting her botanical series, a project that would occupy her through the colder winter months. She looked forward to a riot of summer colours inside her studio while the days outside turned bleak.

Turning into her street at the end of the day Franny saw Dee walking along with little Josh by her side. The pair were holding hands. Immediately Franny remembered the events of the early morning. The buzz created from a day spent sketching and people-watching in the beautiful March sun nosedived and fizzed.

'Hello, Mrs C,' Dee called to Franny's open car window as all three arrived at their driveways simultaneously. 'Was lovely to see you this morning.' She sported a cat-who-swallowed-the-cream grin.

Franny stopped the car at her gate, beckoning the pair over. 'Hello again, Dee, hello, Josh,' she said, getting out of the car. 'Just coming home from school?'

'Mum's at work so I had to pick him up,' explained Dee. 'He's not keen on the after-school club just yet.'

Josh made a miserable face. 'I'll never be keen,' he murmured.

Dee rolled her eyes.

'We need to talk,' said Franny to Dee. 'I guess I should thank you for today.'

'I guess so,' said Dee. 'You don't like that lady much, do you?'

The bluntness of this statement took Franny by surprise. She did not dislike Di, she just disliked the sadness and pity that crept into the other woman's eyes whenever they met. And more than that, and harder to admit, was the fact Di's life sometimes reminded Franny of all that she had lost in her own. She knew her old friend deserved to live life as she always had but that option was lost to Franny now. The reminder of this was too painful to ignore.

'I wouldn't say that. I just don't feel the need to see her and I certainly don't need to have coffee with her.'

'Who *do* you like to see?' Dee was grinning again.

'No one, especially teenage smartarses. Now what's this Poppy business Friday?'

Dee gave a quick shake of her purple head, inclining it towards her brother. 'Why don't you go inside and get changed, Joshie,' she said, handing him a key. The little boy began to protest but his sister cut him off. 'Get changed and we'll play Ball for a little while before Mum gets home.' Her tone was cajoling.

'I thought he didn't like basketball,' said Franny, remembering Dee's comment from the other night.

'That would be Ball with a capital B,' said Dee. 'A game he made up himself.'

Josh became animated. 'The basketball is the pumpkin carriage. It takes Cinderella to the ball.'

'We watched the 1950s Disney film,' said Dee in explanation, 'now he's obsessed. All we hear is bibbidi bloody bobbidi boo.'

You did, did you? That's interesting, thought Franny, remembering the throwaway line she'd made about Charles Perrault and Cinderella the other night after the Oscars.

'The fairy godmother turns the mice into horses,' continued Josh, strident in his defence. 'It's so cute. And beautiful.'

Dee gave Franny a what-can-you-do look then shoved the little guy. 'Off you go,' she said. 'Otherwise you can just do homework.'

'Okay, okay,' he took off, a comically large school bag dragging on the ground behind him.

'So, explain yourself,' Franny said to Dee.

'It's nothing. One of my BFFs from my old school is having a party and Mum's rostered to work. She won't let me catch the train. I've organised a lift home but can't get over there. I really need to go.'

'Need?'

'You know. I don't want them to forget me.'

Franny looked at the young girl for a long moment then sighed. 'I'm going to check with your mum on this. That's a stipulation.'

'Maybe that's not a good idea,' said Dee.

'I thought you said you're allowed to go.'

'I am but . . .'

Franny realised Sallyanne might not object to where Dee was going but she might object to who was taking her.

'I see. Well, if your mother has a problem with me taking you, I guess I won't be taking you,' said Franny. Escaping this new entanglement was not the worst outcome she could think of.

'But you owe me,' whined Dee.

'Not my problem. It's between you and your mum.' She used the clicker on her keys to open her gates. 'What time does she get home anyway?'

'Tonight? Around six,' said Dee.

Franny made a face. Right on Tanqueray time. 'Is she home tomorrow?'

'Think so.'

'I'll speak to her then. Gives you time to pave the way.' She got back in her car then popped her head out the window. 'One other thing, Dee.'

The young girl's face was sullen. 'Yes?'

'Real friends don't forget you just because they don't see you all the time. Believe me.'

8

Boy trouble

Late the next morning Franny was in her bathroom getting ready to go out to lunch when the front-gate buzzed.

'Bloody hell,' she said to Bathroom Frank, mounted in a frame by the medicine cabinet. In this photograph, her husband was immersed in an azure swimming pool. Arms folded on the edge, he looked into the camera, squinting against the sun and sporting a gigantic smile. 'It's like Piccadilly Circus around here sometimes. Who the hell can that be?'

Still in bare feet, she padded to the console near her front door. She strained to see the intruder but only glimpsed a blonde head.

A voice crackled through the intercom. 'Mrs Calderwood, it's Sallyanne, from next door. Can I have a word?'

Franny looked at her watch. She normally gave herself an hour before lunch to browse the second-hand bookstore around the corner from Bello Cielo. 'I'm on my way out actually,' she said.

'It'll only take a minute. Dee mentioned you might pop over but I have a meeting in the city that could drag on. I don't have your phone number and I didn't want to mess you about.'

Franny took a moment to consider her options. Sometimes, after a good Tuesday lunch, she liked nothing better than to nap for a few hours then work in her studio till the middle of the night. Other times she could read almost an entire book or binge back-to-back movies, stopping only for a walk around the block with the dogs before dark. Whichever way she looked at it, neighbourly visits were not high on her afternoon's wish list of activities. Cutting her losses she decided now was a good opportunity to get this little chit-chat out of the way.

'Come on in,' she said.

Sallyanne had definitely pulled herself together. Her hair was freshly blow-waved and she wore a navy pants suit, accessorised with discreet gold jewellery. Her makeup, though carefully applied, did not quite conceal the dark shadows beneath each eye.

'Well you scrub up all right,' said Franny without really thinking.

The other woman laughed. 'Thanks, I guess. I'm dressed for battle.'

'Sorry?' said Franny.

'I'm seeing my ex and the solicitor.' Sallyanne reddened at this admission and moved the topic along. 'So, Dee said you wanted to see me. Everything all right?'

Franny stepped back so her neighbour could enter. As she did so Sallyanne's attention was snagged by a huge framed poster hanging by the front door.

'You're a fan of Mr M and Timmy then?' she said, a note of surprise in her voice.

'Pardon?'

Sallyanne pointed to the poster behind Franny's back. 'Timmy Tuggernaught and Mr Marmalade. You're a fan? When I was a teenager I used to babysit some twins next door and they were obsessed. I must have read those books a hundred times. A poster like that would have earned me one hell of a tip.'

'Well, back then merchandise wasn't the big deal it is today,' said Franny. 'You had to be in the trade to get your hands on something like that. Not like now, with characters plastered on every second lunch box and beach towel. All bloody landfill of course.'

'You were in the trade then, like a bookseller . . .' Sallyanne's voice trailed off as she looked at the words beneath the image of a ginger-furred cat and ginger-haired boy—'by Frances Calderwood'—then looked back at Franny. 'Oh, goodness. You're that Mrs Calderwood. You created them.' A huge smile transformed her face and Franny was struck by how very pretty the younger woman was beneath what was probably a mix of exhaustion and anxiety.

'Well the cat created himself, to be fair, as in he was based on our real pet, but yes they were my books,' said Franny. Generally, she was quite happy to discuss the works, they harked back to a very happy, productive time in her life but now, in the face of the fan-girl from next door, she felt cautious.

'Anyway, it was all a long time ago . . . and you're here to discuss Dee.' She walked towards the kitchen, giving Sallyanne no option but to follow. 'Can I offer you a water?' She pulled out one of the stools for her visitor.

Wrong-footed by the change in topic and location, Sallyanne turned down the offer of water, saying she could only stay a minute. 'As I said, Mrs Calderwood. Is there a problem?' All traces of the joyful smile were gone.

'No problem and, please, call me Franny. I just heard Dee needs a lift to a party next week and I'm prepared to be the chauffeur but I wanted to check you really were okay with her going. She said your only issue was the idea of her being on public transport alone, but you know teenagers. I wanted to hear it straight from the horse's mouth.'

Sallyanne's face relaxed and she released a breath. *Just like the daughter*, thought Franny, *no poker face.*

'How on earth do you know about the party?' asked Sallyanne. 'Is she pestering you, making a nuisance of herself?'

'No, no,' said Franny. 'To be honest she got me out of a scrape yesterday. Helped me dodge having coffee with a friend. Along the way, however, she saw the opportunity for a bit of quid pro quo, shall we say. Smart cookie you've got there.'

'Hmm,' said Sallyanne. 'Smart when it comes to getting what she wants. Wish she'd apply those smarts to her schoolwork more.' Sallyanne fiddled with the gold chain around her neck. 'Anyway, I feel this is too much of an imposition. She can miss one party.'

'Look, I'm just paying her back for the favour she did me. I won't be making a habit of it, I can assure you.'

Sallyanne shrugged. 'Okay, if you're sure you don't mind.'

'We should exchange phone numbers,' said Franny, grabbing a pen and jotting down the numbers Sallyanne recited, both her own and her daughter's. 'I'll text you so you have mine.'

'Thank you,' said Sallyanne, who looked down at her watch and blanched. 'God, I have to go.' The words came out in a groan.

'Not looking forward to seeing the ex then?' Franny moved to escort her guest to the door.

'Understatement of the decade,' said Sallyanne. 'If I had my way, I'd never see him again.'

'And the kids?'

'I don't think they'd be that bothered right now either but that could always change. Either way, it's not an option, not with all the bloody lawyers and counsellors involved.' Her eyes darted around in a panic. 'God, where are my handbag and phone?'

'You came empty-handed,' said Franny as she opened the door. 'Calm down.' She put a hand on the younger woman's back. 'Seriously, Sallyanne, you do need to calm down a bit. Otherwise you won't be thinking straight in this meeting and that's how the bastards get the better of you.' Sallyanne's eyes welled with tears but Franny put one long finger up in the air. 'No, no, no,' she continued. 'Crying's just as bad. Remember WALAWAP?' She gestured to the poster behind her.

Sallyanne nodded her head. 'It was Mr M's motto in life: *watch and listen and wait and pounce*,' she said in a quiet sing-song. 'That was his secret to catching mice and birds.'

'Winnie the Pooh doesn't have the monopoly on profound statements when it comes to literature's talking animals,' said Franny, deadpan. 'WALAWAP comes in handy in all kinds of situations, believe me.'

Sallyanne gave a bemused smile. 'Maybe,' she said. 'I guess it's worth a try.' She looked sad again.

'Exactly. Try it then you can come back and tell him how it went,' said Franny, a rush of sympathy momentarily skewering her rational thinking.

'Tell who, tell . . . ?'

'Mr Marmalade of course,' said Franny, practically pushing Sallyanne out the door. 'Make sure the gate clicks behind you.'

Bello Cielo was busy for a Tuesday. Even the few tables on the street front, taking in views of delivery trucks and drug dealers alike, were occupied.

'What's the deal, Paolo?' asked Franny as her waiter, also co-owner of the establishment, placed a cold glass of prosecco on the table before her. 'What's with the hordes?'

'The hordes, Signora Franny, help pay the bills. Not all diners are as loyal and consistent as you.' Paolo leaned in conspiratorially and Franny breathed in his familiar cologne, a mixture of clean linen and cedar. 'My beloved business partner Jenna is dating'—Paolo mimed quotation marks in the air—'a manager from one of the hotels nearby. They do a lot of conferences and workshops. You know the type, lanyards around the necks at breakfast, knickers around the ankles by midnight.' Franny half laughed and half choked on the first sip of her drink. 'Long story short,' continued Paolo, 'we've become one of their recommended venues for lunch in the area. Today's lot are ophthalmologists, I believe. Something to do with eyes.' He crossed his to emphasise the point.

'Well I'm glad they're keeping you busy, old friend. Hopefully Jenna doesn't tire of this girlfriend too soon,' said Franny.

'Exactly,' said Paolo, topping up Fran's nearby water glass and waving a menu in front of her. 'I've asked her to try to keep her fanny exclusive for six months at least. Just till they book all their Christmas parties. Now, you getting something off the specials board or you want to see this, even though you know it by heart?'

Franny did know the menu back to front. Bello Cielo had been one of her and Frank's favourites, dating back to when Paolo's father and uncle worked the floor. 'BC' as they affectionately called the place, was a go-to destination for long Sunday lunches or when friends came to town. Tucked down an alley running parallel to a popular tourist strip, it was a locals' hangout and its consistency in everything from décor to menu to staff expertise was something

Franny treasured. The waiters were briskly efficient; quick quips and quick service their trademark.

After Frank died, Franny's first visit back was something of a milestone for his widow. *If I can handle this,* she had thought, *maybe I haven't lost everything after all.*

Both Paolo and Jenna had been working that day. Having heard about Frank's accident from another customer, they'd greeted Franny with hugs and shining eyes but very few words. Instead, they'd seated her at a small table wedged against the bar, one that she and Frank had never chosen. Jenna had then brought out a bottle of Taittinger and poured three glasses, raising hers towards a wall of black-and-white photographs nearby.

'To Frank,' said Jenna.

'To Frank,' echoed Paolo.

Franny had realised she was looking at a newly added image to the wall: Frank and Paolo Senior, who had died just six months before.

'May they finally discover that perfect fucken negroni together,' said Paolo quietly, 'and stop criticising the way I make mine.'

Franny had let out a relieved sigh. She had dined there almost every Tuesday since.

This week her choice was tuna carpaccio with baby capers and charred sourdough, followed by a stew of barramundi and mussels. Paolo was scribbling out her order when the sommelier, Ben, arrived by his side.

'Where am I taking you today, Lady Franny?' he asked, peeking over Paolo's shoulder to see what she had ordered.

Franny adored Ben. He wasn't much more than a kid, still in his twenties, but his scholarly approach to wine appreciation amused and impressed her and he had a childlike sense of wonder that she admired and sometimes envied. If the restaurant was unexpectedly quiet or if Franny lingered past coffee and dessert, the two whiled away an hour or so tasting from the new bottles dropped in by hopeful distributors. Ben loved Franny's tales of worldwide wine-drinking escapades and she loved his proclamations on 'terroir' and 'mouth feel'. Delicious and diverting, these conversations soothed her soul.

'I've come over all pescatarian today,' said Franny. 'Paolo talked me into the stew.'

'You won't be disappointed. And I see you're starting with the tuna. Fancy trying an Eden Valley Riesling with that? The notes of lemon blossom will cut through the richness of the tuna nicely I think.'

'Ah, Benjamin, my dear boy, your words are like music. Bring it on.'

Ben took a deep bow and departed.

Paolo looked on in amusement then said, 'He's going, you know?'

'No,' said Franny. 'We haven't even made it through petit verdot yet.' She stuck out her bottom lip.

'You and I both knew it was only a matter of time. I told you not to get too attached.'

Franny felt genuine sadness. Ben, having never met Frank, was one of the few people in her new life she could be her old self with. When her husband's name came up in her anecdotes and recollections it was welcomed with curiosity and amusement, not sorrow and pity.

Over lunch Franny leafed through her most recent copy of *The New Yorker*, tucking into a huge article on curatorial bickerings at New York's Metropolitan Museum of Art while also tucking into her aromatic stew. Finishing off a second glass of riesling, she pushed her plate aside and surveyed the dining room. Most tables were empty now, the office types and conference crew returned to their various grindstones.

Benjamin, polishing glasses behind the bar, looked up and caught her eye.

'Un café?' he mouthed silently, and Franny nodded.

Within minutes a squat little glass of coffee stood before her, a small biscotti tucked against its base.

'Paolo told you I guess,' said the sommelier. 'It's my last week.'

Franny's lips arranged themselves in a straight line. 'Yes, he delivered the news along with my prosecco. You're making a huge mistake.'

'You don't even know what I'm doing, so how can you know it will be a mistake?'

'You've still got a lot to learn. Just look at this coffee for God's sake.' She flicked the glass with her index finger.

Benjamin looked at her for a minute then laughed. 'That's an absolutely perfect short black and you know it.'

'You are a cocky little so-and-so my friend. What have you got for me to taste today? Better be good.'

Benjamin went behind the bar and returned with two tasting glasses and a bottle of white wine. Franny put on her spectacles to read the label's fine print.

'Take a seat,' she said, approvingly. 'What's he going to do, sack you?' She flicked her head in the direction of the kitchen.

Benjamin sat down and poured a small amount of wine into each glass then swirled his around. Franny inhaled a nostril full of grapey goodness before taking a sip.

'Ooh this is good. Italian?'

'Of course,' said Benjamin. 'You know what Paolo's like.'

'Is that why you're going?' she asked. 'Too much Italian?'

'The opposite, actually. I'm going to Italy to try to get some work during vintage. You know, get my hands dirty. Ideally, I'll end up in Montalcino; I've got some contacts there.'

'Tuscany,' said Franny, clapping her hands in delight. 'All right, I'll stop being so bitter and twisted about it all then. Is that everything?'

'Well, no,' said Benjamin, a proud grin spreading across his face. 'It looks like I've lined up a junior sommelier job at Locanda Locatelli in London. It's a Michelin.'

'Shut the front door,' said Franny, swatting at him. 'That is fantastic.' She turned in her seat, bellowing Paolo's name over her shoulder.

The owner rushed from the kitchen, hastily brushing crumbs from his shirt front.

'Signora, what's the problem?' he said, his voice low as he glanced over at a lingering couple feeding each other tiramisu between sips of champagne. 'And what's going on here?' Paolo wiggled his fingers at the collection of glasses and bottles in front of his seated employee.

'Oh relax. He's indulging one of your oldest, most revered customers,' said Franny, swirling the final drops in her tasting glass. 'Can you believe the adventure he's going on? You're just jealous.'

Paolo nodded his head. 'It is true,' he said with a solemn, ecclesiastic tone. 'Signora may well be our oldest patron.'

Franny threw her napkin at him.

'This pinot bianco is delicious,' she said, nodding to the wine Benjamin had poured her. 'Put it on my bill, Paolo. Let's share the whole bottle: celebrate.'

Sommelier and restaurateur looked at each other warily. Franny was in one of her expansive moods. They'd been down this path before.

An hour later, the wine finished and a glass of Moët & Chandon Grand Vintage 2009 downed by owner, customer and sommelier alike—'to really say bon voyage'—Benjamin escorted a slightly swaying Franny out to a waiting taxi. As he opened the car door for her she took his hand.

'You'll have a wonderful time,' she said, eyes suddenly filled with tears. 'My husband and I had our honeymoon in Tuscany. A lot of good memories. Maybe send me a card via Paolo?'

'Of course, of course,' Benjamin said, giving her hand a firm squeeze. 'And I'll be sure to toast you when I'm there.'

'Toast my Frank,' she said, climbing clumsily into the car and shoving on sunglasses even though it was six o'clock and the sky was a blueish grey.

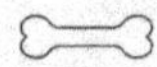

As soon as Franny let herself in the front gate she knew something was amiss. Whisky failed to launch himself on her like a hairy juggernaut, ears flat, bum waggling. The pet door at the back of the house meant both dogs had complete run of the property, indoors and out, when she was not at home, although Franny suspected her bed and the sunroom couch were as far as either ventured.

She was about to call their names when Soda appeared from the side of the house, quickly overtaken by a high-speed Whisky who landed at Franny's feet with a thud. The smaller dog's teeth grinned around a worn-out pink-and-blue tennis ball that Franny failed to recognise. She bent down to look at it, nearly toppling over in the process, as Whisky turned on his stocky little legs, inviting chase. Uncharacteristically, he didn't come back when he realised the strategy was unsuccessful.

''Ello, 'ello, 'ello,' said Franny in a cockney policeman's voice. 'What's this then, Soda? Where's your pal?' Soda's huge chocolate eyes gazed adoringly at Franny, her slab of pink tongue lolled out. 'You're panting, old girl,' said Franny. 'What's going on?'

In the taxi on the way home Franny had been tossing up whether to brew herself a strong tea then walk the dogs or pour herself a pinot and fire up season four of *Breaking Bad*. As she watched Soda amble off to the backyard she realised the only thing she was really fit to do was scrub off her makeup and hit the hay. The Italian wine, so delicious going down, now formed a dry, sour coat on her tongue. She felt the beginnings of heartburn at the base of her throat. Letting out a deep sigh, she followed the dogs.

Franny heard Whisky before she saw him. A begging whine emanated from underneath her prized hydrangea, a bushy tail just visible amidst the shrubbery. As Franny was about to shout at him to 'leave the bloody plant alone' she heard a little voice sing out, 'My turn, my turn, Whisky. I've got the ball.'

With that the pink-and-blue ball flew over the fence from the neighbours' side and Whisky tore out from beneath the plant, catching it in mid-air. Ignoring Franny's presence and radiating cocky glee, he dashed back under the hydrangea.

'Okay, okay,' said the little voice on the other side again. 'You know what to do.'

Franny heard snorting and snuffling, watched the tail bobbing in and out of sight, and wondered what the hell was going on.

'No fair, Whisky, you have to give it to me. It's my turn,' came the voice again. 'Want another treat?'

Placing her jacket on the ground, Franny kneeled to get close to the garden bed and the fence, struggling for a view line amidst plant life and wriggling dog. She soon noticed a hole the size of a mango had been dug beneath the wooden palings. Whisky was absorbed in a trio of complicated manoeuvres made up of moments of frantic digging, small nudges of the ball into the hole and quick snatches to grab it back. Leaning closer, experiencing a wave of heartburn as she did so, Franny saw a tiny hand, presumably belonging to Josh Salerno, shooting in and out under the fence as well.

'You don't play fair, doggy,' said the little boy again and this time a tiny biscuit in the shape of a bone shot through the hole. Whisky lurched at it and the small hand grabbed the ball. 'Hee hee, hee hee,' said Josh, followed by, 'Ready? Ready?' The dog was already shoving past Franny, well aware of the joy to come. Once again, the ball sailed over the fence. It bounced once before ending up in the terrier's mouth. He dashed back to the hole, ready to start again.

'Okay come on, Whisky, give me the ball.' Josh's patience impressed Franny. She often found her dog's obsessive, exhaustive ball shenanigans challenging.

Seeing an opportunity to play a trick, Franny gently but firmly moved the dog out of the way. The next time the boy's hand came under the fence she touched one finger lightly.

'That's it, that's it, boy, give me the ball,' said Josh, mistaking the sensation for Whisky's snout, no doubt. When no ball was forthcoming the hand poked through again. 'Come on, Whisky.' This time it was the child who was whining. 'Give me the ball. I have to go in for dinner soon.'

Franny grabbed the little boy's hand in a lightning move and growled. Josh pulled away with a panicked cry. Franny fell back on the earth, laughing raucously.

'Don't want to play anymore?' she teased.

Josh's voice quivered. 'Who's that?'

'It's Franny. Whisky's owner. I see you've dug a hole.' Franny struggled to get to her feet. She wasn't used to combining so much physical exertion with so much barramundi and booze.

'Whisky started it,' said Josh, whiney again.

'It's all right, matey,' said Franny, feeling benevolent towards young boys after her conversation with Benjamin. 'This dog is known to be a bad influence.'

She heard something being scraped along concrete and suddenly Josh's bright blond head appeared; he hugged himself to the fence with chubby golden arms.

'Whisky's not bad, is he? He just likes to play,' he said, slightly breathless from all the exertions.

'You're right,' conceded Franny. 'He just likes to play. He gets bored when I'm out.'

Josh looked back towards his house. 'I thought so,' he said. 'I was just helping him.'

'Of course you were,' said Franny, 'but I wouldn't want that hole to get too big. I wouldn't want him running away.'

'That would be bad,' agreed Josh. 'Our dog Luna was not even allowed in the front yard unless I kept her on her lead.' Suddenly his little face clouded over. 'I miss her.'

'I bet Whisky and Soda would have liked her,' said Franny. 'Where'd you get that coloured ball?'

'It was Luna's. Can I have it back please?'

Franny looked down at Whisky, whose mouth bulged with blue and pink. 'Drop it,' she said sternly. The dog swung its head from side to side, the tuft of hair between its ears forming a quiff. 'I said drop it.' Whisky plopped the ball on the ground, giving Fran a peeved look. 'Good dog. Here you go, Josh.' She passed the ball up to the boy. Immediately Whisky began jumping up and barking, confused to see his owner so blatantly relinquishing this prize.

'Do I have to let him keep it now?' asked Josh, his little face crumpled in a frown. 'He seems upset.'

'We can't always have what we want, Josh. He has to learn that.' The dog continued to whine and bark. 'Tell you what,' said Franny. 'Could you bring the ball over sometime and have a play? I know he'd like that.'

Josh's expression changed from pained to elated. 'Really?' he said.

'Really.'

All of a sudden, a voice called out from the house behind him. 'Joshie. Dinner!'

The little boy pouted his lips.

'You better go, mate,' said Franny. 'You must be hungry.'

Josh shook his head. 'Not really. It's sausages. Yuk,' he moaned. 'Mum normally does better stuff but she says there isn't time with all the unpacking.'

'It'll get better, mate. Things will go back to the way they were.'

Josh's face took on a slightly panicked expression. 'What? Will they?'

Shit, thought Franny, *me and my bloody big trap*. 'Things will get better is what I mean, mate, they'll get better. And Mum will cook your favourite dinners again. Maybe I'll even make you one.' *Get inside and shut your mouth, you crazy woman*, Franny thought, bending down to pick up the still yapping Whisky. 'Off you go. Enjoy your sausages,' she said and flicked Josh's arm to get him moving.

9

Just say no

Inside the world of The Wuthering Club, chat centred on a recent book-of-the-month called *Lullaby* by a French-Moroccan author named Leïla Slimani. Franny would chime in with her thoughts eventually but her first job of work involved scanning all recent comments on the book club's Facebook page, sniffing out the scent of her online nemesis, Nancy Friol.

Nancy lived in the Northern Rivers district of New South Wales and used the image of a flag with a tie-dyed Venus symbol as her profile picture. No matter which book the club was discussing, Nancy managed to shoehorn in a mention of her solar heating, her composting adventures, the yoni eggs she was trying out or her daughter's enthusiastic embrace of the menstrual cup. She was also a big one for doling out unsolicited advice, from how to raise children correctly (she had three and they had all moved overseas, which Franny considered suspicious), to how to maintain a happy marriage (she and her husband of thirty-six years still enjoyed tantric sex sessions), to why club members could no longer use the word 'disabled' in conversation (even if they had a disability themselves).

This week, although the book's themes were motherhood, child-rearing, immigration, domestic violence and mental illness, Nancy had somehow managed to introduce the topic of urban foraging.

'You have got to be kidding,' said Franny, leaning closer to her laptop and peering at the comment. She sat, perched on a stool at the kitchen counter, drinking espresso and nibbling on an almond croissant.

Since her overindulgence at Bello Cielo earlier in the week she had been trying hard to have what she seemed to recall Nigella Lawson calling 'temple days'. Last night, however, the temple had become much too boring so Franny decided a bar should be installed, one specialising in navy-strength gin.

'Can you believe this bloody woman?' she said now, looking over at the photo of Kitchen Frank in exasperation. 'There's a scene with a roast chicken carcass in this novel that shrieks with domestic menace and this Friol woman's going on about dumpster diving at supermarkets. For God's sake.'

Taking a good slug of her coffee, Franny began to type:

> While it's nice to see Wuthering members having fun with the chicken carcass scene and connecting it to urban foraging, I don't really think this is something to trivialise. Obviously, this is the first time in this book where you truly gauge the peril these innocent children are in. This is where we begin to discuss mental illness people!!!! I'm sorry, I just can't be so frivolous about such a sensitive topic.

'Boom!' said Franny with a laugh and closed down the Facebook screen, moving on to check her emails. She knew it would take a while for the comments to flood in, especially from her Northern Rivers pal who, at this time of the morning, was no doubt out tending to chickens or collecting beeswax to make her own cling wrap.

There was a time when attending a book club had been a flesh and blood affair, organised and hosted by her best friend, Anthea, and loved for its ribald conversations and outlandishly congested cheeseboards. All eight members rallied to support Franny when Frank died, helping organise the wake and constantly dropping by with copies of *Tuesdays with Morrie*, bunches of fresh flowers and a bewildering array of William Morris-patterned notebooks. Still, she had refused each invitation to return to their literary gatherings.

When Franny eventually emailed Anthea to say she no longer wanted to organise the group's annual Melbourne Writers Festival adventure, the members took the hint. This had been, after all, a tradition Franny had initiated, adding new activities every year, organising tickets, choosing restaurants, even booking city hotels. Upon receiving the email Anthea immediately phoned her old friend but Franny ignored the call. A week later one final book-club email landed in Franny's inbox, written by Anthea and copied to the rest of the group. *You'll always be welcome. We miss you*, she wrote.

With The Wuthering Club, Franny could be anonymous. Her Facebook nom de plume was 'Lady Marmalade', her profile picture a pen-and-ink sketch of her long-dead cat.

Franny enjoyed discussing books and ideas, always had, but now she could do it without all the pitying glances and enquiries as to 'how she was doing'. Early into her widowhood the sad, concerned eyes of others sometimes had the power to undo her anew, a risk she could ill afford. She also got to skip the feeling that conversations regarding 'couple stuff' shut down each time she entered a room.

The unexpected cherry on top, of course, was how obnoxious she could be online. Facebook was the watering hole for all the moral-campaigning, permanently outraged, advice-giving, mantra-mumbling social-media zealots she abhorred. The big-game hunter inside of her could not resist the chance to take a shot each time one naïvely stumbled across her sights.

Someone's having a birthday. Four horrific words filled the subject line of the email. Franny's eyes flicked to the sender. Who else but Margaret, sister-in-law and self-proclaimed keeper of all family milestones?

> Darling Franny,
> We're not long off from your day of days now. I think I mentioned on the phone to you recently that there's a quilt thing coming up and I might come to town. Only yesterday I realised that it's the weekend before your birthday. Isn't that the bomb as my grandkids say! I can take time away from the quilting gals on the Saturday night so what shall we do—dinner at your place (I'll pick something up or we can order in) or maybe a slap-up meal in Chinatown? Your choice. I'm in your hands. Ping me the names of places you like and I'll make it happen. (PS: Just don't make it for the Friday because that's the quilters' fancy dress dinner where they give out awards for Best in Show. I'm going as Scarlett Johansson's character from The Avengers, Black Widow. Can you believe it? Can't wait!) Love to Whisky and Soda. Hope you're keeping well.
> Kiss, kiss, Margs

Franny groaned, the sound building to a crescendo, bordering on a screech. Whisky, napping on his owner's still unmade bed, came running from the bedroom, barking excitedly. Soda, seated close to Franny's feet, stood up, head cocked to one side.

'No, no, no, no, no, no,' said Franny. 'This will not be bloody happening.' She reached down to give each dog a reassuring ear scratch. 'Doggies, this will not be happening.'

She took her empty coffee cup to the dishwasher and placed it inside then walked over to Kitchen Frank and picked up the frame. 'What's worse?' she said. 'The idea of your sister sausaged into black pleather—there'll be a wig involved, mark my words—or me enduring three hours watching her slop dumpling sauce down one of her Trent Nathan Resort linen shirts while she reminisces and cries? Happy birthday to me.' Franny put her fingers to her temple to faux shoot herself before putting down the photograph and returning to her laptop. She untied and retied her hair in a bun, then nibbled on the skin of her thumb.

After cracking her fingers like a concert pianist, she wrote,

> Darling Marg,
> How kind you are to be thinking of me all the time, especially when you have so much on your plate. The quilt festival sounds great. You girls really know how to have a good time. I can just imagine you wowing the ladies in your black jump-suit. Hope there'll be a burly Thor on hand! As for the birthday dinner idea, alas, lovely as it sounds I'll be away that weekend myself. My online book club is having a once-in-a-lifetime, in-the-flesh gathering in Hobart and I thought, what the hell, I'm in. You know you are always telling me to get out and do more . . . well this is me doing it. Should be fun. Of course, I'm devastated to be missing you. Still, there'll be a next time. Much love to Mark, Carrie and all the grandkids.
> Stay well, Franny XXX.

'She might not swallow that but at least it buys me some time. Talking about time'—Franny removed her reading glasses and gave a whistle—'bed-making, shower-taking and it's off for a walk.' She looked out the kitchen window at grey, cloud-filled skies then down at the two dogs now obediently at her feet. 'We'll stay local. Looks like rain.'

An hour later, bundled up in a hooded jacket, pockets bulging with tennis balls and treats, Franny and the dogs headed out the door. The walk to the park was spent fuming over Margaret's email and muttering about interfering so-and-sos. The walk home involved panicked strategising to escape the dreaded dinner. Back in Ipswich Street, Franny saw Sallyanne hosing down her car. Up closer she realised Josh was inside the small sedan, painstakingly polishing the windows. Her stomach gave a small dip as a vague memory tippy-tapped against her consciousness. Something about the child and a ball?

As Franny and her entourage approached the gate, the little boy caught sight of them and broke into a huge grin. Within seconds he was scrambling out the car door.

Franny's vague memory swiftly morphed into clear recollection and she silently cursed the bouts of sentimentality that sometimes afflicted her when drinking.

'Franny, Franny,' shouted Josh in his cartoon-cute voice. 'Hello, Whisky. Hello, Soda.' He bent down to let the dogs lick his entire face, his small hand still gripping a bottle of Windex and a cleaning rag.

'G'day mate,' said Franny. 'Helping Mummy with the chores?'

'Yes, I'm the best at it she says. Plus, I get a dollar.'

'A dollar?' said Franny. 'Nice work if you can get it. Don't let me distract you.' She turned to key in the security code on the pad beside her gate.

'Mum's going to take me to the pet shop. I'm going to buy Whisky his own new ball.'

By this time Sallyanne had noticed all the activity and turned off the hose. She came around to where her son and neighbour stood. 'Hello, Franny. Nice to see you.'

Franny gave a tight smile. 'Hello to you. I see you're both working hard.'

'Yes, well this one's particularly motivated.' She nodded her head towards Josh. 'He hasn't stopped going on about his puppy play dates.'

Franny noted the reference to more than one date with alarm. What the hell had she got herself into? 'Yes, well,' she said, 'we'll get there eventually. For now, we've all got weekend jobs to do no doubt.' Again, she turned towards the gate. 'See you soon,' she called over her shoulder and was gone.

Once inside she unpacked the dogs' things, washed her hands, then glanced at the clock. Nearly one o'clock; too early for a drink? A crisp German riesling was calling her name from the fridge but Franny had a painting of a Protea species she was itching to begin so she switched the kettle on instead. The firewheel tree, officially known as *Stenocarpus sinuatus*, was more like a miniature firework display than a flower; she had discovered it while exploring the Australian Forest Walk in the Botanic Gardens. Leaving the kettle to boil, Franny grabbed the laptop and headed to her studio. She wanted to download some photos of the plant taken on her last visit to the gardens so she could enlarge them to recreate its vibrant red ribs accurately. Plugging her phone into her laptop on the studio desk, she caught the vague sound of crying from the driveway next door. Edging closer to her open window, Franny heard little Josh sniffling and moaning to his mother. Words like 'Whisky', 'doggies' and 'why not' migrated her way. She closed the window and went back to the kitchen to finish making the tea.

A few hours later the light was beginning to wane. Franny stretched her arms above her head, arched her back and took a swig of ice-cold tea. Flicking on a lamp and heading to the en suite to wash her brushes, she marvelled, once again, at the way time vanished when she worked this way. These moments were precious, moments where she remembered what it was to feel happy.

Her mind still absorbed in a world of hues and brushstrokes, Franny jumped slightly at an eruption of noise from the front-gate buzzer and the dogs' barked response. On autopilot, she moved to answer. 'Yes,' she said distractedly into the speaker while also trying to shush Whisky and Soda.

'Franny, it's Sallyanne from next door. Mind if I pop in?'

Immediately regretting her daydreaming, Franny snapped back into the here and now; no point pretending she wasn't at home.

'Of course. Come in.' She pressed the security button and opened the front door. The dogs bounded out to accost the visitor. 'Sorry. They've been cooped up for a few hours,' she said.

Sallyanne made no attempt to stop and pat or acknowledge the pair. *Face like thunder*, thought Franny.

Standing at the front door, Sallyanne said, 'I won't come in. Just wanted a word.' Her voice trembled with emotion.

'Please,' said Franny, stepping back and nodding Sallyanne inside. 'It's getting cold.' She headed towards the kitchen, calling for the dogs to follow. 'Pull the door shut after the two beasts, will you?' she added.

'The beasts are actually what I wanted to speak to you about,' said Sallyanne.

Franny stood behind the island bench, glad for the buffer. *Time for a drink*, she thought, already pulling tumblers from the cupboard. 'G and T hour. Can I tempt you?'

'Franny, Josh is really upset and confused. You've really disappointed him.' The woman would not be distracted.

'Let me just grab the Tanq.' Franny headed to the drinks trolley for the bottle of gin while an exasperated sigh leaked from the other woman.

'Look, I'm sure it's no big deal to you but Josh doesn't have a lot of friends. When someone makes promises to spend time with him, he really takes it to heart,' she said.

Franny returned to her station to mix the drinks. She pushed one glass over to her visitor. 'I'm not sure I'd say promises were made, Sallyanne. You know how it is, you just say things in the moment.' She took a slug of her drink.

'That's not how it works with an eight-year-old,' said Sallyanne.

'What do you want me to say, dear? Maybe if he hadn't been hanging over my fence . . .'

'Actually, that was going to be my suggestion precisely,' said Sallyanne, red dots now burning on both cheeks. She pushed the untouched gin and tonic back towards her hostess. 'You obviously value your privacy.' She waved her hand around the lovely room. 'Maybe it's better for everyone if I just keep him out of your way. And if you refrained from making empty promises.' Her eyes filled with tears.

Bloody hell, thought Franny, *I've walked onto the set of a telenovela.* 'Sit down and have a bloody drink,' she said gently to Sallyanne, moving around to sit beside her.

Sallyanne wiped her eyes and looked at the glass tumbler hesitantly. 'I should be getting back,' she said quietly. 'Joshie's in the bath.'

Franny reached across the bench, grabbed the Tanqueray bottle and topped up her own glass. 'Cheers,' she said, raising it to her neighbour. Sallyanne shook her head gloomily but clinked her glass to Franny's anyway.

'Look, I did mean it when I said the boy could come over now and then. Just not today because I'm working. I didn't realise it was such a big deal.'

A couple of renegade tears escaped Sallyanne's eyes. 'I know you probably think I'm massively overreacting, Franny, and maybe I am. But Josh has been through a lot recently; I'm overprotective. I don't want him disappointed or hurt anymore. He deserves a break.' She took a sip of her drink and gave an appreciative sigh. 'This is really good.'

'I'll just ask straight out,' said Franny, her eyes moving to Kitchen Frank as if for reassurance. 'Is there something wrong with him? I mean, he seems like a great kid, normal and all, maybe a little smaller than your average bear, but what would I know? Half the world seems to be on some kind of spectrum now. Either that or they're allergic to dairy.'

Sallyanne sat back on the stool and ran her hands through her hair. 'Thank you for saying that, the good kid part, not the spectrum. Or the dairy.' She gave Franny a censorious look. 'He is great and there is nothing wrong with him.' She mimed inverted commas around the word wrong. 'But he is kind of sensitive and gentle and, well, not a boy's boy, if you know what I mean. He's on the short side for his age and not into football or setting fire to insects. He likes music and dancing and painting and dolls.'

'I see,' said Franny, throwing Kitchen Frank a knowing look this time. Sallyanne saw the glance but said nothing. 'So, am I to understand that in this so-called inclusive, politically correct, no-more-personal-pronouns world in which we are living, some things in fact do not change?'

'That's right,' Sallyanne said with a sad smile. 'In this post-gender, post-fact world, little boys still get tormented in the playground for being themselves. He had it rough at his old school and he had it rough at home. I want that to change now.'

'Home? Surely not Dee,' said Franny. 'She seems genuinely devoted.'

'Dee's more protective than I am, when she remembers to be.' Sallyanne laughed. 'No, sadly, it was his father. Josh's behaviour made Danny uncomfortable and Danny made that known, loudly, aggressively and regularly.' She polished off her drink.

'What an arsehole,' said Franny, 'if you don't mind me saying.'

'Ha! He gives arseholes a bad name. Couldn't agree more.' Sallyanne pushed back her stool, preparing to leave. 'Anyway, that might in some way explain why Joshie's a bit over-eager when it comes to company. He's seeking out kindness, at least that's what his counsellor says.' Immediately the tears returned. 'Bugger,' she muttered, rubbing roughly at her eyes. 'I've gotta get this under control. Anyway, I'm sorry for dragging you into it but it's probably best you understand the situation up front. Dodge that bullet and all the rest.'

Franny sipped her drink. 'I hope it's not too nosy but where are your folks in all of this?

'Dad's dead and Mum's interstate. She's not in great health so we don't see too much of her. And Danny's family . . . the cousins are great, I know Joshie is missing them, and Danny's mum is okay in small doses. She was kind to Josh so maybe that's another reason he's gravitating towards you.' Sallyanne gave Franny a cautious look. 'I think he is missing his nonna.'

'Hmm, not sure I'm nonna material but go on,' said Franny.

'Not much more to say. Basically, with everything blowing up, the extended family might end up in the collateral damage column. It's going that way currently.' Sallyanne held out her hand formally to Franny. 'Thank you for the drink and sorry again for the mother-bear act. I'll get out of your hair.'

Franny looked at the other woman's hand and shook her head. 'What's for dinner?' she asked.

'What?'

'I believe sausages were on the menu the last time I spoke to Josh. He was not impressed.'

'He's not crazy about tonight's menu either. Supermarket-bought chicken schnitzels. Why?'

'Let him come over here. You said he likes to paint, didn't you?'

'He loves art and I appreciate the thought, Franny but, like I said.' She made a little patting movement against her heart.

Franny put both hands up in the air in a stop motion. 'Listen, one of my best friends was a Joshua.' A memory of Don teasing her hair into a towering top-knot while Gary poured champagne flashed across her mind. 'We need more sensitive men. My husband was a stellar example.' She looked over towards Kitchen Frank. 'I know the kid probably has an early curfew but let me cook him a little pasta and he can fiddle around in my studio or play with the dogs.' She looked at the clock. 'It's half past five now. I'll have him back at yours by eight or so. Is that too late?'

'You have a studio?' asked Sallyanne.

'Yes. I'll show it to you when you bring him over. Would he eat carbonara?'

'He'd devour carbonara. Franny, are you sure? I'm still nervous that—'

'Let's leave it to Josh. If he enjoys it and understands the concept of working quietly then maybe he can come and paint every now and then, and entertain these mutts,' she said, nodding towards her two bored, dozing dogs. 'Actually, if you get him over here in the next fifteen minutes, he can feed them. I like to delegate.'

Sallyanne looked close to tears again. Franny grabbed her by the shoulders and marched her to the door before any more seepage occurred. 'Buzz the gate when you're ready. He can be in his jim jams.'

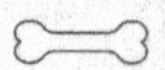

'Why's the pussycat wearing an eye patch?' Josh was examining every inch of Franny's studio with forensic intensity.

'He lost the other one in a knife fight with a Pomeranian. It's a long story.' Franny stood framed in the doorway, watching her diminutive visitor with amusement.

The small boy gave her a suspicious look but let the topic go, too distracted by the mountains of papers and pads, the crowded jars of coloured pencils and pens.

'So, you want to do some drawing while I start on dinner?' said Franny.

'Are we really having carbonara? With cream and everything?' Josh bent down to throw the pink-and-blue tennis ball he had brought along. Every time the child moved Whisky was at his feet, dropping the ball with obsessive persistence, committed to making the most of this splendid turn of events.

'All the trimmings,' said Franny. 'Where do you stand on parmesan?'

'Yuk,' said Josh theatrically. 'Smells like spew.'

Franny tutted. 'Only the cheap one in the can smells like that. Wait till you try my Pecorino Romano.'

'Pecker who?' said Josh.

'You're a pecker,' she said, grabbing a plastic container and handing it to the boy. 'Choose some paper and pens and throw them in here, then come out to the kitchen and draw for me. We'll keep the paints for another day, when you haven't just had a bath.'

Josh scrutinised the objects on offer with the focus of a De Beers diamond grader. He was dressed in flannelette pyjamas featuring retro space rockets and a kewpie-like boy in a spaceman's suit. The contrast between his cheery outfit and studious expression sent Franny back to her pasta-cooking with a broad grin.

'So, you're a bit on the arty side I hear,' said Franny once Josh was settled on a high stool at the bench. The water for the pasta was close to the boil as she finely chopped pancetta to add to her sauce. She had made herself a large white-wine spritzer in deference to her babysitting responsibilities.

'I'm not arty. Don't say that,' said the little boy quite seriously, putting down his pencil. 'Daddy doesn't like people who are arty.' He pronounced the last word as *art-tee*, emphasising it with an unattractive drawl.

Franny blew out a long, slow breath, picked up her wine and took a slug. 'Is that right?' *Daddy sounds like a complete moron*, she thought. 'Daddy sounds like he's a bit confused about what arty means. That happens. Some of my favourite people have been arty.'

'Like who?' he asked, resuming work on his portrait of Whisky. The dog was proving an uncooperative subject, unwilling to sedately pose, preferring his constant ball-dropping routine punctuated with a little backside licking.

'Well, there's me. And my husband, Frank. He was very arty, although he liked to use words for art more than pictures. And I've had friends who were arty and made clothes, and friends who were arty and dressed up in costumes, and friends who were arty and made movies. Dee tells me you play piano; arty musical people are among my favourites. In fact, I'd go as far as to say that arty people are some of the best people. It would be a boring old world without them.'

Josh looked thoughtful. 'Is that Frank in the picture in your studio? The one where you're in the white dress but you've got a black wig on?'

Franny spluttered a laugh and touched her white hair. 'That is indeed Frank,' she said. 'But that's not a wig. That's what my hair looked like when I was young. Then it turned white.'

The little boy peered closely at her over a chopping board that was now covered with spring onion and garlic. 'But one bit stayed black,' he said, pointing at the stripe running from her right temple. 'Is that still young hair?'

Franny felt the conversation going off topic. She was not in the mood to discuss follicles and grooming with an eight-year-old. 'Something like that,' she said. 'The point is, being arty'—she emphasised the word—'or artistic or good at painting or drawing, singing, dancing, you name it, it's all fantastic. You should be proud of it.'

'One of the boys in our class is artistic,' blurted Josh. 'He doesn't like anyone touching him.'

Franny looked at the kid to see if he was taking the micky. He was not. 'I think you'll find that child is autistic, Joshua, not *artistic*, though he could be both. That's a topic to discuss with your mother. Speaking of, she promised me you'd feed the dogs. Hop to it!'

Josh beamed and jumped off his chair, nearly landing on Whisky in the process. 'Really? Really? What do they eat?'

Franny pulled a plastic container of rice and chicken mix from the refrigerator. Soda's finely tuned senses led her to amble over from the couch to get involved.

'Okay, first we retire this thing from play,' said Franny, coaxing the soggy pink-and-blue ball from her terrier's mouth. 'Go put this in your bag to take home,' she told Josh.

Whisky let out a small whine but remained focused on the container of food. While the little boy was feeding the dogs, Franny took a peep at his drawing. It was in a cartoon style and quite good.

'You need to add eyebrows,' she said as Josh washed his hands and resettled at the bench. 'They add a lot of character.'

'What's character?'

'You know how Whisky sometimes looks confused and sometimes looks naughty?'

'Yep.'

'Well, that's character and his eyebrows help with it. Watch me.' Franny pulled some faces, drawing her dark brows into an angry frown, then shooting them upwards in a look of wild surprise. Josh began to giggle. 'See how much my eyebrows move around,' she said. 'They help you know what I'm thinking and feeling.'

Josh ran his finger across his own very blond, very straight little brows. He scrunched his face up, then opened his mouth wide in surprise. 'Mine don't move,' he said with disappointment. 'Mine are broken.' He put his pencil down with a thud.

Franny walked around to his side of the bench and cupped his chin in her hand. *Frank would bloody adore you*, she thought, not for the first time that evening. 'They're not broken, you duffer, they're just still growing. Look at Whisky.' The dog was busy licking its arse. 'Well, when he looks up,' continued Franny, making a disgusted face. 'He doesn't technically have eyebrows but you add them anyway, for fun and for character. You exaggerate. Know what I mean?'

'I think so,' said Josh. 'Mum always tells me to stop exaggerating.'

'Wise woman I'm sure. May I?' She reached down to grab a pencil and deftly added some eyebrows to the picture. One was cocked and one was straight. Immediately the terrier took on a look of utter confusion. Josh clapped his hands.

'Now he looks like I've told him there's no dinner,' he said, holding up the piece of paper.

'Exactly,' said Franny. 'But in real life I don't think he'd take the news so calmly.' While Josh stared at the drawing with renewed concentration Franny stared at him and a long-buried memory washed over her, literally buckling her at the knees. She put out a hand to grab the back of a kitchen stool, steadying herself before inhaling a deep breath. 'Talking about no dinner,' she said in a weakened voice, 'we better crack on and get you fed and home to bed.'

10

Lost loves

Tilly was the biggest secret in Frances Calderwood's life. If she couldn't talk about Frank, she could barely think about her baby girl. Perhaps father and daughter were together now, a concept that simultaneously broke and warmed her ageing heart.

Most people assumed Franny was not the maternal kind, and they weren't so far from the truth. She and Frank had taken a good few years to decide to procreate. All the debating and deliberating became irrelevant once the pregnancy test divulged its news. The pair's delight turned them into giddy children themselves.

Franny's myriad artistic skills transformed their apartment's spare room into a nursery fairyland. She continued to work, feeling energised by the new life growing inside her. Frank pandered to her every whim, driving her crazy at times with his endless offers to run baths or brew tea. They both saw this baby in the same way, one final perfect addition to their private, happy world.

Five months into the pregnancy, Tilly was named. Franny needed to know who she was talking to. The name was a family one, as in it belonged to a rabbit she had had growing up, named by her Irish father after his favourite cow back home. 'Good enough,' said Frank when he learned this provenance. 'Our rabbit was called Bugs so we couldn't call her that.'

When Tilly died, three hours after she was born, a chasm opened up in Franny's heart that she thought might require surgery if she was to survive. She demanded to go home within forty-eight hours of the birth, any physical discomfort she felt numbed to insignificance by the searing pain accompanying each and every breath.

Frank too had been close to the precipice in the weeks that followed. While Franny knew he had grieved deeply for Tilly, he seemed to fear for his wife more. After their tiny daughter's birth, then death, Frank had dragged himself away from Franny's hospital room to make some heart-crushing phone calls. On his return, he found his wife's door partly open. Getting closer, an animal-like keening could be heard. Peeping inside the room he saw his majestic Franny kneeling on the bed, rocking back and forth. She clutched a white crocheted shawl to her milk-tender breasts. Franny saw him at the door but did not stop. Instead, she held the shawl out towards him, her banshee sounds increasing. Frank was aware of footsteps rushing down the hall. He stepped back quickly, shook his head at the approaching nurse, then entered the room and quietly shut the door.

For some couples, a thing like this can mark the end, an experience of such devastation and pain that they cannot go on together, cannot bear the loss reflected in the other person's eyes. For Franny and Frank, it was different. Their child had gone but she left them with a precious gift, fusing them with a closeness of such intensity it was hard to fathom.

Within a fortnight of the loss they were on a Greek island. For Franny, it was the only path she could bear. The questions and conversations, the shock and concern were too much for her to handle at home. Frank's sister, Margaret, had done the heavy lifting in their stead. Flying down to clear out the most painful items in the apartment, corresponding and conversing with the friends, family and colleagues still reeling from the news. She and Anthea, the only person Franny had spoken to directly in the wake of Tilly's death, became a grimly focused team. Anthea got a local house painter over to return the nursery to a simple spare room. In later years Franny would sometimes find herself imagining that scene: her best friend standing at the door and weeping, watching the roller do its work, smoothly and quietly replacing an enchanted forest with stark, white gloss.

11

Border crossing

Franny was in the backyard, hosing down the dogs after an early-morning beach walk, when she heard Sallyanne's voice from over the fence, calling her name.

'Rushing to get out to the movies, dear. Can it wait?' she called back.

Sallyanne's head popped over the palings, her hair turbaned in a towel. 'I just wanted to thank you again for the other night. Joshie definitely enjoyed himself.'

'He's very welcome. Glad he had a nice time. Look I have to go. There's a new Catherine Deneuve on at The Grand at eleven. I like her now she's chubbier.'

'You're terrible, you know that don't you?' said Sallyanne. 'Listen, come over for dinner with us tonight? It's my first proper break from work in a week or more. You'll be our inaugural house guest. Please.'

Franny, bending down to dry out Whisky's ears, hesitated briefly but could not come up with an excuse on the spot. 'Is it those schnitzels?'

'No, it's not those schnitzels. It's roast chicken and scalloped potatoes, the kids' favourite.'

'Hmm. Sounds acceptable,' admitted Franny who had a penchant for spuds in all their guises. 'I'll bring the chardonnay. What time?'

'It's a school night, is 6.30 p.m. too early?'

'Not at all. Do you need dessert? There's a wonderful Italian patisserie next door to the movies.'

'I hadn't thought about it but that sounds fantastic,' said Sallyanne. 'Don't get carried away.'

'Just a humble cannolo or two. See you then.' She headed indoors.

'Your sister is at me again,' Franny said, scrubbing determinedly at a wine stain on her favourite grey marl tracksuit pants. Laundry Frank snoozed on from his sun lounge, undisturbed by the chatter.

Upon returning from the movies she had opened her email to discover a new missive from her sister-in-law Marg.

> Hello Franny,
> I cannot believe you're going to be in Hobart just when I'm in Melbourne. What are the chances? Still, this gives you the chance to see Eleanor's new place. You remember Eleanor . . . she came to see La Bohème at Mrs Macquaries Point with us all that time—when we met up in Sydney. Frank was quite taken by her from memory. You know she's moved to Tassie now??? I'll tell her you're coming; she'd love to see you. I'll just pass on your email and phone details to her and I'll SMS her contact details to you so you can set something up. You won't believe her new place . . . Battery Point, fifteen mins up the hill from Salamanca Market. Amazing apartment in an old schoolhouse there. I think Errol Flynn was once a student. You'll love it. And you'll get to meet that new bloke of hers, Marty. He's a retired orthopaedic surgeon or some such. Loads of spondoola. Anyway, can't wait to get a snapshot of

the two of you together. And, don't you worry, I'll send you
one of me in my costume, with or without Thor!
Love, Margs xxxx.

'She thinks she's got me now, the wily old mare,' continued Franny, wringing out the pants and throwing them inside the washing machine. 'She's using Eleanor to trap me. If I say no to seeing her then I'm admitting I'm not in Hobart. Why did I bloody well choose Hobart?' She leaned forward and rubbed suds off Frank's photograph. 'In other news, I'm off to dinner next door. Can you believe it? Never rains but it pours. Still, it will be nice to have someone else doing the cooking and washing up for a change. You don't exactly carry your weight anymore,' she said, leaning forward and lightly kissing the frame.

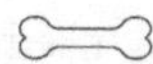

Franny knocked on the Salernos' front door just after half past six, heartened by the smell of buttery goodness in the air. Dee opened it, only to be pushed sideways by her little brother, rushing to present a large sheet of paper to the visitor.

'This is for you, Franny,' he said, holding his artwork up high so Franny could get a better view. 'I've been working on eyebrows.'

With her hands occupied by boxes and bags Franny couldn't take the paper from him. Instead she bent down for a closer look, emitting a few 'oohs' and 'ahhs' in appreciation.

'For God's sake, Josh-man, let Mrs C in the door, would you? No one cares about eyebrows,' said Dee, grabbing his small outstretched arm and steering him out of the way.

Franny and Josh both stopped to look at her.

'Well that's not strictly true, Dee. Eyebrows are crucial to facial character in artwork,' Franny said. She looked down at Josh and gave him a courtly nod. 'But I wouldn't mind getting rid of the rum baba and cannoli before handing out appraisals.'

'I know what cannolis are but what's a baba and what are appra-zels? Are they like Cheezels?' asked Josh, excited at the prospect of new food treats.

Before anyone could reply Sallyanne appeared further along the hallway, wiping her hands on a tea towel and saying, 'Would you two let the poor woman in? Sorry, Franny, they're less house-trained than the two at your place.'

The townhouse was long and thin, its bland and featureless interior already familiar to Franny, who had nosed around during an open-for-inspection a couple of years earlier.

'The Constantinou family used to live here,' she said, stepping around a smallish black-and-orange BMX bike and a nest of trainers and other shoes. 'Lovely family. Cyprians. All dead or moved elsewhere now of course.'

A memory flashed across her mind. Young Gina Constantinou weeping on Franny's doorstep, explaining that Vassilis and Eleni's home of thirty years would be knocked down: her dad was dead, her mother in a nursing home with dementia. Gina's brother, Bill, was keen to capitalise on the booming property market. Within a few months the old lemon and apple trees next door were gone, along with the yellow-brick house and its faux marble patio. Two mass-market townhouses appeared instead; the builder's brochure listed the model as The Vogue, Franny preferred to call it The Fugue.

She placed a white box stencilled with the name 'Abruzzo Bakery' on the small, risen ledge that covered one half of the kitchen island, screening a double sink tucked in on the other side. 'You've done a good job of unpacking,' she said looking around. 'Looks like you've been here for ages.'

'Is that a veiled way of saying the place is a mess?' said Sallyanne with a good-natured smile. She reached out to take a bulging tote bag from Franny's other hand.

'On the contrary. I thought you'd still be at the boxes phase.'

'Well thank you for noticing,' said Sallyanne. 'Not everyone appreciates my efforts.' She gave Josh a dirty look. 'They prefer to go around criticising my cooking instead.'

Josh opened his mouth, poised to argue his case, but Dee was too quick. 'Whatcha got there?' she asked, directing her nose to the canvas tote.

'Supplies for the adults,' replied Franny, moving to join Sallyanne by the sink. 'I've taken the liberty of bringing some libations,' she told her hostess. 'Hope you don't mind.'

She pulled out two bottles, one of Tanqueray No. Ten and one of Dolin Dry Vermouth, along with a stainless-steel cocktail shaker and a tall, skinny box. 'I like to bring housewarming gifts that benefit me too.' She undid the box and pulled out two elegant cocktail glasses. 'Hope you like martinis, Sallyanne. Here, Dee, make yourself useful.' Franny handed the girl a bottle of chardonnay, adding, 'Grab some ice while you're putting this in the fridge.'

Soon both junior Salernos were settled on stools at the bench, eyes glued to Franny as she made the drinks. Their neighbour's tote bag was like Mary Poppins' carpet bag, but instead of a hat stand and potted plant, Franny produced a jar of olives and a packet of toothpicks. When she sloshed vermouth around each glass then tipped it down the sink, each child looked astonished. Their mother stood back studying them, her face in a broad grin.

'Let's sit down for a minute and enjoy our drinks,' she suggested, inclining her head towards a grey, L-shaped sofa and a low coffee table nearby. On the table was a bowl of nuts, a bowl of potato chips, a Disney Princess water bottle and a Spiderman action figure.

'Don't mind if I do,' said Franny, picking up the drinks and letting the youngest member of the household lead the way.

'Cheers to you. And thank you again for being so kind to us all. We really appreciate it,' said Sallyanne. Franny said nothing but her cheeks turned pink. 'This is fantastic, by the way,' continued her hostess, taking an appreciate sip of her drink. 'Danny wasn't much of a social drinker and he certainly never thought to make me something like this.'

'Really?' said Franny, looking genuinely dismayed. 'Frank and I had a pre-dinner cocktail no matter what. When he was working on the election trail he'd often call me from interstate and we'd share them over the phone.'

'He was a politician then?' asked Sallyanne, handing the bowl of chips to Franny who declined. Josh leaned in and grabbed a bulging handful.

'God no,' said Franny, smiling. 'He was a speechwriter for a while, years ago now. It was something he fell into. Good money. Long hours. Too much travel. Quite the boys' club in those days of course. They probably had a lot more freedom than today's lot.'

'I bet you have some stories,' said Sallyanne, her eyes glittering. Franny noticed she was already two-thirds of the way through her drink.

'Not suitable for these ears.' She gestured towards the children. 'But yes. There's some gin left in the shaker. How about a top up?' She ambled over to the kitchen to retrieve it. 'The only thing you're missing is some artwork,' she said once seated, surveying the bare walls while sipping her martini. 'Cheers anyway. Thank you for having me over.' She clinked her glass against Sallyanne's then held it out to the children who were making do with iced water.

Franny was dressed in a pair of raw silk cigarette pants in muted gold and a ruby-coloured velvet blouse with a mandarin collar. Her long white hair with its distinctive black stripe was pulled up in a high chignon and a turquoise and amethyst dragonfly swayed beneath each earlobe.

Josh ignored the toast, his little hand on autopilot, already reaching out. 'Can I see your earrings?' he asked.

'They look delicate, darling. Why don't you just admire them from afar,' said his mother, giving Franny an apologetic look.

'No, no, he's fine,' said Franny, undoing a gold hook and passing over one of the earrings. 'My husband Frank had them specially made for me by a friend, many years ago now. The dragonfly represents good luck, you know. They were his gift to me for my first major exhibition.'

'You showed your art as well as produced the Mr Marmalade books?' asked Sallyanne while her son, tongue stuck out in concentration, examined the small piece of jewellery, turning it over and over in his hand.

'Painting and exhibiting were my first loves, actually, but then Marmalade and co. came along, plus a few other book series, and I somehow lost the habit. For a long time most of my artwork was linked to something commercial or to a brief. In recent years I'd started working in a gallery part-time, but painting just for the love of it had fallen by the wayside.'

'Joshie said you've got quite a collection of art supplies over there,' said Sallyanne, taking a sip of her refreshed martini. 'So does that mean you still work professionally? I think you mentioned it being a work day when I came over the other evening.'

'I don't work for pay anymore if that's what you mean; I just work for pleasure. The weekends tend to be when I really knuckle down. I'm painting a series of plants right now. That particular day I had a protea I was itching to start on.'

Franny felt a renewed rush of self-consciousness about the clash she and Sallyanne had almost had. Josh had been charming company in the end and the dogs were exhausted after all the attention. She found herself looking forward to him visiting again.

'You look young to be retired,' said Dee.

Her mother made a small choking sound on her martini but Franny just laughed.

'Well I'll take that as a compliment, young lady,' she said. 'As it happens, I'm nearing sixty-five. I retired when my husband died.'

'How long ago was that?' asked Sallyanne. 'If you don't mind me asking.' She moved forward a little in her seat.

Franny sat further back in hers, sipping once more from her drink. 'Almost three years ago. Hit while riding his bike.' She looked over at Josh who was no longer playing with the earring and was staring intently at her. 'The driver was not in his right mind,' she whispered to Sallyanne then, reverting to a normal level said, 'What about you, Sallyanne? I think the kids said you're an emergency nurse?'

Sallyanne took the conversational baton with aplomb. 'I'm what they call an after-hours coordinator these days,' she explained. 'It's a bit less physically taxing than ward nursing and the hours are more flexible for me now I'm . . .' She waved her hand around in a general way. Franny understood and nodded. 'Anyway,' she continued, 'I've started at St Michael's. You know it?'

Franny did know it. Though pronounced dead at the scene, the ambulance was still obliged to take Frank to the nearest emergency department, which happened to be at St Michael's.

'Yes,' was all she said then she slugged down the last of her cocktail. 'Well that was delicious if I may say so myself.'

'It was,' agreed Sallyanne. 'Maybe we should have some food before I start slurring. Pop on some music, honey,' she said to Dee. 'Nothing with bad language.'

Josh clapped his hands together. '"Can't Stop the Feeling!", "Can't Stop the Feeling!",' he said, jumping up and down.

'Jesus, Josh. There's more to the world than Justin Timberlake,' said Dee.

'But he's the best to dance to,' said Josh, already doing a little robot walk behind the sofa.

Franny smiled as his sweet, high voice began warbling something about sunshine and pockets and soles and feet. 'Dinner and a show,' she said. 'I love it.'

Josh gave his sister a triumphant look, continuing to jig around.

'Dee, how about that dinner-party mix you found for me on Spotify?' suggested Sallyanne. 'Nice and mellow. We'll keep the stage show for after dinner.'

Franny put out her bottom lip in a gesture of solidarity but said to Josh, 'Sounds like a good idea. You can work off the scalloped potatoes.'

Dinner served, chardonnay poured and inoffensive jazz playing in the background, Sallyanne settled herself at the table and proposed a toast. 'Well you two,' she said, holding up her glass and taking the time to look each child in the eye, 'our first proper dinner in our new house with our first proper dinner guest.' She raised her glass towards Franny. 'Well done to us. I think we're doing okay.' Her eyes shone suddenly with unshed tears.

Franny caught Dee's eye just as the girl was about to open her mouth. She raised her eyebrows in tandem with her glass.

'Well from the outside looking in I think you're doing remarkably well . . . organising the move, setting everything up here, and keeping up with a demanding job as well,' said Franny. 'Hugely impressive. Wouldn't you agree?' She clinked her glass against Dee's iced water and then against the tumbler of milk next to Josh's plate.

'S'pose so,' mumbled Dee.

Josh, cheeks already bulging with potato, nodded enthusiastically.

The meal was indeed delicious and Franny expressed her appreciation by using a finger to scoop up remnants of cheese and cream from the edge of her plate. Josh looked on with admiration.

'Whisky taught me that trick,' she said, standing up to clear everyone's plates. Sallyanne protested but Franny said it was the least she could do. 'Anyway,' she added, 'Dee will help me, show me where things go, won't you, dear? And Josh can get set up to dance.'

Dee glared at her mother but said nothing, just pushed out her chair and stomped towards the dishwasher, salad bowl in hand.

Sallyanne, two glasses of wine under her belt, was beaming. 'Come on, Joshie,' she said. 'Let's see you tear up the rug.'

By the time everything was cleared and Josh had changed the music Dee was preparing to flee. 'Gotta go do my homework,' she said. 'Better say goodnight.'

'Don't be rude, darling,' said Sallyanne, twist-dancing to the Justin Timberlake beat emanating from the speakers. 'You said you'd finished. Plus, we have a guest. Plus, you should have a dance.'

Josh began gyrating across the lounge-room rug, little hands hooked in the waist of his jeans, cowboy style.

'As if,' said Dee, rolling her eyes. She slumped down on the couch beside Franny, projecting disgust at the sight of mother and son's joint balletic forces.

'She's got some good moves.' Franny pointed to Sallyanne, now spinning her giggling son across the floor.

'Puh-lease,' said Dee, putting her hands across her eyes to block out the shame.

'I think she's pretty impressive in a lot of ways, but what would I know?' said Franny. 'Anyway, speaking of moves, have you got all yours worked out for Friday night? I'm assuming you still need that lift.'

'Definitely,' said Dee. 'I mean, if that's still okay.'

'A deal is a deal,' replied Franny. 'Got an outfit planned?'

'Something everyone's seen like a gazillion times,' grumbled Dee and jutted her chin out towards her mother. 'She says we can't afford anything new.'

'Poor diddums,' said Franny and gave a little pout. 'There are children starving in Africa you know.'

'Yeah well there are girls buying Chloé online at my school so swings and roundabouts I guess,' said Dee haughtily.

Franny raised her eyebrows. She had heard Elouise mention this Chloé. 'All right. I remember what it was like, even if you don't believe me.' Narrowing her eyes, she looked at Dee and said, 'If you were a nicer child I might even be tempted to help.'

Dee looked Franny up and down, from the black-striped hair to the bare ankles and ballet pumps. 'Really? How?'

'Don't look at me like that, you brat. I happen to have quite a few vintage bits and bobs you might like. A Glomesh shoulder bag for starters and a Wrangler denim jacket my goddaughter's always eyeing off. And don't even start me on jewellery. You can come over and take a look before you go.'

Dee's eyes widened. 'I know those brands,' she said. 'They're, like, old-school famous.'

'Is that so,' said Franny, feigning surprise. 'Well who'da thunk it? Anyway . . . up to you.'

12

After party

When Friday night arrived, Dee was seated in the passenger seat of Franny's army-green Skoda. Behind her, the windows of the car were fogged from Whisky's and Soda's combined panting.

For more than an hour the young girl had trawled through two tightly packed wardrobes in Franny's smallest spare room, discovering a cache of incredible clothing and accessories collected over the years. At one stage, holding up a gold lame jumpsuit and a velvet halter neck evening gown against herself, Dee had bemoaned the fact she was shorter than Franny by five or so inches. 'You must have been smoking when you were young,' she had blurted then giggled and put a hand to her mouth in embarrassment. 'I mean not that you're not great looking now or anything but . . .'

Franny, seated on a bed once saved for guests—now more often used by Soda—had looked down at her long, lean legs clad in navy Adidas track pants and said, 'You work with what you've got kid.'

Now Franny watched as Dee carefully examined her reflection in the car's side mirror, tucking her hair behind her ears to show off the wares. She was wearing her white jeans again, this time matched with a borrowed Wrangler denim jacket. One wrist was dwarfed by a stack of Franny's thick plastic bangles and large triangular yellow earrings hung from each earlobe.

As she started the car, Franny could feel her passenger's eyes on her, seemingly examining her profile.

'Ever leave the house without these two?' Dee asked eventually, nodding back towards the dogs.

'Those two, as you call them, are superb company,' said Franny, checking for oncoming traffic and heading out of the drive. 'They don't talk back. You cannot imagine how charming that can be.'

'Funny. Dad used to like that about Luna, our dog that died,' said Dee. 'He's a big one for not talking back too.'

Internally, Franny debated which way to respond. A quick check on directions now or an innocuous query about the party would shut this discussion down. Instead, guided by either her conscience or the age-old conversational power exerted by car interiors, she took it further.

'You miss him, your dad?' she asked.

'I miss Luna more,' said Dee, opening up the small suede clutch purse she had also borrowed and pulling out a lip gloss.

Franny chuckled. 'Tough talk,' she said. 'I hear he was a bit rough on your brother.'

Dee, who had pulled down the visor to use the mirror, looked at her sharply. 'Mum told you that?' she asked, clearly surprised.

'Yes.'

Dee said nothing for a moment, just nodded her head slowly. 'Yeah well, she ignored it for long enough. I mean, who calls their own son a faggot?' She slammed the visor back loudly and Whisky gave a bark. 'Sorry,' she mumbled. 'I just . . .'

'I can imagine,' said Franny, eyeing the car's navigation system to check the route. Dee leaned towards the radio, hand out to change stations. Franny growled, 'Never touch another woman's radio. You can turn it up though.' 10cc's 'I'm Not in Love' blared from the speakers and Franny started to sing. Dee gave an eye-roll but, surprisingly, joined in.

Twenty minutes later, with the party house in sight, Franny said, 'What's the story with booze and dope tonight? I get the sense you see yourself as a bit of a Sid and Nancy type but you are, in fact, underage. You should be careful.'

'What's a Sid and Nancy?' asked Dee.

'Not important right now.' Franny groaned. 'Answer the question.'

'The answer is that I covered all of this this afternoon—with my actual mother.' Dee opened the car door and got out, turning at the last minute to say, 'Thanks for the ride though.'

Franny watched her run towards the front steps of the house where she could just make out two teens in a passionate embrace. 'You're welcome,' she muttered and restarted the car. 'And so is your poor mother.'

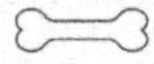

Franny poured the last drop of a Tasmanian pinot noir into her glass and began shutting down her laptop. She had been grazing on cheddar cheese and a box of Ritz crackers for a few hours, while devouring an Elizabeth Strout novel for The Wuthering Club. Surprised to see it was after eleven o'clock, she had wandered to her studio to google ticket prices for an upcoming watercolour and gouache exhibition before heading to bed. Within minutes, however, the siren call of Facebook had its way, alerting her to the news that Nancy Friol had taken the bait.

Beneath Franny's comment about the chicken carcass, Nancy had written:

> Actually my son recently told me one of his colleagues (a professor at Berkeley!!!!) is doing studies to show poor people that it's feasible to eat foraged greens. I think we'd all agree the public health benefits could be immense.

Two Tanquerays and three glasses of stalky wine under her metaphorical belt, Franny was feeling liquid gold inside and reckless.

> Four words: Not. The. Faffing. Point.

She was careful to avoid actual swear words for fear of being slung out of the group.

> I think we're meant to be talking about the actual contents of the actual books we're reading on this page, dear. Maybe you should look for a group called, WOMEN WITH SONS AT BERKELEY. I'm sure there is one. And if the best advice your so-called professors have for POOR PEOPLE—as you so eloquently call them—is digging up driveway weeds for dinner, maybe it's time they swapped places with these folks!!!!

As she sat back in the old leather office chair, chortling to herself, Franny heard a strange noise outside. She turned off her desk lamp and crept over to the window. The warm, hairy bulk of Soda suddenly pressed against her leg, the old dog cocking its head as the unmistakable sound of retching drifted over from the driveway next door.

Looking over at Studio Frank, Franny whispered, 'Five bucks that's the girl in the yellow triangle earrings.' His strained but smiling face gazed back at her. 'All right, all right, I'll go take a look,' she added.

Moving first to the bedroom where she knew Whisky was out cold, Franny quietly closed the door to stop the dog from causing a ruckus. In the kitchen, she pulled on her moccasins and placed an almost-finished bowl of risotto on the floor to occupy Soda, then headed outside. The retching had subsided, replaced now with a sob.

'Dee, is that you?' she stage-whispered, pushing open her gate.

A hiccup boomeranged in response. Franny waited for her eyes to adjust to the dark. The Salernos' hall lamp sent a sliver of light across the front yard. Upstairs, in what she knew to be Sallyanne's bedroom, a weak strip of light seeped out beneath the blinds.

'Honey, it's Franny. Are you okay?'

Dee was on her hands and knees near the garden tap. 'Keep away,' she said in a croaky voice. 'I've spewed.'

'I gathered that.' Franny moved closer and held out her hand to help up the young girl. 'Come on, let me get a look at you.'

The white jeans had grass stains on them and Dee's lovely young face was streaked with mascara. She wore only one earring.

Franny put a hand on each of Dee's shoulders and looked intently into her bloodshot eyes. 'You okay, Dee? Just pissed, not hurt?'

Dee wiped at her eyes and ran a denim sleeve across her mouth. Sobered by the shock of vomiting and possibly realising whose jacket she was using as a napkin, she suddenly looked aghast. 'God, sorry,' she croaked. 'I'll get it dry-cleaned, I promise.'

'Don't worry about that now,' whispered Franny. 'What's going on?'

'Nothing. I think someone put something in my Coke.'

'Do not confuse old with stupid,' said Franny, looking around for the clutch purse and missing earring. She found only the purse. 'Is your mother at home?'

'Think so. Her shift ended at 10 p.m.' Dee started to cry. 'She's going to lose her shit. I'll never get out of the house again.'

Franny looked up at Sallyanne's window then back at Dee. 'If I get you inside do you promise we have a big talk about this down the track but, right now, you get your act together?'

Dee sniffed and nodded. 'How?'

'I'm going to create a distraction out back, it'll attract your mum. In the meantime, you let yourself in. Got a key?'

'Mum said she'd leave it under the mat,' sniffed Dee.

'Maximum security then,' said Franny. 'Anyway, good for us right now. Wait till you hear all the commotion then get inside. Wash your face, throw on PJs and brush those teeth. And for God's sake, stop the blathering.' She turned and rushed quietly back through the gate.

Opening her back door, Franny turned on all the garden lights then rushed to the laundry and pulled out a couple of dried kangaroo strips from what she called the 'dogs' pantry'.

'Whisky, Whisky,' she called, stomping loudly towards the bedroom door. The little terrier barked and scratched, demanding liberation. Soda ran up and down the hallway, confused but exhilarated. 'Outside, outside,' said Franny in a deliberately zealous tone, freeing Whisky and shooing both dogs towards the backyard. After throwing the treats in two different directions, Franny headed over to the garden hose and, while both dogs barked and bounded, she shot a mighty spurt of water upwards into the night sky. Unable to let a sprinkler or spout of water go un-attacked since puppyhood, Whisky tore over and, dropping the kangaroo remnant, began barking and growling crazily, simultaneously jumping in the air. Soda joined in with a few booming woofs and somewhere, across distant lawns and fences, a neighbour's dog joined in. Next door, the patio light came on and, despite the cacophony, Franny heard the Salernos' backdoor creak open. A minute later a tousled blonde head peeped over the fence.

'Franny,' called Sallyanne. 'Are you there? Everything all right?'

Franny turned the hose off. 'What?' she called.

Sallyanne was hanging over the fence now, trying to drag herself forwards for a better view. 'It's me, Franny. Sallyanne. Is there a fire or something? Are you all right?' Her eyes flicked anxiously to the hose in her neighbour's hand.

'Oh, right, a fire,' said Franny and threw the hose to the ground. Whisky made one final snap at it. 'Um, no, I was just . . . I didn't give the dogs their second walk today. I was giving them a bit of exercise before going to bed.'

Sallyanne stared at Franny in clear disbelief. 'Do you know what time it is?' she asked. 'You scared the hell out of me.'

'Did I?' Franny arranged her face in an expression of innocent befuddlement. To be fair, the dramatic shift from gentle pinot buzz to emergency rescue service was taking its toll on her system; she could do with a Panadol and a lie down. *This one'll be calling the men in white jackets for me after this*, Franny thought before saying, 'I'm very sorry. I'm not used to neighbours being in bed this early on a Friday night.' It was a low blow, brought on by panic. Behind Sallyanne's pale, annoyed face Franny saw new lights coming on upstairs. Dee had clearly made it inside so now she was just playing for time.

'Well,' said Sallyanne with a deep sigh. 'I guess I should stop cramping your style.' She dropped back to the ground on her side of the fence with a thud. 'Dee SMSed me when she got to the party. I should thank you for that.'

'No problem,' said Franny. 'Did she tell you about the dress-ups? We found some great pieces for her—'

'Franny.' The other woman cut her off. 'I was asleep when all this started. At least as asleep as you get when your sixteen-year-old's out on the town. Maybe we can talk about this tomorrow.'

The back door creaked again and Franny heard Dee call out, 'Mum, what on earth are you doing out there in your PJs? I've been sneaking around 'cause I thought you were in bed.'

Genius, thought Franny, *she's turning it around so her mum's the one in trouble. This kid is good.*

'Oh, hello darling,' said Sallyanne. 'I was just talking to Fran. She was doing some . . . well I don't know what she was doing but she's finished now. Let's say goodnight and go inside.' Franny heard feet shuffling, then Sallyanne added, 'Wow, you're all scrubbed and ready for bed.'

This time it was Dee's head popping over the fence. 'Hi, Franny, thanks again for the lift. I've got some bad news,' she said. Her hair was held back in a polka-dot headband and she wore a sky-blue onesie. Her cheeks glowed pink.

'What is it, dear?' asked Franny. 'I know no one else had the same outfit as you so it can't be that.'

Dee smiled wanly. 'No, I think I lost one of the yellow earrings.'

'They were from a flea market in the eighties,' said Franny. 'I really wouldn't worry.'

'You've had them for over thirty years?' said Sallyanne from between the palings. 'Oh Franny, I'm so sorry. We'll try to find replacements.'

Franny saw a chance to crawl out from beneath her earlier, insulting Friday night jibe. 'I woke you up. She lost an earring. Let's call us even. It's not like I wore them anymore.' She winked up at Dee. 'Goodnight, ladies. Don't make too much noise in the morning.'

13

Sick and tired

Franny sat back on the sofa and sighed contentedly. She had had such a lovely weekend. Marg, thinking her sister-in-law was in Hobart and apparently too distracted by quilting escapades to bother nagging about the Eleanor catch-up, had left Franny in blissful peace.

Somehow this had made the time feel more precious than ever and Franny had used it productively. Her protea painting was one of the best things she'd ever produced, she was sure of it, and her mind crackled with ideas for larger, related works. On top of this she had rediscovered Max Richter and kept his *24 Postcards in Full Colour* album blaring while she worked. The roast duck only recently delivered by Old Kingdom for a very early dinner was an absolute triumph and she had decided to celebrate the whole damn pleasure of it all with a bottle of 2011 Heemskerk that had been stashed for just such an occasion.

Now she leaned forward and picked up her flute of sparkling chardonnay pinot noir. Looking over at Lounge Room Frank, she took a large gulp and gave him a wink. Then the phone rang.

Franny eyed it from across the room, hardly daring to breathe, let alone answer the thing.

'Darling, are you there?' Margaret's voice called out from the answering machine after a dozen or so rings. Her sister-in-law was one of the few people who still called the landline. *Note to self,* thought Franny, *get rid of that bloody phone; never delivers anything but bad news.*

'What a shame. I was hoping to catch you,' continued Margaret. 'Anyhoo, I've been thinking about your birthday. I just cannot abide not seeing you so I'm extending my stay in Melbourne. I'll still be here when you get back from Hobart, isn't that great? To be honest, I thought you'd be back tonight but maybe it's tomorrow. Regardless, I'm here all week now, we'll have an absolute ball. Ring me once you're back in the nest and we can work out the details. Toodles.' She hung up.

Sitting stiff-backed on the sofa, Franny stared glumly into space for a good fifteen minutes while determinedly making her way through the last of the Heemskerk. Finally, she hauled herself to her feet, all the time muttering 'Why God, why?' She packed up the remains of the duck feast and downed a quick nip of Bowmore whisky before calling the dogs for a walk.

'We need some fresh air,' she said to Soda, adjusting the old girl's lead. 'And your mistress needs a fresh plan.'

Earlier, Franny had spotted Dee and Josh finishing off their Sunday afternoon with a spot of weeding in the front yard. Now, as Franny emerged through her gate, Whisky straining at his lead, Soda plodding quietly next to her owner, she could hear the pair bickering over a long-handled gardening tool.

Upon seeing her, Josh instantaneously forgot about gardening feuds and called out. Franny responded with a tipsy aye-aye-captain wave.

'Hello, mister,' she said as Josh bounded over to pat the dogs. 'Mum's got you working I see.'

'We're weeding for dim sims,' he said. 'Mum said if we got this chore done by the end of the day she'd get us fish and chips for dinner from Spud and Sea. It's the best.'

Franny's mind was moving a bit too slowly to keep up with this conversation. 'You can't beat a good dimmie,' she replied. Then, noticing Dee stamping down a cardboard box full of weeds nearby, said, 'How you doing, Nancy?'

Dee removed her foot and slowly walked over. 'I still don't know who Nancy is but I'm doing fine,' she grumbled, looking pointedly towards Josh who she obviously didn't want to hear about her after-party nausea adventures.

The little boy was oblivious, immersed in a cuddle fest with the dogs, but Franny was reminded of the fact she owed Dee a serious talking to. Hadn't that been the deal? Just as she was forming these words, Dee jumped in.

'How about you?' she asked. 'You seem a bit funny.'

'Do I indeed?' said Franny, exhaling. 'Well, that's because I'm bloody miserable if you really want to know. My sister-in-law's in town and is harassing me.'

'Oh,' said Dee, not sure what to do with this information. 'You don't like her?'

'She's okay. I just don't want to see her.' Franny shrugged her shoulders and crossed her eyes. 'Long story,' she added.

'You going for a walk?' asked Josh. 'Can I come? Dee, can we go?' He jumped up and down like a puppy himself.

Dee raised her eyebrows, looked at Franny, then turned towards the weeding detritus littering the front garden. 'Does Franny want us along?'

'Franny doesn't mind. What about your mum?' The words were

barely out of her mouth before Josh was gone, sprinting to the house for permission.

Within minutes three humans and two dogs were off walking, Josh and Whisky a good half block ahead of Franny and Dee, who waited patiently for Soda to do her business on the nature strip.

'Thank you so much for Friday night, Franny, you saved my butt. I'm sorry I haven't been over, I didn't want Mum to be suspicious,' said Dee.

'No problem at all, dear. But I have to say, I wasn't pleased to see the condition you came home in. You're much too young to be carrying on like that. Actually, there's no good age to be carrying on like that.' Franny fumbled with a tight roll of small plastic bags before giving up and saying, 'Have a go at this, will you, Dee? I seem to be all thumbs today.'

Dee took the bags and squatted to pick up Soda's fragrant gift to the neighbourhood. 'I'm not the only one carrying on from what I can tell,' she mumbled, straightening up. She had noticed Franny's bloodshot eyes and off-kilter demeanour.

The comment caught Franny by surprise. She resumed walking, noting that deliberate concentration was required if she didn't want to sway.

This effort unplugged a memory. Frank had once accused her of 'carrying on'; it was at Elouise's fifth birthday. Franny had organised a spectacular unicorn cake for her goddaughter and spent hours on the morning of the party helping Anthea decorate the backyard and organise the games. Then she had sat back, in a folding chair on the lawn, and drunk copious amounts of rosé. As ten little girls swirled and twirled around the house and garden, she had watched them gobbling lollies and screeching maniacally. Eventually, the sun got too much for her and Franny stumbled inside. Feeling tired and nauseous, she had disappeared into the master bedroom and wretched into the en suite's toilet. Frank, who had only arrived for the cutting of the cake, found her sitting on the tiled floor sometime later, makeup smudged and hair awry. Apparently, one of the little girls had run out to Anthea, looking frightened and babbling that 'the lady with the pink drinks was making yukky sounds' in the bathroom.

'What the hell is going on, Fran?' Frank had said upon finding her. 'This is a kids' party, not a place for this kind of carry-on.'

Franny had looked at him, her eyes full of tears and her heart sad that he had not immediately understood the situation. Pulling herself to her feet she had turned on the bathroom taps, washed her face and rinsed out her mouth.

After a few minutes Frank had said, 'Seriously, Fran. What were you thinking?'

At that moment Franny had looked at her husband and, just for a fleeting second, hated him.

'Nothing's going on, my dear. Sorry for the carry-on. It's been a long day; guess I got a little over excited.' She had left him then and walked back into the kitchen where Anthea stood making a pot of tea.

The two friends had looked at each other briefly, then Anthea had walked over and put her arms around Franny, enveloping her and whispering in her ear, 'I know honey, I know. You try so hard. You don't have to, you know, but I appreciate it. So does Ellie.' Anthea had stepped back then and looked her friend straight in the eye. 'I'll always love you and never judge you, Fran. You don't ever have to doubt that.' Then she grinned unexpectedly and added, 'I say that assuming you had the good grace not to throw up on the new carpet!'

A sad smile spread across Franny's face at this memory.

Dee interrupted her thoughts, saying, 'Seriously, Franny, are you okay?'

'What? Of course. Just a bit tired.' The words slurred a little.

'Your turn to have a party?'

'I think the young people call it a pity party actually.' Franny laughed. 'I went from celebrating to drowning my sorrows and wracking my brain. Probably not the ideal combination.'

Franny told Dee all about her ingenious sidestepping of Marg's birthday onslaught, including the lie she had given about book clubbing in Tasmania. Just as she was lamenting aloud the fact that she had nearly got away with it all, Dee interjected.

'Not sure I understand why you want to avoid someone so keen to spoil you,' she said, 'but I do know about dodging family. Maybe I can help.'

'How?' said Franny, reaching down to unclip Soda from her leash; they had walked as far as the park.

'Mum would have to be involved.'

'Go on.'

'Well, why don't we get Mum to call your sister-in-law from your phone, pretend we're being sneaky while your back is turned. We can say we've heard about her plans but we're actually organising to surprise you and take you away for your birthday this week, down the Peninsula or something. Would that work?'

'It's kind of convoluted,' said Franny, 'and I don't know that Sallyanne needs the aggravation. No, I'll work something out.' She sat down awkwardly on a swing. Josh noticed and ran over, Whisky close on his heels.

'Let me push, let me push,' he cried, crouching and heaving against Franny's rear end.

Trees, cricket nets, picnic tables and wood-chip-covered ground flew back and forth past Franny. Whisky barked madly, confused and delighted at the sight of his mistress, airborne.

'Josh, stop pushing, make it stop,' Franny called out after a few moments, her tone slightly panicked. She dragged her feet along the ground to slow things down.

Josh stood to the side, disappointed the fun was ending so abruptly. 'You push me now,' he said as Franny stood up.

She shook her head and placed one finger over her lips then weaved her way to a rubbish bin nearby.

'Look away, Joshie,' said Dee, leaning down to grab her brother's hand and Whisky's collar. 'This ain't gonna be pretty.'

14

Hide and seek

The following evening Franny was sitting on the Salerno family's sofa when Sallyanne got home. Josh kneeled beside her, his nose almost touching a large picture book on her lap. Dee, seated on the floor, had her homework spread across the coffee table but she was edged so close to Franny's knees it was clear she too was engrossed in proceedings. The house smelled delicious, like basil, tomato and garlic.

'Cough, cough,' said Sallyanne, throwing her keys into a bowl on the kitchen bench and letting a couple of bags drop to the floor. 'Anyone remember me?'

Josh jumped up and ran to his mother, wrapping his arms around her while she patted his head.

'Franny's telling me all about Timmy Tuggernaught and Mr Marmalade,' he said. 'They're famous, you know.' He dragged on Sallyanne's arm to take her over to the lounge.

Franny took off her spectacles, closed the book and stood up. 'I thought Josh might like a copy, might even have a go at drawing a picture book of his own,' said Franny. 'Hope you don't mind me barging in.'

Before Sallyanne had a chance to reply, Dee spoke up. 'I asked her over, Mum. We've got a favour to ask. But also, she's helping with tea.' Her eyes flicked over to a saucepan quietly simmering on the stovetop.

Sallyanne's face took on a confused expression. 'She's what?'

'Sorry, dear,' said Franny. 'We're overwhelming you. Why don't you sit down and one of us can make you a cuppa.' Franny flicked her chin towards Dee, indicating just who that someone should be.

'Okay,' said Sallyanne, happy to submit.

Over cups of English Breakfast and a few mini-packs of salt and vinegar chips, Dee explained the situation, along with her plan.

'I know it's asking a lot, Sallyanne, and you're more than welcome to say no. But Dee would not be dissuaded,' said Franny eventually.

'Let me get this right,' said Sallyanne. 'You want me to call this Margaret, pretend I've swiped Franny's phone, then say we're winging her away for a birthday surprise. Is that right?'

The other three nodded, Franny less emphatically than the children. She was on the verge of telling Sallyanne to forget the whole thing when the younger woman said, 'Okay, hand over the phone.'

Within minutes Marg's booming voice came over the loudspeaker. 'You've called Margaret Calderwood, previously Mrs Roxborough. I cannot come to the phone right now but if you leave a message I'll get back in a jiffy. Bye bye!'

Sallyanne looked over at Franny, who just shrugged. Dee made flicking movements with her fingers, urging her mother to crack on. Clearly and quickly, Sallyanne delivered her message to Marg, stressing the fact that she must not spoil the surprise, then hung up. She did not leave her number.

'Well that was odd but hopefully it does the job,' said Sallyanne. 'Now what's going on with that saucepan?'

'Oh bugger,' said Franny, 'I completely forgot about it. The sauce should be ready.' She jumped up and headed into the kitchen.

'Franny's making us a put-her-next-to-her sauce to say thank you,' said Josh. 'It's for spaghetti.'

'Put-her-next-to-her?' said Sallyanne with a laugh. 'Better not let your nonna hear you pronounce it like that. It's *puttanesca*, honey, and it's one of my favourites.' She got up from the armchair and joined Franny at the kitchen island.

'Hope you don't mind,' said Franny, stirring the sauce with a wooden spoon and setting a pot of water to boil. 'The kids thought it would be okay.'

'Mind?' said Sallyanne, bending down to pick up her abandoned bags and empty the contents on the bench. 'I was planning on giving them omelettes, with a little salad on the side.' Josh, who had shadowed her, groaned. 'Yes, not your favourite, Joshie, I know. Spaghetti wins by far.'

Once the pasta was on the boil Franny said goodbye and headed home. The Salernos begged her to stay but she insisted Whisky and Soda needed feeding and walking. Back at home, the smell of tinned dog food in the air, Franny leaned on the kitchen bench, gin and tonic in hand.

'Well, my love,' she said to Kitchen Frank, 'you wouldn't believe the hullabaloo that's gone into me avoiding spending my birthday with your sainted sister.' Her gaze shifted to a stack of CDs on the shelf nearby. The last one Frank had ever bought her was in there somewhere, a young duo from Chicago specialising in 1940s and '50s rhythm and blues.

For the last twenty years of their marriage Frank Calderwood had cooked his wife a birthday dinner then taken her out to see a band. He always bought her a CD or some other memorabilia to remember the night. Frequently, they danced. Never did they invite anyone else along.

The year after he died Franny acquiesced to spending her birthday with Anthea, David and Elouise. Their nagging had been incessant. Frank had been gone nine months. The birthday dinner was held at Anthea's home. Between an Ottolenghi Chicken Marbella and a very fancy store-bought lemon tart, Franny ducked out to the bathroom. En route, her eye fell on a new photo frame on the hallway table. She stooped down to peer at it then stepped back, one hand out to steady herself against the wall. The photo showed Franny's face looking a little drawn beneath her golden tan. She wore a white strapless dress and a large silver and turquoise necklace. Each brown shoulder was obscured by a man's hairy arm, Frank's on one side, David's on the other. A glossy black-and-white collie sat at their feet, pink tongue lolling as it looked up adoringly. Franny stared directly at the camera, Frank smiled over at her and David grinned down at the dog. It was a charming photo—the light was lovely, the moment candid. Franny remembered the day well. The first barbecue of the summer. The first weekend together since the Calderwoods had flown back from an unwanted and unhappy sojourn on a Greek island. That moment in that hallway Franny knew she'd never spend her birthday with another person again.

Franny's afternoon to-do list involved an almond croissant and homemade café latte in bed, accompanied by an episode of *Vera* on her laptop. As she waited for the water to heat in the coffee machine and pondered warming the croissant, a text message on her mobile phone interrupted with devastating news.

> Marg: Your house phone is ringing out, I don't know what's going on with your answering machine, and all yesterday your mobile went straight to voicemail. I didn't bother leaving messages because I figured you'd see my missed calls and get back to me. Of course, you didn't! Are you back from Hobart now? Or maybe you've gone somewhere else . . . ? Anyway I'm not worried about you or anything but my hotel is really not that far away and I'd hate to miss you if I didn't have to. I've decided I'll pop over sometime today/tonight, JUST to check if you're home, JUST in case.

Franny looked up at the clock; it was almost four and it was her sixty-fifth birthday. She had spent most of it out with the dogs, walking the cliffs by the bay, stopping for fish and chips, traipsing around plant nurseries and picking up groceries. By abandoning her house and keeping her mobile phone switched off she had hoped to dodge any unexpected visitors. Returning home in the late afternoon, gate locked and blinds drawn, Franny felt the birthday storm had been avoided. Her decision to turn the phone back on was an acknowledged risk but a few persistent souls still sent birthday wishes. Her plan was to write down their names and text them a thank you—some other time. So much for that.

By keeping an extra-low profile for the last few days, forgoing lunch at Bello Cielo and dodging Marg's various entreaties, Franny had started to believe that Dee's outlandish plan might indeed have worked. Such naivety mocked her now. She should never have underestimated the commitment to meddling that her quilt-loving, pleather-wearing in-law was capable of.

She turned off the coffee machine and walked over to the rug where Soda was absorbing the last of the afternoon sun. Lying down, Franny rested her head against the dog's furry warmth and stared at the nearest photo-Frank.

'Fuck it,' she suddenly declared, 'I refuse to go down without a fight.' With a grunt from herself and a snort from Soda, she was back on her feet, grabbing her bag, keys and dogs and heading for the door. As she backed out of her driveway, Franny saw Dee and Josh arriving home from school.

'My sister-in-law's still coming around,' she called out the car window. 'Can you believe it? The cheek. I have to bolt.'

Josh tugged on his big sister's sleeve, his eyes wide. Dee looked down at him and made a shushing noise. 'Can we come?' she said to Franny through the open window.

In the back of the Skoda the dogs were apoplectic, desperate to get to the kids outside. Franny looked around anxiously, checking the street for signs of a Marg invasion. 'Whatever, whatever, just get in,' she said, pulling off the minute the pair were in the car.

'Where are we going?' said Josh, his voice slightly muffled by Whisky who was determinedly licking his face.

'No idea,' said Fran. They had reached the nearest shopping strip. She pulled up in a car spot on the side of the road and looked into the rear-view mirror. Two kids, dressed in school uniforms, sat squeezed between two overly affectionate and dishevelled dogs. Was this what her birthday had come to? What her life had come to?

Leaning forward, Franny rested her head on her arms on the steering wheel. Dee waited a few beats then unclipped her seatbelt and reached out to touch one of Franny's now-shaking shoulders.

'Franny, you okay?' she said, her voice sounding fearful and concerned.

Abruptly Franny sat upright, her previously silent giggles morphing into a roaring laugh. Whisky, completely discombobulated by everything that had happened in the last ten minutes, pointed his black nose to the roof of the car and howled, causing Josh to jump in surprise. Suddenly and joyfully the Skoda was filled with the sound of three humans screaming with laughter.

'I've SMSed Mum to tell her where we are,' said Dee once the outburst was over. 'She says to come over for dinner when the coast is clear.' Franny caught Dee's eye in the mirror and shook her head. 'Also, Mum says that if you refuse, she'll report you for child abduction.'

Silence ensued.

'Best birthday ever,' Franny eventually muttered while Josh clapped his little hands together in glee.

They looped around the block a few times then drove back towards Ipswich Street, Franny slowing to a crawl as she prepared to make the turn. 'Shh,' she said, 'keep your eyes peeled for any movement.' Her eyes darted frantically.

'You're not going to see anything from here,' said Dee. 'And if you get closer and she's there she'll see you. Just let me out.' She put her hand on the car door as if to exit.

'What the hell are you doing?' said Franny. 'What if Marg sees you?'

'Marg,' said Dee, emphasising the name sarcastically, 'does not know who the hell I am, remember? Let me out.' She jumped out of the car, slinging her schoolbag over her shoulder. 'Keep going to the next block. I'll meet you there.'

Five minutes later, parked but with the motor quietly idling, Franny and Josh watched Dee as she briskly walked towards them. Glancing behind her, she climbed into the car and said, 'Quick, pull into someone's house or something. Marg had a taxi in your driveway, Franny, and she was peeping between the gates. She's probably right behind me by now.'

'Bloody hell,' said Franny, 'I feel like I'm in *The Italian Job.*'

Josh, who was kneeling on the car seat, peering out the back window, cried, 'A car just turned the corner, Franny. Go, go, go!'

Franny planted her foot and sped halfway up the street, turning into a driveway alongside a trio of units. She stopped breathing while a small yellow hatchback passed by, its panels covered in the decals of a local real estate agent.

'Josh, you moron,' said Dee, 'that's not a taxi.'

Franny released her breath and the dogs jumped around manically. 'No, but this is,' she suddenly hissed. 'Everyone duck.'

Just then a cab sailed by, its passenger recognisable by her distinctive auburn hair; she was busy on her mobile phone. As the taxi disappeared from view, Franny's own phone buzzed with a message. Still crouched in her seat, she read the words on the screen.

> Marg: Stopped by your house Franny darling. Worth a shot. Looks like you're out of town after all. Not that I ever doubted it of course LOL!!!! That family next door must really be something. I look forward to seeing LOTS of photos from this surprise trip. Figure I'm not ruining the surprise now. Mxxx

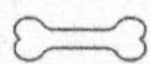

'Happy birthday, happy birthday, happy birthday to you.' Sallyanne and Dee's rendition of the song was halting and tuneless as they struggled to sync the words with Josh's slow plucking of his miniature guitar. Tongue out, face red, the little boy looked up every time he got a note right, checking audience reaction. The birthday girl tipped her champagne glass towards him, nodding encouragingly.

The dinner had been simple but delicious: a roasted leg of lamb and fresh salad full of plump black olives, fragrant basil and plenty of fetta. The birthday cake was less of a triumph. A team effort between brother and sister, the sponge failed to rise or retain any discernible moisture, and the pair's subsequent decision to cover it with Nutella instead of standard chocolate frosting rendered it a highly sugared choking hazard. Nevertheless, a last-minute suggestion—by Franny herself—to serve each slice with ice cream saved the day. As the Salernos limped towards the end of the song, Franny refilled her glass and raised it for a toast.

'Well, you lot. Today you saved my bacon and replaced it with lamb. And you serenaded me along the way. I am honoured indeed.' She leaned over to refill Sallyanne's glass but the other woman flattened her palm across the top of it.

'No thanks, Franny. I know my limits,' she said.

'Hmm,' replied Franny. 'Guess the rest is up to me then.' She filled her glass to the brim then slurped.

'You could have shared some with me,' muttered Dee. Sallyanne gave her daughter a side-eyed glance and the young girl stuck out her tongue.

'So, think you'll hear anything else from the dreaded Marg, Fran?' asked Sallyanne. 'Will the photos be enough?'

While dinner cooked Franny and the kids had changed outfits three times, from swimming costumes to pyjamas, choosing different bland backgrounds around both of their homes and gardens, not to mention inside and outside their cars, in an effort to produce a set of convincing holiday snaps for Franny to slow-drip her sister-in-law. The final shot had been of Sallyanne and Franny triumphantly holding a bottle of Taittinger. Beach towels, dog leads and a pair of boy's board shorts were slung over the door behind them, a final touch in holiday-house production design.

'At least you don't use Instagram, Franny, so you don't have to pin it,' said Dee. 'Marg can't check where the photos were taken.'

Franny didn't answer for a moment. Her attention had gone to the familiar knight on the bottle of French champagne, his sword brandished against its backdrop of gold-and-red foil. In almost three years this was, she realised, probably the first time a bottle of her precious Taittinger had been opened in a mood of gaiety and celebration rather than sorrow and desolation. Looking up at the trio before her she felt a mixture of gratitude and surprise.

'Sorry, what were you saying, Dee?' asked Franny.

Josh answered. 'Pinning it. You can show people where you are under your photos.' He was alternating between plucking at guitar strings and picking around the corners of remaining birthday cake.

'Josh,' said his mother, slapping his hand away from the food, 'that's enough. And I hope you haven't forgotten you're not allowed on Instagram and you must never ever put your location on anything—computers or phones.' Her voice had risen sharply, causing the little boy to put down his guitar and stare at her, bottom lip stuck out.

'I was just telling Franny . . .'

'I know, I know, come here.' Sallyanne held out her arms to him and, slowly, he shuffled over to sit on her lap. 'We just don't go telling every Tom, Dick and Harry where we are, okay? It's important you always remember that. It's not safe.'

'Ah,' exclaimed Franny who had been looking on bewilderedly. 'Stranger danger. I see.'

'Not always strangers.' Dee was muttering again. She looked at her mother and rolled her eyes. 'I'm going to bed.' Standing up, she shifted her gaze to Franny. Hesitating then leaning in to kiss the older woman on the cheek, she said, 'You're not the only one dodging family. Happy birthday, Mrs C. It was fun.'

15

Costume dramas

Franny was in the pharmacy when she learned about Story Week. Perusing the calcium tablet selection, she noticed Sallyanne and Josh in the queue for the cash register. She felt a surprising pang of happiness at seeing them. Since the whole birthday bedlam of the week before she had given her neighbours some space, figuring they could do with a break from her.

Sallyanne and Josh appeared to be arguing, the little boy folding his small arms and turning away from his mother. Within seconds his eyes met Franny's and he bolted over, leaving a cardboard display of vitamins teetering in his wake.

By the time Sallyanne had finished at the check-out and joined them, Josh was jumping up and down on the spot and saying, 'It's the best day of the year and I'm gonna look lame.'

Sallyanne looked over her son's head at Franny with a weary expression. 'Let me guess. He's on about Story Week,' she said. 'It's all I've heard about for days on end.'

'He might have mentioned it in passing.' Franny leaned in and stage-whispered to Sallyanne, 'I believe you are forcing the poor child to assemble a costume from his everyday wardrobe. I'm considering notifying the UN.'

Josh's arms were hovering near their angry-fold position again. 'What's the UN?' he said, tone grumpy. It was clear he sensed they'd be indifferent to his plight. When both women broke out in giggles his suspicions seemed confirmed. Waving a five-dollar note that his mother had given him earlier, he turned and flounced off, yelling, 'I'm going to the bakery' over his shoulder.

'Woo,' said Franny. 'He knows how to turn it on.'

'Yes. Not quite the angelic little darling you've been seeing up to now,' said Sallyanne. 'He's just going to have to get used to me having less time and money, frankly, for all this stuff.' Her mouth made a funny sideways grimace. 'They both are.' Watching her son pass through the sliding glass doors of the pharmacy, she said, 'I'd better go. In this mood he's likely to binge on jam donuts and what I don't need now is the addition of a sugar rush.'

Franny laughed. Josh's dramatic exit had endeared him to her even more. It had also given her an idea. 'Just when is this momentous event?' she asked.

'Monday. Why?'

'Would it annoy you if I offered to help? Friday tends to be my supplies day. I pick up anything I might need for the weekend. If he can tell me what he's after before that I can have a think and a scrounge round and Josh can help me make something on Saturday. If you want . . .' Franny's voice trailed off. She made a show of examining a bottle of chewable calcium.

Sallyanne looked at her for a moment, apparently weighing something up, then said, 'This is just rewarding bad behaviour you know . . . and you are making me look bad.' She held up a finger as Franny prepared to butt in. 'But if you really don't mind, that would be brilliant. I have to work during the day Saturday. Would it be really pushing the friendship for you to keep an eye on him? Dee's home too but it would be a relief to know she has back up.'

Back up? Franny realised she was morphing from voluntary creative consultant to formal babysitter. Before her hackles had a chance to rise, however, she admitted to herself that the costume project was pretty appealing. Fancy dress parties had once been a specialty in the Calderwood household. When Frank died the sewing machine was forced into mourning with its owner.

'Yes, yes, that's fine.' She flicked her hand as if batting away an annoying fly. 'It's a one-off after all. Seems to me Miss Dee said something about becoming a costume designer. Maybe she could help too. Keep her out of trouble and all.'

'I know you don't want to become stand-in granny,' said Sallyanne unexpectedly. 'And I promise it won't be like that. But this really is the sweetest idea and I promise we won't take advantage of you. Actually, maybe we can turn Dee into the sewer of the family and she can be in charge of all the fancy dress events from now on. Teach a girl to fish and all.' She leaned in and kissed Franny lightly on the cheek.

After the pharmacy, Franny headed to the cinema but, ensconced in one of the plush purple chairs, she found it hard to focus on the action on-screen. In her mind she went over her studio inventory, thinking about what fabrics she had lying about and wondering if her sewing machine needed servicing. When the credits rolled, she didn't even bother stopping in to explore her favourite wine shop next door.

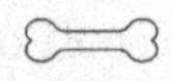

That evening, while Franny watered her back garden, Josh hung over the top of the fence 'brains-storming', as he called it, ideas for costumes.

'What are you standing on?' said Franny. 'You look wobbly. Why don't you just come over?'

The little boy looked down at his feet, swaying backwards precariously in the process. 'It's a big plant pot. Doesn't have anything in it yet.' He regained his balance then his head and arms disappeared. The next moment Franny realised he was calling from her driveway to be let in.

As she resumed her watering, Josh threw the ball for the dogs, simultaneously delivering a detailed explanation of the outfit he desired. It was Little Red Riding Hood; a new animated version of the story had been at the cinemas in recent months.

Franny gave an involuntary groan that she covered with a cough. Theoretically she knew they lived in more tolerant times and her own love of the flamboyant and camp was unquestionable but, after sixty-five years on the planet, she was also a realist. A kid who had previously been bullied for being a tad 'different' might do well to choose something a little more conventional for his first foray at the new school. She swore under her breath at this thought process, disappointed at her cowardice, and then she was struck by a brilliant idea.

'Okay, fella, I've got it. Be over here midday Saturday ready to work. Bring your sister and your appetite. Tell Mum I'll feed you.'

16

Made to measure

The big table in Franny's studio was cleared of all current projects and a third stool had been added. The sewing machine, dusted off from its perch in the laundry, sat at the end closest to the windows, a pile of fabrics and detritus on the floor nearby. A huge square of paper with something drawn on the underside was clipped to the old easel.

In the kitchen, a shoulder of lamb was already in the oven, commencing its four-hour, slow-cooking journey. Franny was plonked in her office chair, marvelling at the fact she had already been up for six hours.

'Hell's bells,' she said to Studio Frank. 'I'm not used to this kind of running around. It's exhausting! Yesterday was bad enough but I think I've got everything we'll need. Thank God for op shops, hey? Hopefully the extra-long walk this morning will keep the hounds at bay and we can get on with work.'

Just then her intercom system sounded. She picked up the photograph and gave it a smacking kiss. 'Wish me luck, darling,' she said, heading for the door.

Dee let out a 'wow' as she entered the studio. On arrival, she had been the picture of teenage surliness and disinterest, eyes glued to her phone screen, 'I'm just dropping him off' her only words of greeting. Now, the phone had disappeared and she looked around, eyes and mouth wide.

'I forgot you haven't been in the studio before,' said Franny. 'Make yourself at home.'

'Told ya, told ya, told ya,' squealed Josh, dancing around the room, Whisky hot on his heels.

'We'll need to decide on a creative soundtrack,' said Franny. 'Choose something.' She pointed Josh towards a shelf full of CDs.

'Are they little books?' he asked, clearly confused.

His sister let out a snort. 'No, doofus, they're music, just an old-fashioned way for playing it. Let me have a look.' She glanced over at Franny who shrugged and winked.

Within minutes the Salernos had learned to use the player and Bill Wyman's distinctive bass notes on 'Miss You' filled the room. Josh flicked his tiny hips and bobbed around the room accordingly.

'Nice choice,' said Franny. 'You know this album, these blokes?'

'Dad likes to call himself a "Stones man",' said Dee.

'Not all bad then.' Franny reached over to turn the sound down as Mick Jagger's falsetto 'ooh oohs' got a little too loud. 'Anyway, are we going to make a costume or what?'

Josh clapped his little hands together, sing-songing the words 'Little Red Riding Hood, Little Red Riding Hood' over and over again.

'Yes, I've had a thought about that,' said Franny.

Dee, standing behind her brother, put protective hands on his shoulders and looked directly at her. 'He really wants this,' she said, enunciating each word very clearly.

Franny patted the air in front of her like she was quietening down an orchestra. 'And he shall have it. I'm simply suggesting an exciting twist. Sit down.'

With both children seated, Franny made a flourish of turning around the giant piece of paper on the easel. 'Voila,' she said. 'How about being Red Riding Hood and wolfy grandmother all in one?'

In thick black marker pen she had hand-drawn the outline of two identical figures, back and front views, each with Josh's distinctive hair. On the front image, she had coloured in a long-sleeved red cloak with a huge bow at the neck. Down the centre of the cloak ran a row of toggle buttons like those found on duffle coats. A plaited side bun was drawn on each side of the boy's head and he held a wicker basket in one hand.

The rear view showed the boy as wolf-in-grandma's-clothing. He had pointy high ears, a big nose, whiskers, teeth and dark glasses. A frilly collar hugged his chin, leading down to a long-sleeved floral night gown.

Josh got up for a closer look, practically shoving his nose into the paper. 'Huh?'

'Super cool,' said Dee, rocking back in her chair for a broader view. 'He's going to be sweet Red Riding Hood at the front and mean old wolf at the back. I get it.' She looked at Franny then nodded slowly. 'Right. I get it,' she repeated.

'That's not gonna work,' moaned Josh. 'How's that gonna work?'

'O ye of little faith,' said Franny. 'Watch and learn.' She sorted through items from the pile on the floor and spread them on the table. An old nightgown was already cut in two and she held up a beautiful piece of white organza ribbon to attach as a collar. Josh took it from her gently, running it under his chin with delight. Then Franny spread out a huge swathe of red velvet fabric. 'These are old curtains I found at the op shop yesterday. This, sir, is your cloak.' She wrapped the fabric around herself and bowed. 'As is this.' She grabbed at an old duffle coat with the number 25 stitched to the back. 'Well at least when I get the buttons off.'

Grabbing a box from one of the shelves, she continued her show-and-tell. 'Brown felt for nose and ears,' she said, 'black wool for hair and dark sunglasses because you don't have eyes at the back of your head. And then there's the question of teeth. To be honest, I'm still struggling with those but I'm thinking we cover rigatoni with white felt and stain it yellow. What do you think?'

'Still don't get it,' said Josh, bottom lip stuck out.

'God, J-man, how much more obvious does it get? Franny's going to sew it so the front is the cloak, attached to the nightie at the back.' She grabbed the floral fabric and pushed it against his back and held the red velvet against his front. 'When you walk towards people you'll be Red Riding Hood. When you walk away, you're the wolf. Genius!'

Her brother's small face took on the look of someone receiving the word of God. 'Oooh I get it now,' he said, grabbing some black wool and bunching it against his head. 'And I get to have buns.'

'That's right, little bro, you get to have buns.' Dee pinched both of his cheeks and he squealed.

After some speedy measuring and pinning Franny got the kids to work then began sewing.

Dee sat close beside her, working on the felt ears while also paying close attention to her neighbour's movements. Cutting out the pieces Fran had already marked up with tailor's chalk, she said, 'I'm doing textile and design at school but we never do anything fun like this.'

'Bet your machines aren't this ancient,' said Franny, pointing to her battle-worn Husqvarna.

'Ours have lots of buttons and dials,' said Dee, 'but they look flimsier. This one smells great.' She took a deep sniff of the air.

'Ha! Sewing-machine oil and a lot of dust I would say,' said Franny. 'I've had this machine for at least thirty years. My friend who was a fashion designer gave it to me.'

'You know a fashion designer? Who?'

'Dead now. Her name was Cecily. You wouldn't have heard of her. She was a lot older than me. Had a store in London in the so-called swinging sixties. Worked for Mary Quant for a while. I met her when she moved back here to retire in the eighties. All a long time ago now.'

'Who's Mary Quant?'

Franny flicked a sticky-note pad and pen over to Dee. She spelled the name out. 'Q. U. A. N. T. Look her up sometime. If you're into design you'll need to know about her. Miniskirts, hot pants, pantyhose; you name it, Mary designed it. Check her out on IMDb too. I'm pretty sure she designed for a few movies.'

Over the next couple of hours Franny and the Salernos beavered away, pinning, chatting, sewing and stuffing. The Rolling Stones were replaced by Marvin Gaye, Josh took a 'ball break' with Whisky and Soda, and afternoon clouds sent shadows across the workroom.

'Okay, Master Salerno, get up on the table,' said Franny eventually. 'Let's see where we're at.' The little boy held his arms in the air as the costume was slipped over his head, covering his striped T-shirt and shorts. Franny stood back to examine her handiwork. 'Still all the trimmings to add but we're getting somewhere,' she announced. 'Let's add your bits, Dee.'

Dee had rushed home at one point to grab a velvet headband belonging to Sallyanne and this now had two big ears attached to it on one side, coils of thickly plaited wool on the other. The wolf's giant nose was super glued to dark sunglasses, picked up at a two-dollar shop by Fran the previous day.

'Put your back to me, Joshie, so I can attach these,' Dee told her brother then flattened his hair close against his head and rammed the glasses in tight. 'What do you reckon, Fran?' She stood back beside the older woman, hands on hips, head to one side.

'It will be better when we add the big red bow and organza collar but I think we're on to something. Here, hold this, Josh.' Franny placed the wicker basket in the little boy's hand. Dee's creativity had flourished here too; she had made faux food parcels from chequered tea towels and added shiny red apples, pilfered from the kitchen counter at home.

'Let me see, let me see.' Josh was threatening to jump from the table. Franny, nervous of flying pins and loose tacking stitches, rushed forward to deposit him on the floor.

'Let's go to my bedroom,' she said. 'You can look in my big mirror.'

'Grrr, grrr, hello, hello.' Josh twirled around, alternating from gruff wolf-like growls to sweet little-girl hellos. 'I love, love, love it,' he said, swinging the basket to and fro, admiring his reflection.

'Here, look at your wolf-face,' said Dee. She had taken a photograph of the back of Josh's head on her iPhone and held it out for her brother to enlarge and examine. His eyes grew wide.

'I'm going to be the best,' he whispered, awestruck. 'I might win the prize.'

While he explained how a book voucher was on offer for the most creative costume in each year level, Franny gingerly removed the costume and folded it in a neat pile on the bed.

'You have to do a presentation on the story though too, Joshie, don't you? It's not just about dress-ups,' his sister reminded him.

Franny watched as Josh's expression changed. 'I forgot that bit,' he said, sinking onto the bedroom floor and burying his face in the ever-present terrier.

'Let's go to the kitchen,' said Franny. 'We need to celebrate, and check on the lamb.' She grabbed the little boy's hand, dragging him to his feet.

Delicious aromas of rosemary and garlic filled the kitchen. Franny opened a bottle of Chandon Brut Rosé and poured herself a glass. Dee looked at her with puppy-dog eyes. 'Just one small one,' said Franny, grabbing a second champagne flute from the cupboard. Josh made do with a concoction of soda water, fresh mint and orange slices and they all raised their glasses in cheers.

'Okay, what's the problem?' asked Franny eventually. 'What's the big deal about a presentation? You obviously know the Red Riding Hood story.'

Josh scooped out a slice of orange and sucked on it, saying nothing.

'He doesn't like speaking in front of the class,' said Dee. She leaned forward and whispered to Franny, 'He got heckled at his old school.'

Franny looked over at Kitchen Frank. *You'd know what to say,* she thought. *Inspire me.* Josh continued to fuss with his drink.

Franny took a big gulp of her sparkling wine. 'I think you're a star, Master Salerno,' she said finally. 'And you know what makes a star?' Josh looked at her, his expression solemn but interested. 'Talent and preparation, that's what. You've got the costume part nailed, if we do say so ourselves. Now you just have to add the pizazz. Go out back and run the dogs around while Dee and I pack up the studio and get dinner happening. Soda and Whisky can be your audience. Rehearse your piece then do it for us while we eat. What do you say?'

Josh scrunched up his nose. Unconvinced.

'Go on, Joshie. I think Franny's right. You've got this,' said Dee.

'I guess . . .' muttered Josh, slurping the last of his drink and climbing down from the stool. 'But if they laugh at me.'

'If they laugh at you I'll set Whisky on them,' said Franny, also polishing off her drink. The small dog backed up the threat by giving the boy's bare leg an enthusiastic lick.

17

Too much of a good thing

'I won, I won, I won.' Josh was beside the car before Franny could let herself out. Her body had spent another Monday at yoga followed by the botanic gardens but her mind had roamed elsewhere, concerned about a small boy in a schoolyard close by, facing his fears armed only with a basket of apples.

Bending down now, she said to him, 'Won what? Calm down, what are you talking about?'

Josh stilled himself, staring at her, mouth open in disbelief. When Franny winked, he jumped into her arms. They hugged enthusiastically.

'I think it's fair to say that most of the mothers hate me now,' said Sallyanne, arriving behind her excited son. 'You may get some commissions out of this.'

Franny straightened up with a groan. 'Bloody knees,' she said. 'So, our hard work paid off. I'm delighted to hear it. You know Dee did a lot of the work, Sallyanne. Our budding costume designer.'

'So Josh told me. She's got basketball practice this afternoon but we'll definitely celebrate when she gets home. Can you join us?'

'Please, please Franny,' said Josh. 'We're having my favourite: chicken nuggets.'

'Wow you really know how to tempt a girl,' laughed Franny. 'Maybe I'll just opt for a drink?'

'Now don't be like that,' said Sallyanne. 'They're homemade. More like crumbed chicken balls in fact.'

Franny pulled a face and said, 'Josh, no one told me chickens have balls.' The little boy squealed with delight, setting off the dogs on the other side of the gate.

After dinner, the dishes done and both children exiled to their bedrooms, supposedly completing homework, Sallyanne nodded towards the fast-disappearing bottle of pinot grigio and said, 'I know I said I wouldn't have one earlier, but I think I fancy a glass after all.'

Realising there wasn't enough for two decent pours anymore, Franny said, 'Come over to my place. I need to water the garden and you can sneak a cancer stick.' Before Sallyanne could protest, Franny leaned in and whispered, 'It's okay, your secret's safe with me.'

Back at Franny's, a pair of negronis prepared and the sprinkler doing its work, the two women sat at a small outdoor table near the fence farthest from the Salernos. Sallyanne dragged deeply on her cigarette, staring into the air.

'Earth to Sallyanne,' said Franny, waving a hand in front of her neighbour's face. 'Penny for them.'

'Sorry, what?'

'Penny for your thoughts. Not a saying you hear anymore I suppose.' Franny swirled the twist of orange in her drink. 'Something on your mind?'

Sallyanne flicked ash from her cigarette and glanced furtively towards her yard. 'Only more ex-husband dramas,' she said. 'Danny's pushing to see Josh without me, as long as he has a social worker present, and I think he'll pull it off. I didn't want to tell Joshie till Story Week was done. I wanted him to enjoy something for a change.'

'You don't think it's a good idea?'

'Danny really traumatised that kid. Josh isn't ready to see him again. And Danny hasn't earned the fucking right.' She took one more drag on the cigarette before butting it out dramatically. 'Sorry, Fran, excuse the language.'

Franny laughed and placed her hand on top of the other woman's. 'Do you have a good lawyer?' she asked casually. 'Someone experienced?'

'I'm using a friend's brother. He's helping us for free.'

Franny sat back in her chair, sipping slowly on her drink and considering Sallyanne. 'My father was a bastard,' Franny said out of the blue. 'Heavy drinker. Heavy hitter. Took most of it out on my mother.'

'God, I'm sorry.'

'Please, honey, it was a lifetime ago—more than your lifetime, in fact—and no harm done, at least not to me. Of course, women had to put up with that shit in those days. You don't anymore. One of Frank's old pals is a pretty hot-shot lawyer type. His name's Alexander. Mind if I have a talk to him?'

Sallyanne's eyes filled with tears. 'I don't want to impose, Fran.'

'Please. It would be my pleasure. Your son's one of the only people I can bear talking to these days.'

Sallyanne let out a sob-tinged laugh.

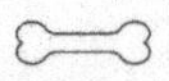

The Grand was running a ten-day Spanish film festival so Franny popped in to see a documentary about olive oil production in the province of Jaén. Tastebuds tingling in the aftermath, she went directly to the well-heeled shopping strip nearby, picking up ingredients for a recipe of steamed coral trout and chorizo dumplings kindly supplied by the festival's olive oil sponsor.

'The bottle of albariño to wash it all down was my own stroke of genius, of course,' she told Kitchen Frank while unloading the groceries. 'I can't believe we never got to this region, my love. Olive oil farms you can tour like vineyards, renaissance architecture as far as the eye can see.' She ran a link of cured sausage under her nose, inhaling it like a good cigar. 'Right up our alley!'

Franny gave a fleeting glance towards the refrigerator door where a chunky wine-bottle-shaped magnet gripped a business card for the local animal hospital. Once upon a time the magnet's purpose was to clutch a piece of paper where both Calderwoods jotted down names of places they randomly heard or read about and thought worth visiting. Every few months they took it down and spent a weekend researching the places together and discussing their merits. Sometimes this research turned into solid travel plans, sometimes it got filed for another time. Always, a clean sheet of paper went up on the fridge.

The last list had been incinerated in the kitchen sink, victim of a Redhead match. That was almost three years ago.

'Now,' she said, glancing at the kitchen clock, seeing it was only half past four. 'Is it too early for sherry?' Her eyes moved to Kitchen Frank. 'Just a plain old Tio Pepe while I'm cooking. Practically compulsory. This recipe is ludicrously complicated.'

By six o'clock three glasses of chilled Tio Pepe had been consumed, the albariño was one glass down and the chicken consomé was heating on the stove, ready to receive the steamed trout and dumplings. Initially Franny had considered eating outdoors but her energy had waned so she was setting a place at the kitchen bench when the intercom buzzed.

'Not dinnertime visitors,' she moaned to Whisky who, as always, was close by during food preparation. 'Yes, who is it?' she said into the contraption.

'It's me, Mrs C. Dee. Can I come in?'

Franny groaned. 'Everything okay, dear? Not an emergency, is it?'

'No, but I have some earrings for you. I won't stay long.'

Soda, sleeping in a strategic location between kitchen and lounge, stood up slowly, wagging her tail. Whisky barked.

'Well the mutts have me outvoted,' said Franny. 'Come in.'

Once inside, Dee took a deep sniff of the air. 'Wow what are you making? Smells delish.'

'It's Spanish steamed coral trout with chorizo dumplings and lemon yoghurt,' said Franny. 'Just a little recipe I stumbled across.'

'Sounds posh for a weeknight.' The youngster peered over Franny's shoulder towards the kitchen.

'Yes, well, one likes to make an effort. What's this about earrings?'

Dee produced a paper bag from behind her back and held it out. 'Mum found these at an op shop. Picked them for you. They're not identical to the ones I lost but they're pretty cool.'

Franny nodded for Dee to follow her over to the kitchen bench where she removed a small box from a bag emblazoned with the name Belinda's Collector Closet. Franny knew the place, she had sold a few pieces of her and Frank's 1980s clobber there in recent years. It was where spendthrift women driving 'moonlight blue' Audis went when they needed to unload the impractical Louis Vuitton backpack they'd purchased for five thousand dollars and never used. From what Franny had seen, students with too much disposable cash were the shop's main clientele.

'I would not call Belinda's an op shop, dear. And these'—she held up large, beaded earrings in the shape and colour of lemon segments—'are Kenneth Jay Lane according to the tag. Designer. What's your mother up to?'

'Told you they were cool. What's this stuff?' Dee had wandered over to the green bottle of Tio Pepe sweating on the bench. 'What does palomino fino mean?' She removed the lid and took a sniff.

Franny, struggling to coax one of the earrings into the half-closed hole in her ear, said, 'White-grape variety. The most important one for making sherry.'

'Sherry?' Dee wiggled both eyebrows and smiled. 'Never tried it. Can I?' She was already picking up Franny's empty glass.

'Voila!' said Franny, finally getting the earring attached. 'What do you think?'

'Love it. Let's have a drink and I'll help you with the other one. They really suit you, Mrs C.'

It had been a long time since anyone bought Franny jewellery. She felt unexpectedly giddy, although what role the wine and sherry were playing was difficult to determine. She ambled over to the pot of consomé, well and truly boiling now, and turned it off.

'Okay, have a snifter.' She grabbed a vintage gold-stemmed sherry glass from the cabinet and poured, then filled a wine glass with white for herself. 'Cheers,' she said and raised her glass. 'To designer lemons.'

Dee decided sherry was not for her but the albariño proved to be much more what Franny called 'approachable'.

'I weaned myself on to sherry, truth be told,' she explained, slopping steaming consomé into a shallow bowl and placing a piece of trout and a chorizo dumpling on top. She placed the dish in front of Dee. 'Try it with this.'

'Oh my God.' Dee spoke through a mouthful of wanton wrapper and tender fish. 'To be honest, the recipe sounded kind of gross but it tastes really nice. Here, you have it. It's your dinner.'

Franny shook her head. 'No, you go on. I'm not hungry anymore. Happens a lot when I cook these days, maybe it's age.' She zig-zagged over to a wall mirror nearby to admire herself in the earrings. 'I have the most amazing yellow mini-dress that would go with these,' she said and hiccupped. 'Not that I'd wear it anymore.'

'It's a bummer you're so tall. Everything's too long for me.' Dee was munching on chorizo and finishing off her wine.

'I don't know. That particular dress was always a bit short. Come try it on.' Franny sloppily filled her and Dee's wine glasses with the last of the bottle. 'Bring your drink,' she sang out and sashayed from the room.

Forty-five minutes later, with Cat Stevens blaring in the background, clothes flung all over the front room and Dee dressed in a biker's jacket and harem pants, a mobile phone buzzed. 'That's me,' the girl said, scrambling through the mess to find it. She looked up from the screen. 'Mum's wondering where I am. Man, it's almost seven and she's serving dinner. Gotta go. I said I'd only be a few minutes.' Her head swivelled and she looked longingly at all the fashion treasures.

'Keep that outfit,' said Franny, feeling both magnanimous and sleepy. 'And here.' She shoved the famous yellow mini at Dee. 'You're welcome to this too. Looked great. Needs a stitch or two to fit you properly. We'll do that together one day.' She wanted the girl gone now.

'Really?' Dee bent down to gather up her own clothes from the floor and lost her balance for a second. Franny laughed and shooed her out the door.

Franny lifted her head off the floor like an ancient turtle reluctantly peeping out from its shell. The scarf she had scrunched under her head as a makeshift pillow was caked with drool. She had passed out on the floor of the spare room, surrounded by clothes. The insistent buzzing on the intercom was taking a while to penetrate her consciousness.

As her eyes focused, the first things Franny saw were a shot glass and bottle of vodka standing sentry on the side table, the empty albariño bottle leaning precariously against silver-framed Spare Room Frank.

She stared blankly at what she thought of as her husband's sexiest Woodward and Bernstein moment, a candid image captured on the campaign trail, Frank's tousled hair skimming his opened shirt collar, two lanyards around his neck and a pen sticking out of his mouth. On the wrong day this photograph could deliver a real gut punch. Most days. Looking at it now she struggled to recall what had happened in the two or so hours since Dee had left the house. She thought she had tried on a few outfits. She knew she had downed a few more drinks.

The buzzing noise came again and, somewhere else in the house, she heard her mobile phone ringing. Whisky began to bark.

Franny was aware of her sour breath and could feel the hot clamminess of her skin. She struggled to sit up and get her bearings.

Deciding the door was more urgent than the phone, she made her way to the intercom, pressed it and croaked out a hello.

'Franny, it's Sallyanne. Let me in please.' The words came in clipped, low tones.

Franny realised her phone had ceased ringing. 'Was that you on the mobile?' she asked.

'Yes. I've been calling and buzzing for ages. Let me in please.'

Franny looked down at the two dogs now gathered at her legs and blinked hard. It dawned on her that she was in no way sober. 'Um, I don't think that's a good idea, dear. I'm a bit . . . under the weather.'

A loud intake of breath came from the other end of the intercom. 'Let me in this gate now or I will go around and climb over the back fence. The choice is yours.'

'Okay, okay, keep your knickers on.' She buzzed to let her visitor in then unlocked the front door.

Sallyanne didn't wait for a formal invitation. She was through the door and in the kitchen within moments, turning on bright lights as she went. The place smelled like stale grease and seafood. Everything from Franny's Spanish cooking adventure lay strewn across sinks and benchtops, including Dee's half-eaten meal, now cold and congealed.

Sallyanne spread her hands wide like a magician, taking in all the mess. She looked at Franny with large, open eyes. Eventually, head on the side, she said, 'Well?'

The lights really were bright. Franny felt as if she were on the set for one of the forensic procedurals from the BBC she liked to watch. She moved to a stool at the kitchen bench and sat down. 'Well what?' she said. 'Since when do you care about my mess?'

'Great question,' said Sallyanne with a nasty little laugh. 'Really good question.' She picked up a cleanish glass from the bench and filled it with tap water then handed it over to Franny. 'Drink this for God's sake and wipe your mouth. There's something'—she wiggled her finger at Franny and grimaced—'hanging around it.'

Franny's cheeks reddened. She wiped her mouth and drank the water, because she really needed to not because this blonde was ordering her. Eventually she said, 'Can you tell me what's going on?'

'Well, I guess you're right in a way. I'm here about your mess and the fact I don't want my daughter dragged into it.' Franny looked as if she was going to interrupt so Sallyanne held up a finger to silence her, then continued. 'My sixteen-year-old daughter came home late for dinner tonight, red-eyed and slurring, dressed like an escapee from a psych ward and smelling like a mix between an op shop and a bottle shop.' Again, Franny tried to interrupt. Again, Sallyanne wagged a finger in warning. 'She told her sweetheart of a brother to "shut the fuck up" when he asked what was wrong with her and now, in one of my proudest child-rearing moments, I have been forced to put her to bed with a bucket beside her because she has developed the bed spins.' Sallyanne raised her eyebrows to reinforce her point.

'Dee says you gave her sherry—who the hell still drinks sherry?—and some other shit while feeding her trout and playing dress-ups. All in all, I think it's fair to say, yes, I do indeed care about your mess'—she shoved the plate of unfinished dinner towards Franny—'but only when it comes to the effect it has on my child's life.'

Sallyanne stopped for a beat and stared at Franny. 'Obviously, you have a drinking problem. But it's not my place to interfere. It is, however, my place to keep my kids away from it. And to tell you that, under no circumstances, do I ever, ever want to see you giving my kids booze of any type again. Got it?'

Franny tipped forward on her stool a little so she could use the bench as a support to help her stand. Doing so she caught a whiff of the trout and chorizo and understood immediately what the hot prick at the base of her throat was signalling. She tried giving Sallyanne a look of fury but suspected it came across more like panic. Rushing to the laundry, Franny heard Sallyanne call out, 'I'll let myself out, Mrs Calderwood. Enjoy the rest of your evening.'

18

The bigger picture

As she waited for the long arm of the parking boom gate to rise and allow her access to the art gallery's car park, Franny's mind went over the previous night's skirmish, or at least the parts that had stayed with her.

She knew Sallyanne had accused her of having a drinking problem. That was pretty rich for someone who hardly knew her, for someone who had burst into her neighbour's home and accosted her. *The cheek of it*, thought Franny. *Who the hell does she think she is?* It was galling the way some of Sallyanne's words had looped through Franny's brain all morning.

Grabbing her drawing satchel from the back seat of the car, Franny headed into the gallery and up the escalator to the home of nineteenth-century European paintings. A small group was gathered, clipping sheets of paper to drawing boards, readying themselves for the tutor's brief chat about great artists and their use of light.

Franny showed her membership card to a black-clad girl holding a scanning machine, who smiled through a mouth full of braces and told her to take a seat. Sketching in this environment was one of Franny's favourite things to do. There was something about the smells and sounds of a big public gallery, the quiet shuffling of viewers moving from one work to the next, the hushed conversations, the lingering aroma of coffee from the café downstairs.

Here, the world behaved differently. Outside, workers hurried past, their eyes glued to phones, confirming meetings, counting steps. Outside, tourists bickered over where to eat or what to see while taxi horns blared and trams disgorged passengers. The world, its thoughts and movements, rushed and roiled. Inside the gallery there was quiet, even the noisiest of children hushed by teachers, parents or friends.

Here, people stopped, people stared. They looked carefully at things and read the fine print. They listened to quietly spoken tour guides or turned to each other and murmured brief comments, even pecked a quick kiss. There seemed to be, to Franny, a pace and approach to the business of life, its contemplation and consideration, that was akin to a place of worship.

When Frank died she came here often in the early days, spending hours reading every label in the Ancient World collection, sometimes eating sandwiches on the lawn, sometimes poring over books in the gift shop or sampling the cafeteria cake selection, sometimes downing champagne in the dimly lit bar. She had wept silently in the sculpture garden and stood unseeing before a painting of colonial settlers as the shock and horror of her life's loss crackled through her like electricity. Eventually some of the guards became familiar, occasionally nodding as she passed by. One of the baristas knew her coffee order. One of the bar staff knew the pinot she preferred. She still visited regularly, for this monthly drawing class or when a new exhibition opened. She still felt the balm of the place.

Today the balm had its work cut out. Franny's hand hovered above the page, her pencil teetering expectantly as she stared at the sight of a distressed ewe standing guard over its dead lamb, a murder of crows lurking nearby. The light in the work was remarkable, a bruised and muddy sky against stark white snow and the frosty breath of the wretched creature. Franny's mouth was dry, behind her eyes there was a subtle ache. Her classmates, dotted around the room, had their heads bent as they concentrated on works chosen to study and inspire. The tutor, an open and sunny woman with a blunt blonde fringe and bright, orange-painted lips, caught her eye and wiggled her eyebrows. Franny gave a grimace and rubbed a hand across her stomach, the international symbol for feeling peaky. She packed up and nodded goodbye.

In the cafeteria, she ordered a chai and took it to the quietest corner she could find. She thought back on the day before, the pleasure of the movie, the delight of the cooking, the tang of the wine. It had been fun to see Dee all dressed up, her smooth young skin resuscitating the form and flow of the old fabrics. Franny had enjoyed the delight on the young girl's face. She couldn't completely recall pouring the child drinks but there you had it; she couldn't completely remember a lot.

The sketching class cost fifty dollars, even for paid-up gallery members like Franny. She resented dropping out today, normally she ensured she was in good form to attend. Now she had allowed that annoying harpy from next door to get in the way.

'That's it,' she said aloud, slamming her hand on the flimsy café table, causing an elderly man nearby to frown disapprovingly over his newspaper.

Back in the car she vented loudly and lengthily as she exited the car park. 'That woman has no business coming into my home and passing judgement on my life,' she told the rear-view mirror.

Back in the house, unpacking her art materials onto the laundry bench, Franny yelled, 'What we do in our own home is our own business. Isn't that right, darling?' Laundry Frank continued snoozing under the knickers. 'When I'm locked behind my precious door I do not expect neighbourhood children descending on me willy-nilly. It's not like I'm out there forcibly leading them astray. Enter at thy own peril, that's my motto.' She picked up the photograph and gave it a kiss. 'Or here's an idea: don't bloody enter at all!'

It was six o'clock when Franny checked the letterbox, decided she would have a simple dinner, preferably involving carbohydrates, then go to bed early. This day needed to end soon.

Among the flyers for various pizza delivery and gutter repair companies she saw an envelope bearing unfamiliar handwriting. Her name appeared in block letters on the front. The sender's name, Angela Caliendo, was similarly written on the back. The sender's address, Franny noted, was only about three suburbs away.

Back in the house Franny put some water on to boil for pasta and poured herself a soda, not sure her stomach could handle a gin and tonic. Sitting at the kitchen bench she popped on her reading glasses and opened the intriguing letter. Within seconds she regretted this decision with her entire being.

'Jesus, Mary and Joseph. When is enough enough?' Franny whispered to Kitchen Frank, wishing for a moment this particular image—her husband in the boob-covered apron—was not so ridiculous. She needed something to bolster and reassure her. As she rubbed her hand back and forth across her lips, she felt a slight tremor running through it.

She stood up and turned off the gas beneath the saucepan. Picking up her glass of water and the letter, hand still trembling a little, she moved through the house, closing blinds and checking doors. The dogs had been fed early and were asleep head-to-head along the sofa. She looked at them fondly, envious of their carefree lives, then headed into her bedroom. She lay down on the bed on her belly, the letter spread out in front of her, and began to read it once more.

Dear Mrs Calderwood,
I write to you because of the thing you sent back in the post the other week. Don't worry, while putting excrement in the post is illegal, I have managed to convince everyone concerned not to involve the authorities. I don't think you'll have any visits from law enforcement as things stand.

My name is Angela Caliendo and I am aunt to Chris Pavlos. I do not need to explain who he is. Firstly, I would like to offer my deepest condolences on the loss of your husband Francis Calderwood. You are always very much in our family's thoughts. I hope you can believe that.

Chris's mother is my sister, Sandra. She does not know I am contacting you, neither does Chris, and in fact by all rights I should not be. I should not even have your contact details. But, someone somewhere recognised my desperation and has gone out on a limb to help me. I hope my contacting you will not put them at risk too.

I will get straight to it Mrs Calderwood—I BEG of you to reconsider your response to Chris. As much as it pains me to say it, it is true that my son was the person who introduced him to drugs, and it's fair to say it was my son who led him astray.

Nicholas, my boy, has always been troubled. I won't go into that now. But Chris was always a good kid. Only when he became unemployed and depressed was he vulnerable to his older cousin's influence.

Chris is back on track now. You have my word on that. His behaviour while incarcerated and his response to the rehab program makes him eligible to pursue some further education, maybe have another shot at life. Funny thing is, he won't do it. He won't take these positive steps without the green light from you. That's what his letter was about. He doesn't think he has the right to move on.

Mrs Calderwood, I know this is a huge thing to ask. You don't know him, you don't know us. But my sister is a wonderful woman, innocent of all of this, and her son is at heart a beautiful boy. It's my son who has brought this family so much trouble over the years. This last thing is, however, too much.

I feel I must tell you that Sandra has been diagnosed with breast cancer, it is the stress I think. She is my best friend as well as my sister and I truly believe she needs to see her boy doing okay if she has any chance of fighting this thing.

Please consider my request, my plea, Mrs Calderwood. I ask you as a woman, perhaps a sister and friend, if not a mother. I guess I am being selfish. I can't live knowing my son has ruined not only his life but all of these people's as well. Someone must come out of this okay.

I cannot ask you to put yourself in our shoes because that would be impossible for sure. But maybe you can for a moment think about Chris. He'll lose a lot of his twenties to prison but there is still time for him to have a future. He's not a lost cause, Mrs Calderwood, I promise—but I am not sure what will happen to his mental state if he does not hear from you. He doesn't know about the 'thing' you sent back. He thinks you just didn't respond, or at least haven't as yet. It's not too late, Mrs Calderwood, for any of us. Please consider.

Yours in sympathy and in faith,
Ange Caliendo
angecal@gmail.com

19

A friend in need

While technically it was a day to be working on her art, there was no way Franny could focus. The letter that had arrived the day before from Aunty Prick, the name already designated to Ange Caliendo, replayed across her mind again and again, like the annoying advertisements that ruin your favourite television show.

Refusing to give in to naval gazing or rumination, she opened up her laptop on the studio table, deciding to visit The Wuthering Club and post a few notes about *An Isolated Incident*, a novel she had devoured the week before.

Besides her initial whispered outburst to Kitchen Frank the night before, Franny had not said another word to her dead husband, or at least the photos of him, about the letter or her thoughts on it. Her goal was to push the whole thing aside, pretending nothing had happened, no letter received. While achieving the goal was proving tricky—even in the shower that morning she had found herself muttering 'no, no, no you don't' when tears threatened—she was determined not to acknowledge or share the outrage and distress she was experiencing, not even with the dead.

This morning, plastering on a smile and sipping from an extra-sweet iced coffee, she quipped to Studio Frank, 'Ooh, I see Nancy Friol has left some droppings. Our hippy head girl is suggesting we read something called *The Clarity Cleanse*.' Franny clicked on the link to the book embedded in Nancy's post. 'Oh perfect,' she shouted, waking Soda from a sunlight snooze nearby. 'It's something called a Goop Press Book. I believe that means Gwyneth Paltrow recommends it. What's next, "Embracing Your Anus"? For God's sake.'

Franny scrolled through the comments attached to the post. Midway down, one of the group's administrators, Mindy Delfrate, reminded Nancy that monthly title suggestions must come from the fiction category. Saying that, she was 'sure members welcomed other thought starters for supplementary reading'.

Franny looked again at the link to *The Clarity Cleanse*. 'Recipes targeted at congestion in the areas said to be most affected by anger—liver, gallbladder, lungs, kidneys and pancreas,' she read aloud. 'I have some thoughts starting, but I don't think Mindy would want to hear them.' In disgust, she slammed shut the lid of her laptop, just as Soda got to her feet and Whisky came rushing into the studio, barking excitedly and dancing around at the window.

Moving towards the curtains, Franny peered out at her driveway in time to see a small blond head pass by. The intercom buzzed and both dogs exploded in a chorus of barks, keen to let the visitor know they were at home.

Franny glared at them. 'Bloody traitors,' she said in tone more amused than annoyed. Since her run-in with Sallyanne she had not seen much of 'the people next door' as she had taken to thinking of them. She'd also been telling herself the peace and quiet was a relief. Today, however, she knew she could do with the distraction, and quickly buzzed in Josh.

'Franny, Franny I have something to show you. It's my prize,' said Josh, barging through her open door a few moments later. He waved a large hardback book of Newt Scamander's *Fantastic Beasts and Where to Find Them* at her. 'It's the illustrated edition, the special one, because my Story Week voucher was for fifty dollars.' The small boy plonked the tome on the ground then submitted to the dogs' enthusiastic welcome licks, from his knees to the tip of his nose.

Franny watched the trio and thought once again how much Frank would like this pint-sized neighbour. Biting her bottom lip, she bent down and busied herself with rescuing the new book from the mêlée. At the kitchen counter, she slipped on her glasses and flicked through the pages, bending to inhale the magical new-book smell while admiring a fiery coral phoenix, its wings and plumage filling two glossy pages.

'You can watch Olivia illustrating this on YouTube,' she called to Josh as he extricated himself from tails and paws. 'She uses copperplate etching.'

He climbed up on a stool beside her. 'Who's Olivia?'

Franny pointed to the name on the front cover of the book. 'Olivia Lomenech Gill. She's the lady who drew all these wonderful creatures.' Franny pointed to another page where a giant emerald dragon soared above seaside bathers. 'Look her up when you go home.'

Josh pushed his bottom lip out. 'Can't we do it together? I just got here.'

Franny looked at the clock. Nearly midday. 'I haven't even started work yet. Half the day's gone. Anyway, where's your mum?' This was her real concern. Was the boy allowed to visit anymore?

'She's at work and I know she said I shouldn't bother you so much anymore.' At these words he looked down sadly at the dogs on either side of his stool. 'I know you're too busy and everything but you did make the costume and that's why I won. I thought you'd kinda wanna see the book. That's all.' With dramatic flair, he slid slowly off his stool.

'All right, monkey, hang on.' Franny put her hands under his armpits and lifted him back up with a grunt. He was remarkably light. 'You're still allowed to visit me?'

Josh shrugged. 'Yeah, why? Did you tell Mum I couldn't?'

'No, no, nothing like that. I just think she was a little grumpy with me the other day. After Dee came over to visit.'

'Oh, you mean the night Dee smelled funny and wouldn't eat her dinner?' Franny nodded uncomfortably. 'Mummy was angry with her, not you. Dee told me to shut up you know! She used a bad word.'

His look of indignation sent Franny into peals of laughter. She leaned forward and kissed him on the cheek. 'You, my friend, are the bee's knees. Feel like sharing toasted sandwiches for lunch?'

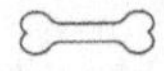

Monday morning's yoga class had been sublime. Calliope was exploring something called Yin Yang and Franny's muscles felt longer and more supple than they had in years. After the weekend she had had, swapping toasted sandwiches for a buttery chardonnay after Josh had left on Saturday, then eating her bodyweight in fish and chips on Sunday, she needed to do something wholesome. Her commitment to 'not letting Aunty Prick's letter get to her' had sent Franny into overdrive in terms of eating, drinking, weeding, bathroom scrubbing and dog walking. She had purchased a nineteen-hour audiobook of Arthur Conan Doyle's gothic tales and was already eight hours into it.

'I'm going to have to stop coming soon,' she told the lycra-clad teacher when class ended and people were rolling up mats and stacking cushions.

'Franny, no,' said Calliope, looking genuinely upset. 'Is something wrong?'

Franny laughed. 'The opposite. I'm too okay if anything. You're doing too good a job. Keep coming to this class and I'm in danger of living forever. I certainly don't want that. I'm already running the risk of making old bones.'

The yoga teacher gave Franny a bemused look. 'You know your birthday popped up on my calendar recently. Did you just turn sixty-five?'

'Keep it down, keep it down,' said Franny. 'I keep telling that lot I'm seventy-five.' She nodded her head towards a trio of chatting women in floral yoga pants all walking out the door together.

'Why on earth would you do that?'

'When they thought I was their age they kept inviting me to things. Now they think I'm an old lady.' Franny mimed air quotes around the term. 'So they won't be seen dead with me. The old detest the elderly, it reminds them too much of what's ahead. Anyway, it's perfect really. Can't believe I haven't tried the strategy before.'

Calliope released a bell-like laugh. 'You're a very unusual person, Frances Calderwood. Is there something specifically objectionable about Karen, Rhonda and Marianne? Something I should know? They've always seemed quite sweet to me.'

'Exactly.' Franny screwed up her face and made for the door. 'They're quite sweet and I'm quite sour. A poor mix all round. Om shanti. See you next week.'

Outside Calleidoscope Yoga Studio, rifling through her bag in search of keys, Franny noticed a now-familiar lilac head in the window of The Chicken Joint. She slipped through the door behind a trio of workmen and tiptoed towards her quarry.

'Bunking off are we?' she whispered in Dee's ear.

'Christ, Mrs C, you scared me.' The girl's attention had been completely focused on a basket of hot chips and her iPhone. She looked Franny up and down, taking in her outfit. 'More yoga?'

'Very perceptive. What about you? More delinquency?'

Dee pulled out a note from her pocket and waggled it in Franny's face. 'Actually, I had a dentist appointment. Mum just dropped me here. I'm catching the late bus to school.'

'Well that's something I guess.' Franny leaned over and stole a chip. 'How is your mother by the way?'

'Still pissed with you if that's what you're asking. I'm banned from accepting alcohol of any type from you in case you haven't heard. And I'm not even meant to be alone with you if you're drinking.' Dee mimed someone knocking back a large drink to embellish her point. 'In fact, she doesn't want me coming over to your place at all when she's not around. What happened between you two? Mum went on and on about you having "problems".'

Franny's cheeks reddened abruptly. 'I didn't have problems till you lot moved in.' She spat out the words.

Eyes wide, mouth in a grim straight line, Dee placed her phone in the pocket of her school dress and pushed aside her stool to leave. 'You know, I was actually thinking about you earlier.'

'All good I hope.' Franny tried to make her tone contrite.

Dee shrugged on her school backpack. 'I was remembering that woman you ran into here the other week. Was Di her name?'

'What about her?'

'I was thinking that if you're someone people try so hard to catch up with then you can't really have that many "problems", as Mum calls them. You must at least be a good friend.' Dee's glance went to the window. People previously milling at the bus stop were now gathering bags and belongings; the number eight was on its way. Looking back at Franny, Dee said, 'But maybe I was wrong.' Then she shoved past Franny, not bothering to say goodbye.

Franny's return from the botanic gardens that afternoon coincided with Josh and Dee's return from school. Not a complete accident. Franny had picked up a beautiful colouring book from the gardens' gift store, along with a grow-your-own-tomatoes kit, a child's wet weather poncho in a ladybird design, two pairs of socks decorated with wombats and a hideously overpriced candle, supposedly fragranced by alpine eucalypt.

'Hey, Salernos,' she yelled out the car window as she pulled into the driveway.

Josh's face broke into a grin and he waved enthusiastically. 'Hi Franny,' he called.

Dee kept walking.

'Hang on a minute, will you?' Franny hurried to get out of the car, dragging a couple of gift bags from the back seat. 'There was a sale on. I picked up a jumble of stuff. Come in and see if there's anything you want.' She sounded pleading, even to herself.

'Got snacks?' asked Josh.

Dee looked at the bags then at Franny. 'No thank you, Mrs Calderwood. We've got homework and I promised Mum I'd peel some potatoes.' She grabbed her brother's hands and steered him towards their house. 'Bye.'

Josh dropped his schoolbag and sat on it. 'I wanna go to Franny's. I wanna have snacks.'

Franny swayed the gift bags to and fro, as if she were dangling barbecue chicken in front of the dogs. 'Come on. Not for long. I've got spuds. We can get them ready together.'

Josh was on his feet, breaking free of his sister's grip. 'Whisky, Soda,' he yelled, heading for his neighbour's gate.

Inside the house, Franny poured two big soda waters, filling the glasses with ice cubes and slices of lime and orange.

'Aren't you having one?' Dee eyed Franny slyly.

'I fancy a tea, actually.' Franny switched on the kettle and pulled an unopened box of green tea from the back of a cupboard. 'It's an antioxidant, you know.' She busied herself, putting together a plate of cheese, crackers, sliced apples and strawberries and a big bowl of chilli-lime cashews.

'Yum,' said Josh as he created little sandwiches from the combination. 'It's like a party.'

'Speaking of, where are these gifts you say you bought?' Dee was scrolling through her phone and crunching on an apple wedge. The look she shot Franny was defiant.

His sister's tone seemed to send a direct signal to the small boy's emotional radar, somehow alerting him to the fact something was askew, even if he had no idea what it was or why. 'She didn't say gifts, Dee Dum, and you sound greedy. Mum says that's not nice.'

'Mum says a lot of stuff. One of them is that we shouldn't be in this house when she's not here.' As Dee spoke her thumbs danced across her phone.

'Okay, young lady, I get it. You're angry with me. If I apologise will you drop the act?' Franny placed a triangular tea bag into a slim china cup.

'The stuff about Mum not wanting us here is true. No act, and you know it.' Now she was glaring at Franny. 'But you also seem to think we're more trouble than we're worth. So there's that.'

Josh looked at the two females staring intently at each other. Tears filled his big blue eyes. 'What's happening? Why are you saying all this?' Jumping off his stool, he ran around and wrapped his arms around Franny. Whisky, who had been hoovering up crumbs by his feet, chased behind, jumping up on Franny, enjoying this new game.

Franny put a hand down to ruffle Josh's hair. 'It's okay, honey. I was angry about something this morning and because of that I was rude to Dee. I upset her. It was very wrong and I'm very sorry.' She looked over at Dee. 'I am sorry, Dee. I did not mean it. Can you forgive me?'

'Come on, Dee Dum,' said Josh, running around and hugging his sister. 'Franny's really sorry.'

Dee dragged her brother up onto her lap. He barely fit. 'I don't know,' she said, grabbing both of Josh's ears and waggling them. 'Did she say she'd make mash?'

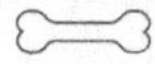

An hour and a half later—both kids satiated by their after-school feast, supplemented with a little taste-testing of creamy mashed potato—Dee's phone rang. She was settled on the lounge-room floor with a textbook beside her. Josh was in the kitchen, playing with Whisky and telling Franny about his day.

'Hang on, Joshie. Be quiet for a sec,' said Dee.

Franny could not hear what Dee was saying but her expression looked troubled. Immediately she felt a pang of guilt that the children were acting against their mother's wishes. Did Sallyanne somehow know? She walked over to the young girl and mouthed the words, 'You okay?'

'Hang on, Mum. Mrs C. is here now. Yep, yep, I will.' She handed her phone to Franny. 'Mum wants to talk to you,' she said, her face pale. She signalled for Josh to come sit with her on the floor.

Franny readied herself for a dressing down. 'Sallyanne?' she said curtly.

'Thank God. Franny, I think we need your help.' The other woman's voice was low. She sounded panicked.

Franny's mind changed gears. 'Okay, all right, what is it?'

'I'm at work. I'm trying not to freak.'

'Just tell me what it is and we'll go from there.' Franny looked down at Dee and Josh and gave them what she hoped was a reassuring grin.

'Danny's been calling and texting all day. I tried ignoring it all but now he says he's at the house. Your lawyer friend, Alexander Dempsey, has shared the news with him that any visits with the kids are being delayed. He's going ballistic. Demanding to see "his offspring" and wanting to know "who the fuck" is interfering with his family. I didn't think he knew our address yet but I guess it was just a matter of time. I'm scared, Franny. Can they stay with you?'

'Bloody hell. Of course they can. No question about it. Hang on for a second.' Franny moved the phone away from her ear and bent down to the two anxious children. 'I'm just going to pop into the other room for a moment. Stay here.' She smiled again.

In the bedroom, she returned the phone to her ear. 'Do you think he's actually dangerous? It's just there's a complete knob over the back fence, Shawn Dimitriades. He's a pain as a neighbour but he's a bloody respected cop. He might be home. Can I call?'

Sallyanne didn't hesitate. 'Call the whole street if it means my babies are safe.' She let out a sob. 'I'm knocking off. I'll be home in half an hour. See you then.'

'Sallyanne, Sallyanne, don't hang up.' Franny moved to her studio and stood sideways by the window, straining to see out to the street. A black Mustang filled the Salernos' driveway. 'Listen, call before you get here, before you're in Ipswich Street. I'll tell you if the coast is clear. Okay?'

Another sob made its way across the phone line. 'Thank you so much, Franny. Please . . . keep them safe.'

One phone call and two SMS messages later, Franny was nestled on the couch in her lounge room with Dee and Josh, the television on low, Seinfeld doing some patter about old people driving in Florida. At one point, blue lights had briefly illuminated the windows and loud voices could be heard but no actual words made it over. The dogs went crazy at the window but Franny and Dee insisted Josh stay beside them on the couch. When a man came to the door Franny and he spoke in low murmurs. She scribbled something on a piece of paper and handed it over; then it was silent, everyone gone.

'Well that was exciting,' she said, turning the television to mute and calling Soda over for a chin scratch.

'I don't understand. What's going on?' Josh was up from his seat and running to look out the window.

Franny gestured to Dee to stay where she was. 'It's okay, guys. It looks like we might have had a burglar in the street. The police came. Nothing happened. It's all over.'

'A burglar, like a robber?' Josh stepped back from the window as if it were on fire. 'Where? At our house? Where's Mummy? Did he take my bike?' He ran back to Dee and climbed onto her knee.

'It's okay now, honey, really.' Franny sat beside him, smoothing his hair. 'We're very lucky. We have a policeman for a neighbour and he thought he saw something fishy and contacted his police friends.'

'But why did Mummy call before? How did she know?'

For the first time since meeting him, Franny cursed the fact this eight-year-old was so clued-in. 'She knows the policeman. He called her first to check if anyone was at home.' Josh did not look convinced but she powered on. 'Anyway, they came by and took a look and now everyone's gone. No one took anything and Mummy's on her way home from work, safe and sound. And you still have a bike.' She gave a rakish wink.

In fact, Franny had just sent a message to Sallyanne, parked two blocks away, giving her the green light. As brother and sister cuddled on the couch, the intercom sounded then their mother was flying through the door.

Josh exploded into stories about cops and robbers and being scared. Sallyanne gathered both children in her arms. Putting her mouth against Dee's ear she whispered, 'You okay, sweet girl?'

Dee looked back towards Franny, who had returned to her position in front of the noiseless television. The young girl's eyes brimmed with tears. 'We're okay, Mum.' She nodded her head a few times. 'Franny was here.'

20

Close encounters

Autumn was making a show of itself. Franny sat in the backyard and contemplated the Boston Ivy. Its annual blaze of colour was a miracle of which she never tired: one day a verdant but sedate companion in the garden, the next a crimson flamboyance. She often photographed the leaves so she could paint them later. Within a month or two the colourful gala would end, leaves dropped and covering the lawn, the dowdy and damaged back fence exposed like poorly darned underwear.

'We'd be heading to the Dog and Duck soon,' she said, picking up her Waterford gin balloon and taking a long, appreciative sip. Soda, splayed beside the stool where Franny's feet were propped, raised her head and looked at her owner quizzically. 'It's all right, honey,' said Franny, reaching down to scratch the dog's ear. 'I was talking to the old man, not you.' She swirled the ice cubes in her glass and took another sip.

Franny and Frank had headed into country Victoria in autumn for years to attend a duck and pinot weekend at the Dog and Duck pub. They'd started doing so after the area was decimated by bushfires, the locals in need of city cash and tourists' bums on seats.

The Calderwoods had bonded quickly with the owners of the pub. Bev and Darren McIlroy, The Macs to their friends, were ex-city folk who had sold everything to pursue a life's dream. When that dream turned to cinders the couple's insurance company and adult children were surprisingly in sync in terms of being obstructive and fatalistic. The new Dog and Duck scored lower on the quaint metre than it's eighty-year-old predecessor but much higher when it came to fire proofing and guest-room plumbing. The inaugural duck and pinot dinner was a fundraiser organised in part by Frank's 'hot-shot lawyer' friend, Alexander. The dinner was an out-and-out success, and the Calderwoods returned year after year, reversing Frank's beat up four-wheel drive between an ever-growing collection of Audis and Porches.

'It looks like a bloody luxury-car showroom, not a country pub car park,' Frank had said on their last visit. 'We're lowering the tone. Might have to start parking down the road from now on.'

The last time Franny had been there was almost exactly three years ago. Back then she had also marvelled at the Boston Ivy's blaze. Back then it had reminded her to finalise their Dog and Duck weekend plans. Back then she and Frank had returned from the trip, tired but elated. Back then she had hardly looked up from unpacking when her husband called out something about jumping on his bike and 'nipping round to the shops'.

Finishing the gin and tonic, Franny held up the heavy crystal balloon and examined the prisms of pink light flowing through it. The glass was part of a set of four, a gift from Anthea and David following a trip to Ireland. Once upon a time Franny had saved them especially for when the foursome dined together. Now she kept three of the glasses in a box in the laundry.

She shook her head as a couple of fat tears escaped her eyes. Sitting in the yard like a piece of garden furniture was not helping her state of mind. She looked down at the dog now collapsed back into sleep and ruffled her blonde head. 'Okay, pooch,' said Franny, 'let's waddle inside and rustle up something for dinner that stretches our culinary skills.'

The gay fizz of the aspirin was mocking her. She downed it in one gulp to show it who was boss. Even by her standards Franny had tied one on the night before.

For more than two hours she had slaved over Julia Child's version of boeuf bourguignon, browning lardons, quartering mushrooms, and coating and frying beef. With around seventeen ingredients to busy herself with, time had flown. By the time the meal was ready Franny had swapped gin and tonic for cabernet sauvignon and lost all interest in food. Over a kilo and a half of what basically amounted to stew was now in a Tupperware container in her fridge.

'Note to self,' she said to Bedroom Frank, bending down to rummage for a scarf in her wardrobe's depths. 'When it's midnight and I start thinking Roku on ice and an Aretha Live at Fillmore West marathon is a good idea, it never is.'

Franny straightened up and was hit by a nauseous burning in the back of her throat, the cruel stepsister of last night's iridescent buzz. She grimaced at the photo.

'Dorothy Parker was right, darling, the best way to avoid a hangover is to stay drunk.' Blowing a kiss, she left the room.

Survival was her only goal today. If she could walk the dogs and change the bedsheets, she would consider herself an overachiever. A few hours of back-to-back movies on her iPad in bed, supplemented by cups of tea and, later, something carb-laden to eat, would constitute her agenda.

Experience told Franny she wouldn't feel human until evening. Then the inevitable remorse would kick in and she'd start beating herself up about wasting her time and ruining her health. This would be the moment when the shower got cleaned or a yoga retreat was researched. She knew the drill, had the T-shirt. For now, a dog walk where she didn't pass out was her priority.

By the time Sallyanne and Josh buzzed the intercom that evening the sun was setting and Franny was downing another dose of aspirin while very, very tentatively wondering if a small serve of bourguignon could be stomached.

When he entered, Josh held a huge bunch of colourful gerberas and a white envelope with her name written on it.

'These are for you,' he said proudly, gesturing for her to take the items off his hands. 'They're for welcoming us into the neighbourhood.'

Franny's eyes met Sallyanne's. Obviously, Josh still did not know what had really happened with his father the other night.

'Thank you, young man. I accept these on behalf of Ipswich Street.' She took a bow, a move she instantly regretted. Her head could not cope with the downwards swooping. 'Come into the studio,' she said after a moment, remembering the kitchen and lounge room still bore evidence of her Julia and Aretha-loving activities. 'I have the perfect vase in there.'

With everyone seated around the large table, and two dogs hovering nearby, Franny told Josh how beautiful the flowers were.

'I knew you'd like them,' he said. 'Maybe you could paint them. And look at the card, Franny. There's something in there.'

Inside a card printed with the words 'thank you' was a photograph of a stocky black-and-white pug. Franny looked at her guests with a confused smile.

'That's Luna,' said Josh, beaming. 'Our dog. I thought maybe one day we could paint her together, you know, if I gave you a picture.' His expression was hopeful.

Exhausted and feeling the kind of sentimental vulnerability only a good hangover could deliver, Franny got up and found a large jar of coloured pencils and a thick drawing pad for the boy and said, 'Why don't you do some preliminary sketches now while I grab the vase from the en suite and talk to your mum?' Before he could ask what preliminary meant, she added, 'And preliminary means practice.'

Josh nodded enthusiastically and got down to work.

Sallyanne followed Franny, stopping in front of a group of floral paintings lined up beneath one of the windows. 'You're really building up this collection,' she said. 'They're so beautiful. Would you exhibit?'

Franny found the vase and began filling it with water. 'I can't see that happening,' she said, then lowered her voice. 'After all, who'd want to get involved with some weird old dog lady with an obvious drinking problem?'

Sallyanne moved closer to Franny, lowering her voice as well. 'Hmm, I've been meaning to bring that up.' She looked back to make sure her son was engrossed in his artwork. 'I can't say I'm sorry for being angry at you in terms of giving Dee the booze, Franny. I was angry at her too, for going along with it. And scared, actually. I've been relying on her a lot lately, with Josh and everything. It was an uncomfortable reminder of just how vulnerable she is.

'Even if we park the fact that Dee's underage and it was an outrageous act on your behalf'—she widened her eyes and nodded her head to emphasise the point—'did you know all the research today shows your brain is still developing up until your mid-twenties? All in all, I really can't tolerate that happening again. You do get that don't you?'

Franny nodded, making a show of keeping her lips sealed, and Sallyanne moved slightly closer, putting a hand on her arm.

'But I did want to say how very, very grateful I am that you were home the other day, that the kids were with you and that you stepped in when Danny turned up. If anything had happened . . .' Her voice trailed off, eyes glistening.

Franny plucked out one of the gerberas, pretending to show Sallyanne some detail on it. 'Now don't go upsetting yourself. We were completely fine, and I was happy to help. I would always help.' She looked over at Josh's bent head and serious expression. 'As I seem to recall saying before, your two kids are probably the only people I enjoy spending time with these days,' she added, the words ringing surprisingly clear and true.

Uncomfortable with the conversation's direction, Franny suddenly clapped her hands, startling two dogs and an eight-year-old boy. 'Okay, Joshie, let's have a look at where you're getting to with this masterpiece,' she declared.

21

Going places

The driveway gates were open, and Franny was checking the letterbox before climbing into her car and heading into town to see a matinee of *The Happy Prince*. Determined to get herself back on track, she was dressed in black linen pants and a long turquoise frock-style jacket. Her white hair was gathered on her head, wrapped in a thin crimson and turquoise scarf.

'Whoah,' said Sallyanne who, unseen by Franny, was crouching near her front fence, wrestling with a recalcitrant garden hose. 'You look amazing, Fran. What's the occasion?'

Franny stood up from the letterbox and gave a dismissive shrug. 'Don't be ridiculous. I'm just going into the city to see a ballet. I can't look like the wreck of the *Hesperus* all the time.'

Her neighbour laughed. 'I don't know what that is but you never look like the wreck of anything.' Sallyanne wiped her hands on her tracksuit pants and walked over. 'Ballet in the daytime? I didn't know there even was such a thing. You go often?'

'Once every few months. I also go on a Monday night occasionally. They tend to have earlier shows so I train it in in the late afternoon, have a little something to—' Here Franny stammered.

'Something to eat . . . and then head to the Arts Centre. You've never been?'

'Sadly no. I am a cultural ignoramus. Plus, I suspect it's a bit out of my price bracket.'

'Like all the so-called high arts it is indeed prohibitively expensive for most hard-working people. Shits me no end. Still . . . one of the perks of old age.' Franny rummaged in her handbag and pulled out a small card. 'Pensioner's discount,' she said with genuine glee. She looked at the other woman and chewed on the side of her lip. 'Actually, I was thinking about Dee earlier when I was getting gussied up.'

'How so?' said Sallyanne.

'The Ballet Centre runs tours. You can see the costumiers in action, visit the fabric rooms. She tells me she wants to be a costume designer. I thought she might like it, maybe get a tad inspired.' Franny threw her bag through the passenger-side door of her car and moved around to the other side to climb in. 'The only problem is they happen mid-morning or lunchtime Tuesdays and Thursdays from memory, not ideal with school I guess.'

'Not ideal with my work timetable either, but it would be good for her, open her eyes to the realities of that world. It's not like I have any idea and she needs to be more motivated. Stop mooning over the friends she's left behind.'

'I guess I could take her,' said Franny, aiming to sound indifferent. 'Surely we could convince her teacher of the value. I mean, I'd enjoy it anyway. Dee would just be tagging along.' At this point she made to get into the car but looked back at Sallyanne pointedly. 'You'd have to trust me of course.'

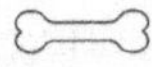

When the mobile rang and Franny saw her sister-in-law's name come up she knew she would have to answer. All the recent obfuscating had gone on too long. Marg was a force and would not be ignored.

'Darling, hello,' said Franny, swinging her legs into the car and putting the keys in the ignition. 'Hang on a tick, will you? I'm just going to fire up the engine which means the Bluetooth should kick in. I might lose you for a second.' Normally this was a trick Franny used to curtail annoying chats—intentionally cutting the call off instead of connecting it—but she meant it this time. Her afternoon spent watching lithe dancers dressed as river reeds and marvelling over choreography and backdrops had left her feeling buoyant and, therefore, vulnerable to a chat.

'Huh,' said Marg when she realised Franny was back on the air, 'I thought you might be cutting me off.'

'Perish the thought,' said Franny, negotiating her way out of the supermarket carpark. 'I had a particularly cantankerous netball mother waiting for my parking spot and thought she might ram me with her SUV. How's tricks?'

Unused to Franny's encouraging tone, Marg sounded a little flustered. 'Good thanks, Fran. You sound good too. Where've you been?'

'The Australian Ballet's production of *The Happy Prince*. Bloody marvellous matinee. Have you seen it?'

'Can't say I have but I've heard good things. How was the artwork and costumes? I know you love all that.'

'Divine luvvie, divine. Such a sad story yet they've managed to find the light. It's supposedly aimed at the kiddies but it's wasted on them if you ask me. There was a touch of Brett Whiteley to some of the backdrops and the bodies of those youngsters—just so bendy! Anyway . . .'

'Anyway indeed, I'm delighted to see you getting out and about. Speaking of, how did your birthday adventure with the neighbours go? I'm still shocked you agreed to such a thing.'

Franny thought back to the staged photos of beach towels and holiday-house settings. 'Oh well, it was a distraction for the poor dears. They've had a bad trot. Marital problems and a pending divorce etcetera. I did it to help.'

Marg guffawed. 'Doling out kindness to strangers. Should I be checking under your bed for alien pods?'

Franny smiled to herself, once again reminded of her sister-in-law's wicked humour. 'Shut up, you old bitch. I can be nice.'

'Just not to family, is that the policy?'

'Did you ring about something in particular or was blanket character assassination the sole aim?'

'I rang to see how you are, dear. I still have your birthday present here to send and, well, I had a few other odds and ends I was hanging on to for you. Wondered if I should throw them in too.'

'Odds and ends? You haven't made me another quilt, have you?' Franny's mind went back to the purple-and-lime embroidered monstrosity she had received two years ago when Marg was experimenting with her new Janome. Even Soda wouldn't sleep on it. 'I mean, I appreciate the thought but there is just the one of me.'

'Not a quilt. Don't panic. It's a pile of books, actually.' Marg paused for a beat. 'Lovely coffee table and travel books about Scotland and all its writerly connections. I'd been buying them for Frank, and for you, for the big trip. And, well . . .' Marg's voice trailed off momentarily and Franny looked stonily at the traffic ahead. 'Well, the anniversary is coming up and I was looking at them. Wondered if you'd like them anyway. There really are some stunners there, everything from *Diary of a Bookseller* to James Hogg's collected Highland journeys. That one cost nearly two hundred dollars.'

'I'll pay you back,' said Franny sharply.

'Franny, don't.' Marg's voice went quiet. 'You know I'm not talking about the money, it's just a real treasure and it's going to waste here. I just thought you . . .'

Ahead of Franny the traffic lights turned green and she took off too quickly, almost careering into a cyclist trying, inexpertly, to avoid car doors and tram tracks. She hit the brakes, causing horns to blare in her wake.

'Marg, I'm in city traffic. Can't talk now. Send, don't send. Do what you please, you do anyway.' She pressed the Bluetooth button to end the call then stuck her finger up at the driver in the car behind her. In response, she was treated to another serve of horn.

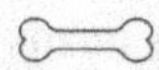

'Get a move on child, we're going to be late.' Franny, having ditched her usual routine to get this excursion off the ground, already had the car running and was halfway down the driveway. 'I told you ten o'clock.'

'Soz,' said Dee, slipping awkwardly into the passenger seat, a huge denim satchel squashing Franny's arm.

'What the hell do you have there? We're not going away overnight.'

'I brought a sketch pad and my mum's good camera. She doesn't usually let me use it.'

Franny looked over at the young girl and noticed her flushed face and bright eyes. 'You look fevered. Not contagious, are you?'

'Bloody hell, Fran, you love to throw shade. I might have spent a little too long blow-drying my hair.' Dee's hair was indeed sticking up at a considerable height.

'Your attempt at a mohawk, I presume,' said Fran, flicking on the indicator and heading out into the road.

'Hardy har har. Like you're the style influencer.' Dee flipped the car's visor down to check her reflection in the mirror. 'I just wanted a, you know, a look for today.' She turned to Franny who was dressed in a ruby-red turtleneck and geometric silver earrings. 'Don't pretend you didn't put a bit of effort in.'

'You do go on,' said Franny, keeping her eyes on the road. 'So, a camera, hey? Didn't pick Sallyanne for a snapper. When does she find the time?'

'She doesn't now. Hasn't for a while. She always says she bought it to take pics of us kids but she's actually quite good. You should get her to show you one day. Naturally the Neanderthal always said it was a waste of money. He threatened to pawn it all the time.'

'Indeed,' said Franny. 'In terms of today I'm not sure you'll be allowed to use a camera at the Ballet Centre. We'll have to suck it and see.'

'God that's a gross thing to say. What does it even mean?'

'"Suck it and see" is not gross. It simply means to try something and see how it goes. Taste it to see if you like it, I suppose.'

'Sounds like blowjobs to me. You shouldn't say it.'

Franny exploded with laughter. 'Well, we're off to a good start. And you said "throwing shade". I know what that means. My goddaughter already told me.'

'Woo hoo, welcome to three years ago.' Dee's tone was narky but in the reflection of the window Franny saw the grin on her face.

'Know anything about where we're going?' asked Franny.

'I looked it up online. Might be okay.'

'Glad to hear it. I've done that online tour too. Not half as good as the real thing. Plus, if you're lucky you'll get to talk to some of the staff.'

'My teacher wants a report on it. Gotta ruin every bloody thing.'

'Think of it as a magazine article, like you're a journo doing interviews. It's a good excuse to speak to people and you might extract even more information. Maybe one day you could do some work experience there.'

Dee opened her window and stuck her head out.

'Did you hear what I said?' Franny poked the young girl in the arm.

'Yeah, yeah, to you everything is just sooooo easy.'

Franny snorted. 'Things are never easy. What the hell gave you that idea?' She glanced sideways at Dee but the girl remained stubbornly silent. 'But they don't have to always be hard either. You just have to jump in and have a go. Have a go and do the work. That's the secret. What, are you scared to put yourself forward and speak to these people? I thought you had a bit more gumption than that.'

'I'm not scared of some idiots with sewing machines. Who do they even think they are?' The words came spitting out.

'I see.' Franny concentrated on the traffic piling up ahead. The sound of the wind rushing through Dee's window filled the car.

Finally, the girl said, 'They're not going to want to talk to some kid. Some suburban dickhead.'

'My dear girl, suburban dickheads, as you call them, are the engine room of the arts, and make up many of its brightest stars.' Franny grinned at this thought. 'You think I was always this magnificent?' She took her hand off the wheel and waved it theatrically against her person, Vegas showgirl style. 'I am my own creation just as you will be yours. People like the costumiers we're about to meet are slaves to their work. It's a vocation. Getting them to talk about it will not be the problem. Getting them to shut up could be tricky. The only reason I would discourage you from pursuing this career is the money, if that's what's important to you. Only the really top tier make big bucks. In Australia, that tier is wafer thin.'

'Well I'd only want to be top tier.' Now Dee's tone was belligerent.

Franny laughed. 'That's the spirit. Let's go meet some dickheads.'

Franny barely got a word in on the way home. The tour had been a success. A group scheduled to take part cancelled at the last moment meaning she and Dee had the guide, Nico, to themselves. That's if you didn't count the three quietly spoken ladies from country New South Wales who were still part of the group. Those poor dears never stood a chance.

'OMG the pointe-shoe room. How amazing was it?' Dee was wriggling in the car seat while flicking through brochures and other paraphernalia she'd harvested from the foyer of the Primrose Potter Australian Ballet Centre. 'It was too much! But probably my favourite things were the wigs. I'd never have the patience. And the tulle, so much tulle. How lucky were we to see that prima ballerina being fitted in front of our eyes? Wasn't it just everything, Fran? It really was too much.'

Franny's eyes darted from the teenager beside her to the traffic ahead. 'Me thinks there was too much sugar in the jam,' she joked.

When the tour ended she had taken Dee around the corner for an early lunch at the art gallery's tea room where they devoured egg and watercress sandwiches, followed by house-baked scones with jam and cream.

'And you!' Dee pointed dramatically at her driver. 'What about you and the whole, "Oh yes I created a set design for a ballet once" comment? What the actual? I thought those other ladies were going to curtsy. Even posh boy Nico seemed impressed.'

'Don't be ridiculous,' said Franny, though her cheeks coloured slightly. 'Those women were simply old enough to have kids into Mr M and Timmy T at the time, that's all. They remembered the characters' names. It was a silly little school-holiday ballet program one year. No one serious saw it.'

Franny had blurted out the comment while looking at a photograph of a cat puppet used in an *Alice in Wonderland* ballet. The creature reminded her very much of the giant Mr Marmalade she had created years ago.

'Anyway, this trip was for you, young lady. Think it was worthwhile?'

'God yes. I don't even want to go back to school. It's so boring.'

'Please share that titbit with your mother, won't you? I'll be more in the good books than ever.'

'She's not pissed with you anymore, you know. How could she be after, well, after Dad rocked up and was such a moron? You know Josh still doesn't realise what happened?' Dee gestured like her head was exploding. 'Kids, huh?'

Franny let out a guffaw. 'Kids indeed. What are they like, hey?'

'Yes, yes you think I'm a kid too.'

'Me and the entire legal fraternity but please, continue.'

'You know what I mean. He believed what everyone told him. We protected him from it all.' Dee turned her face away and looked out the car window. 'He deserves that.'

Franny looked over at the young girl beside her and a lump formed in her throat. Thoughts of her own father. Dreams for her own lost child. Emotions flooded in.

'All kids deserve that, my love, including you,' she said. Dee shrugged. 'Sallyanne would do anything, is doing *everything* she can to protect you, you know that, don't you?' *Even when she's having a go at me*, she thought. 'It's not the easy thing she's doing, Dee. You'll see that one day.'

'Jesus Christ,' Dee exploded. She looked back at Franny and her eyes were red-rimmed. 'It's not the 1950s. I do get it.'

Franny took a deep breath but said nothing.

Dee continued, 'I just don't think she gets a medal for marrying such an arsehole and fucking up our lives. Or for being such a doormat. Even now he's got the house and we're poor. He's still at home, my home, and I'm living in a shitbox, surrounded by strangers. We don't even see my cousins anymore, did you know? Mum won't tell them why she left. Doesn't think it's fair on Dad. How about what's fair on us? They all think she's a bitch now when it's him that . . .' She let out a sob.

Although the sign for Ipswich Street was up ahead, Franny pulled to the kerb and applied the handbrake. She undid her seatbelt and put her arms out to Dee. 'Come here,' she said quietly.

Dee shook her head.

'Come here.'

Finally, the girl slid over, manoeuvring herself into an awkward hug; the car's centre console was in the way. 'I miss bench seats,' said Franny.

'What?' sniffed Dee.

'Nothing.' Franny patted the girl's back as she did Whisky's during a thunderstorm. 'There's a lot going on in that lilac head of yours isn't there, little lady?' She tugged on some of the gel-hardened spikes of hair now poking into her shoulder. 'And there's a lot going on for that mum of yours.' She eased Dee back upright, licked a thumb and ran it under the teenager's eye where mascara had skidded haphazardly.

'Gross,' squealed Dee, then laughed. She moved back to sit properly in her seat, pulling down the visor to look in the mirror. As Franny handed her a tissue, she swiped at her face and said, 'Sorry. What a sook.'

'You're not a sook, dear, you're in pain and you're going through a lot. I understand that. Let's backtrack. Remember how an hour ago we were having a fantastic time?'

Dee nodded.

'Well, let's remember that and the fact that all kind of lives and worlds are ahead of you. Okay? And Sallyanne will do anything she can to make it all happen.'

'She doesn't know about that stuff.' Dee's composure returned in tandem with her teenage belligerence.

'She knows enough. And you have other people in your life. People who will help.' Franny clapped her hands. 'Hey, let's do something nice for the Salerno girls.' She released the handbrake and resumed the short drive home.

'What?'

'It's Mother's Day soon, isn't it?'

'Probably. So?'

'So, let's have a little party at my place.'

'How is that "something for the Salerno girls"?'

'You and Josh can help me plan it and we'll make sure there's some fun for you too.'

'Can I wear your clothes?'

'You can wear my clothes.'

22

Wrong number

Ange Caliendo, unexpectedly, had a Kathleen Turner-style voice. Franny cursed herself for noticing this almost as much as she cursed herself for answering an unknown mobile number to begin with. Her thoughts had been elsewhere when the call came in, Max Richter blaring through the studio and her eyes scanning paint brushes, looking for the perfect tool.

'Mrs Calderwood, it's Ange Caliendo,' the woman said for a second time, a little more loudly than the first.

Franny, phone tucked awkwardly under her chin, wiped her hands on a rag and moved to turn off the CD player. She hesitated then said, 'You should not be ringing me. The letter was bad enough.'

'I know, I know and I'm sorry, I truly am, but I find I can't let this go.' The words came out in a tumble. 'You got it then, the letter? You read it?'

Franny sat down heavily on her old leather chair and stared at her taxidermied cat. 'Yes I got it,' she said finally. 'I was already considering making a formal complaint. And now you have my phone number as well—'

'Yes, yes,' the other woman interrupted. 'It's wrong, I know. I strong-armed the person involved. They're family. Please don't take this to the authorities. It's not their fault. I just want to help. And then . . .' She hesitated for a moment. 'There's the matter of the dog excrement. That's not exactly legal either.'

Franny could not believe what she was hearing. 'Are you . . . are you threatening me? Are you ringing me in my own fucking home and threatening me? Jesus, woman, this so-called family of yours is something else. Goodbye.'

'Mrs Calderwood, Mrs Calderwood, Frances,' the other woman shouted down the line. 'Please don't go. Please.'

Franny sighed. 'Look, I think you laid out your sob story in the note. What more is there to say?'

'I know you must be angry, Mrs . . . can I call you Frances?'

'No.' Franny took pleasure from this one cruel but simple word.

'Okay, Mrs Calderwood. I can imagine you're angry but I really do beg you to reconsider. You would be helping us more than you know. There is more than one innocent victim here.'

Franny stood up. She needed to pace. 'Please do not tell me that little prick Christopher is innocent. Please do not tell me you're comparing him to my husband Frank.'

'Well, no, of course not, but, as I said in the letter, I'm the mother of the person who set Chris on this path and—'

'Yes and you must be very proud, dear,' Franny cut in.

Ange Caliendo said nothing for a moment. Franny could hear her breathing. Finally, she said, 'Actually, Nicholas is dead now, Mrs Calderwood. He died of an overdose six months ago.'

Franny was standing by Mr Marmalade, rubbing one of his stiff, hairy ears. She closed her eyes and took a deep breath. 'I see,' was all she said.

'Do you, Mrs Calderwood? I hope so. Helping Chris is more important than ever now. We can't lose them both.'

'What does my forgiveness have to do with your nephew? It sounds like he's doing fine without me.'

Ange Caliendo was speaking quickly again. 'No, not really. His father refuses to speak to him and his mother, my sister, my God, it's tearing her apart. And now she is sick. Do you have a sister, Mrs Calderwood?'

For a moment Franny was surprised to find Anthea's name flash through her thoughts. 'I do not,' she said.

'Well, that's a shame. But most likely you have a best friend? Either way it's Sandy—Sandra—who's suffering the most. I can't bear it. I can't. I have to find a way to give her son back his future.'

For a moment Ange Caliendo's words had been breaking down Franny's defences, tiny arrows breaching her carefully constructed fortress. Now, she exploded.

'Future? That fucking arsehole's future? You want *me* to worry about that? What about my future, Mrs Caliendo? What about Frank's future? While we're talking about it, what about my whole fucking life?' Here Franny's voice broke. She ended the call then threw the phone across her studio table.

23

Show business

Josh had been at Fran's place for three afternoons in a row. Sallyanne was forbidden to know what he was up to.

'Leave him be,' said Franny when her neighbour popped a blonde head over the fence to check her son wasn't getting in the way. 'He's on a mission and it's something for you. He guarantees me he's also doing his homework.'

Sallyanne laughed. 'He'd do the other kids' homework too if he could. There's no problem there. I was just worried that Dee was offloading her babysitting duties on you when I'm not around.'

'She's not that wily yet and, no, she has her own things taking up her time.' Franny wriggled her eyebrows mysteriously. 'Can I still have her Saturday, by the way? Then on Sunday we'll have everything ready for you.'

'I still feel very self-conscious that you're doing all of this, Franny. Are you sure I can't give you some money, or at least help?'

'Money? Don't get your hopes up, dear. Your Mother's Day this year will be a decidedly jerry-built affair.'

'Knowing you I very much doubt it,' said Sallyanne. 'Anyway, I must bring something. Tell me what.'

'Are we allowed champagne or is that forbidden?' Franny waggled her finger up and down like a scolding schoolteacher.

Sallyanne raised her eyebrows. 'Not gonna let that one go, are you?' she said. 'Okay, I will bring some bubbles.'

'Excellent. Now go away.'

The kids had devised the menu, poring over the Calderwoods' hundred-strong cookbook collection. Many of the books bore traces of Frank's culinary adventures; the telltale wineglass and gravy stains across their pages a memento so painful to Franny's eyes she preferred to find recipes online these days.

'The Duke of Wellington was a famous English soldier and aristocrat, you know,' said Franny as she and Josh worked on their illustrated place mats for the occasion. Each of the four guests would have a bespoke artwork to eat from, one that listed the day's feasting items as well as the date, plus an idiosyncratic portrait of Sallyanne. Today Josh was working on his depiction of her as a superhero nurse. His mother's hair was tucked beneath a boxy cap and a long red cloak sailed out behind her as she flew across what he assured Franny was a hospital building. It looked a lot like a gingerbread house.

'And he liked beef so much they called a dinner after him?' The little boy's eyes remained on his creation as he spoke.

'I think so, but they also say it's because the dish is shaped like a wellington.'

'A what?'

'A wellington. You know, a gumboot.'

'What's beef got to do with gumboots?' He put down his paintbrush and stared at Franny quizzically.

Feeling the conversation skidding off the rails, Franny said, 'So, have you got your act together?'

Jumping out of his seat, excitement levels too high to keep him contained, Josh said, 'Yes, yes, yes, yes, yes. I know all the words and Dee got me a black pleather cap from the two-dollar shop. Mummy's gonna love it.'

He had a Mother's Day performance planned, a singalong with P!nk on the track, 'Get the Party Started'. Rumour had it the song was one of Sallyanne's favourites during her nurse-training years.

Pumping the air with his fists and adding some complicated foot moves, Josh sang to Franny about how everybody was 'dancing' for him.

'All right, don't peak too early, little man,' she said, pressing her hands lightly on his shoulders to subdue him. As always, the child made her grin.

She looked at her watch. 'I think you better head home. The placemats are all finished, aren't they?'

'Well I could still—'

'One of the things about being an artist is knowing when to stop and put something out into the world, Josh.' She looked at the final piece and clapped appreciatively. 'I'll hang this to dry and see you back here in three hours. Let's synchronise watches.'

'I don't have one,' Josh mewled.

'Not a problem. Wait here.' She dashed into her bedroom and came back with an old-fashioned wind-up alarm clock topped with two fat silver bells. 'I've set it to go off three hours from now.' She handed it to him and began shoving him towards the door. 'Check Dee has the blindfold, won't you? Now shoo.'

Once he was gone Franny got down to business. The beef had been cooked the night before and now sat patiently in the refrigerator, swaddled inside its pastry blanket. Thanks to Josh, the devils on horseback were wrapped and ready to bake. The rosewater-infused pavlova base was in the laundry, covered by a pristine white tea towel. All she had to do was whip the cream and slice the strawberries, peel the spuds and prepare the beans, arrange the flowers, set the table and . . . Franny looked at her watch again and did some calculations. Somewhere in the schedule she would need to have a shower. Would there even be time for a drink? Looking over at Kitchen Frank, his barbecue tongs blazing, she thought of their well-choreographed days of entertaining.

'I'm not quite the same Ginger without my old Fred,' she said.

At half past five on the dot the Salernos arrived. The children had covered Sallyanne's eyes with a scarf and Josh was attempting to twirl her on the doorstep. Fearing a mishap—the woman was juggling a champagne bottle, a bunch of flowers and a jumping terrier, after all—Franny stepped in to relieve her of her cargo.

'Hang on, Joshie,' she said. 'Let's not send Mum head over heels before the fun even begins.'

Franny ushered the trio over to the kitchen bench and settled the blindfolded Sallyanne on a stool.

'See to the lights like we planned, darling,' she told Dee, a vision in tight black jeans, shimmering hooded jacket and gigantic diamond-shaped earrings.

Dee obeyed, then rushed to light half a dozen candles in tall holders on the dining table. Franny gently uncorked the champagne and poured it into two crystal flutes. She filled another two with sparkling apple cider.

'Okay, Joshie, let her rip,' she said.

With signature flamboyance Josh whipped the scarf from his mother's eyes, crying, 'Ta da!'

As Sallyanne adjusted to the light she took in a deep breath. 'Wow,' she said, and stood up to take a closer look.

A small row of chairs was set against the glass doors leading to the garden. The doors themselves were decorated with fairy lights, and black and silver balloons bobbed lethargically from as many points around the room as possible. A large hand-painted 'Happy Mother's Day' sign was pinned to one wall.

'Happy Mother's Day, Mum,' said Dee, handing Sallyanne her glass. Dee tipped her flute forwards to say cheers and saw Sallyanne's eyes dart to the bench behind her. 'It's all right, Mumma Bear, it's crappy apple.'

'Crappy apple,' repeated Josh, his glass gripped between two small hands. 'Happy Mother's Day, Mummy.'

The four of them clinked glasses.

'Wow,' repeated Sallyanne, 'I'm speechless.'

'This is only the beginning,' said Franny, pulling out bacon-wrapped prunes from the oven and arranging them on a platter. 'We've got canapes and then the shows begin.'

'Shows?' asked Sallyanne.

'I'm first. I'm first.' Josh bit into the devil on horseback—naturally, he had chosen the menu item specifically because of the name—and grimaced. 'Yuk! Where are the Cheezels?' Dee handed him a bowl of the chemically coloured delights.

With refreshments enjoyed and all three females seated on the row of chairs, Josh disappeared into Franny's room. Within minutes the beats started and P!nk came blaring out of Fran's CD player. The little boy re-emerged, sliding across the floor, halting in front of his mother. His hair was hidden beneath a shiny faux-leather cap and a gold chain, complete with a giant dollar sign, hung round his neck. Miniature Elvis-style sunglasses covered his eyes and at least three fingers on each hand sported a plastic gold ring. His black T-shirt was rolled up to show his tiny midriff, his black tracksuit pants were cut off at his calves creating an incongruous pirate effect. He bounced to the music, singing loudly.

Sallyanne squealed and clapped with delight. By the time the final chorus came around she was dancing beside her son, both of them sing-shouting. As the track ended, she picked him up and hugged him, saying, 'Brilliant, Joshie, just brilliant.'

Initial excitement over, the group moved on to dinner, with the expected oohs and aahs as they made their way through layers of puff pastry, buttery mushrooms and tender eye fillet. Josh's request for tomato ketchup was initially shouted down but Franny relented, admitting finally that, yes, beef Wellington probably was 'a bit like a giant sausage roll'.

As soon as the meal was finished Dee disappeared into another room. Sallyanne tried to help Franny with the dishes but her hostess declined, telling her to relax in the lounge room with her son. A short time later Franny and Josh made eye contact across the room. The little boy gave an exaggerated wink then said, 'Back in a minute,' abruptly abandoning his mother. Franny came over with a clean champagne flute and a bottle of Taittinger.

'Ooh la la,' said Sallyanne as she accepted the drink. 'You're pulling out all the stops.'

'Tatt was Frank's favourite,' said Franny. 'I always keep a bottle on hand for special occasions.'

'I'm truly honoured.' Sallyanne clinked her glass against Franny's. 'You really have made this special. Thank you.'

'You're welcome, dear. Mothers deserve to be celebrated. Besides, occasionally I miss putting on spectacular home dinners.'

'You used to entertain a lot?'

'Relentlessly at times. Frank was chronically social. Like a disease. Loved nothing more than cooking for friends. He'd pore over recipe books for weeks, working out themes, steeping and marinating. Drove me bloody mad.' She took a gulp of champagne. 'But he'd do it just for us as well. We never shied away from linen tablecloths and a candelabra on a Wednesday night.' She gave a girlish laugh.

'What was your role?'

'When it was just us I cooked too, but he was definitely better when it came to the big events. Then I'd help with a bit of cold larder, but my main job was front of house: table decorations and music choice, organising the cocktail bar and flowers, the lights in the garden, "set dressing" as he called it.'

'You wouldn't do it now?' Sallyanne waved a hand around the room, indicating the lovely atmosphere created. 'You clearly still have it in you.'

Franny shook her head and looked out towards the darkened garden. 'God no. Could you imagine? All those people milling about, comparing it to the old days and feeling sorry for "poor old Franny", reminiscing or bloody weeping about Frank.' She gave a theatrical shudder. 'Not on your nelly.'

Sallyanne put her drink down on the coffee table and leaned forward. 'Would that be so bad? Reminiscing about Frank?'

Heaving herself up with a sigh, Franny walked over to the wall and switched on the garden lights. 'Frank was the really social one, the one who loved a crowd. I just went along for the ride. I liked the show, his show. No, listening to other people bleat about him these days, needing me to comfort them, sitting through their anecdotes . . . pure torture.'

'Once you did it a few times, though, that would all die down. People get used to a new normal pretty quickly, you know.'

Franny walked back to the coffee table and picked up her glass. 'A new normal.' She nodded her head slowly. 'Right.' She gulped champagne. Refilled the glass. 'I guess they could forget what it was like here before. Forget what we were. People do, don't they?' Her eyes filled with tears.

Sallyanne realised her mistake.

'Oh Franny.' She made to stand up, her arms outstretched. 'I'm sorry. I didn't mean . . .'

'Nothing to be sorry for, dear,' Franny whispered, turning away quickly. 'Ready in there?' she shouted and moved over to the CD player to change the music.

Shirley Bassey's 'Hey Big Spender' came blaring through the speakers and Franny angled one of the lamps to mimic a spotlight. Dee stalked into the room, dressed in a long denim jacket with a map of the world stitched on the back. She wore huge silver sunglasses and a black felt fedora. Up and down the room she strode, eyes straight ahead like a fashion runway veteran. As Shirley sang the iconic lyrics, Dee turned her back on her audience and shimmied out of the jacket. Beneath it she wore a spectacular knee-length silver sequinned cocktail dress. She threw the sunglasses and hat to one side and slipped her feet into a pair of high, silver platform shoes stashed near Franny's drinks' trolley. Hat and glasses gone, Sallyanne saw her daughter's hair was parted starkly to one side and slicked down against her head. Thick licks of black eyeliner flew from the edges of her eyelids and her lips glistened with frosted, icy pink lipstick.

Dee resumed her runway walk, staring fixedly ahead of her as if the entire French fashion press were archly taking notes. As Shirley hit a crescendo, the young girl stopped dramatically and pointed to the other end of the room. From the shadows appeared the smallest and dandiest of the big spenders, his diminutive frame encased in an equally diminutive black tuxedo. Around Josh's neck was a blue-and-gold cravat and he gripped a huge brandy balloon in one hand, a long black cigarette holder in the other. A little hand-drawn moustache snaked along his upper lip.

Imitating his sister's solemn modelling style was not an option. Instead, Josh strutted and pranced, emphasising the idea of someone 'popping their cork' by jumping up on to the couch, causing Sallyanne to erupt with laughter. Franny stood in the corner and grinned. When the song ended, she turned down the sound, allowing Ms Bassey to quietly croon about impossible dreams in the background.

Brother and sister turned to their mother, joined hands and bowed. Josh added some flourish, alternating between extravagant air kisses and puffs on his imaginary cigarette.

'A little fashion show to display Miss Dee Salerno's hair, makeup and styling skills,' said Franny as she re-joined the group. 'Well done, team.' She and Sallyanne clapped their hands in appreciation.

'I'll say well done,' said Sallyanne, standing up to hug and kiss her children. 'That was amazing. You guys look amazing.' She twirled her daughter around. 'This all Franny's stuff you've commandeered?'

'Some of it,' said Dee. 'The good stuff.' She ran her hands up and down her dress and jutted her head forwards to show her mother the two oversized diamante hoops in each earlobe. 'But some of it's from the op shop—Josh's suit, of course—and some of it I sewed myself.'

'You did? Like what?'

'I found the map of the world fabric and sewed it to the jacket, and I embroidered it a bit. Also, I had to alter Josh's suit to fit.'

'That's very impressive. No help from Franny?' Sallyanne looked over at her neighbour who responded by holding up her thumb and forefinger to indicate *just a smidge.*

'I made something from scratch for you too, Mum,' said Dee, 'for Mother's Day.'

Sallyanne raised her eyebrows.

'Go grab the box,' said Franny.

Dee disappeared towards the hallway again and returned with a smart white box tied with a wide, white ribbon. 'Happy Mother's Day,' she said, handing it over.

Inside layers of frothy pink tissue paper was a short cotton skirt with an elasticised waist. The fabric's design showed a reworking of William Morris's 'Strawberry Thief', the thrushes and strawberries oversized, the background a bright cobalt-blue.

'It's super basic,' said Dee quickly. 'Franny said this skirt pattern is one of the easiest you can start with, but I can style it up. I'll show you.' She grabbed her mother by the sleeve and pulled her towards Franny's bedroom. 'Come on.'

When the pair returned Sallyanne was wearing the skirt and every other element of her outfit had been changed too, even her shoes.

'Oh, Mummy you look so cute,' said Josh.

'I love it, she hates it,' said Dee, twirling her mother around.

Sallyanne appeared breathless, with her cheeks flushed and hair mussed where Dee had apparently whipped clothes up and over her head. 'I don't hate it. I love the skirt. I'm just not sure about the combo.' She looked down at her bare legs and white trainers, the skirt, a loose short white T-shirt and a cropped denim jacket. In her ears were two large plastic hearts. 'It's a bit young maybe.'

Franny stood back and peered as if she were a judge on a reality television show. Josh went and stood next to her, placing his forefinger against his lip to demonstrate the seriousness of his ponderings.

'Mr Salerno,' said Franny, turning towards the little boy, 'as fellow judge, do you agree with me when I say that Sallyanne here looks fresher and prettier than she ever has since moving to Ipswich Street?'

Josh cocked his head on the side and pressed his lips together. He still had the cigarette holder and took an extravagant puff on it before stepping forward and examining his mother closely. He then peered up at his sister and puffed again.

'Hmm,' he declared eventually. 'Dee Salerno, I think the work you've shown us tonight is beyond compare. This woman has never looked better. It's a yes from me.' He reached out his small hand to shake his sister's. She got the joke and shook back.

'There you have it,' said Franny. 'The judges have spoken. Never looked better. First prize to Dee.'

A while later, the children sent home to brush teeth, do homework and ready themselves for bed, Franny and Sallyanne sat on garden stools wedged against the fence furthest away from the Salernos' house. Each woman nursed a glass of red wine. Sallyanne dragged on an illicit cigarette.

'Again, Franny, that was amazing. The things you achieved with those kids. The way you spoiled me. I don't know what to say. You're a marvel.'

Franny brushed off the compliment. 'Please. I had a ball. They're not bad company, for kids.' She made a face as if she were tasting something sour.

Sallyanne grinned, then moved forward and lowered her voice. 'Are they? Do you think they're, well, they're okay? I mean with all the shit that's gone down, I do worry.'

Franny thought back to her conversation with Dee on the way home from the Ballet Centre tour. 'It's funny, isn't it? At the beginning I feel like children are something that happen to you, the parent. You're the main character if you like and they're part of your storyline. But there comes a time when they start to be their own people and have their own storylines. I think that must be a tough juncture. From then on, I think you just have to be on hand with plenty of love and attention. Kids are resilient, from what I've observed and, at the risk of sounding like an *Oprah* episode, they just need to feel "seen".' She gave a snort-like laugh. 'But what the hell would I know?'

Franny swirled her wine, watching the crimson liquid ebb and flow around the inside of the glass. *Do kids ever stop being part of their parents' storyline*? she wondered and her thoughts turned, unbidden, to Ange Caliendo and Sandra Pavlos. *Would they ever have any peace? Would The Evil Prick have peace? Did she care?*

'I've been wondering about that,' said Sallyanne, bringing Franny back to the here and now.

'Sorry, what?' Franny slugged back more than a sip of red wine.

'You wrote amazing kids' books, you're a magician with my two. Forgive me if I'm overstepping, but did you never consider having your own?'

Franny lent back on her stool, resting her head on the garden fence behind. 'Wow, I haven't been asked that one for a while.' She smiled. 'Why don't you have kids? Almost makes me feel like I'm in my thirties again. Thank God I'm not.'

Sallyanne took a puff on her cigarette and nodded but said nothing. A thin trail of smoke escaped from her nostrils.

Franny swirled wine in clockwork circles. 'I had a child, actually. A daughter.' She sipped more wine.

'Had?' Sallyanne's voice was gentle.

'Mm . . . she died soon after she was born. Minutes after. All very unexpected. Very tragic in that mundane way these things are.'

'Oh Franny. I'm so sorry.' Sallyanne reached forward and put her hand on the other woman's knee. 'I cannot even entertain the thought.' Her voice broke. 'When was this?'

'Oh decades ago now. Tilly'd be, I don't know, around thirty if she'd lived. Not much younger than you.'

'I'm nearly forty but thanks for the compliment,' said Sallyanne. 'But you know exactly how old she'd be . . .'

'I do indeed.'

'So where is she? Tilly, you said? I mean, were you living here?'

'No. Not here.' Franny looked around at her garden affectionately. 'This was Frank and my happy place. But she's close by. With Frank now, as it happens.'

'They're buried together?'

'Yes. We have one of those family plots. Can't wait to get there myself. You've probably driven by the cemetery off Main Road on the way to work. Lots of big gum trees.'

'I've noticed. It's quite beautiful.'

'Probably all the dead-people nutrients in the soil. You should see the way the roses grow over there. Very Stephen King. Makes you wonder.'

Sallyanne leaned forward, coughing and spluttering through a mouthful of wine, giving most of it to the lawn. 'Bloody hell, Franny. You really are the worst.'

'Oh please. You're a nurse. You get it.'

'I know we're meant to be famous for our macabre humour but I'm afraid I never did well in that department. Nursing still takes it out of me emotionally, to be honest. One of the many reasons I like my current role. Anyway'—she lit another cigarette, took another sip of wine—'you never tried again?'

Franny shook her head. 'Nope. Never tried again. I felt the universe had spoken.'

'No, Franny, it's not like that. You have to know—'

Franny held up her hand to silence the other woman. 'I know, dear. I've had this conversation many times before. Let's not.'

24

The truth hurts

'It's only me. Can I come in?'

For a moment Franny didn't recognise the voice on the intercom. It felt like months since she'd heard it. 'Elouise, is that you?'

'Yes. I'm back. And I come bearing gifts. Belated birthday gifts. Let me in.'

Franny looked at the clock. Having encouraged Sallyanne to enjoy a rare lunch and afternoon movie with a girlfriend, Franny had promised to make dinner for Josh and Dee and it was almost five o'clock. She only had an hour left and was running wildly late. The day before, Marg's Scotland books had arrived in the mail, an occasion marked by Franny hitting the Bowmore whisky while looking through them that night, occasional tears dampening the pages. As a result, exhaustion hummed within her. It was three o'clock before she had found the energy to peel off her pyjamas and brave the shower. An unexpected visitor was the last curve ball she needed.

'Oh, honey . . .'

'Aunt Fran, for God's sake.' Elouise's tone was growing impatient; Franny buzzed her in.

'Hello, pups,' said Elouise as both Whisky and Soda competed to be the first with their hellos. She got as far as the hallway before falling to her knees to be covered in canine kisses. Noticing the pile of books thrown messily on the floor, she looked up at Franny standing above her, tea towel in hand. 'What's this lot?' she asked.

'Books Marg sent over in the mail. She's been collecting them for me apparently.' Franny moved to stand in front of the pile but was too slow. Elouise snaked her hand around her ankles and grabbed one.

'*The Scottish Bothy Bible*?' she said, holding up a hardback book, its cover the stark photograph of a simple stone building set against a brooding landscape. 'Seems like an odd choice.'

'Yes, well they were for a trip we'd planned. Ages ago.' Franny attempted to shift the dogs and haul Elouise to her feet as she spoke. 'Don't know why she sent them now, bloody fool. Better off going to a second-hand book store.'

'You and Marg were going to Scotland? I didn't know that.' Elouise's tone was one of pure disbelief.

'Not Marg and me.' Franny walked back towards the kitchen, assuming the young woman would follow.

She did not. Instead, Elouise continued to go through the collection, examining the titles, forming them into a neat pile. When she looked up there were tears in her eyes.

'Uncle Frank and you were going? Is that it?' She moved to join Franny at the kitchen bench.

Franny looked at her goddaughter then returned to slicing mushrooms. 'It was a retirement thing. No biggie, as you young people say.'

'Oh Fran, I'm sorry. I think everyone and anyone would call that a biggie. You wouldn't still go, to Scotland I mean?' Franny's chopping continued, silent and methodical and Elouise took the hint.

'So, you look busy. Making enough food for an army. What gives?' As she spoke, she dug into her tote bag for her godmother's gifts.

'The kids next door are coming for dinner. I'm keeping an eye on them while their mother is out.'

'You're what?' Elouise placed two colourfully wrapped parcels on the bench in front of her and stared at Franny in disbelief.

'It's nothing. They're good kids and she's a single mum. I'm just helping out.'

Elouise moved around to the other side of the bench and helped herself to a glass from one of the cupboards. She slammed its door then moved over to the tap for some water.

Franny stopped chopping and looked at her. 'For God's sake, Elouise, what's the problem?'

'What's the problem?' Elouise stood very still, watching the water fill then overflow the glass. 'What's the fucking problem?'

Franny stared at her. Elouise was patience and good manners personified. She never swore in front of her godmother, not even the time Franny dropped her off at high school and shouted out the car window, 'Make sure you use that ointment. Don't want a rash like that spreading' then drove off cackling loudly.

The young woman walked back to where the gifts were. She picked up her bag and pulled out her car keys. Laughing gruffly, almost an animal-like grunt, she said, 'People who love you beg to see you. People you've been friends with for decades beg to see you. People who need you beg to see you. My mother has begged to see you.' Here, her voice cracked but she continued. 'Mum misses you. She needs you. Do you know Dad was rushed to emergency with chest pains while I was gone? Do you know how often Mum has cried in my arms over the loss of you and the loss of her beautiful friend Frank?' Now Elouise started to cry. 'For fuck's sake, Fran.'

She shook her head. 'You hardly ever cooked when *we* came over. Frank did it. And now here you are, cooking for strangers.'

Franny butted in. 'They're not strangers.'

Elouise shook her head again, biting on her bottom lip. Finally, she sighed and said, 'I'm allowed in to fix your Wi-Fi and listen to your rants while some random kids get, what? Is it Franny's famous mushroom tagliatelle you're cooking for them? Do you know that's my favourite, by the way, or is that one of the things your constant boozing has erased from your memory?' She let out a sob. 'A single mother, big bloody whoop, Fran. Maybe if Dad dies and Mum's a single mother you'll let her back in? What do you say?'

Elouise pushed the gifts towards Franny then headed for the front door. 'Happy birthday, Mrs Calderwood,' she said in a sarcastic tone. 'One is from me, one's from Mum. She got you Apple AirPods. Maybe your *new* friends can set them up for you.' She slammed the front door behind her.

25

Save the date

The date on the calendar was stalking her, she could feel its predatory eyes. She took down her ridiculous Cairn calendar and stowed it on a studio shelf. She kept her phone on silent, placing it face down on the table so the date couldn't ambush her from the screen. She told herself things would be different this time, yet she was stockpiling essentials and not answering the door. When the anniversary hit it was like a king-tide wave. Franny could see it coming but couldn't run. She had neither the strength nor the skills to escape to higher ground.

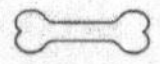

Many of the cupboards around the house are open, she sees this when she comes to. She has been looking for reminders, crying over books and photos, clasping belongings to her breast. She has watched their favourite movies, ranting at Frank till she falls asleep on the lounge-room floor. She started with champagne from a flute and ended, she thinks, with vodka from the bottle. She has howled and scared the dogs. *My God where are the dogs?*

Franny sits up cautiously on the sofa and looks around. She has to take it slowly. One fast move and who knows? Whisky is whining by the back door. *Is that what woke her?* She slides her knees onto the carpet then uses the coffee table as a leaning post to help her up. Soda has been asleep, or keeping watch, by her side. The old dog looks at Franny unblinkingly then joins Whisky at the door. It is dark outside. *Has she fed them? Is the dog door open? Perhaps they need the toilet? Does she need the toilet?* Franny stands and staggers, aiming for the back door.

She doesn't bother putting on the outside lights. Doesn't want to be seen. She knows Dee tried to come by at some point in recent days to return the silver dress. There was a text message about it. Just like there was a text message from Aunty Prick. She wonders where her phone is. Hopes she didn't flush it. She puts a hand in her dressing-gown pocket, feels the weight—*thank God.* Whisky whines again.

'Okay boy, do your thing.' Both dogs speed out the open door.

The fresh air is a shock. Franny feels she should sit down. She turns quickly, her leg catching on the iron plant pot in the shape of a swan. She feels it, the clean cold slice down her calf. She crumples to the concrete, rolls up in a ball, quietly cries. For a moment there is no pain. She thinks she might sleep. Then the stinging starts, and she senses the blood, the ooze and the feeling of letting go. It feels like a lot of blood. She fumbles for the mobile in her pocket, calls Elouise.

The girl doesn't wait to hear details, just says, 'I'll be there. I'll come.' In fact, she calls an ambulance. They arrive at almost the same time, the ambulance without lights or siren. Franny has passed out on the back patio, the dogs on either side of her. There is a pool of blood and urine forming an almost artistic outline around her legs.

Groggy on the gurney, Franny sees Sallyanne run from the house next door, still dressed for work. Her neighbour is calling out to Elouise.

'Is that Franny? Is she okay?' Sallyanne's voice is full of concern. 'You have blood on your face. Is it yours? Are you okay?' She reaches up to touch Elouise's cheek.

Franny is being trundled towards the ambulance doors. Elouise brushes the back of her hand against her face, sees it smeared with red. 'I have to go, to follow them,' she says, nodding to the paramedics.

'Please,' says Sallyanne. 'She's our neighbour. Our friend. Is she okay?'

Their voices are floating over to Franny, mixing with those of the paramedics. She catches the occasional word or phrase. 'Of course,' Elouise says in a flat voice at one point, 'you must be the one with the kids.'

More words are exchanged. Franny hears Elouise introduce herself tersely. 'I'm the goddaughter, for what it's worth. She obviously didn't mention me.'

Then Elouise is calling out to the paramedics, 'I'll see you there.' The pair, two young women, look up from their busyness and nod. Back inside the house they have already talked to the girl and gauged the situation as they applied an emergency torniquet.

Elouise looks at Sallyanne's polo shirt, complete with hospital insignia. 'You medical?' she asks. 'She should have called you instead of me.' She begins walking towards her car. Calls back, 'Gotta go. Sorry.'

'But, Elouise, what happened? Is she okay?' Sallyanne is pursuing her, voice louder.

'What happened?' Elouise makes no effort to lower her voice. 'She got pissed and fell over. PFO, isn't that what you nurse types call it in the trade?'

26

Reality bites

'Stop fussing, Anthea, for God's sake. I'll get to it all in a few days.' Franny struggled to sit up higher in her bed.

The room was not big and, with Frank and Franny's old queen-sized bed squeezed into it, as well as a small, old-fashioned dressing table, floor space was at a premium. The doors to Franny's robes were part-way open, clothes shoved in untidily, the arm of a man's suit jacket reaching out onto the floor. In the bright, sober light of the day, the whole thing made for a depressing tableau.

'You won't be doing anything in a few days, Fran, face it. And the district nurse will be here in the morning and certainly won't want to see all this.' Anthea Martini waved a well-manicured hand across the dressing table cluttered with half-empty wine glasses, a whisky bottle, crumpled tissues and a photo album. 'Just let me clean up.'

Franny's cheeks burned red and she turned her head away to look at Soda who peered at her from the station she'd set up by her owner's bedside. The retriever let out a whine.

'It's all right, old girl,' whispered Franny. 'They'll all be gone soon.'

'No one's going anywhere for the moment, *old girl*, so you better come to terms with that here and now. You've made sure the house will be full of visitors for a while to come.' Anthea sat down on the bed, careful not to disturb Franny's leg, which was elevated on a pillow. Anthea pushed a hand through her immaculate hair then looked more closely at her friend. 'You look like hell, by the way. Have you seen that bruise on the side of your face? You were really bloody lucky this time, Fran. That could have been your temple or an eye speared by that ugly old swan. Thought of that?'

'That swan is gorgeous, thank you very much. Frank and I bought it from a local artist when we did that driving holiday up north years back. In fact, didn't we buy you and David one too?'

Anthea blushed a little but maintained eye contact. 'I always hated that thing. Looked like something that had melted in a house fire. You're the one who goes in for all that artsy stuff. David gave it to one of his juniors at work. Anyway, that's neither here nor there. We were talking about you dive-bombing a piece of iron in your backyard because you were too drunk to see straight. Let's talk about that.'

Franny groaned and shifted her leg a little. 'I'm tired. I need to rest. I've been through a lot, you know.' She arranged her face in a pathetic expression.

Anthea stood up and straightened her long denim skirt. 'Haven't we all, dear?' she said sarcastically.

Before biting back, a memory poked its way into Franny's consciousness. 'Anthea, did David have a heart attack while Ellie was away? She said something about him going to hospital.'

'Oesophageal spasms, not a heart attack. The symptoms seemed similar initially. Didn't want to take any chances.' Anthea began piling debris from around the bedroom into a black plastic bag.

'Well that's good news. Food allergy or something, is it? Like reflux?'

Anthea looked over at Franny and frowned. 'It's probably linked to anxiety, actually. They're looking into it.' Before Franny could respond in some way she continued, 'Look, don't worry about it, all right. Just worry about you.' She swept the final few items into the bag and left the room.

A few hours later Elouise knocked lightly on the half-open bedroom door and entered.

'Franny, you awake?' Soda gave a woof and Whisky came running in. 'Down,' said Elouise sternly. 'No jumping on the bed.' The small terrier cocked his head in confusion but remained earth bound.

'I'm up, I'm up,' Franny mumbled. 'What time is it?'

'Nearly six. We've made you some dinner. We'll give it to you then go.'

'We?'

'Mum and I, obviously. She's still here.'

'What's obvious about that?'

'The house was a sty, Fran, and you had no fresh food, though the booze supplies are pretty healthy. We had to clean up. Also, I walked the dogs before I brought them over this morning but that's going to have to do them for today. I've got an essay to work on.'

'Is there a nurse or someone coming tomorrow?'

'Yes, they have your mobile.' She nodded towards the iPhone on the bedside table, sitting beside a glass of water and vial of pills. 'They'll ring if there's a problem, otherwise someone will be here around ten. I think it will be a female because she's going to help you bathe as well as dress your wound.'

Franny put her head in her hands and groaned. 'Help me bathe?'

'I see a lot of sponge baths in your future,' said Elouise in a cartoon fortune-teller voice. Then she saw the expression on Franny's face and relented. 'It'll only be for a few days. Until you get your strength back and she thinks you've got the hang of it. She'll bring a special stool to sit in the shower and so forth.'

'A stool in the shower; at least I know the title of my memoir now.' Franny grimaced. 'Anyway, how do you know all this?'

'Because we're on your paperwork as next of kin, dear godmother. The blessed Marg is preparing to come down but she couldn't get away immediately, something to do with arrangements re grandkid minding so, for now, we get all the gory details—and the jobs.'

Franny made an effort to move her leg and get out of bed. When Elouise tried stopping her she said, 'I have to go to the loo. Is that allowed?'

'Only if you use these, remember?' Elouise grabbed a pair of crutches the hospital had supplied. 'When you've finished come out to the lounge room and see the set-up.'

In front of the television in the lounge room, Elouise and her mother had created a comfortable nest on the sofa where Franny could sit, propped up by pillows, a footstool in front of her and a tray to the side, furnished with landline handset, a bottle of water and the television remote. The day's newspaper and a couple of current magazines sat in a neat pile on top of a patterned throw. Franny's spectacles and handbag sat beside them.

'Do you want to sit down here and see if you're comfortable? I made my ginger chicken, you can eat it there.' Anthea bustled around the kitchen arranging crockery and a napkin on a little foldable tray table. 'Like a G and T to go with this?'

Franny, easing herself slowly onto the couch with the aid of Elouise, looked back at her friend in surprise.

'Get a grip, woman, I'm kidding,' said Anthea. 'While you're on those antibiotics and painkillers you're off the booze.' She brought the tray over and set it up. 'And you should be off it generally, if you ask me.'

'Don't take that schoolmarm tone with me, Anthea Martini. I've held your hair back while you vomited Bacardi into Danny O'Halloran's mother's bathtub.' Franny tried to push the tray away but found herself hemmed in by the thing.

'I was fifteen years old for God's sake.' Anthea nudged the tray back against her friend and turmeric-coloured sauce slopped slightly over the edge of the bowl.

'Okay, girls, let's not fight.' Elouise took a seat on one of the armchairs and leaned into Franny. 'Look, none of us wants to be in this situation, on that we can all agree.' Franny harrumphed while Anthea sniffed exaggeratedly. 'So,' continued the younger woman, 'let's just get through this as best as we can. Aunty Fran, you attempt to be gracious and appreciate the efforts of others. And Mum,' she looked over at Anthea and raised her eyebrows, 'maybe you could hold off on the sermons for a week or two.'

'No one needs to be here for a week or two.' Franny gripped the small table tightly as she spoke. 'I'm sure once the nurse comes she can set me up with things and I'll be fine. Things can go back to normal.'

'Fine? Normal?' Anthea's voice rose high in disbelief. 'How do you figure that? Firstly, your idea of normal is carrying on like a pissed Miss Havisham. Secondly, you can't walk more than a few steps right now. You've got no hands free with those bloody crutches. One fall and you'll pull the stitches out and create a whole new world of troubles. Plus, you have two dogs used to being walked within an inch of their lives. How are you going to be fine?'

Franny couldn't hide her shock at the bitter tone in her friend's voice. 'I, I can pay someone or'—suddenly she thought of the Salernos—'or the kids next door can help. Have you spoken to them?'

Elouise and Anthea looked at each other. Elouise opened her mouth to speak but her mother held up her hand.

'Look, Franny,' Anthea said, her tone noticeably gentler, 'there's a lovely card up on the kitchen bench from that little lad next door, Joshua, is it? Ellie got it when she popped over to their house earlier.'

'Yes,' said Franny, her face attempting its first smile in over a week, 'he's quite the artist. He'd love to help.'

'Yes, well that's not quite how it's going to go. I don't think you'll be seeing Joshua for a while.' Anthea sat down beside her old friend.

'What do you mean? What's wrong?'

'The mum said she wants to give you some space,' said Elouise. 'I think this'—she gestured to Franny's injured leg—'has put the wind up her.'

'This . . . ?' Franny's voice trailed off quietly. She began nodding her head in understanding. 'Right, right. I get it.' She looked down at her plate of food. 'Well, this chicken looks great and it's getting late. You two should go.'

'Franny.' Anthea put her hand out to cover her friend's. 'It's okay. They're just neighbours and they've only recently moved in. She's on her own with two kids. It's a bit much for her I imagine. To be fair, she hardly knows you. Give it time. After all, we're here to help.'

'And the girl will come in and walk the dogs after school each day. I said you'd give her fifty bucks a week,' said Elouise. 'Mum's paid her for the first two in cash. You can organise it after that.'

'Fifty? Right. Thanks.' Franny played with her food.

'I've set up everything out the back so she won't be in and out of the house. But someone will have to buzz her round,' Elouise nodded towards the intercom at the front door, 'till Marg gets here; reckon you can manage that?'

'Yes, of course. That's good. No need to come into the house. I get it. Thanks.' Franny leaned forward for the remote control and turned on the television.

27

Duty of care

Nurse Leslie Atherton was from Lancashire but had lived in Australia for close to twenty-five years. She had arrived as a newlywed with her husband and two-year-old daughter. She loved the place, could never imagine moving back home. This was home now.

All this and more Franny had learned within the first fifteen minutes the woman had been in the house. Franny was hell bent on hating her.

'So, Mrs Calderwood, I—or my colleague Meenakshi if I can't get here—will be coming to dress that wound for at least the next week to ten days. We all lose a bit of elasticity and collagen as we age. I'm sure the hospital explained how more mature skin can take a little longer to heal. We just have to be careful and patient.' The nurse was crouched beside Franny's leg, continuing to work as she spoke. The two women were in the lounge room where the light was best and where Franny could stretch her leg out on a footstool covered in a clean, white towel.

Franny stared at Leslie, estimating there could only be a decade's, at most, age difference between them. Fuming, she studied the crisply ironed short-sleeved shirt, the official lanyard around the nurse's neck, and the black nylon trousers that strained at the thigh seams. Franny abhorred short-sleeved shirts.

'Thank you, Laurie. You can be sure I'll do everything in my power to minimise the time you have to spend here.'

'Leslie.'

'What?' said Franny.

'My name is Leslie, dear, not Laurie. You've gotten confused.'

In Franny's mind a movie played out, one where Soda knocked *Leslie* off her feet then Whisky got hold of the lanyard around her neck and ran around in ever-tightening circles until the woman's eyes bulged and her tongue lolled out. 'Of course, Leslie. My mistake. Not quite as pretty a name so I'll remember it that way,' she said.

The nurse stopped unrolling gauze and looked over her spectacles at Franny but said nothing. There had already been a testy moment in the bathroom when Leslie questioned her patient's insistence on unboxing a new tube of Diptyque Eau Rose Shower Foam for her ablutions.

'We're not in some urine-tinged nursing home now, dear. I'm still allowed civilised things,' Franny had said.

Leslie had given her the kind of look you give a child you feel a bit sorry for. 'Mrs Calderwood, it's nothing like that.' Her voice was calm and friendly. 'It's the perfumes and chemicals and what not. You have more than a few abrasions.' Franny had not seen the full array of bruises and grazes beneath her clothes until the nurse had helped ease them off. 'I'd rather use this boring old stuff to be safe. Posh stuff can sting.' Leslie held up a nondescript bottle of cleanser.

Now, as she was packing bags and checking paperwork, Leslie turned and said, 'All right for food are you, Mrs Calderwood? Got something to nibble on? It's tricky when you have such a serious wound and you're on your own, in the house I mean.' Her eyes darted over to Lounge Room Frank. 'And it can take a while to master the crutches.' Glancing down at her watch, she added, 'Should I whip you up a sandwich or something before I take off? Nothing fancy but . . .'

'Thank you, I'm fine. My . . .' She was about to say best friend then hesitated. 'My friend Anthea has left me supplies.'

'Good-o. Well, as I said, Mrs Calderwood, we'll have you up and about in no time. As long as you take care.' Through her purple-rimmed spectacles, the nurse took a final glance at some papers in her hand then looked pointedly towards the drinks trolley nearby. 'Of course, you know that alcohol diminishes the body's resistance to bacteria so is best avoided when it comes to wounds healing.' She looked up then, a big open smile across her face. 'But with the meds you're on as well, you'll also know to steer clear. There'll be plenty to celebrate when you're back on your feet.'

Leslie opened her mouth to speak again but Franny interrupted, yelling, 'Whisky, Soda.' The two dogs came running.

Nurse Leslie had already suggested the 'animals' be kept outside as they were a 'falls risk' but now Franny leaned over and, stifling a moan of pain, grabbed a tennis ball on the floor beside her chair and said, 'You dash, Laurie. I'll distract these two.'

The other woman frowned. 'It's Leslie.'

'What's that?' Franny sat up as tall as she could manage, holding the ball aloft in the air.

'You just called me Laurie again.'

'I don't think so, Leslie.' She emphasised the woman's name heavily. 'Maybe your hearing's going. It starts at our age. Off you trot, and thanks again.' Franny threw the ball in the direction of the kitchen and, as the dogs scurried after it noisily, she made a shooing motion to the nurse.

'You're in and out, all right, Dee? That goddaughter Elouise made it pretty clear, there's no need for chit-chat, no need to bother Franny. Check the dogs' water out the back and make sure their pet door is unlocked so they can come and go. Take them for a thirty- or forty-minute walk and that's that. No mucking around. And leave those ear buds behind. You need to have your wits about you crossing roads and so forth. You need to be aware of traffic and other dogs.'

Sallyanne's voice seemed to be coming from just outside Franny's gate. Franny was in the studio where Anthea had left the windows open to 'get rid of the stench of booze' as she had been at pains to explain. Apparently, a rogue bottle of whisky was discovered during clean up, empty, on its side in the en suite sink. To be fair Franny could still detect a whiff of something Speyside in the air. It made her feel slightly nauseous.

She looked down glumly at the calendar she was holding in her hand. She had hoped to replace it on the wall but the throbbing in her leg had been so intense after the short hobble through the house that she'd been forced to sit down and catch her breath.

'Jeez, Mum, I have walked a dog before,' Dee was saying, and Franny could imagine the teenager's frustrated eye-roll accompanying the statement.

'Yes, but these are not your dogs. If something happened to them . . . which reminds me, don't let them off the leads at the park.'

'Why?'

'Just don't risk it.'

'And are you for real that I can't pop in to see Franny? That seems mean, and rude.'

Sallyanne's voice dipped lower. All Franny caught was something to the effect of 'We've spoken about this, Dee. Give it a rest.' Then, in a louder voice, Sallyanne said, 'Remember, honey, I'm leaving for work in an hour and I don't want Joshie here on his own.'

Franny wondered if other neighbours were aware of her house arrest. *Had they seen the ambulance? Did she care?*

At that moment, Josh's little voice called out. He must have run from his house to hers. 'Why can't I go with Dee, why? I want to see Franny and walk Whisky and Soda too.'

'Darling, keep your voice down,' said Sallyanne. *Maybe the whole of Ipswich Street didn't know what was going on after all.* 'We've been over this till we're both blue in the face. Franny is recuperating—which means getting better—from a very bad cut on her leg. She needs peace and quiet. And this is Dee's first walk with the dogs. She needs to concentrate. I want you to be a good and helpful boy and just do as you're told. Next week, when everyone's got the hang of things, you can probably go with her. Okay?'

'What about if I just visit Franny instead? I'd be good.' *Was that the stamp of a small foot?* 'She could still have a piece of quiet.'

'Peace *and* quiet, doofus,' said Dee. 'Now scram.' Franny heard a little whimpering and then the intercom buzzer sounded. Leaning heavily on the crutches, grimacing all the way, she made it to the front door. Saying nothing, she buzzed Dee in the gate.

Franny could hear the girl's footsteps along the driveway. They paused once or twice, apparently Dee was trying to peep in the side windows, but the blinds were down. By the time she reached the back of the house Dee was being assaulted by much barking and tail wagging.

From her vantage point Franny could just see Dee moving around, talking to the dogs, checking their water and the small, fur-rimmed pet door. Franny knew Elouise had left the two leads, a couple of rolls of paw-patterned plastic bags and a small packet of treats on the garden table. As Franny adjusted her crutches, wondering if she should return to the studio or to her bed, she realised Dee was again trying to see in. *She is a stubborn one all right,* she thought with a smidge of admiration. Dee peered through the glass doors that separated the lounge room from the patio and garden. The only things visible would have been Franny's pile of pillows and books on the couch, plus a folding tray table sporting a tea pot, a mug and a carton of long-life milk.

Dee looked over her shoulder towards her house then tapped quietly on the window. For a moment Franny considered responding. Dee tapped a little louder and Whisky barked and jumped up on her.

Suddenly Dee seemed distracted by something behind her. Franny watched as the girl spun around, realising Sallyanne was hanging over the shared fence. Whatever was said between the two—Franny could make out Sallyanne's mouth moving but couldn't catch the words—the result was that Dee snapped to, clipping the leads onto the dogs' collars and briskly heading towards the gate.

Sallyanne continued to watch, presumably as her daughter exited onto the street. Then for a little while she remained dangling over the fence, apparently lost in thought. Finally, her head moved, bird-like, as movement inside the other house caught her eye.

Dressed in a nightgown, leaning heavily on crutches, long white hair plastered to her head, Franny was at the glass doors. The two women's eyes met. Sallyanne froze, perhaps not sure what to do next. The decision was instantly taken from her. Franny closed the gauzy drapes and moved clumsily out of sight.

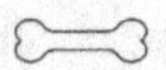

When Anthea let herself in through the front door she found the mistress of the house seated at the breakfast bar, bad leg propped on the stool beside her, crutches nearby. Franny had a bottle of Tanqueray, a can of tonic and a crystal tumbler in front of her.

'God you've become punctual in your old age,' said Franny in way of greeting. She peered over at the kitchen clock. 'Six o'clock on the knocker. Want one?' She held the tumbler towards her visitor.

'Don't tell me you're drinking, not on all those meds.' Awkwardly, Anthea made her way over to the kitchen, struggling to balance handbag and keys, a small insulated esky and a bunch of native flowers. She plonked everything in a heap on the bench and stared accusingly at her friend.

'Keep your knickers on. It's just the one and a light pour at that,' said Franny. 'More of a suggestion of a gin than the real deal.' She made a show of moving the green gin bottle out of Anthea's way. 'I'm assuming that's a no from you then.'

Anthea stared at her silently, for longer than was comfortable, then said, 'You've got a mushroom and thyme risotto, some roast pumpkin and cumin soup, a lasagne and some more of that ginger chicken curry. There's also bits and bobs to make a salad and some of those microwave pods of rice.' She began lifting plastic containers out of the esky and arranging them on the bench. 'Oh, and I bought some milk, bananas and another loaf of bread. You okay for tea and coffee? Still drinking that Genovese stuff?'

'Yes, I'm still drinking the Genovese stuff but I have plenty, thank you.' Franny tipped some more tonic into her glass. 'You know you don't have to do all this, Anth. I can just get stuff delivered.'

'Including booze, I suppose.' Anthea was stacking items in the refrigerator as she spoke.

'Anthea.' Franny took a quick sip of her gin. 'I appreciate everything you have done, I really do, but I don't need the holier-than-thou act, okay? If you don't want to stay for a drink, then feel free to go. No one could blame you.'

'That's an interesting choice of words. What exactly would I be blamed for and who would be doing this blaming?' She slammed the defenceless bananas into a large ceramic bowl.

'Good God, Anthea, forget I said anything.'

'Franny, Franny, Franny.' Anthea gave a sarcastic laugh. 'How can I possibly forget when it's been so long since you said anything to me? I have to hang on to this moment for posterity if nothing else.'

The anger in her friend's words created a prickling sensation in Franny's guts. She looked at this woman who had once sat next to her on the back seat of the school bus, who had once helped write her wedding vows, who had once rushed into a room with a pregnancy test in her hand and screamed, 'It's positive, it's positive, I'm pregnant', then danced around in circles while they both laughed and cried. In that moment, a deep and heavy wave of exhaustion swept through Franny. Anthea needed so much. Deserved even more.

Wincing as she lifted her leg off the stool, Franny just managed to grab the crutches before they clattered to the floor. 'Thank you for all you've done, Anth. I mean it,' she said. 'My leg is killing me and I'm going to bed. You should take the flowers for Ellie. She's earned them. Hope you don't mind letting yourself out.' She took one last slug of gin before hobbling towards her bedroom.

28

Women's issues

When Marg arrived, she did so with a bang, quite literally. Franny was expecting her that afternoon and had taken an extra Endone tablet for the occasion. Slumped sideways on the couch, a golden retriever on one side of her, copy of *The New Yorker* on the other, she was startled awake by the sound of something hitting the windows at the studio end of the house. Whisky was already up there, barking his lungs out while, simultaneously, the mobile phone on the coffee table rang out, Marg's name flashing up as the caller.

Franny looked at Soda through heavy eyes. 'I'm sorry you have to deal with all this,' she said to the dog who looked back, eyes full of sorrow. Franny picked up her phone and said, 'Hello, Marg, hold your horses, I'm coming.' Her mouth tasted like the bottom of a cockatoo's cage, as the saying went, but there was no time to freshen up. Leaning on her crutches, she moved slowly to the front door to admit her dreaded Florence Nightingale.

Marg's hair was dyed a glossy auburn and cut into a bob so thick and precise it looked like a doll's wig. Her dead-straight fringe skimmed the top of thick yellow frames on overtly branded Prada spectacles. *You look like a red panda*, thought Franny, before saying, 'Darling, hello. You really shouldn't have come.'

'Shut up, you old windbag,' said Marg, the wheels of her large black and white polka dot suitcase nearly knocking Franny off one of her crutches. 'They told me not to expect a warm welcome.'

'They?' Franny flattened herself against the wall like a villager taking shelter as the tanks rolled in.

'Anthea and Elouise. Who else?' Marg thumped her gigantic handbag on the floor beside her suitcase and looked back at Franny. 'Jesus, look at that thing on your face.' She winced.

The bruise was working its way through a sunset of colours and had reached a deep yellow and purple now. From an artistic point of view, Franny found its metamorphosis quite mesmerising.

Determined not to be thrown off course, she said, 'I'm glad everyone is discussing me.'

'No, no, Fran, please don't start the very minute I walk in the door. Can I at least have a cuppa before you train the guns on me?' Marg bent down to accept some love from Whisky and Soda. 'At least they're happy to see me.' She looked up at Franny and winked.

An hour later the two women were seated in the lounge room, an empty coffee plunger in front of them, alongside two mugs and a plate covered with crumbs from Marg's homemade Anzac biscuits, ferried from her Blue Mountains' kitchen.

'So, this isn't great, is it?' Marg munched on a biscuit and nodded towards Franny's leg, now resting on a footstool. 'Care to explain?'

'What's to explain, Marg? I took a tumble. It's happened to us all at one time or another. It's just there seems to be an age where you no longer fall or go arse over tit, for that matter. Instead, you *have* a fall and you become a *falls risk*. Actually, there's no need to make a big deal of it.'

Marg looked down at her coffee mug. 'It can't be like this every year, darling, you know that.' Franny squirmed visibly and looked away. Her sister-in-law continued. 'You shut up shop when it first happened, and I understood. When you closed all the blinds and turned off all the phones that first month I put it down to the shock. All very W.H. Auden, and I say that with no disrespect. But now.' Marg swept her hand around the room. 'Now, Franny, life must go on. It's been three years. You must find a different way. This is becoming dangerous and, frankly, worrying.' Marg leaned forward and tried, unsuccessfully, to put a hand over Franny's. She sat back and stared out at the garden. 'I'll leave it alone for now but you know I'm right,' she said, more quietly than Franny knew she was capable of. 'You don't want to face it, but you know I'm right.'

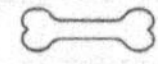

Constant babble, the movement of people, annoying television programs and even more annoying conversations now dominated Frances Calderwood's life. Naturally, Marg and the relentlessly positive Leslie got along like a house on fire. Who could have guessed that the nurse had relatives in the Blue Mountains and Marg was all too familiar with the 'darling' teashop they ran? The pair had so much to talk about, sometimes in cheery, too-loud voices, sometimes in whispered, irritating hallway conflabs. One thing they completely agreed on was that it was about time Franny 'joined some clubs' and 'got some hobbies', just basically 'got out more'. The day before, Leslie had stumbled upon her patient's room of 'paints and pencils and other stuff' and declared it was 'a start'. Even Marg had had the good grace to look abashed at that.

No doubt Leslie was now completely up to speed with the whole 'annual meltdown' saga and, one afternoon, Franny even overheard

Marg telling her about 'the family next door'. Marg and Leslie were outside Franny's bedroom window, the former taking off to get groceries, the latter on her way inside to dress Franny's wound.

'For a moment there they seemed to be all over her. Even took her away for her birthday, which seemed over the top,' Marg had said. 'All very odd. Sometimes you have to wonder if they were after her money.' Marg lowered her voice a tad. 'You know, seeing she doesn't have grandkids and so on. You do hear about that kind of thing.'

Leslie made a tutting sound. 'Surely not. The mother's on her own, isn't she? If there's been a lot of, well, you know, imbibing, it makes sense she doesn't want to take that on. Not around the children.'

'Hmm. Maybe. I know that's what Anthea thinks.' Marg had sounded unconvinced. 'Either way, it's probably for the best. I mean, it's not like having them around helped in the long run, is it?'

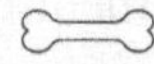

The Wuthering Club's most recent book had been discussed without input from the Ipswich Street member. Reading an article about its controversial author in *The New Yorker*, Franny decided to opt out. The book was one of the previous year's blockbusters, its plot dealing with a woman who becomes addicted to booze and pills following the death of her husband and daughter. There was a supernatural twist; the central character still saw her dead loved ones or something like that. Franny decided an interrogation of this particular subject matter was something she could live without.

Nonetheless, she flicked to the club's Facebook page, curious to see what the gang made of the book and find out what they were reading next. Franny might be off her feet but could still feed her brain. Sipping pinot noir slowly and appreciatively from the tall, porcelain coffee mug on her bedside table, she breathed out a relaxed sigh for what felt like the first time in too many days.

Thankfully, Marg was a self-declared 'early to bed kinda gal' so she toddled off to the small spare room around half past nine each night. Only then did the house start to feel like Franny's domain once more. She stalked it, awkwardly and a little painfully, a wretched old lion in the dullest enclosure of the world's saddest zoo.

Today marked her best day since the fall. The nurse's home visits were over, the heaviest painkillers used up. The bruised side of her face was only slightly yellow, the discoloured hue of a smoker's lounge room, and the crutches were finally tamed. Her movements were less like a newborn giraffe finding its legs, a crucial development for her evening ramblings. With her balance improved and head cleared Franny could finally dig out the special edition Mac Forbes Yarra Valley pinot noir stashed in the laundry cupboard. It was behind a box of old newspapers she kept for lighting the outdoor fire pit. This part of the house stayed the coolest and Franny had paid almost three hundred dollars for the case of six bottles. She was keeping it for special occasions. In Franny's mind no occasion in recent history was more special than this.

She thought back on the final session with Leslie, an awkward encounter to say the least. Sitting back and looking at Franny's leg, possibly admiring her handiwork, the nurse had said, 'That's going to be tender for a while, Mrs Calderwood. You should be prepared for that. And you'll need to build up your strength.'

Franny, tired of all the indignities, concerned looks and ministrations, wanting this period of her life to be over, crumpled up and thrown in the bin like a failed drawing, had grumbled, 'Yes thank you, Leslie. I'll go slowly.'

Eager to see the back of the nurse's ugly short-sleeved shirt, Franny was surprised when, instead of readying to go, Leslie looked directly into her eyes and said, 'You're made of strong stuff, Frances; may I call you Frances?'

Franny laughed. 'Let's face it, you're finishing up, you can call me what you like. You've probably called me worse at some points.'

Leslie smiled a little, but not very much. 'See, there you go, you're a tough cookie. Strong inside and out.' She tapped her chest. 'Marg says you've barely mentioned the pain in the time she's been here. She also says you won't accept much help.'

'Marg likes to say a lot of things but maybe she'd be better off—'

Leslie interrupted the rest of the diatribe by holding up a few sheets of paper covered in handwriting. 'Marg did not mention this.'

Immediately Franny knew what it was. 'How dare you? That is private property. You cannot be going through—'

Again, Leslie interrupted. 'Frances, I was not going through anything.' She folded the letter and tucked it gently beneath Franny's thigh so it was barely visible. 'Actually, if you didn't keep leaving your crutches in your room and hopping about like a wallaby I would never have seen it. When I went to retrieve them from the floor near your bed earlier I saw the papers under the bed. And yes, I read the letter.' Here Leslie flushed and held two hands up in surrender. 'I'm ashamed to say it's true, I'm an incorrigible stickybeak.' She took Franny's hand, still looking intently at her. 'But I'm also genuinely the soul of discretion. You have to be to do this job. I'm sorry I read it but it did make me wonder. On top of Frank's anniversary, it seems like you've been dealing with much more.'

Franny's first impulse had been to bluster and protest. *Who the hell did this lanyard-wearing hussy think she was?* But then she had slumped back against the chair and shrugged wearily. 'You haven't mentioned this to Marg?'

'Goodness no,' said Leslie.

'Good. Don't. I mean it.' Franny closed her eyes and breathed deeply. 'She called me too, that bloody Ange woman. Can you believe it?'

'Was this before your accident?'

'Yes but I can't blame her.' Franny picked up the letter and placed it inside the cover of a book on her tray table. She slumped back. 'She may be guilty of other things but this,' Franny pointed down to her injured leg, 'this is all my own creation.'

'This is what I mean, Frances. Your compulsion to internalise and carry everything within. There are other ways. People want to help.' Leslie rubbed Franny's hand gently. 'I think Marg wants to help.'

Franny appreciated the nurse's good intentions. At the end of the day Leslie had provided some pretty intimate assistance when Franny needed it most. The woman was kind and patient and had put up with less than polite behaviour. Franny had waved her goodbye with the gift of a bottle of gin. 'Oh Tanqueray, my favourite,' Leslie had said. 'Don't tell Marg. And especially don't tell that friend of yours—Anthea.'

In bed now, Franny welcomed the opportunity to forget about nurses and letters and whatnot and focus instead on The Wuthering Club conversation which had, perhaps unavoidably, strayed from the plot of the most recent novel to the stories surrounding its author. Initially there had been rumours that he had faked certain writing credentials and, more disturbingly, a history of childhood trauma. These were then overshadowed by the news he had been discovered masturbating behind a marquee at a prestigious literary festival. By a Booker Prize winner, no less.

Club members weren't sure if this should affect their opinion of his writing. One member was 'dying' to see the movie adaptation of the book while another posted a link to a video where the author gave writing tips to other wannabes. Media ruminations about his lies and indiscretions also generally mentioned his Clark Kent-type good looks. The Wuthering Club was not above examining such claims for themselves.

Franny hit a link to conveniently provided video footage while sipping her wine. It was smooth and earthy, with a tiny touch of violet for elegance. She moved it around her mouth slowly and appreciatively, sliding it down her throat with luxuriant ease. Her self-prescription allowed for one large glass. The goal was to savour.

Definitely got crazy eyes and each of his buttons looks about to pop. If he's such a big shot, where's his stylist, or at least someone who cares enough to tug on his shirt? Franny switched from the link and back to The Wuthering Club's page, not bothering to listen to the writer's words. Seeing slivers of hairy belly poking through his checked shirt was all the information she required. *Definitely something not quite right there*, she decided.

Staring at the laptop screen, seeing but not reading an exchange of comments about a famous feminist author who was suspected of having a boob job, Franny's mind turned to a book club of another kind. It must have been close to a year since she visited The Shelf, the private group page kept up by Anthea and the seven other members of Franny's old book gang. Clicking over to it now, seeing the familiar cover image of nine women, Franny included, snapped at the opening night of the movie adaptation of a Patricia Highsmith novel, she felt a pang.

Things were simple here, just a log of books the group had read and posts about ones they were considering down the track.

Occasionally there'd be a personal photograph, mostly of a grandchild with a book, otherwise the images pertained to the group themselves—snapshots of them huddled around cheeseboards, selfies taken at writerly events, a recent close-up of Anthea on the balcony of a surfside beach house. The caption read: *Day one of The Book Shelf's annual weekend away #reading #napping #chocolate #wheresthewine? #booklovers.* Franny noted the photograph was posted only four weeks earlier. Franny had instigated that tradition; she wondered who organised it now.

Scrolling further down the page she saw a post from Anthea about one of their shared favourite authors, Jeanette Winterson. Meaning to click on the story link, she missed and jumped to Anthea's personal page instead. Suddenly an image blindsided her. The photograph was an old one, Frank in his very early forties, holding a tiny baby and smiling joyfully at the camera. He was waving the child's delicate wrist in the air, a diminutive victorious gesture for Miss Elouise Martini who had just survived her baptism. The post was a couple of weeks old, just the picture and a couple of sentences typed beneath:

> Remembering our darling Frank this week, the best friend, godfather and Scrabble partner a gal could ask for. Always loved, forever missed. A chasm in our lives that never goes away. We're drinking Tatt tonight for you, beloved friend.

'Darling, you're still up?' The bedroom door banged open and Marg barged in.

Franny jolted in the bed, the laptop bucking against her hand, almost spilling the illicit cup of wine.

'Bloody hell, Marg. Ever heard of knocking?' Franny slugged back the last of the wine and ran the back of her hand across her mouth.

Waste of good booze, she thought. Immediately her eyes searched out the bottle wedged discreetly between the bed base and the side table. A stack of books and a mohair throw masked it nicely. She exhaled a breath then looked up at her sister-in-law again, now skulking at the other side of the bed and trying to peer at the laptop. Franny snapped it shut. 'Seriously, what the hell do you want?'

Marg straightened herself and stuck out her bottom lip like an offended toddler. 'I saw the light on and was worried. I just wanted to—'

'Snoop. You just wanted to snoop.' Franny was furious at the disturbance. Her eyes still swam with the image of Frank and baby Elouise. She took off her glasses and rubbed the lenses with her bedsheet.

'I'm so sorry, Mrs Calderwood. I didn't see the do-not-disturb sign on the door. Please don't tell my supervisor.' Marg turned in a huff and padded back the way she'd come. Her feet were bare but the rest of her was ensconced in a huge, velvety magenta dressing gown. When she left the room, she slammed the door pointedly behind her.

'You look like a walking roll of carpet, by the way,' Franny yelled.

Late the following morning Franny was sitting at the small desk near the window in her studio half-heartedly flicking through bills and hospital paperwork. Her sister-in-law's silent treatment had gone on for almost three hours. In Marg's mind this was a punishment, in Franny's it was manna from heaven. Marg's bad humour was not serious enough to wreck her appetite, or diminish her sense of hospitality, therefore a delicious smoked salmon, cream cheese and capers bagel still made its way to Franny's studio, delivered amidst sulky footsteps and ostentatious harrumphing.

Chomping on it now, Franny caught the sound of Marg's mobile phone ringing at the other end of the house. Minutes later a voice called out, 'Back in a minute' and Franny heard Marg bustling out the front door, the two dogs on leads behind her.

Grabbing a crutch, she used it to lean forward and peek through the studio windows. Though Franny had not painted anything for at least a month, one was still open to let fresh air in, allowing her to hear the voices at the top of the driveway. She was pretty sure they belonged to Marg and Sallyanne. It seemed Sallyanne was taking the dogs. Franny could only hear murmurs, so she hobbled into the en suite where the window delivered driveway acoustics at their clearest.

'Not exactly making me feel welcome but what was I to expect?' This was Marg's voice.

'Difficult for everyone I guess.' Sallyanne was replying now. Franny could not catch everything said but she did hear the phrase: 'A bigger problem than people realise. I've seen a lot of it while nursing over the years.'

A car drove by, muffling the next segment of conversation, then Marg's voice was audible again. 'Well I completely understand your point of view. I know your generation of mothers is very sensitive about who you leave the kids with. Rightly so, of course. Still, we appreciated the dog walks. Sure you don't mind today? I'd do it myself but I don't like to take my eyes off "her indoors" as they say.'

Franny didn't hear the next part of the exchange; another car went by. When she heard Sallyanne speak again it was to say: 'Dee's got an exam I want her to focus on. It's only for a couple of days.'

'Well that's probably how long I have left here,' said Marg. 'I can sense I'm outstaying my welcome.' Suddenly Whisky and Soda started barking, possibly at another canine passer-by. When Marg's voice reached Franny's ears once again, she said, 'Shame because she loves kids. Seemed surprisingly attached to yours.'

'Do you think that's part of it? The no kids thing?' This was Sallyanne speaking.

'Well, I . . . I mean . . .' Marg sounded uncharacteristically tongue-tied.

'It's okay, I know about Tilly,' said Sallyanne. From that point onwards the voices dipped dramatically in volume and Franny's crutches prevented her from getting as close to the small, elevated window as she would have liked. Momentarily she lost her balance, knocking a jar of thin brushes off the lip of the sink. It hit her slippered foot and bounced, avoiding a smash. Moaning in frustration, she bent and gathered up the wreckage. Seconds later, Marg's voice rang out: 'Thanks again, Sallyanne. Just buzz and I'll come out and grab them.'

A short time later Franny heard the coffee machine gurgling. She was still in the studio, now sitting in front of the easel staring at her abandoned painting, when Marg walked in.

'I'm making a latte. You want one?' Marg walked over and examined the work in progress. 'Is that a tiny hand hidden in the details of that flower?' She leaned in, nose-to-canvas, to look more closely then moved over to a collection of works propped along the wall nearby. 'This series you're working on is genuinely amazing. Does Darrien ever hound you to show?'

Franny shrugged and rose from the chair, retrieving her crutches and heading for the door. 'He gave up a long time ago. Doesn't know about this lot. Coming?' Her body language made it clear she wanted Marg out of the room. 'Anyway, I don't do it to exhibit.'

'No but you used to,' said Marg, 'and these are wonderful. You should start showing again.'

'Next topic please.' Franny shooed her towards the kitchen. 'And where are my dogs?'

'Sallyanne's taken them for a walk. Dee couldn't make it today.' Turning the coffee grinder on, Marg focused on her task.

'Hmm, is that who you were gossiping with outside. Sallyanne?'

Marg finished frothing milk and looked up. 'Heard us, did you?'

'Snippets.'

'You're full of surprises you know that, Frances Calderwood? I'm surprised that woman knows so much about you. Didn't realise you confided in anyone anymore.'

'It just came up one day. I was not confiding.'

'The loss of your only child just came up. Find that hard to believe.' Marg placed the latte in front of Franny and offered her some sugar.

'I don't take sugar and you know it,' said Franny, pushing the bright-blue bowl back across the bench.

'Thought things might have changed,' said Marg. 'Seems like there's a lot I don't know these days.'

29

Back to basics

Franny leaned against the doorframe of the spare room and watched her sister-in-law struggling to jam an avalanche of clothes and other items into the polka-dot suitcase. During her time as nursemaid in Fran's home, Marg had also managed to sneak out for the odd spot of retail therapy and the results were overwhelming her.

'Sit on it,' said Franny, moving over to the bed where the suitcase lay.

'I might have to get you to post a few things back.' Marg was battling with a pair of tan leather boots, attempting to flatten them into the case's outside pocket. Her eyes slid, almost guiltily, to a nearby chair where a bag of toiletries stood abandoned beside a fat magenta pile of dressing gown. Looking back, she saw the corner of her sister-in-law's mouth twitching upwards. Simultaneously both women erupted into laughter.

'I'm sorry, Marg. That garment is actually very regal, I shouldn't have made the carpet comment.' Franny wiped tears from her eyes and eased herself onto the bed.

The last two days had passed almost peacefully, Marg making sure Franny had everything necessary for life on her own, fussing around the house, filling it with flowers and cleaning it to luxury holiday-rental standards. She had also nagged Franny back to her painting routine, delivering a series of gourmet dishes to the invalided artist while she worked.

'No, you're probably right. The one thing about living on your own is not having anyone to give you unvarnished feedback, don't you find? Even a useless husband like Darryl could sometimes be useful that way. He had a pretty good eye.' Still holding the boots in her hands, she sat down heavily on the bed too. 'I know my taste verges a little on the loud at times.' She checked Franny for a response but got none. 'And then there's my backside; it's always been like towing around a mini-caravan.'

Looking over at Marg, dressed in floral-patterned leggings and an oversized mauve sweater that reached midway down her thighs, Franny was struck by the look of almost teenage frustration on her face.

She patted her on the leg and said, 'Frank always loved your style. He called you the family rainbow. I like a little colour myself.'

'You.' Marg let out the word with a sigh of frustration. 'You're like one of those bloody models they bring back from the 1960s and '70s, all cheekbones, long, tanned feet and skinny thighs. On you everything ends up looking arty.'

'Doubt I could make that dressing gown look arty.'

Marg hit Franny lightly with one of the shoes. 'You really are a bitch.'

'Also, your arse is lovely, like two freshly baked buns. Mine seems to be growing rectangular. Some people have a washboard stomach, I have a washboard arse.'

Marg chuckled. 'It does seem to have dropped a bit. I thought that was just from all the bed rest.'

'Now who's a bitch?' Franny grabbed one of the boots and hit Marg back. 'Seriously, though, who cares? Shouldn't you be over all of this by now, woman? You're sixty-eight or something. If you're not comfortable with yourself at this point, when will you be?'

'Is that your way of saying no one cares anymore anyway? That I should give up? I get that feeling from my kids sometimes. They roll their eyes when they hear me talking about shopping for new clothes. It's like, why bother?'

Now Franny whacked Marg. 'Oh for God's sake, what do they know? I bet no one told Jane Fonda to "give up" when she was knocking on seventy.'

'I'm no Jane Fonda.'

'No, you're Margaret Roxborough née Calderwood and you're a magnificent specimen. You're fit, healthy, vibrant and gorgeous.' Franny touched the other woman lightly on the leg. 'And, more than that, you have a personality that other people are drawn to.'

Marg looked down at her lap balefully. 'Penelope Black said I had a matronly bosom and that it enters the room before I do. I overheard her talking to someone.'

Franny looked at her sister-in-law in amazement then roared with laughter. 'Oh my God, a matronly bosom. I haven't heard that one before but only a woman would say it about another woman. Let me guess, this Penelope person is bird-thin and small with dyed silver-blonde hair and an awful marriage. Probably does Pilates three times a week and has a small white dog, an oodle of some variety.'

Marg looked genuinely impressed. 'It's a Poochon actually, cross between a toy poodle and bichon frise. And she doesn't admit to the marriage being bad, but we all know he had a fling with his dental hygienist a few years ago.'

'Poo-shon! That is not a real thing.' Franny's tone was incredulous. 'And I assume she stayed because of the money.'

'Well, when the teacher comes to your house to deliver private Pilates classes it can get *very* expensive.' Marg winked.

That night the two women enjoyed a farewell dinner. Franny ordered roast duck from Old Kingdom and insisted on opening a bottle of sparkling shiraz. 'It's basically bubbly Ribena,' she said to Marg who looked at her in disbelief. 'All right, with a tiny little kick. You know I'm okay now, Marg. Let's enjoy ourselves, it's fine.'

Sitting outside on the patio, sipping the shiraz and watching the setting sun, Marg looked towards the fence separating Franny's house from the Salernos. 'Should I SMS that Sallyanne woman saying you'll walk the dogs yourself now or do you need another week? I'm sure the youngster's enjoying the money.'

Franny picked up a ratty tennis ball and threw it to Whisky, who had been silently and patiently staring at it for five minutes from across the lawn. 'Cut her loose if you don't mind, Marg. I can drive Whisky and Soda to the off-lead park and let them run free. Probably best to get back to normal as soon as possible.'

Marg nodded and took a sip from her fluted glass.

'What?' Franny asked.

'I didn't say a word.'

'Exactly. A world's first.'

'Put the claws back, Franny. We've been doing so well.'

Franny had the good grace to look contrite. 'You're right. I apologise.' She held up her glass in a gesture of cheers. 'I just think it's better if I keep myself to myself as far as they're concerned. They were always a bit needy.'

Marg nodded and again said nothing.

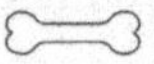

Franny stood in her driveway leaning on a wooden walking stick topped with a hand-carved duck's head. It was something she and Frank had picked up at a Dog and Duck pinot weekend from a folk artist who sold his work through the pub. For years the thing had hung ornamentally on the back of the toilet door, now it was called into legitimate service. Waving goodbye to Marg's taxi she looked down at the stick and said aloud, 'We joked about who would be the first one to really need this didn't we, darling? Well, at least I didn't use it to beat your beloved sister with.'

Just then the Salernos' car pulled up and Franny saw Josh waving frantically at her from within. She used the cane to wave vaguely then continued towards her gate.

Inside, plonking herself down near the silver-framed photograph of Lounge Room Frank, she said, 'Husband oh husband, we are finally home alone. It feels like months, but I know it's only been a few weeks. Seriously though . . . my idea of hell.' She looked around at the pristine house, noting a trace of Marg's trademark Paris by Yves Saint Laurent perfume in the air. 'Close to it anyway.'

Waiting for the water to boil for dinner that night, a nice, elegant spaghetti aglio olio she'd been craving in recent days, Franny poured herself a double-sized Tanqueray, picked up the remote control and began hunting for a killer. Marg, who 'couldn't understand the appeal of dead bodies', had commandeered the main television throughout her stay, subjecting Franny to a diet of cooking competitions, antiques and gardening, supplemented by shouty current affair shows hosted by men and women with ostentatiously lacquered hair. Franny was ready for some grit.

While Franny had been laid up a new British crime thriller had launched so she clicked the link to watch a preview. The scene that greeted her was comfortingly familiar: body of a dark-haired girl in a red mackintosh splayed on a country roadside; cut to suitably craggy male detective staring into an open fire, bottle of Laphroaig whisky balancing on a footstool nearby; cut to scenes of a ramshackle fishing boat crewed by dubious-looking characters. *Yep*, thought Franny, *just the ticket*. She returned to the main menu, leaving the screen on silent, pleased she would have something suitable to accompany dinner.

The image of the Laphroaig label stayed with her. The effects of her recent 'Swan Dive', the name she'd given to the accident, were too fresh to consider dabbling with any of the 'brown drinks' just yet, but the whisky stirred up memories.

'It was Laphroaig that got us going on the whole Scotland trip idea wasn't it, darling?' She picked up Lounge Room Frank and stared at the image. Her memory went back to a wintry dinner at David and Anthea's house. Both couples had gorged on oysters Kilpatrick followed by wild salmon with new potatoes and were sipping on cognacs and whiskies beside the fire in the Martinis' living room.

Picking up a bottle of Laphroaig from the coffee table and removing its lid, breathing in the smoky aroma, Frank had said, 'God the peat in this is out of this world, Dave. Imagine what the distillery must smell like.'

David, who had been fiddling with the fire, had mumbled, 'You should go find out. There's plenty of distilleries on the island where it's made.'

Frank had taken another sniff from the bottle, replaced the lid and looked at his wife. 'What do you say, darling girl? You and me in a hire car, barrelling around the Scottish isles, eating neeps and tatties, and drinking with the lairds and locals?'

Franny had looked at her husband to see if he was serious. 'Nobody else, just the two of us on a Highlands road trip, beautiful scenery and bonny accents on the radio?' Frank had nodded. 'And it really would just be us and we wouldn't have to cook or entertain, and I could bring my sketchpad?'

Franny remembered jumping up from her seat and rushing over to smother her husband in kisses.

'This, my dear, is exactly the kind of thing that makes me glad I married you,' she cried, while her best friend had rolled her eyes theatrically and told them to 'get a room'.

Snapping out of her reverie, Franny returned the photograph to the table and looked at the frozen television screen. She picked up the remote and went back to the main menu. Suddenly she couldn't stomach a hard-boiled detective working the Scottish borders.

'I think I'll find something a bit more Mediterranean, goes better with dinner,' she muttered to herself.

30

Party of one

A week later, Franny was feeling physically much more herself. Her first walk back at the beach had gone without incident. If anything, it had been exhilarating: the moss and lichen of the rock pools had resembled beading and brocade, sparking ideas for future paintings; small, doll-sized waves had rolled into shore, ending flat and gentle at her feet.

Later, sitting outside Beachcomber, both dogs exhausted, damp and sandy at her feet, she looked at the fern-shaped swirl on her caffe latte and almost cried with relief. *You flew close to the flame this time, old girl*, she thought.

The idea of losing her independence, the carefully orchestrated routines that now anchored her life, had been keeping her awake. Lying in bed a few weeks before, listening to the well-meaning Leslie and Marg outside her bedroom door, discussing her 'wound maintenance', Franny had experienced a feeling of premonition so profoundly chilling she had tugged her doona up tight beneath her chin. When, a short time later, Marg could be heard in the driveway calling goodbye to the nurse, Franny had turned to Bedroom Frank and said, 'Imagine your whole day being in the hands of others, my love. And not even others like us.' As her lovely young husband stared out a Tuscan window, she added, 'At least one indecency you've been spared.'

This afternoon heralded a return to the botanic gardens. With the weather turning cooler and the days shortening, Franny regretted the warmer weeks she had missed while recuperating, leg up, in bed or on the sofa. Still, the change of seasons was something she relished, and she tended to look forward to a Melbourne winter, the afternoon light so often stark and pure. When spiked by snow on the nearby ranges, its crisp clarity could enliven her. It could also evoke memories.

While it wasn't winter yet, Franny knew from experience that sitting still beneath a giant cypress or fern for a few hours could soon leave you feeling chilled. Rummaging in the coat closet, looking for her favourite old, knitted hat and scarf, scenes from the winter she and Frank rented a caravan by the coast slammed through her mind in brutal waves.

The younger Calderwoods had dreamed of owning a holiday house but lacked the necessary capital. Believing you could 'get the vibe' in other ways, Frank had surprised his wife with three-months' rental of a Viscount twenty-four-foot caravan at Gumnut Gully Park on the Great Ocean Road. For ten out of the twelve weekends the couple packed an esky, filled a thermos and headed along winding cliffside roads, Franny delighting in the smell of eucalyptus mixed with sea air. When the evenings dipped to below one degree and Frank had decreed the tiny electric bar heater too dangerous to run all night, Franny had taken off to the local hippy surf shop to purchase the hat-and-scarf set. She'd worn the rainbow-coloured duo to bed most nights, prompting Frank to say it was like sleeping with a knitting Nancy. Franny had said she'd knit one for his pecker if he needed it.

That winter lived in Franny's memory as one of the greatest ever. It was too cold and primitive for most of their friends, so they had only each other to play with. They hiked in the national park, bought fresh fish at the co-op on the pier, played cards by candle-light on their dinky Laminex-topped dining table and got to know the locals at the nearby pub. Frank won the pub's pool competition three weeks in a row and Franny painted a portrait of the owner.

Closing the closet door, Franny shrugged on a long down coat and wrapped the scarf around her neck. Though the Skoda's heating was top-notch, she liked keeping all the windows down while the heater baked her feet, a practice Frank had loathed and ridiculed. Even now, anytime she pushed the tiny lever and the window slid down, cold air rushing in, she imagined ghost-Frank tensing beside her and smiled. *I wonder if he feels me still annoying and goading him from the great beyond*, she thought. *Hope so!*

Looking at her supply bag beside the front door Franny realised her polaroid camera was missing. She'd planned to explore its kitschy effects that afternoon. Moving tentatively but efficiently when indoors without the walking stick, she returned to the studio and rifled among stacks of papers and detritus in search of the thing. Her eye landed on the shape of a dog's head among the piles. Franny picked up the sheet and examined it, Josh's grubby but accomplished doodling filling the page, and stared. Immediately the sight of the boy's little tongue poked out in concentration came to mind. She grinned anew at the memory of him confusing someone being autistic with someone being artistic, then gathered up five or so similarly decorated sheets, folded them roughly and threw them in the bin.

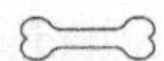

At the gardens, Franny procrastinated by visiting the café-kiosk for a disgracefully overpriced coffee and muffin. Pigeons pecked around her table, the sight of their waddling rears momentarily reminding her of Marg. She laughed at her wickedness then realised she should ring and check in on her sister-in-law. The woman had put her life on hold for a couple of weeks there and deserved some recognition. While thinking about this Franny's attention became snared in a conversation going on behind her.

'It'll do. There's hardly any difference anyway. Just drink it so we can enjoy the sun.' The first speaker's tone was impatient, almost scolding.

'There's a great difference, dear. I can't abide Earl Grey with sugar. Can't you get me another? Or I'll go. I can go. I don't really like tea in polystyrene either, if I'm honest. Maybe they'll give me a proper cup.' The second speaker's voice was reedy, Katharine Hepburn in the latter years. Franny heard sounds of awkward shuffling. Pretending to reach down for something in the bag at her feet, she turned to glimpse the subjects of her eavesdropping.

A little bird of a woman with flyaway white hair was struggling to get out of one of the café's spindly outdoor-dining chairs and manoeuvre herself behind a wheelie walker. She was shaky on her feet but her hand was steady as it reached towards the take-away cup on the table.

'All right, all right, you win. I'll get it. Just sit down.' The bird-lady's companion was in her late fifties, early sixties in Franny's estimation. She had steel-grey hair cropped close to her head and was dressed in all black, right down to a functional black backpack and black-framed sunglasses. Franny found herself wondering whether the two women were relatives or employee and employer. The answer was no clearer when the woman in black said gruffly, 'Well, give me your purse. They won't give me another one for free.' She snatched the bird-woman's handbag, pulled out a purse and huffed off in search of a replacement Earl Grey.

The bird-woman eased back into the chair and sighed. Looking down at her hands, she fiddled with a sparkling diamond on her bony ring finger. At that moment Franny realised she was staring. Grabbing the first thing she could from her bag, the camera, she sat up and the movement caught the other woman's eye. Her small bow-like mouth gave a half smile, which Franny returned, adding extra wattage.

'Beautiful day for this time of year, isn't it?' said Franny. 'Good old Melbourne.'

'Personally, I'd rather be sitting indoors,' said the other woman. 'Too cold for me out here but my friend is a fresh air devotee. Was a time cafés were for sitting in, now they seem like backdrops. Anyway . . . I just do what I'm told.' She shrugged forlornly.

Franny gave a half smile and returned to her coffee. Something Frank's mother used to say came to mind: 'old age ain't worth the wait'. She took a final mouthful, crumpled the muffin wrapper, gathered her things and headed towards the garden's main entrance. On the way she encountered the Earl Grey procurer, carrying a ceramic mug while studying her mobile phone.

Leaning in, Franny tapped the woman on the shoulder. 'I think your friend is cold,' she said. 'Take her inside the café, for God's sake, if that what she says she wants to do.' Franny walked off, her walking stick thudding lightly against the asphalt. The other woman just stared.

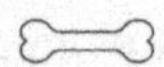

For an hour or so Franny worked away, sketching and photographing while dealing with the odd query from a tourist wanting to know where the bathrooms were, which gate was nearest a tram stop and where they might find a koala bear. By three o'clock she decided she'd had enough. Her leg was stiff and aching; the small folding stool she used for what Frank like to call her 'plein air posturing' seemed far lower and more uncomfortable than before. She realised she needed to get back to yoga with Calliope. With a stab of guilt, she also realised she had ignored a stream of calls and emails from the young teacher, concerned after she missed classes in the weeks surrounding the Swan Dive. Packing her things back inside her supply bag, Franny decided to pick up a little something as a form of apology from the garden's gift shop before she went home.

Browsing among the shelves of linen tea towels, plush penguins, model trams and heirloom tomato seeds, Franny's walking stick brushed against a display of wet weather ponchos. Momentarily she stared at them, wondering why they seemed so familiar, then remembered a previous apology-gift buying spree in this same shop. *Maybe I should be nicer to people*, she thought, *it would be cheaper.* Choosing a set of essential oils in bush scents, plus a coffee table book filled with shirt-free muscular men doing yoga poses against rugged landscapes, she took the gifts to the counter.

In the car, driving home, Johnny Cash came on the radio. As he sang about walking the line Franny's mind went back to the bird-lady and her carer-cum-tormentor from earlier in the day. She felt an unexpected surge of anger flood through her system but its source was unclear. After all, she didn't know the situation of the two women involved. Had no right to judge. Catching her eye in the rear-view mirror she decided to talk it out with Frank.

'I don't know why it got to me so much, to be honest, darling.' She turned the radio down to better order her thoughts. 'There could be a whole *Flowers in the Attic* thing going on with those two. Maybe that old biddy tormented the younger one for years. Or maybe she's just a demanding old so-and-so who's never happy. Maybe she hasn't paid the other woman's wages for six months. God only knows.'

Franny pulled up at a set of traffic lights and watched as a group of young girls in school uniforms walked past. 'You'd have a whole back story concocted by now, wouldn't you, my love?' she continued. 'Something about the older woman being the stepmother to the younger one. Adultery and betrayal galore. But really, the younger woman could just be having a train wreck of a day. Maybe she had terrible news herself this morning. Maybe her blood tests came back abnormal or the cat died. Maybe hanging around a café with an octogenarian was the last thing she felt like. You just never know what's going on with people, do you?'

Franny glanced over at the car beside her. The couple in the front seat were speaking intently to each other, as if in disagreement. Suddenly the woman on the passenger side slammed her hand down on the dashboard with considerable force. Involuntarily, Franny flinched. Simultaneously, three other things happened: the light turned green, the couple erupted into laughter and a small boy in a booster seat behind them came into Franny's view. He stuck out his tongue and glared at her as their car sailed past.

'See what I mean, darling,' she said. 'You just never know.' She looked over at her empty passenger seat, sighed, then turned up the music. 'Whatever way you cut it, maybe both those women today were out of choices.'

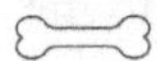

The working week was coming to an end and 'Drive with Karl' was in full flight. Franny's most despised politician had hit the headlines the day before after 'exposing' a funding program that enabled teenagers from refugee backgrounds to paint murals across a series of state-owned housing estates. Karl wasn't sure this was an appropriate use of taxpayers' money. His callers thought 'graffiti' should not be encouraged. Janice from McKinnon rang in to say her son Tyson had been fined for spray-painting a wall of the local railway station. Why, she wondered, was that not art? How could she secure her son some funding? He was, after all, a very talented boy who just hadn't found his calling yet.

Abandoning the paintbrush in her hand, Franny stood up and switched off the radio. 'For God's sake,' she said to Studio Frank. 'The world is going to hell in a handcart. I can't listen. It's not even funny anymore.' In the ensuing silence she heard the heft and wheeze of a vehicle pull up out front, followed by the tinny screech of sliding metal doors. Immediately, Whisky was at the window barking his little guts out while Soda ambled over and stood by her owner. Franny moved to get a better view. The night before she had indulged in some light 'riesling retail', her name for a delightful combination of online shopping paired with a few glasses of German white wine. Spurred on by another episode of Nigella, a burning need for cheese fondue had come upon her. As a result Franny would soon be the proud owner of a ceramic Heidi-branded fondue pot, charmingly illustrated with goat herders and mountain tops. 'It's too soon for that delivery,' she said to Whisky, nudging the terrier sideways so she could get a better view of the driveway.

Outside the day was grey and windy. A young man in a black Sikh-style turban wrestled with an unruly bunch of large silver and white balloons. He headed towards the Salernos' driveway, setting off a renewed bout of Whisky's barking. Franny silenced the dog with a stern 'shush'. Minutes later Sallyanne headed out towards the van alongside the now empty-handed young man. She signed an electronic gadget and took a cardboard box from him, waved and returned indoors.

Franny looked over at Studio Frank. 'Looks like someone's having a party,' she said.

Later, while getting changed from dog-walking gear into a Friday night YouTube concert and cocktail ensemble, Franny bent down to examine her injured leg. The scar formed a long, swollen line, reminding her of the piping on hot cross buns, if that piping was an angry purple-red in colour.

'What's good for scars? Aloe vera?' She looked over at Bedroom Frank questioningly. 'We had some somewhere, didn't we?' Pulling on the black velvet leggings she reserved for weekend nights, she finished dressing, tying a sash around the waist of a cheongsam-type blouse. She moved over to her bedside table and rummaged through its contents. At least a dozen bookmarks and twice as many hair ties and bobby pins were in there, mixed up with old cough-lolly wrappers, two pairs of over-the-counter reading glasses, a jumbo pack of aspirin and one miniature tennis ball she had obviously confiscated from Whisky one night before bed. No aloe vera.

Franny groaned in frustration then remembered Frank's old bedside drawers, which were crammed into a corner behind the door in her bedroom. A vision of him lathering gel all over himself after falling asleep in a deck chair at Anthea and David's country property came back to her. Besides having the squat piece of furniture moved when she was setting up her studio, Franny had barely touched the drawers since the week her husband died. His reading glasses were in there, as was the novel he'd been halfway through, plus the favourite little hair comb he always kept in his back pocket. The hospital had returned that as part of his 'belongings', the scent of California Poppy Oil still lingering on its tines. She took a deep breath and moved towards the seemingly benign item of furniture.

How one small constellation of wood, screws and handles could affect her so deeply was hard to fathom yet Franny knew, since her husband's passing, that she had become part of a silent, bereaved army, each member clinging to some personal talisman or memento mori that might never be abandoned. She comforted herself with stories of women who wore items of their late husband's clothing for months after they died or the mother who slept under her drowned son's doona cover, unable to wash it and lose his scent. Indeed, didn't one of Frank's uncles continue to cut out the daily newspaper's crossword puzzle for almost a decade after his wife passed, just because she had loved them so?

Yes, she avoided going near this set of drawers. Just knowing Frank's most mundane and everyday belongings rested inside made it something of a shrine, one she chose not to disturb. Imagining him reaching out at any time to grab his book and 'speccies' was comforting, as if he had only just stepped out of the room. The fact he would never perform this domestic ritual again was irrelevant; the combination of potential and memory was what mattered. Some days Franny needed to pretend her husband was still there, other days she needed proof that he'd been there to begin with.

She went straight to the bottom drawer. The contents of the top one she knew off by heart, its ordering fixed in her mind the way a tray of instruments must be for a surgical nurse.

This other drawer was neat, the product of Frank's more ordered mind. It contained a notebook, a pencil and a small stack of post-cards from various travels he'd bought but never sent. A banged-up wallet was tucked beside these, two old driving licences inside, plus a tiny snapshot of Mr Marmalade as a kitten. Franny smiled at the cat's round, golden face.

Digging deeper, she was intrigued to find a stack of old letters and postcards, even some weather-beaten aerograms covered with her handwriting, probably sent to a hotel somewhere while Frank travelled for work. At the bottom of the pile was a still crisp-looking white envelope, the writing across it clearly Frank's. His loopy, generous style spelled out the words, *To Franny, always my love.* She pulled her hand away abruptly, as if she had been scorched by some-thing on a hot stove. Then, breathing in and out twice, slowly and deeply, she picked it up, sliding out the handwritten letter within.

My darling girl,
I'm writing this to you on the morning of my 60th birthday. You're in the other room, fussing with breakfast mimosas before we head off to the fish market. I can hear you rattling about and swearing at the new puppy. I warned you a Cairn would be a handful but you wouldn't be told. Can never be told! One of the reasons I love you.

I'm not sure where I'm going with this. Part of me is spooked by the whole big six-o thing. You know Dad died at 59 from heart failure. I think I've been on eggshells this whole year at some level . . . only admitted it to myself in the last few weeks but I tell you, when I blow out those candles on the cake at Bello Cielo tonight, I'm going to do it with gusto, and more than a little relief.

You were gorgeous this morning. What's new? you'd say but it's always worth remarking on. The way you bounded in with those gifts, surprises you've probably been squirrelling away all year, and you looked like a teenager, all long legs and cotton pyjamas. How my heart soared. I don't know how many people ever get to feel the kind of love you shower on me. You pay attention to me in a way I don't even pay to myself. Just presenting me with Peter Temple's last book was testament to that fact. I remember tearing out the review from the newspaper and stashing it somewhere but then I'd forgotten all about it. Not you though, you remembered me mentioning it and voila it appears. I don't think, in all our years together, you've ever missed a step when it comes to supporting my dreams, desires and ambitions. It's almost too much sometimes but I love to be spoiled so don't ever give up.

So why am I writing this? Because I need to tell you again and again all you mean to me, all you have meant to me. How much I love you. I need you to know how much I appreciate your love for me but also our love together. How much I appreciate the blessing we received when we met at that house party all those years ago. Imagine if that rat-like punk couple hadn't decided to root in the bathroom? We would never have been two strangers, stumbling out to the garden for a pee. I would never have been embarrassed when you found me, willy out, spraying the lemon tree. I would never have watched those green eyes of yours look me up and down like a judge at a prestigious cattle show. And I would never have panicked and pissed on my shoes. They were vintage Converse you know!

Even those shoes bring it all home. You bought me Converse trainers for our first wedding anniversary. Always such a fabulous smart arse!

You're loved by so many people, it's one of the things I adore about you. Yes, this morning you were whingeing AGAIN about having a party and why can't we just celebrate alone but you know you adore it. You adore people, some of them at least. You say you don't want to give a speech because they all just come to see me and you're a loner at heart but it's not true. You're discerning, I'll admit it, but once you've chosen someone for your team then that's it, come hell or high water, and it's one of the things I admire so much about you.

Why else would Anthea and David have asked us to take care of Ellie if anything ever happened to them? After all, David's sister was a bloody mothercraft nurse or whatever they called them back then—but there was still no one Anth would prefer raising her daughter than you. That's not nothing, my love!

I feel like loving you has made me a better man, is that too corny to admit? If I died tomorrow—please God don't let me die tomorrow, I'd really like to read the Temple book for starters—I'd never change a day I lived with you.

Okay I'm pausing here because <u>of course</u> there's one day I would change and I would have her and I would have you and she would be at this birthday party tonight and she could speak instead of you and I could marvel at our miraculous daughter and the way your light shines in her. How you glow together, making me so proud.

And now I'm getting maudlin. Perhaps this is not a letter I will share with you after all. I'll sit on it, maybe try again later. You're singing out from the kitchen and I think I smell pancakes and bacon frying. You're frying and I'm crying, there's a country song somewhere in there.

Oh Franny, I have to get all of this out. I'm 60 and we made it to this milestone together and tonight I will watch you as you charm and dazzle the people who love us and you will shower them with attention and remember all their kids' and pets' names and you'll know who's going where and doing what and you'll encourage them and tease them and torment them and I will stand apart, Taittinger in hand (if David hasn't drunk it all, the bastard), and watch and know you are the greatest gift I could ever have dreamed of and everything you bring to my life, and everything I see you bring to others, is everything I'll ever need.

Oh my Franny, you make me believe in a benevolent God and we all know I'm a raving atheist. Thank you for getting me to 60.

Xxxx F!

Franny sat down heavily on the bed, letter in hand. She didn't dare look over at Bedroom Frank, the sensation of being winded already making her lightheaded. Seeing his gorgeous young face right now would have God knows what effect. She gulped in air, glancing around, wishing she had a drink.

Eyes back on the letter, she re-read the part about speeches and Bello Cielo. A mass of memories crowded her mind like a heavy-handed movie montage. Frank's sixtieth began at seven in the evening and lasted until four the next morning. Later that day the Calderwoods hosted an afternoon recovery barbecue at their home. 'Hence the fish market,' Franny said to herself.

She remembered the beautiful Sophia Webster wedge-heeled shoes she wore on the night. *Whatever happened to them?* popped into her feral brain.

She remembered Frank wiping away tears as his old mate Jeff spoke of their years in the advertising and political worlds, Frank's way with words and knack with ego-laden clients. From memory Jeff called Frank one of the world's last true gentlemen and then got a little misty himself. He said they'd both had their ups and downs in life, but Frank weathered his with courage and grace. Grace. The word had struck Franny at the time. Not normally one used to describe a man, unless he was a ballet dancer. She had loved it then and loved it now. She gulped once more. Poor Jeff. What the hell had happened with the lung cancer? Had she even bothered to check in with Di? Di, who on the night of Frank's sixtieth, organised an extravagant cake in the shape of a typewriter. Di, who had stayed sober till the bitter end so she could drive the birthday boy and his carload of gifts home. Di, who had done nothing wrong in the last few years except try to be Franny's loyal and present friend.

Dropping the letter on the bed beside her, Franny leaned forward, head in hands, eyes to the floor. Guilt sent a wave of heat through her body. Regret formed a lump in her throat.

Suddenly, her head snapped up. 'For fuck's sake,' she said. 'This is it in a nutshell, isn't it? All the problems of all the people. Even now. I can't have just a moment to focus on my dead fucking husband. What about my poor, poor Frank?' She grabbed at the letter once more, re-reading his words, straining to imagine his voice as he called her his darling girl, remembering their lost but precious Tilly.

Standing up, she finally looked over at Bedroom Frank, tears erupting with brutal force. She couldn't stop, wasn't breathing properly. The dogs appeared in the bedroom door, Whisky jumping up on the bed, sniffing at the letter, Soda nuzzling against Franny's leg. Her sounds were frightening them.

'It's okay, my loves, it's okay,' she said eventually, through hiccups, stroking both their ears at once. 'The old lady's just missing her Frank.' Hearing the name, Whisky's head cocked to one side and his brown eyes darted around the room. Franny's heart broke anew. Grief, pain, anger—they pushed out against her chest with physical force. She threw down the letter again and scooped up the dog. 'Oh, my little terrorist, I know, I know, you miss him too.'

Still hugging Whisky's squirming, stocky body close to her chest, Franny moved awkwardly out towards the kitchen. Within seconds she realised her recovering leg and a ten-kilo Cairn terrier were not a match made in heaven. She dropped the dog clumsily then lurched on.

The kitchen bench was strewn with ingredients for a lemon and spinach risotto she had planned. Going directly to the refrigerator, Franny pulled out the bottle of riesling from the night before and poured a large glass. Slugging greedily, she surveyed the distinctive little red-and-white sack of Spanish Calasparra rice that Frank had loved to cook with when the budget allowed. Costing more than fifteen dollars a kilo, it was an outrageous indulgence, but handling the little cotton bag it came in, and making sure she had Ligurian olive oil on hand to complement it, were the pleasures she relied on now, the rituals and affectations that got her through the days.

Franny finished the glass of wine and looked over at Kitchen Frank. The big rubber breasts on his apron jutted out like pink-tipped cannons. 'Oh, my angel,' she said, her voice ragged from crying. 'What would you think of your darling girl now?'

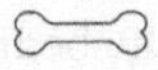

Whisky's barking broke through her sleep. Franny and the dogs had been out early, walking the beach cliffs for almost two hours, stopping on the way home for a newspaper and coffee, a bag of doggy treats and two almond croissants. Back home she had made a cup of tea and sat down in the lounge room for a moment's rest. Whether minutes or hours had passed since then she was not entirely sure.

The night before had been a restless one, no risotto made, no additional wine drunk. The 'crying and wailing', as Franny thought of it, had left her stomach churning and head sore. In the end, retreating to her studio, Franny painted and sipped green tea till the wee hours of the morning.

'Bloody hell,' she said to Lounge Room Frank. 'What's the kerfuffle?'

Hoisting herself up from the sofa where she'd dozed off, she went to the back door in search of the noise maker. Soda, previously snoozing alongside her owner, shook herself and half-heartedly followed.

Whisky's scruffy rear end poked out beside the hydrangea. The way it moved, all twitching and jiggling, indicated some kind of digging was underway. Immediately Franny remembered the hole beneath the fence where Josh, Whisky and a pink-and-blue tennis ball had initially bonded. She tipped her head back and sighed in frustration. *Note to self, get the bloody thing fixed!*

Opening the door, she headed into the garden, but before she could call out the dog's name, Franny noticed activity on the other side of the fence. Pop music played and the smell of barbecue wafted over. Bobbing black and silver balloons were just visible.

'Gem, can you bring the paper towel out with you?' Sallyanne's voice sang out.

'Sure thing,' came another female voice. 'Will I bring the veggie burgers now too?'

The Salernos' back door banged and Franny's attention returned to her dog. Whisky was really going for it. *Digging towards China*, Franny thought and grinned when she realised this was probably a politically incorrect saying now. She wanted to halt the ruination of her garden bed, but not at the cost of anyone next door realising she was there.

'They'll think I'm eavesdropping on their bloody party,' she said to Soda quietly. Pondering this dilemma, Franny heard a familiar little voice saying, 'Just one more Cheezel and that's it.'

Ah ha, thought Franny, *the plot thickens*. She moved over to the fence and tapped her dog's rear. Whisky glanced back momentarily before returning his snack-based focus to the hole beneath the fence.

'Whisky, stop it,' said Franny. 'Get out of there.' The dog's wiggling ceased momentarily but only because the sound of a Cheezel being crunched could be heard.

'Whisky, come!' Franny's voice was quiet but stern. The terrier edged back a microscopic distance from the fence.

'Franny, is that you?' Josh could not contain the excitement in his voice. 'Hello, Franny, are you there?'

Shockingly, Franny felt a lump form in her throat. It felt like forever since she'd heard that little cartoon voice. She coughed and said, 'Hello, Josh. How are you?'

'I'm good, Franny. It's my birthday. Mummy's making burgers.'

'That's nice.' She stopped herself before adding the word 'darling'. 'You're nine then?'

'Yup. Naughty nine, Mum says. She got me an easel, you know, like yours but a bit smaller. I can be like you now, a proper artist.'

'That's a perfect pressie,' said Franny. 'All you need is a smock and a beret.'

'A what?'

'Nothing. Doesn't matter.'

Suddenly another voice chimed in. 'Joshie, what are you doing? I thought you were going to help me set the table.' Franny heard Josh scuffling a little on his side of the fence. Whisky smashed his nose into the hole again and then the same voice added, 'You're not messing around with that dog again, are you? I thought Mummy told you to stop.'

'I'm just giving him a Cheezel, Aunty Gem,' said Josh.

Footsteps came towards the fence. 'God, Josh, the two of you have made quite a mess of this. Sallyanne,' the voice got louder, 'have you seen the mess your son and that mutt next door have created?

You're going to have to do something about it. The thing'll be over here before you know it.'

'Whisky's not a mutt,' complained Josh. 'He's my friend. Isn't he, Franny?'

Franny bit her lip. Suddenly she felt like the neighbourhood weirdo, snooping around where she wasn't wanted.

More shuffling from the other side of the fence then the woman's voice, presumably Aunty Gem, said to Josh, 'Are you talking to someone, Joshie?'

'He's talking to me.' Franny kept her voice low and even. 'The mutt's owner. And I agree this is a mess. They've all but mutilated my hydrangea. I'll get it seen to next week.'

'Oh sorry, I didn't realise anyone was there,' said Gem. 'Obviously, it's none of my business.'

'Doesn't matter. I hadn't realised things were so bad,' said Franny. 'Anyway, I have to go. Happy birthday, Josh. Enjoy your burgers.'

Josh pushed his face up between the fence palings. 'Want one, Franny? You could come over. She's melting cheese on top.'

For an awkward moment there was silence, both adults unwilling to be the first to speak. Sallyanne's voice split through the moment. She yelled out, 'What the heck are you guys up to over there? These buns aren't going to butter themselves.' Then added, 'Dee, will you get off that phone and get out here now? I won't ask you again.'

Josh pressed up against the fence again. 'Mummy said I had to give you time to yourself, Franny, but you're all better now aren't you? You've had enough of yourself. Come over, it's only the four of us. We have lots to eat.'

Franny looked down at Whisky. Whisky looked eagerly up at her. His nose twitched at the aroma of frying meat and onions.

'Joshie darling, what did I hear Mummy telling you only this morning?' said Gem. 'Franny's very busy at the moment. You're supposed to be leaving her alone.'

Josh made a pained sound. 'But?'

'Say bye bye,' said Gem.

Josh remained silent. A lone Cheezel appeared under the hole in the fence and Whisky dived at it. Franny watched the small yellow ring disappear then grabbed the dog by the collar and said, once more, 'Happy birthday, Josh. Enjoy the easel. And the Cheezel.' Her little neighbour giggled at the rhyme. 'Inside Whisky,' she said, heading back to her house.

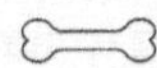

A couple of hours later, when the barbecue smells had dissipated and the music had moved inside, Franny went out to her potting shed and grabbed an old terracotta pot. She shoved it up against the hole in the fence and plonked a bag of potting mix inside to weigh it down. Whisky, her constant shadow throughout these operations, looked on forlornly.

'I know, boy. Gonna have to find yourself another playmate.'

31

Things people say

'The bean soup special, the radicchio salad and a glass of the Nals Margreid Punggl pinot grigio, thank you, dear.' Pushing her glasses up on her head, Franny placed the menu back on the table and looked up at the young blond waiter. 'Where are Paolo and Jenna?'

'One of the wine distributors is flying them and a few other restaurateurs up to the Strathbogie Ranges for some tastings. Is there something I can help with?' He gave her a neutral stare, wary in case she was heading into disgruntled customer territory.

'No, no, they're just old friends. I haven't been in since Benjamin left.'

'Benjamin?'

'The previous sommelier. Anyway, what's your name?'

'Kaden.' He removed the second cutlery setting and wine glass from the table and placed a water glass in front of her. 'Will that be all for the moment?'

Franny nodded and watched the young man head back towards the kitchen. Picking up her *New Yorker* she scanned the contents page, hoping someone amusing like David Sedaris was featured; she felt she needed a lift. Instead there was a large piece on the US postal service and a deep dive into police unions. Franny groaned and flicked to a movie review.

Her phone pinged. It was Anthea, who had been sending brief texts to Franny once a week since the Swan Dive. Franny had been responding in an equally succinct manner.

> Anthea: Did you find someone to fix the fence etc?

Franny took a sip of the wine that arrived at her table and sent a message back.

> Franny: Yes. They're called GOOD NEIGHBOURS. Do fencing and landscaping.
>
> Anthea: Good fences, good neighbours. Nice one. Ideal for you.
>
> Franny: Very funny. Start tomorrow.
>
> Anthea: Okay. Just so you know, I'm off to Blue Mountains for a yoga retreat tomorrow. Away for one week. Ellie around if you need anything.

Though disgusted with herself, Franny registered a pang of jealousy. It was she who had introduced Anthea to yoga. She sent another text.

> Franny: Blue Mountains. Sounds nice. You should pop in and see Marg.

Her phone pinged again immediately.

> Anthea: Marg told me about it. We're going together.

Franny stared at her phone. She felt genuinely churned up and the realisation infuriated her. She picked up her phone, poised to send a sarcastic note about packing earplugs to drown out Marg's snoring, but caught herself in time.

> Franny: Lovely. You two will have a ball. You deserve it.

Anthea didn't respond except to tag a little thumbs-up beside Franny's own sent message. Franny didn't know how to do that herself; she assumed Elouise had taught her mother this techno-trickery.

She was pondering this when her phone pinged again. This time it was Sallyanne.

> Sallyanne: Franny, Sallyanne here. Hope you are well. Just wanted to let you know Alexander Dempsey has been a huge help with the whole Danny 'situation'. The kids don't have to see him for at least four or so months. Such a relief! Thank you again for putting me in touch with him. I will always appreciate it.

As Franny stared at her phone screen, the waiter interrupted, placing a huge white bowl and a small basket of crusty bread before her. 'I'll be back with the salad in a second. Want parmesan or anything else? Another glass of wine?'

Franny looked at her near empty glass and blinked. The day outside was beautiful. Winter sunshine glinted off the tables set along the footpath outside Bello Cielo.

'No, that's fine. Thank you.' She put her credit card down on the table. 'I have some things to do when I get home. You might as well fix the bill up for me now so I can dash as soon as I finish.'

The waiter shrugged, smiled briefly and turned away, taking her card with him.

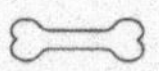

Lenny from Good Neighbours reminded Franny of a British bulldog. His curly red hair was pulled back in a thick ponytail and he wore charcoal-grey overalls and huge mustard-coloured steel-capped boots.

'Hello, Mrs Calderwood. You're looking chipper today.' He held out a ribeye-sized hand for Franny to shake. The two had met the week before when Franny walked Lenny and his colleague Cam around her property, pointing out the work she wanted done and listening to the young men's additional ideas.

'Great news you got the landlord next door to stump up for fixing the fence,' said Lenny, gently nudging Franny out of the way as Cam and another much younger, wiry-looking chap, introduced as Wyatt, came through the gate. Each carried a selection of tools and other hardware.

'Well I didn't give him much choice. And I'm paying the majority seeing it's all part of my grander garden overhaul.' Franny followed the trio inside the yard, opening the back door so the dogs could come out and sniff the visitors. 'This is Whisky and Soda,' she said, and Whisky gave a bark. 'I'll keep them out of your way but if they get a good sniff and a nuzzle with you now, things will play out easier in the long run.'

Fifteen minutes later she was out again with a tray bearing three cups of hot, sweet coffee, a plate piled high with homemade zucchini slice and a packet of chocolate ripple biscuits. 'Knock yourselves out, lads,' she said, placing the bounty on her patio table. 'Just keep the dogs away.'

'The white bamboo's a great choice,' said Lenny, digging into his second zucchini-laden slice. 'You'll just have to keep on top of it, as I said, because it can get to twelve metres high. Still, that's what we're here for if you need us down the track.' He grinned and slurped coffee.

'Yes, a reinforced fence, a nice tall screen of bamboo and a lovely pergola near the back of the yard. My own private Idaho. I won't know myself.' Franny whacked Whisky's nose away from the table of treats.

'You've got a great set-up here, Mrs Calderwood,' said Cam, scratching his thick neat beard and peering into the glass doors at the back of the house. 'I can see you've got a pretty sweet vinyl collection in there. I love it. Old school.'

'Feel free to have a look if you're in and out to use the loo,' said Franny.

Lenny tutted. 'The boys aren't here for their amusement.' He frowned at Cam and Wyatt. 'Speaking of, how about we get to work.'

For a few days in a row, staff from Good Neighbours Fencing and Landscaping came and went, arriving before eight each morning, disappearing for a lunch hour then working onwards till dusk. They kept their radio playing low and their language tame. At one stage Franny heard a 'Jules' would be coming and she thought she would finally be meeting a female team member. Instead Jules, as in Julian, arrived dressed in camouflage pants and a Gough Whitlam 'It's time' T-shirt. He was bald and bearded, with the squat build of a wrestler crossed with a garden gnome. He said little but worked fast, doing everything needed to fit the pergola with plumbing.

Franny tried to keep herself and the dogs out of their combined beards and long hair. On the third day she popped in to see Wayne at The Good Drop and ask what the modern tradesperson liked to drink. Frank always rewarded anyone working at the Calderwoods' house with a quality tipple in the midst of the job; he believed it contributed to a superior standard of work.

'Hello, Franny,' said Wayne when she entered the bottle shop. 'You're in early. Haven't seen you without the car for a while.'

He gestured to Franny's shopping jeep and the two dogs tied up by the front door of the store. 'Does that mean the leg's better?'

'Hello, Wayne. It does indeed. Better every day.' The Good Drop's manager was under the impression Franny had tripped over Soda's lead and fallen on a fence post while out walking somewhere at the beach.

She wiggled her finger to coax the bottle shop manager out from behind his counter and headed over to the beer fridge. 'So, I have a crack team of tradies in the backyard working up a sweat and I thought I'd reward them with something frothy and delightful to finish the week. What do you recommend?'

'Sounds interesting. What are you getting done?'

'I'm getting my privacy back, that's what I'm getting done. The house next door is a rental and, well, you know what it's like. You never know who might be moving in next.'

'Ah, I get you completely.' Wayne nodded enthusiastically, hitting on a favourite topic. 'We've got a bunch of students in the house behind us and they're either burning pans and stinking out my backyard or playing basketball at midnight. Bloody nightmare. The cat's on anxiety medicine.'

'Yes, well my situation's not as bad as that but better to be on the safe side.'

'Actually,' said Wayne, 'I thought you said a nice family moved in a few months ago. I seem to recall you in here buying champagne for Mother's Day.'

Franny felt her cheeks redden. 'Hmm, they're still there, but for how long? No, ever since the old Greek family moved, I've wanted to fix things up a bit. And now's the time.'

Wayne seemed to find this explanation satisfactory. 'Alrighty,' he said. 'Well, the young blokes love fancy beers these days. How about getting some Little Creatures or a bit of Stone & Wood?' He moved over to the fridge and pulled out an amber bottle with a green label.

'Wayne, you might as well be talking another language to me. They both sound like the names of folk songs or kids' storybooks. I'll get a slab of both. Oh damn.' She looked out at the dogs. 'Now I wish I'd brought the car.'

'No problem. I'll get Jessie to drop it over.' He nodded back towards the counter where a black-haired girl channelling the wraith look was restocking the cigarettes. 'She's on her way home in the next hour or so; she can drop the beer at your place.'

The wraith apparently had good hearing. 'What are you saying about me?' Jessie called out in a bright, girlish voice at odds with her zombie-apocalypse fashion ensemble.

'I said you'd happily drop a couple of slabs of beer off to Mrs Calderwood's house on the way home. Okay? She doesn't have her car.'

Jessie agreed to the plan but Franny insisted Wayne carry the slabs out to the girl's car.

'I could do that myself,' said Jessie as she watched her boss heave the beers out of the walk-in refrigerator.

'Of course you could, dear,' said Franny. 'But experience tells me you'll do more than your share of heavy lifting for men over the years. My advice is to get them to pitch in whenever you see a chance.'

'Ha! Love it,' said Jessie. She let out a raucous laugh, revealing a silver tongue stud in the process.

Good God, hope she doesn't swallow that thing, thought Franny, trying not to stare.

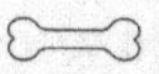

'Jesus Christ!' Franny shouted, startled by the knocking on the window of her studio where she was immersed in a painting. Max Richter blared from her speakers, counteracting the noise of drilling and sawing emanating from the backyard. The dogs were splayed on the patio out back, keeping a general eye on the boys from Good Neighbours and recuperating from their walk to the shops.

'Where do you want it?' Jessie shouted, tapping her car keys against the glass. 'Is someone going to bring them in? I'm not carrying two slabs. Occ health and safety, you know.' She winked at Franny theatrically.

Grinning, Franny held up one long finger to indicate the girl should stay put then headed out to the backyard where Wyatt was standing next to a wheelbarrow, slurping water from a water bottle.

'You wouldn't be a dear and go help the young lady from the bottle shop bring in two slabs of beer would you, Wyatt? She's in the driveway.' Franny looked around for Lenny, wondering if she needed the boss man's imprimatur.

Wyatt's beautifully arched dark eyebrows shot up. Franny hadn't dealt with him much in the last few days and was taken aback by the deep, gravelly voice emanating from an almost delicate frame. 'Happy to help, Mrs C,' he said eagerly then yelled out behind him, 'Just giving the client a hand!'

Jessie was parked on the other side of the road, unable to get closer to the house because of the workmen's vehicles. She leaned against the outside of a boxy white van, fingers flying across her mobile phone. When Franny called to her, the young woman slid the phone into the back pocket of her jeans and moved to open the van's rear doors.

'All good?' Franny turned to look at Wyatt.

He stared straight ahead and grinned. 'I reckon.' A wolfish expression spread across his face as he headed over the road.

Franny shook her head in amusement then frowned when she realised her ever-present neighbour Tarzan lurked in his front yard, trademark stretch of white, hairy belly showing from beneath a faded T-shirt as he half-heartedly watered some flowerbeds. He raised a hand in greeting and winked but Franny pretended not to see, bending instead to pluck at a weed near the driveway. Doing so, she noticed feet in a familiar pair of white trainers hanging over the low fence next door.

'Hello, Mrs Calderwood,' said Dee in a mock-formal tone.

Franny stood up with a groan. 'Hello, Miss Salerno.'

'You know only old people make noises like that when they move about.'

'I am old.'

'Since when?'

'Hardy ha ha. What are you doing hanging around out here like a bad smell?'

'I'm studying for exams, they let you do it from home. And I'm waiting to see Wyatt. We're mates.'

'Really?' Franny looked across to where the young man in question was balancing a slab of beer on one narrow hip while saying something so hilarious it had made a wraith laugh. 'Popular boy.'

'He just gives me a ciggie sometimes. God, not everything's about sex. I don't even like him like that.' Dee jumped off the fence and walked over to Franny, still keeping her eyes on the young couple across the road. 'Who is that anyway?'

'Jessie from The Good Drop. She's new I think.'

'Doesn't look old enough to be driving a car. And what's with the hair? She looks like whatshername from *The Addams Family*.'

'Hmm. What do you care? If she's working and driving she's obviously older than you. More Wyatt's age.'

Dee looked over at Franny and crossed her eyes. 'Whatever.' She fiddled with one of the beaded hoop earrings she wore. 'So, what's going on? Landlord told Mum work was going on next door and we just had to lump it. Then Wyatt said you're putting up a new fence.'

'I very much doubt Mr Kaur told Sallyanne she had to lump anything. And no, it's not a new fence. You'd notice a gaping hole next door surely. It's just some mending and then a bit of a redesign. Upping my privacy and comfort levels a tad.'

Dee grunted but didn't say anything, her eyes back on Jessie and Wyatt, the latter now trying to balance one ungainly stack of beer on top of the other. It was a struggle.

'Why don't you bring one in at a time,' Franny called out. 'You're going to strain something or you're going to drop the beer. Either way, you lose.'

Wyatt put the beers down on the nature strip and gave a shrug before resuming animated chit-chat with Jessie.

'Why do girls always like the pretty morons?' said Franny.

'He's not a—' Dee caught herself before finishing the sentence.

Franny grinned knowingly. 'In my book, anyone who gives an underage child a cigarette is a moron.'

'For the millionth time I am not a child.' Dee's hands went to her hips. 'And you gave me booze. That must make you worse than a moron.'

Franny laughed. 'A million things make me worse than a moron, dear.' She then spun around, put two fingers in her mouth and gave a piercing whistle. 'Hey, Romeo,' she shouted to Wyatt. 'How about we let Jessie go back to her life and you and I get back inside?'

The noise brought Lenny out to the driveway, shadowed by the dogs. 'Jesus,' said Franny. 'What is this? A bloody street party?'

Tarzan could not hide his interest now and had come so close to the boundary of his property he was basically just watering the footpath in front of it. Franny yelled out to him, 'All happening today, Trevor, isn't it?'

Tarzan looked around him in confusion before yelling out, 'My name's not Trevor.'

'That's nice, dear.' Franny gave him a thumbs-up then turned her back on him.

'What's going on?' asked Lenny.

'I don't care to know my neighbour's name,' said Franny, 'and I'm having beers delivered for you boys and Wyatt's helping me get them inside.' She nodded towards the young man now struggling across the road with his burden, legs visibly buckling.

Lenny laughed and headed over to help salvage his employee's dignity. With Jessie pulling away in the van and Lenny, Wyatt, Dee, Soda, Whisky and Franny now all grouped in the driveway, Franny said, 'Shall we just open a couple out here now?'

Wyatt beamed at this idea until he saw Franny wink and realised this was a joke. 'Just teasing,' she said. 'No drinking in the driveway. And no smoking while I'm at it, especially with young girls who are minors.'

Lenny looked over at Wyatt and grimaced. 'Mate?'

'What? She said she was seventeen.' Wyatt gave a sideway glance at Dee whose cheeks burned red.

The expression on Lenny's face suggested an inner struggle to control his temper. 'Wyatt, we'll talk about this later. Mrs C, I apologise on his behalf. This is not the kind of behaviour we pride ourselves on at Good Neighbours. I'm very sorry.'

'Well it's not his fault this one is dumb enough to smoke.' She jerked her head towards Dee. 'But let's all keep to our own sides of the fence, literally, till the job's done and we'll say no more about it.' She looked at Dee. 'I assume you will let this young gentleman concentrate on his work now, Dee.'

The teenager held up her middle finger.

Swatting at it, Franny said, 'Now it's my turn to apologise, Lenny. In Dee's world that passes for a legitimate response. Why don't you lads get back inside, and I'll see you in there. The beers are of course for you to divvy up as you see fit.'

Lenny, who held a slab with the ease of someone holding a tiny kitten, shot out a hand for Franny to shake. 'You're a class act, Mrs C.' He and Wyatt moved back inside.

'Right, I better go too,' said Franny. She looked down at the dogs. 'That goes for you two as well.'

'Did you have to embarrass me like that?' Dee kneeled to scratch Soda behind the ear.

'I just stated the facts, dear.'

Dee shook her head in frustration. 'It's weird not seeing you anymore.' She kept her eyes on the dog as she spoke.

'I'm sure you'll cope.'

When Dee looked up Franny saw the hurt in her eyes. Franny bit her lip and said, 'Yes, it is a bit weird for me too but probably for the best. An old windbag like me is better off on her own. And you lot have plenty to be getting on with.'

Giving the dogs a final pat, Dee stood up. 'It's that Elouise's fault, you know. I think it's the things she said on the day she came back to grab your stuff that got Mum all crazy. I heard Mum repeating them to her mate Gem on the phone.'

'Things?' Franny wondered if this was a topic she wished to pursue but Elouise was famously discreet. Franny was both shocked and curious to see what she would share with little more than a stranger.

Dee coloured, possibly regretting having launched this grenade, then dived back in. 'She said you did this every year around the time Frank died. Said you locked yourself away for a month the first time. She said this time you were pissed and fell over something in the yard and even hinted that Mum should be careful about putting us in the car with you. She said you weren't grandma material or something like that, which seemed kind of rough, to be honest. She even said Mum should start paying for babysitters.'

Franny's eyes opened wide. 'Well, well, my goddaughter said quite a lot, didn't she?'

'To be fair, Mum said she might have been in a bit of shock. You know, because she was the one who saw you first and got the ambo and everything.' Dee shrugged. 'Either way, when we did all the dog handover stuff afterwards, she never said anything else mean to me. Actually, I think she apologised to Mum later so . . .'

Franny gave a small nod. 'Yep. Bit of shock I think. But she's a bit angry with me too. Rightly so, no doubt.'

'I don't know why she should be angry with you, Franny. You hurt yourself, not her.'

'Well, I'm not sure that's true but, regardless, I can understand your mum's point of view. And we should respect it.' Franny reached out and touched Dee on the cheek gently. 'Nice earrings by the way.' She turned to walk inside.

'Did Mum tell you about Dad?' Dee's eyes were shining. 'He has to do an anger management course and something I think's called sensitivity training too before he can see Josh or me. We're off the hook for months Mum reckons.'

'Your mother sent an SMS to say there'd been some progress, yes. I'm glad things have improved.'

Dee stood and looked up at the older woman. 'Now Dad's folks, his whole family, also know what's been going on. The shit's really hitting the fan.'

'I see.'

'Don't you care anymore, Franny?'

Franny looked at the young girl and exhaled. 'Of course I care, honey. I think it's great that you three are getting a chance to settle into your new lives and hopefully this will help your dad too.'

'Sometimes I can't believe all the shit that has happened.' Dee played with her earring again.

'Your dad's not a lost cause, Dee. This could be the thing that snaps him out of it, helps him see the sense in things. I'm sure eventually you and Josh will be reunited with him in some nice way.'

'I wasn't talking about Dad.'

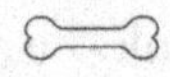

Nancy Friol was up in arms and it was Hilary Mantel's fault.

'She wants us all to boycott reading *Bring Up the Bodies*,' Franny said with a cackle, looking over to Desk Frank, a framed photograph added to the studio in the aftermath of the Swan Dive.

The image was taken by Franny herself, an impromptu portrait snapped as Frank stood reading aloud from a recipe book one day when he had been in the process of planning an upcoming dinner. She recalled wanting to be left alone at the time to concentrate on a series of in-progress photographs she was taking to accompany a work being published in an art journal.

'Look up, dear.' She took the photograph. 'This is an image of an annoying man. I am going to frame it and call it Annoying Husband. What do you think?'

Frank stuck out his lower lip. 'I just want to make sure you're happy with the menu.'

'You just want me to tell you how clever you are.' Moving over to kiss him on the protruding lip, she said, 'Now vamoose and save your Betty Crocker act for someone who cares.'

Turning back to her laptop now, Franny continued skim-reading The Wuthering Club's page. 'Apparently Nancy doesn't understand our ongoing obsession with dead white men and thinks it should end. We should be reading books by or about Indigenous brothers and sisters from our own and other countries as well as,' Franny peered more closely at the screen, 'works from the LGBTQIA community. Hell, that looks like she's added extra letters.' Franny opened another tab in Google and typed in 'LGBTQIA' then looked back at Desk Frank.

'Bugger, I'm behind the times, darling. I'd only gotten as far as LGBTQ but there's an "I" and an "A" now too, did you know? Standing for intersex and asexual or allied, apparently. Trust Miss Right-On-Friol to be up with the latest lingo.' Franny picked up the glass of sauvignon blanc she was drinking and sighed. 'To be honest, darling, I'm kind of with Nance on this one, but not necessarily for the same reasons. I don't think I can face another of those doorstop novels, as much as I love la dame Mantel. Maybe I'm just getting squeamish in my old age but I don't feel I can take another beheading.' She closed the Facebook page and opened her email program, sighing once more.

Since her driveway conversation with Dee two days earlier, Elouise had been on Franny's mind. A precious part of the Calderwoods' life since the day she was born, Frank had called himself the girl's fairy godfather. The passion the pair eventually shared for writing simply strengthened the bond.

Taking another sip, Franny wrote:

> Dear Ellie,
> Guess who? I don't think I ever thanked you properly for all the care and help you gave after my recent mishap. I'd love to get you a gift but God knows what young ones like you are into these days. Send me your banking details and I'll deposit some funds. That way you can pick yourself up something nice. Maybe get a little something for your mum too? Love, F.

Franny shut down the laptop, sipping wine as she watched the screen turn black. 'Well there's a little olive branch,' she said aloud. She looked at Desk Frank. 'Okay, maybe more of a twig but it's something.'

32

And the award goes to

Work on the garden was almost complete but bad weather was hampering operations. The Rolling Stones blasted through the studio, drowning out the sounds of workmen and blustery winds combined. Franny was fiddling about with bottles and brushes in the en suite, meaning she jumped when Lenny appeared at her studio door.

'Sorry Mrs C, didn't mean to startle you. It's just that it's about to piss down, I mean rain, so we're going to pack up and go. Hopefully we can start a little earlier tomorrow.'

Franny looked out the window. Fat drops were already falling from a blackening sky and thunder rumbled. 'Of course, Len, you should go. It's going to get nasty. Text me tomorrow and we'll see what's what. Maybe you should wait till after the weekend.'

'We've got jobs backing up but let me see. We're almost done.' He looked at his mobile phone. 'We made it to three o'clock today, which is better than I hoped. We won't let you down.' He gave a wink.

'I'll miss you boys, you know,' said Franny. 'Even wily Wyatt. Quite the lady killer that one.'

Lenny rolled his eyes before turning away. 'I am not telling him you said that,' he called over his shoulder.

A little later, music still loud, Franny stood at her easel chewing on the end of a wooden paintbrush. The rain was really pelting down, hitting the driveway with such force it splashed back up towards the sky. The studio windows rattled a little and Whisky was nowhere to be seen, having disappeared under the bed in Franny's room at the first sign of lightning and thunder. His famed terrier courage abandoned him when it came to weather. Soda, on the other hand, lolled beside the window, gazing out at the rain, occasionally looking back at her owner with sleepy affection. Storms never bothered the golden retriever, but, looking at her now, Franny wondered if she was also becoming a little deaf. She put down the paintbrush and moved to her desk where she scribbled 'vet, hearing' on a sticky note before returning to the easel. While doing so, she thought she heard a car's brakes screeching. Soda, ears clearly working well enough to notice this too, sat up, pressing her nose against the glass.

'It's okay, honey,' cooed Franny. 'Someone in Ipswich Street can't drive in the wet. Probably bloody Tarzan.' She went back to work while the dog remained upright and alert.

Within minutes the studio lights flickered, and The Rolling Stones halted abruptly. Franny cracked her knuckles and rolled her shoulders.

'You know what, Lady Soda, I think we might call it quits for today. It's a bit chilly and miserable in here for two old ladies. Let's batten down the hatches out back, fire up the telly and have an early dinner. What do you say?'

Soda might not have been a Rhodes Scholar but she recognised the word 'dinner'. Her tail began its trademark slow thump while

Franny stashed supplies in the en suite, closed the studio's blinds and walked out, the dog behind her.

In the kitchen, just as she held a tumbler beneath the icemaker, Franny once more thought she heard something. Going over to the big glass windows looking onto the backyard, she realised a piece of tarpaulin belonging to the boys from Good Neighbours had escaped and was flying around.

'I should probably check everything is tucked up out there too,' she said to Lounge Room Frank. Looking over at Soda, Franny said, 'Stay there and guard the Tanqueray,' before slipping into an old waterproof jacket and walking outside.

It felt a lot later than four-thirty in the afternoon. The sky was a shade of blueish charcoal and the wind had started sending the rain sideways. Franny picked up one of her old garden shovels and threw it on top of the tarpaulin to hold it down.

'You have to go. Please, Dad. I think you should go.' The words came from over the fence.

Franny did a double-take, unsure of what she was hearing.

'Please, Daddy, I'm not going with you today. Call Mum and ask her. You have to go.' Drifting across the fence, muffled by the weather, Dee's voice still sounded tearful. Gently, Franny pulled back the hood of her jacket and strained to listen more intently.

A male voice growled, 'You're my fucking daughter. I can see you when I want to. Don't need that bitch's say-so.' There was a banging sound, the back door being shook, a fist or a foot hitting against it? Franny could not tell. She moved clumsily through mud and new bamboo plantings, trying to get closer to the fence.

'I am your father, you hear? I don't need strangers telling me what to do.' It was the man's voice again. 'Who the fuck do they think they are, anyway?' His words sounded slurred. 'Fucking ponces, interfering fucking ponces and smug bastards. You're my fucking kids. That whore—'

There was another loud bang and Dee cried out. Franny rushed inside her house, grabbing her mobile phone from the kitchen bench.

'Shit, shit, shit,' she said, remembering that earlier in the day she had switched it off as further defence against distractions. She scrambled to bring it to life now, her hands wet, touch slippery.

Shoving it into her pocket in frustration, Franny ran to the studio and looked around desperately. On the shelf beside Mr Marmalade was one of the sharpest, heaviest awards she had ever received. She picked up the ugly bronze and glass thing, felt its heft, and was off. Walking out the front door, she checked her phone again; she had a signal. When the person at the other end of the police emergency number answered Franny made her urgent, whispered plea.

Father and daughter stood on the step outside the family's back door. Danny Salerno had his daughter pinned against the wall, one hand on each of the girl's shoulders. Neither of them heard Franny unbolt the side gate and enter. Dee was sodden, her grey hooded jumper slick against her thin frame. She sobbed loudly.

'I'd say you have five minutes before the police arrive, Mr Salerno,' Franny said. She was behind Danny now, holding the award aloft. Removing his hands from Dee, he spun around.

'Who the fuck are you, old lady?' He stepped towards Franny.

'I'm the *old lady* next door and I'm a friend of your daughter's. You can see you're scaring her. You should go.'

Danny looked at the object in Franny's hand. 'Are you going to hit me with that thing?' His tone was incredulous.

'Thinking about it.'

Danny let out an ugly laugh and stumbled, half falling off the step. Dee slipped past him and ran to Franny who shoved the girl roughly behind her.

'I think you should give your daughter some space, Mr Salerno.' Franny continued to hold the award in the air. She turned to Dee. 'You okay, honey?'

Dee nodded and ran a sleeve underneath her dripping nose. She gulped through tears.

Danny came closer to the pair. Franny moved them both a step away from him. Even through the driving rain she could see how bloodshot his eyes were. His handsome face was unshaven.

'I just want to see my daughter. This is none of your business,' he said.

'Your behaviour is making it my business, Mr Salerno. Surely you can see that.' Franny looked out towards the driveway, hoping to see a police car.

Danny caught her glance. 'You didn't really call the cops, did you?'

'I did I'm afraid.'

He ran his hands through his hair and mumbled, 'I'll lose my driver's licence.'

'At the risk of sounding like a midday movie, I think you're on the brink of losing a lot more than that, dear.'

When he looked back at her, Danny's expression was a mix of anger and confusion.

'Just go, Dad, for God's sake.' Dee, no longer crying, stepped out from behind Franny. She reached up, took the award out of Franny's hand and placed it on the ground.

'Dee's right, Mr Salerno. If seeing your kids is really what you want, as opposed to just trying to terrorise them and their mother, then you should go. Now. Though I'd personally prefer it if you stayed and faced the law.'

'Jesus, you're an interfering bitch, you know that?' Danny lurched towards Dee, hands outstretched. Franny moved to block him but the girl nudged her away.

'It's okay, Franny.' She faced her father. 'Isn't it, Dad?'

Danny Salerno looked at his daughter. Dropping his hands to his sides, he started to weep.

'Dad, please go.' As Dee spoke a car pulled into the Salernos' driveway, its doors quickly opening.

'We're out here,' yelled Franny.

Dee shook her head, face stricken, while her father continued to stare at her and weep. 'Oh Daddy, no,' she whispered and her tears fell anew.

The email back from Elouise was short but not particularly sweet. She wrote,

> Hello Fran.
> It was a surprise to receive this email. You're not usually much of a correspondent. Please don't buy me or give me anything. It's not necessary. I hope you know that. Actually, I've been wanting to apologise for the way I carried on that day when I came with your birthday presents. Maybe I should have been glad to see you cooking for the kids next door? It might have been a good sign of your recovery and me acting like a spoiled teenager put you back a bit. Did it, Aunty Fran? Mum says that's impossible, but she would say that, wouldn't she? At the end of the day I was just jealous I guess, like a kid. You and Uncle Frank were like second parents to me. I know I should be more mature and understanding but it's

> hard sometimes. Maybe you were right about me working with the kids up north. Maybe I'm not mature enough for that kind of work??? They've offered me a six-month placement, from the beginning of next year. Of course, Mum doesn't want me to go. Thinks it's dangerous. Worries about me as a 'young woman on my own'. Too bad you're not around more to make her see sense. Anyway, speaking of Mum, she doesn't need presents either. You know what she needs. Anyway, take care. Did you get the AirPods working? XX Em

Franny pushed the laptop away and reached for her mineral water. She was assiduously avoiding eye contact with Kitchen Frank.

'You want the last of this?' She bent down and handed half a water cracker to Whisky who sat, jammed up against the kitchen stool like the forty-ninth kid at the back of a school bus designed for forty-eight. 'You'll look like one of these soon.'

When the intercom buzzer sounded, Franny jumped, and the dog barked.

'Thank God,' she said. 'Saved by the bell.'

Pressing the buzzer and hearing Sallyanne's voice at the other end diminished Franny's relief a little. Being honest with herself, she had fallen into a hot mess once the initial adrenaline had died down after the Danny encounter. When the police moved in, she had all but collapsed on the Salernos' back step. And when the formalities were over, a trembling Franny had been escorted home by a lovely young officer and dosed up on sweet black tea.

'By the sound of things, you were very brave over there, Mrs Calderwood,' Constable Reyes had said. 'Things could have worked out differently, to be honest though.'

'Yes, it was definitely my Cagney and Lacey moment,' Franny had replied. 'I acted before I thought. Pure instinct, I guess. What else could you do?'

'Not sure what a Cagney and Lacey moment is.' The officer had looked to be in his early twenties. 'But you'd be surprised how many people choose to do very little . . . and I don't necessarily blame them.' Once he'd let himself out, Franny had poured a large Bowmore whisky and sat on the lounge-room floor, a dog on either side of her.

The buzzer sounded again.

'Franny, you letting me in? Everything okay?' Sallyanne's tone held genuine concern.

'Sorry, dear, got distracted. Come in.'

Dodging the dogs, Sallyanne smiled at Franny then followed her to the kitchen bench, her hands full. It had been a couple of days since they'd really seen each other. Both households retreated into themselves immediately after the drama, although a delivery man had arrived at Franny's gate the day before carrying an outlandishly large bouquet of flowers accompanied by a beautiful thank-you card from the Salernos.

'The kids made this for you.' Sallyanne pointed to an ungainly but lush-looking chocolate cake now on the counter. 'And this is, of course, from Joshie.' She held out a painting depicting what was presumably Franny, dressed in a superhero cape covered in dog pictures. She flew through the air, her long white hair with its distinctive black stripe streaming behind her.

Franny was about to protest all the gift-giving when Sallyanne walked quickly towards her and wrapped her in hug. Before another word was said, Franny felt tears shuddering through the younger woman's body.

'Oh Franny,' murmured Sallyanne. 'How do I ever thank you?'

Two strong Darjeelings and a slice of cake each later, Franny had recounted everything that happened on the fateful afternoon and

Sallyanne had outlined the legal turmoil now facing her soon-to-be ex-husband.

'And Dee?' asked Franny, switching the kettle on again and running a finger along the cake's icing, scooping up runoff.

'That kid is made of surprisingly tough stuff I think,' said Sallyanne. 'She has to be conflicted about the state of her dad, I mean she clearly thinks he's got something wrong with him, but she's not talking about that right now. She is, however, talking about you.'

Franny raised her eyes questioningly, continuing to suck chocolate off her finger.

'If you weren't her hero before you definitely are now. She could not believe you came running with that big clunk of an award—you left it behind by the way—but she's also worried about you. Said you looked pretty shattered by the end of it all.'

'Uhf, there's nothing to worry about with me. I just needed a minute to collect myself.'

'You've only recently had a pretty major health emergency,' said Sallyanne, nodding towards Franny's leg. 'And let's face it, you're over sixty-five.'

'For starters, Nurse Salerno, I am not over sixty-five.' Franny spat out the words. 'I *am* sixty-five, on the knocker.'

She glared at Sallyanne for a moment then both women burst out laughing.

'And little Josh,' asked Franny as their giggles subsided. 'Does he know what's gone on?'

Sallyanne's face clouded over. 'Yes, I was pretty straight with him. Felt I had to be. One look at me and Dee and he knew something massive had taken place. I mean, I was a mess. I don't know, do you think I did the right thing?' Sallyanne looked at Franny beseechingly. 'The experts say kids know when there's a major drama going on and if you don't level with them, they make stuff up and generally it is worse than the truth. Often they blame themselves.' She pushed her empty cup towards Franny. 'Anyway, he knows all of it to a degree now. Especially about you.'

'For the last time, there is nothing to know about me.'

Sallyanne smiled ruefully then sat forward in her chair. 'Franny, I need to talk to you about things. I need to apologise.'

The kettle had boiled. Franny busied herself making a fresh brew of tea.

'I did the wrong thing after your accident. I did the wrong thing and I'm so sorry for it.' Here, Sallyanne's voice cracked and tears slipped down her cheeks. 'These days people don't leave their kids with neighbours and that sort of thing. Not like they did when I was growing up. You know what it's like. You don't see kids riding out on their bikes for hours on end without any adult supervision. Hell, you hardly even see them walking to school on their own.'

'Sallyanne, you don't need to explain yourself to me.' Franny pushed a hot cup of tea towards her neighbour. 'In your place I'm sure I would have done the same thing.'

Sallyanne's hand came down hard on the bench in front of her, making the cup rattle. 'That's just it though isn't it, Franny? You wouldn't have. You would never fucking do something like that. You're just not that petty.' She bit her lip, uncomfortable with her language. 'But people talk and people judge these days. It's bad enough being a single working mother. Fail, fail, fail says my score-card. And then, to think I'd *outsource* my kids to *some woman* in the street, well that's how people see it, how they say it. And when I say people I, of course, mean other mothers. So much for the famous sisterhood.' Sallyanne slugged back tea like it was straight vodka then, realising how hot it was, spluttered it out. Patting herself down, she looked around for a cloth to clean up. 'God, sorry Franny.'

Franny grabbed a clean tea towel and wiped the benchtop. Smiling, she then dabbed at Sallyanne's chin like she was a baby. 'It's okay, honey. Take a breath.'

'Anyway,' continued Sallyanne. 'I'm not apologising just because you helped with Danny and Dee this week. I need you to understand that. I already knew I'd done the wrong thing and I didn't trust my gut. I went with my fear and my insecurities instead. The kids have been hating me for it. They've been so angry with me. To be honest, I think that's part of the reason Dee is okay right now. She sees this as irrefutable proof you should be in our lives. She figures there's no way I can wiggle out of it.' Sallyanne looked Franny directly in the eye. 'And we should be in each other's lives, Franny, if you'll still have us that is.'

Looking over at Kitchen Frank, Franny smiled. 'Luvvie, touched as I am by all of this, and can I reiterate that I do not blame you for pulling back, I've been making a mess of my life for quite a while now and you have enough on your plate besides getting involved with that. You were and always will be right to protect yourself and your cubs. I won't hear another word about it.'

'But that's not what friends do, Franny. They don't run away when things get hard. They don't turn their back when things get painful. They step forward.' Sallyanne's tears came again. She swiped at her eyes with the tea towel Franny had left beside her.

'For Pete's sake.' Franny moved in and hugged the younger woman. 'You must stop being so, so hard on yourself. You've got years of self-recrimination and hair-shirt wearing ahead of you, dear. God, you haven't even fucked up your kids yet. Wait till you start believing that. And you haven't mistakenly spent half your forties worrying about frown lines and cellulite. Don't be wasting all this energy already. Save some of it for your fifties at least!'

Sallyanne looked at Franny and started laughing once more, wet sobs occasionally bursting through. 'You're a one-off, Mrs Calderwood, I'll give you that. But seriously.'

'Yes?' Franny sat down on the stool beside Sallyanne and put her chin in her hand in an exaggerated form of concentration. 'Do go on.'

'You have to be straight with us now, with me at the very least. We have to be straight with each other.'

Taking away her hand, Franny sat upright.

Sallyanne continued. 'You have to talk about Frank when you want to, Franny. You have to say his name. We'd love to hear about him. We want to. And we want to know when you're sad and hurting and if other things are bothering you. You don't have to bottle it up.' Sallyanne stopped suddenly, an uncomfortable look spreading across her face. 'Sorry, I didn't mean anything by that.'

'By what?' Franny looked confused for a moment then a lightbulb came on. 'Ah, bottle. I see. No pun intended, hey?' Before Sallyanne could protest, Franny held up one of her long slim fingers. 'It's all right, dear. I know you weren't making a crack. But as we're talking about being in each other's lives, and talking about being honest and so forth, then I guess this needs to be addressed. Speaking of.' She looked up at the clock. It was ten minutes to six. 'Don't mind if I do.' She moved the tea-making equipment out of the way and went to the drinks trolley to grab a bottle of Botanist gin. 'Fancy one?' she said to Sallyanne.

The other woman looked uncomfortable.

'Oh, don't look so terrified. Yes, I've been known to go too far but I'm not giving it up altogether. It's just not happening.' Franny shook her head to stop Sallyanne butting in. 'I like a drink. I like all the things that go with it. What I do in my own time is my own business and, while I would like to think I'd never end up in the—let's call it "situation"—that I did recently, I'm human, which means I cannot make bulletproof promises. Obviously, I don't want anything like that to happen again. But I might fail, or it might take a while. That's just the reality. I adore you lot but I'm not a fairy-tale version of an old lady.'

'You're not an old lady.'

'Good. I'm not an old lady. Even more reason I'm going to have a gin and tonic when I feel like one, while I still bloody can. End of story. I want to be around you and the kids. As shocking as that is to me, I really do. But I also want to live my own life. Without walking on eggshells. I would never put Dee and Josh at risk, I hope you know that. That is the one thing I will always guarantee, but I will not become someone else because it suits you. Do you see?' She opened the gin bottle and sniffed the lid appreciatively.

Sallyanne reached forward and put her hand on top of Franny's. 'I know that, Franny. I really do. But as a nurse, for your own sake, I feel honour-bound to encourage you to pull back a bit, if not completely stop.'

'Well don't. Don't feel honour-bound. Feel like my friend and equal, not my nurse, and shut the hell up. And occasionally have a prosecco with me. I know you youngsters love that stuff.'

'You're incorrigible, you know that don't you.' Sallyanne sat back and accepted her drink, which Franny had garnished with a stalk of rosemary and a slice of orange. After taking one extended sip Sallyanne said, 'Damn it, you really do make a good drink.'

'They make it this way in Scotland, so I hear.' Franny clinked her glass against the other woman's. 'Slàinte,' she said.

Afterwards, with her neighbour gone and another sliver of chocolate cake consumed, Franny replayed her conversation with Sallyanne about parents and how much responsibility they take for the fate and behaviour of their kids. If she had Ange Caliendo in front of her now, Franny wondered, would she be so sympathetic? Would she offer any words of reassurance to the people who had raised The Evil Prick?

So much had happened in recent times that Franny had become blissfully distracted from the plight of the Caliendo and Pavlos families. She wished with all her heart she could leave it that way.

33

Art therapy

Firewheel Number One was the painting Franny considered to be the best in her series so far. She stepped back to look at it one more time before it disappeared into the packing she had specially ordered and was delighted with the intricate details she had achieved, the tiny human hands and faces secreted within the botanical details of the plant. She turned to Studio Frank and said, 'These old paws can still wield a brush, my darling.'

Once she'd finished packaging it all up, Franny added Anthea's details to the massive label the courier company had supplied then attached it to the parcel. Grabbing her mobile phone, she typed out an SMS.

> Franny: I think you should be home with all your chakras aligned by now. Will you be at the house this afternoon between 3 and 5?

Within seconds a response came back and a quick exchange was underway.

Anthea: Yes home safely. And yes I will be home this afternoon. What's up?

Franny: Shooting something over to you. Hope you like it. My way of saying thank you for the other week.

Anthea: Not necessary F. I will always be here for you. Regardless. xx

Franny looked at the text message and shook her head sadly. 'You just cannot be a stone-cold bitch can you, Anthea?' she said aloud. 'Still gotta add the kisses.'

That job out of the way, Franny moved on to the next one on her list, an email to Marg.

Dear Marg,
Welcome home. I know from Anthea the retreat is over. I hope you both had a lovely time. I want to say a sincere, if somewhat belated, thank you for coming to my aid after the Swan Dive. You dropped everything to help someone who probably doesn't deserve that level of care. I won't beat about the bush. I am ashamed at how shoddily I have treated you in recent times. Ashamed and sorry. You have never been anything but kind to me. I often told Frank you were an unexpected asset he brought to our marriage. You've been a sister, in law and in actions, and also a friend. I'm not sure what I can do to make things up to you but I know that I have to. I hope you will let me.

Franny let out a deep breath and pressed send. 'Jesus, this mea-culpa stuff is heavy going,' she said to Studio Frank. 'No wonder the politicians never do it.'

Just as she was about to close the laptop her inbox pinged with a new message. *Bit soon for Marg to be getting back to me*, thought

Franny before noting the sender of the missive was her old gallery pal, Darrien Bromley. She took a deep breath. A few days earlier Franny, buoyed by two glasses of sparkling burgundy and some re-runs of *Sex and the City*, had sent a random message to Darrien along with a couple of photographs of her series of botanic artworks. Almost immediately she regretted the decision but she didn't know how to un-send an email. She clicked on his response now with a mixture of dread and anticipation.

> Dear Franny,
> You'll appreciate how surprised I was to hear from you. Surprised and delighted of course. Here I was thinking you'd had enough of the gallery world, and of me to be honest, when all this time you've been beavering away, creating some of your best work yet. You clever minx you.
>
> You say you have been 'pottering' and hanging around the botanic gardens like a bag lady. Keep it up. You've somehow managed to make this new series traditional and fresh at once. I can already think of a swag of customers who'll go ga-ga for it. And the gardens themselves, we MUST do something with them. Hand clap! I see event tie-ins (did someone say party??????), sponsorships, tea towels, greeting cards, you name it. There is so much to discuss. I'm off to a fair in London tonight so how about I call you when I get back? I'll only be gone for five days.
>
> Obviously, you will not go near another gallery while I'm gone. Not even as a customer or viewer yourself. You're all mine. I have missed you so much and cannot wait to be back hatching plans and swigging champers with you soon. Well done Contessa Calderwood. You're back and I for one am so excited I might need a flat lemonade and a lie down.
> Take care and thank you, thank you, thank you for sending these through. You've given me something wonderful to think

> about while sardined in cattle class (see how much I need a big show $!) for the next zillion hours. Bless you!
> Big kisses xxx Darrien

'Well, well, well.' Franny looked over at Desk Frank and smiled comically. 'He hasn't changed. Still way too over the top. I forgot how carried away he gets. Parties and sponsorships, for God's sake.'

She stood up and went over to her table covered with working sketches. Recently, a Tasmanian Flax Lily had captured her attention. This was the kind of plant Franny loved to depict. At a distance it seemed pretty, with striking lilac-blue petals. Up close, its bold yellow stamen had an ugly, insect-like quality that she would heighten dramatically. Its attractively plump purple berries were in fact quite toxic. The lily's genus name came from Diana, the huntress, frequently depicted carrying a quiver of arrows with a hound at her feet. 'Hello, my lovely Diana,' said Franny. 'Looks like when I'm finished with you, you might be going out into the world.' She gave a wink and left the room.

At a quarter past four Franny's intercom buzzed. After Sallyanne's last visit the two women agreed the children would come to Franny's place after school occasionally, if Sallyanne was working late.

'Don't assume I can do it all the time though, and don't expect me to feed them some kind of organic, gluten-free muck,' Franny had explained to her neighbour when the arrangements were made. 'I'm not staff.'

'Of course not, Franny. What on earth do you mean?' Sallyanne had been surprised and confused by this outburst.

'I just hear, or used to hear, friends complaining about the rules they were expected to follow when spending time with grandkids. Mostly it was their daughters or their son's wives laying down the law. Here were my friends giving up their free time to take care of these kids yet they got treated like mentally deficient, unpaid nannies, not grandparents at all. I don't know when all this started but my point of view is that grown offspring can bloody well open up their wallets and book a place at the local childcare centre if they want a checklist followed and report card given. Otherwise, they can hand over the little darlings to people who love and spoil them and expect a happy, healthy child to be returned.'

Sallyanne had looked at Franny with amusement. 'Okay, you've been thinking about that diatribe for a while, haven't you?'

Sheepishly, Franny had said, 'It used to drive me batty when they'd tell me the special foods they had to buy in and the regimes they were ordered to follow. I mean, you read about entitlement in the press but it's only when you see it in full flight you begin to understand.'

'Well, with my dad dead and mum unwell and living in another state, I've never had the chance to flex that entitlement muscle. Danny's family would help out in the old days but I didn't have to work as many hours then. And, of course, Danny, for all his faults, was around. Although the way he treated Joshie sometimes, I think Whisky would have done a better job. So no, Franny, you won't be getting any checklists from me. Indeed, I am pretty sure when it comes to food, they'll do much better here than they'd do with me at home. In fact, if they could bring me back a doggy bag now and then I wouldn't complain.'

Franny had laughed at that. 'Good to hear.' She'd held out her hand for Sallyanne to shake but the other woman had hesitated.

'What now?' Franny had asked. 'You are not going to go on about the drinking because you know I would never—'

'Not the drinking,' Sallyanne had replied. 'But what about the love and spoiling bit?'

Franny had grinned. 'That I believe I can take care of.'

Franny felt a slight flutter in her stomach as she moved to let the children in. *Get a grip, old woman!* Hands fingering the long braid of hair twined around her head, she told Whisky and Soda to 'sit'.

'Yes.' She spoke into the contraption at the door, her voice low.

'Franny, it's us. Remember, we're coming for tea.' Josh's voice was pitched at its highest. More of an excited squeak.

'Us?' Franny grinned down at the dogs whose backsides jiggled because of waggling tails.

'Josh and Dee, Josh and Dee,' he squealed again. 'Let us in.'

Pushing the buzzer and opening the door simultaneously, she let the dogs rush out to meet the visitors. Josh threw his school bag on the path, allowing himself to be smothered with dog kisses. Meanwhile Dee sidestepped the boy-and-canine-lovefest and headed for the door. She looked at Franny warily before moving into the lounge room and placing her bag on a kitchen stool. Standing beside the drinks trolley, she looked out at the newly landscaped garden beyond.

'Wow, it's all changed. Looks good. You happy?' Dee turned back to look at Franny.

'I'm happy now that you're here.' As she spoke Franny saw the girl's eyes fill with tears. 'This is the part where we hug, dear.' She held out both arms.

When Josh came in and discovered the two of them embracing, he charged directly at them. Franny's still-recovering limb buckled beneath her. She let out a cry, half collapsing to the floor.

'Shit, Joshie, what have you done?' Dee bent down beside Franny, concern spreading across her face.

Josh froze, shocked tears gathering like storm clouds. Franny allowed herself to slide to the carpet before releasing a contented exhalation. She held her arms out to him this time and said, 'It's all right, matey. I just lost my balance.' With that, Whisky jumped on top of his owner, licking her face and neck and Franny looked up at the little boy and smiled. 'Well get in here,' she said.

By half past seven Franny, Dee and Josh had polished off a dinner of lamb chops and minty peas, stacked the dishwasher and practised creating cats' eyes with liquid eyeliner. Now Dee was fiddling with her phone while supposedly doing her homework as Josh thumped a miniature tennis ball around the other end of the house, entertaining an ecstatic Whisky. Beside the armchair, Soda lay by her owner's feet, quietly snoring.

When Dee's phone buzzed, the retriever raised her head in mild curiosity but did not move. 'That's Mum. Go time.' Dee stood up to gather her things. 'Come on, Joshie,' she called out.

Franny was sorry to see them go, mostly because her phone had also been busy during the evening with text messages from Anthea. In deference to her babysitting duties she had vetoed her usual six o'clock radio-silence rule just in case there was an emergency and Sallyanne needed to call. As a result of this she found herself promising to call her old friend once the children went home.

Josh and Whisky reappeared in the lounge room, both looking a little worse for wear. Clearly the ball had secreted itself beside some rarely dusted corner of a room at some point and boy and dog were dusted with cobwebs.

'Come here,' said Franny. She grabbed a kitchen sponge and dabbed at the little boy's face and clothes.

'That's gross,' Josh said. 'You wiped the table with that.'

Franny laughed. 'That's nothing. I wiped Whisky's bum with it this morning. Now vamoose. Go home.'

Josh looked at her aghast. 'You did not?' he said, sounding unsure.

Franny sniffed exaggeratedly, screwing up her face like she was smelling something rank.

'You did not,' Josh whined.

'Don't be such a moron, she's joking,' said Dee, grabbing her brother by the wrist with one hand and throwing his backpack over one shoulder along with hers. 'All right, Franny, we better hustle. Thanks again for a yummy dinner. And for this.' She gestured to the eyeliner stashed in her pocket. 'You're the best.'

Franny accompanied the children to the front door to buzz them out the gate. On the way Josh turned back and wrapped his arms, gently this time, around her waist. 'Do you know how much I missed you, Franny?' he murmured.

'No, how much?' A lump formed in Franny's throat.

'I had a painting of Luna in a frame in my bedroom and I took it out and made one of you and put that in instead.'

Franny crouched down to hug him. 'Really? I'm so touched.' She kissed him on the forehead and smoothed his slightly sweaty blond hair. 'Maybe you can put Luna's back now, considering you can see me all the time again.'

'Why don't you just get another frame from Mum? You doofus,' said Dee. 'Then you could have pictures of them both.'

'But it's my favourite frame,' he complained.

'Bring the frame and the paintings over,' said Franny. 'Next time we're together we'll try to make a new one you like almost as much.'

Josh jumped up and down on the spot. 'Goody, goody, goody.' He clapped his hands. 'When? When? When?'

Franny laughed and gently nudged him towards the door. 'Let's get you home from this visit first and worry about the next one later.'

With the children gone, she poured herself a glass of pinot noir and dialled Anthea's number. While the phone rang it struck Franny that she could not recall the last time she'd sipped a glass of wine at night while chatting to a friend. Sitting down in the armchair, she looked over at Lounge Room Frank. 'I know, I know,' she said.

'You know what?' Anthea said, picking up at the other end of the line. 'That is you isn't it, Fran?'

'Yes, yes, it's me. Hello. Ignore me. I was talking to Frank.'

'You were what?'

'I was talking to his picture. Forget about it. How are you? How was the trip?'

Anthea spoke in a gentler voice. 'Do you speak to his picture often, Fran?'

'Daily, possibly hourly. It's not weird.' She took a sip of wine.

'Of course it's not. Perish the thought.' Anthea's tone sharpened a tad. 'Are you drinking while you're on this call?'

'I'm having a glass of cheeky pinot. It's my first drink of the day if you must know. You'd be having one too if you were here with me so don't start.'

A sigh came through the phone. 'First drink of the day, hey? Is that the influence of the kids?'

'I promised their mother there'd be no drinky-poos while I'm on duty. I'm sticking to my word.'

'Well, that's something then.' Suddenly Anthea seemed to remember the reason for the call. 'Anyway, that painting you sent.'

'Yes?'

'Fran, it's incredible, beautiful, really fabulous. You sure I can keep it?'

'Of course. I wanted to say thank you. Although I may need to borrow it back for a show sometime soonish.'

'Whoa Nelly, slow down. A day of no drinking, or little drinking as yet, babysitting, a painting and now a show. What the hell is going on?'

Franny chuckled. 'The old girl's got a few surprises in her yet. To be honest I wonder what non-drinkers do with their time. I mean, what's their excuse for not being productive?'

At the other end of the line Anthea's voice was muffled, as if she had placed a hand over the mouthpiece. Within seconds she was speaking clearly again. 'Sorry, Fran, that was me nearly fainting from shock. Dave's gone to make me a vodka.'

'Ha! Three minutes on the phone with me and you're an alcoholic too.'

'Too soon, Fran, too soon. But seriously, what's going on?'

Franny sipped her wine again. 'I don't know. I've been working on this botanical range for a while now and just decided to send Darrien a couple of images on a whim. He liked them.'

'Darrien has always adored your work. Him liking it is not the surprising turn of events, Fran, and you know it. What I'm asking is—'

'Yes, yes I get it. Why am I interested in showing again, that's the sixty-four-dollar question.'

'Basically, yes. Hang on.' There was shuffling at the other end of the line and the sound of a door opening and closing. The next minute Franny recognised the unmistakable sound of her friend lighting up a cigarette.

'Anthea Martini, are you smoking over there?'

'Shh, I've just ducked outside with my voddie. You know I only smoke when I drink but I have to go out in the yard. I can't stand the holier-than-thou looks Dave gives me.'

'Reformed smokers. The worst.' Suddenly Franny went quiet.

'Fran, are you there? You all right?'

'I'm here.' She finished the glass of wine but didn't get up for a refill.

'What's the matter?'

'I just had a flashback to Phone Bar. It felt like when we were in our twenties and you spent that year living in NZ. Remember, Anth? We'd ring each other every Thursday night and smoke and drink and talk for hours.'

'Of course I remember. Those were some of the best conversations of my life.'

Without warning Franny began to cry.

'Franny, what's going on? Are you crying?' Anthea's voice had taken on an agitated tone. 'Franny?'

'It's okay. I'm okay.' The words sputtered out in between sniffles.

'Talk to me, Fran. What's going on?'

Franny stood up and walked over to the wine bottle on the kitchen bench. She looked at Breakfast Bar Frank and took a deep breath. Refilling her glass she said, 'I'm just so sorry, Anth. I'm sorry and I'm ashamed. I don't deserve you as a friend.'

'I'm not sure where this is coming from but you don't need to apologise. Not if you're coming back to me now.'

Franny let out a long, shuddering breath. 'I owe you an explanation. And a lot more.'

'Let it out if you want to, hon, but are you sure you want to do it now, over the phone?'

'I'm on a roll.' Franny gave a sad laugh and continued. 'I've been a terrible friend and I've been a terrible godmother. I've let Frank down and I've turned my back on you. I shouldn't have handled it this way.' She took a gulp of wine and walked over to the windows facing the back garden. Her reflection stared back at her, phone in one hand, wine glass in the other, empty house behind her.

'No one can criticise the way someone else handles grief, Fran, and with the love and the bond you and Frank shared, that grief was always going to be horrendous. I can't pretend I would have handled it any better.'

Franny let out a bitter laugh. 'You handle everything better, my friend,' she said. 'You handle life better. Always have. At this age I think it's safe to say you probably always will.'

'I let you push me away. I didn't fight hard enough.' Anthea's voice broke a little.

'That's bullshit and you know it. You're not a doormat. I respect that about you.'

'I was always here though, Fran. I hope you always felt that.'

Franny began to weep again. 'Can I be honest with you?'

'If not now when, woman?'

'I was angry with you. After Frank died, I was angry with you because I blamed you a bit. I know it's crazy and presumably just one of the stages of grief, but there it is.'

Anthea said nothing but Franny heard what sounded like the stubbing out of a cigarette. After a few tense moments Anthea said, 'Do you still blame me? Are you still angry?'

'God no, of course not. It was stupid. It was never your fault.' Franny turned her back on her reflection and faced the lounge room again. 'It was about the bike ride. That's why I was angry. It's sounds so crazy now. It is crazy.'

'You don't have to go on.'

'No, but I feel like I need to explain. Where the anger was coming from.'

'You've already done that. You did it the night that he died.'

Franny put her wineglass down on the nearest surface, shock vibrating through her. 'What do you mean?' she asked.

'You don't remember? That explains a lot.' Anthea sounded like she was struggling to keep her voice steady. 'When we came with you that night to the hospital, when you had to identify the body, his body, you screamed it at me then. You came out of the room where they had Frank and you collapsed on the corridor floor. You don't remember?'

For a moment Franny understood what people might mean about blood running cold. Hers felt like ice in her veins. Flashes of memories crossed her mind, grainy images from a B-grade film. 'Anthea, no, don't.'

'Yes let's, Fran. Let's get this done now and move on. Think of it as a purge.'

Franny sat back in the armchair. 'You don't have to do this,' she whispered.

Anthea bulldozed on. 'The night Frank died he was riding round to the supermarket and to The Good Drop.'

'Anthea, please,' Franny sobbed.

'Every year, when you got home from the Dog and Duck pinot weekend, Dave and I would come over. Every year.'

Franny remained silent.

'And that's what you screamed at me that night at the hospital, darling,' said Anthea. 'You said he popped out to the shops because he didn't have a stash of ciggies in the house for me.'

'Anthea, no.'

'Yes. He was going to pick up some supplies, you said, and if we hadn't been coming over he would have stayed home.' Anthea began weeping now. 'And, darling, maybe you were right.'

For a few moments both women said nothing, just exchanged sounds of tears. Finally, Franny spoke. 'You know I didn't mean it. You know it wasn't true. It was not your fault. Frank's death was never your fault.'

'I know that, honey,' said Anthea. 'You had to lash out at someone. It was Chris the ice addict's fault. I've always known that but still . . .'

Jesus, Franny thought, *what the hell have I done?*

She said, 'Anthea, can you ever forgive me?'

'There is nothing to forgive, my friend, but please come back to life, come back to our lives. If Frank—'

'Okay, don't invoke the spirit of the dead husband just now,' said Franny recovering her equilibrium slightly. 'Believe me, I know he'd be disgusted.'

Anthea hiccup-laughed. 'Well he'd appreciate the whole mourning widow thing for a little while. He'd expect some drama, preferably with a few sets of lacy black underwear thrown in. But he'd never want you to be alone. He'd never want you to be, well, where you are now. And he'd never, ever expect us to be apart.'

'I know and—' Franny tried but failed to interrupt.

'It's time we faced some realities, darling,' Anthea continued. 'The older I get, the more I see life as an accumulation of losses.'

'Is this supposed to be uplifting?'

'Hear me out. My point is that we lose so much along the journey, everything from our pelvic floor control to our eyesight, from beloved friends to husbands.'

'Your point?'

'So we need to be careful now, Franny. We have to hang on to whatever precious things we can, for as long as we can. Do you know what I mean? We've got to jealously protect the things we love. It's now or never.'

Franny let out a long and exhausted-sounding sigh. 'He wrote me an incredible letter, Anth. I have to show it to you. He told me what he wanted for me.'

'Do you mean if he died? Frank wrote you a letter in case he died? That doesn't really sound like him.'

'No, it was nothing like that. You'll understand when you see.'

'When I see? Does that mean I can come over sometime?

'Of course you can!' She paused for a moment then said, 'Look, how about next Saturday night? You, Dave and Ellie, if you can all make it. I'd like you to meet the family next door, my friends next door. Meet them properly. I'll double-check they're free.'

Anthea hesitated then said, 'That sounds lovely, Fran. Really lovely.'

'Can I tell you one more thing before you go?'

'Tell me anything sweetheart. I'm not going anywhere.'

'It wasn't just ciggies he would have been going out for that night.'

'Franny, really, let's leave it.' Anthea sounded tired.

'It was tonic water too. In the car on the way home he did mention not having smokes for you but he also listened to me moan about being full up to pussy's bow with good pinot. We laughed and I said all I craved was a cleansing G and T. But I knew we had run out of tonic.'

'Well, Fran, none of this matters now. It's not relevant. Let it go.'

'I know, Anth, I'll let it go.'

34

The hardest word

Franny looked at the return address on the envelope. There had been a moment's panic earlier when she thought she had misplaced it. When, eventually, it had turned up, crammed at the back of her bedside-table drawer, she had released a breath that immediately morphed into a sob. Now, grabbing the envelope and the letter from Ange Caliendo, still stashed inside the book from Nurse Leslie's last day, she headed to her studio.

'Well, darling, this is it,' she said to Frank in the wedding-day photograph. 'I'm going to use my powers for good instead of evil.'

After her conversation with Anthea, Franny had dedicated an entire morning to painting a tiny portrait of Frank and now it was ready to send. The letter she had written by hand, for Ange to pass on to her nephew, was not terribly long, just two A4 pages. Still, it had taken her a couple of hours and a few re-writes to compose.

'*Ms Caliendos,*' she had commenced eventually, unable to use the word 'dear', '*this is the one and only time you will hear from me. Please believe that and respect it. Please make this clear to your nephew too.*'

Franny had gone on to describe Frank, the life he had lived and the love they had shared. *'I feel compelled to make you understand the very good man we lost that night, you see. If Chris needs a role model he could do worse than my Frank, a man who loved generously and with very little judgement. Frank gave a lot to the people in his life. He gave a lot to me.'*

The painting Franny did of Frank was taken from a photograph of him cooking her dinner inside the tiny kitchen of the Viscount twenty-four-foot caravan at Gumnut Gully Park. She still remembered those pork chops—eaten outside the van in the cold night air, the smell of gum trees mingling with the smell of cooking—as some of the most delicious of her life.

On the back of the portrait Franny had attached a little label that said: *Frank Calderwood: Husband, lover, friend. Gone*. Franny knew that sounded cruel, but she was human and she couldn't let her husband's killer off scot-free. The letter and its sentiments were costing her dearly. He had to know that.

She ended her letter without fanfare, simply laying out the facts. '*This part is for Chris specifically,*' she wrote. '*A good life is one that reaches out and enriches the lives of many others. The decisions you made that night radically changed your own life, Frank's and mine, we know. But what they did more broadly you will never truly understand.*

'I hear you have worked hard to make amends. You have a family who loves you, of that I am convinced. That is the biggest advantage you will have in life. Treasure it!

'I have thought long and hard on whether I can forgive you. And maybe I can. I suspect that I should. What I CANNOT forgive is the thought of you being handed love, support and opportunities and then not making the most of them.

'Because of that night, the world has lost a man who brought joy to others. The way I see it, the least you can do is try to be some kind of karmic replacement. God knows we need it. And, actually, I'm going to try to do the same. In light of this I feel honour-bound to wish you luck and offer you sincere encouragement. For three years all I have thought about is how you killed a part of me that night. Believing that and hating you has killed even more of me. That has to stop now. I'll do my best to get on with things, as must you. More than that I cannot say. Good luck.'

She sealed the portrait and letter in a pristine white envelope, addressed it then turned to Studio Frank. 'Is this what you would have wanted my darling?' she asked him. 'People are always quick to say they know what's on the dead's minds, aren't they? Funny how it often seems to be the exact thing that suits the living. I mean, does Great Aunty Shirley *really* want little half-cousin Mary-Jane singing the theme from *Frozen* at her funeral? And yet.' Grinning, she went over to the photograph and picked it up. Looking closely at the young couple inside the frame, the grin slinked away. Franny was left biting her bottom lip.

She released a shuddering breath then said, 'All right, the time has come, the deed is done. I'm off to walk the mutts and post this bloody thing.' Kissing Frank's image lightly she added, 'And, while I might not be one hundred per cent sure what you would have wanted, I know for sure what you wouldn't have. I'm sorry, darling. Forgive me.'

EPILOGUE

The happy hour

Nancy Friol's husband was dead. The minute Franny read the post she found herself wondering if too much tantric sex had played a role.

'Jesus, I'm a nasty old bitch,' she said to Breakfast Bar Frank then returned her attention to the laptop, automatically moving the cursor over the tie-dyed Venus symbol and clicking.

Nancy's personal Facebook page was already covered in messages of condolence. Some of the names Franny recognised from The Wuthering Club. Part-way down she saw a post from the much-lauded son in Berkeley. His name turned out to be Marley. Franny bit back a smart-arse comment and concentrated on his words.

> I'll be back in Australia in two days. In the meantime, I wanted to thank you all, on behalf of Mum, for your words of sympathy regarding the passing of our dad and her husband, Clive Friol. Over a long and happy marriage of 36 years they weathered many storms, from Mum's breast cancer to the car accident where we lost my brother, Fergus. Some of you will know he was just 17. Mum knows there has been an outpouring of grief from her Facebook friends and has asked me to thank you. Dad's stroke last week came out of the blue. He was happy and healthy the day before. Mum,

> in her usual positive way, is glad he didn't hang around to suffer 'just for her sake' as she puts it. They were an amazing couple. Dad the lawyer, always so straight and Mum, well . . . you guys must know what she is like. Anyway, she is having some time off social media but insisted I wish you all love and light. She also told me to say Dad's spirit animal was a Tawny Frogmouth, so if you see one unexpectedly in your garden in the next few days you must shout out HELLO, CLIVE. These were her instructions to me word-for-word. I do what I am told. Thank you again for your kind wishes. I'll sign off by referencing a quote from a book I know Mum loves, Mitch Albom's The Five People You Meet in Heaven. It's something about dying not being the end of everything because what happens on earth is only the beginning.

Franny pushed herself back from the table and stared up at the ceiling. 'No one gets through this life without taking some serious body blows, do they, darling?' she whispered to Frank. 'You were always better than me at giving people the benefit of the doubt. Remember that time you cried in the traffic because the woman in the car beside you was howling while you were both waiting at the lights?' Pulling the laptop towards her, preparing to write, she looked over at his photograph, tears in her eyes. 'God you were a sop sometimes!' She laughed manically.

Franny clicked on the message box on the top right-hand corner of Nancy's Facebook page and began to type.

> Dear Nancy,
> Franny Calderwood here, fellow member of The Wuthering Club. You might know me better as Lady Marmalade. I see that your husband, Clive, has died. I just wanted to say how sorry I am to hear that.

Franny sat back for a moment, wondering if she should just end her message there. Instead, she typed:

> From your comments and your son's it sounds like you and Clive had a lot of fun together. As I get older I realise how rare and important that is. I am also sorry for the other losses and hardships you've experienced in your life. You never reference those in any of your posts, which I understand, of course, but your energy and positivity for life is remarkable and, dare I say, admirable. I truly hope you can maintain it now and be comforted by it. My husband died three years ago and no one would say I have handled it well. I won't sugar-coat it: his absence cuts me to the quick at some point every day, but I think I am getting closer to seeing the light. Somehow, I think you'll get there faster. I genuinely hope so. And I'll keep my eyes peeled for Tawny Frogmouths. Take care and come back to The Wuthering Club when you're ready. Franny.

Franny closed the laptop and looked around her. Up until an hour before, the kitchen had looked like a team of hungry bears had been through and ransacked it, every cupboard open, every pot used. Now it was reasonably serene.

Entertaining, she discovered, was a different beast when tackled on your own. Her successful hosting of Mother's Day for Sallyanne had been buffered by the help and distraction of Dee and Josh. This time around the flight was a solo one and the experience was as lonely and exhausting as she had spent the last three years imagining it would be. But it was also, at odd moments, quite satisfying.

'Well, I reckon we've done it,' she said now, easing herself off the kitchen stool and rubbing her aching back. Whisky, who had succumbed to boredom and fallen asleep near her feet, jumped to attention.

'You know, little matey, I think you and I, and her ladyship Soda, should have a bit of a W-A-L-K before the guests arrive later. See if we can't wear down a little of your terrier energy.' Whisky put his head to one side and wagged his tail. 'Let me just text Ellie and make sure she's organised the cake and remind Sallyanne to bring the ice.'

Pre-planning, early organising and outsourcing were the three things Franny decided would make the Saturday night dinner party, and any future such events, work for her.

'Look away, darling,' she said to Breakfast Bar Frank, picking up her mobile phone and scrolling through her contacts. 'I know you liked to do and organise everything yourself but it's a new regime now.'

On Thursday she had shopped for the food and drinks. On Friday she had cooked as much of the meal as possible, polishing glasses and setting the table while eating a packet of corn chips for dinner that night. This morning she had purchased and arranged the flowers before cleaning the house.

Her outfit for the evening was laid out on the bed. Choosing it brought on a pang. What she wanted to wear was one of her glamorous kaftans with its big batwing sleeves. What she decided on was velvet pants and a closefitting merino wool jersey.

'Guess if I am going to be pulling things in and out of the oven and pouring drinks myself I should do so without the risk of combusting. Nothing ruins the vibe of a dinner party like a trip to emergency,' she said to Bedroom Frank, then made a tiny violin-playing motion.

Calling for Soda, Whisky already scratching at the front door to escape, she grabbed the dogs' leads and headed out.

Checking in with herself Franny realised she felt tired but pleasantly so. Her slow-cooked beef cheek was, based on her most recent taste test, delicious and she was eager to see what everyone thought of the kid-friendly cocktail she had invented: sparkling apple cider with a sprig of thyme and a slice of orange. She had downed three of them the night before.

As the dogs ambled along on autopilot towards the park they normally went to, Franny tugged on their leads.

'No, no, this way,' she said. 'Your old mistress needs a quicker walk today. I must have already done one million steps getting this bloody dinner together.'

At her small local park, the rainbow lorikeets were staging a town-hall meeting. The tallest tree was alive with their loud bickering, prompting Whisky to bark and strain against his lead, vainly hoping to bring home a parrot.

With both dogs running free, distracted enough by birds and odours to give her some peace, Franny sat down heavily and gratefully on a piece of fitness equipment designed for people to do sit ups.

'Well it works well for sit downs too,' she muttered to herself, then closed her eyes to let the very last of the day's sun warm her skin.

'Bloody hell!' Franny bolted upright. Heavy dog paws rested on her thighs and the snout of Cindy the Staffordshire Terrier loomed at her, ready to plant some wet dog kisses.

'Cindy, Cindy, get off her. Heel,' Antonio's voice called out. The dog ignored him.

'Alrighty, little lady,' said Franny, gently shoving the tank of a canine off her legs and back onto the ground. 'Show some restraint.'

As Antonio walked towards her, Franny realised Whisky and Soda were by his side, Whisky jumping up and down excitedly.

'Franny, ciao,' he called out. 'Haven't seen you here for a long time.'

'Hello to you too. I can tell from Whisky's reaction you're still carrying around those bits of dried liver in your trouser pockets.' Franny screwed up her nose. 'Disgusting!'

Antonio grinned and bent down to the dog. '*Sedersi amico, sedersi.*' The terrier grudgingly lowered his hairy backside to the ground and snatched at the dog treat being offered. 'Your little pal here doesn't think it's disgusting.'

'Yes well that dog has been known to eat his own vomit so he's hardly Gordon Ramsay. Anyway, how are you, Antonio? How is Nella?'

'She is good, I am good. You know, just getting on with it. We've got a trip planned, going back to Sicily in a few weeks so that's keeping her busy. Giving her something to stress about.' Antonio chuckled. 'What about you?'

'I'm pretty good, actually. Been painting a lot. Had the garden re-done.'

'Ah, I would like to see it one day. And you should see ours. Nella got a cubby house built out back for the grandkids.'

'Isn't there only one?'

'Yes, but she has ambitions.' He laughed again.

'Where is Cindy going while you're away?' asked Franny.

'Ach.' Antonio hit his palm against his forehead. 'Don't talk about it. She's breaking my balls, excuse the language. We're taking her to a new place and Nella is sick with worry. I thought we'd be free when the kids moved out but that wife of mine loves the bloody dog like it's another one of them. Frankly she worries about Cindy more than she did about them.'

Franny grinned, paused, then said, 'What about if she stayed with me, with us?' She pointed a few metres away where Cindy, Soda and Whisky clustered around a gum tree, staring fixedly upwards into its branches like bodyguards checking for snipers. 'You know they get along.'

Antonio looked at Franny and raised his eyebrows. 'We couldn't. No. I mean . . .'

'Yes you could. Ask Nella.'

'Want to come back now, have a vino, we could talk about it?'

Franny looked at her watch. It was almost six o'clock. She still had to do her hair and feed the dogs. Her dinner guests were due at seven.

'Actually, I've got people coming over,' she said.

'Sure, whatever. Another time.' Antonio whistled to his dog. 'Cindy. *Andiamo*,' he called.

Franny touched his arm lightly. 'Seriously, I'm having a dinner party. They're coming at seven. How about tomorrow? Sometime before dinner. I'll text Nella beforehand. Maybe I'll have leftovers to bring.'

'Leftovers you say,' said Antonio. 'I always did like it when you guys entertained.'

'Don't get too excited. This time it's me cooking, not Frank.'

'True,' said Antonio with a cheeky grin, 'but I'll take my chances. After all, he must have taught you something.'

FRANNY'S VERSION OF
Botanist gin and tonic

Adapted from Bruichladdich Distillery, Islay, Scotland

Pour 1 × shot (and a half, depending on your mood) of Botanist gin over a liberal amount of ice in a large chardonnay wine glass. Add a slice of orange and a sprig of rosemary. Finish with a small bottle of Fever Tree Mediterranean tonic. Sit back and relax!

FRANNY'S
Mushroom tagliatelle with thyme

Wing the measurements.

Tagliatelle
Button mushrooms
Dried forest or porcini mushrooms
Thyme, fresh preferably
Full cream
Garlic-infused olive oil and a knob of butter
Dry white wine

Boil the kettle and pour hot water over the dried mushrooms in a small bowl. Let them steep for a while. Meanwhile, cook the pasta to your liking. Run it under cold water to stop from sticking. Fry the button mushrooms in a little garlic oil and butter. Add the thyme and salt and pepper to taste. Drain the dried mushrooms, chop them a little and add, with a glug of white wine. Have a slug yourself while you're at it. Add pasta, then cream. Serve with radicchio and fennel salad. (Consider a Bellarine pinot noir on the side.)

Acknowledgements

I used to say invoices were my favourite things to write; that may now have to change to acknowledgements. Fun does not begin to describe the creation of *Happy Hour.* Writing it has brought so much joy to me, and I have a village to thank—those who helped nurture that joy, getting it ready to go out into the big brave world.

Like Franny, I'm blessed with exceptional friends, those I call my sister-girls. Thank you; hopefully you know who you are. Special mention to the Derry girls, Jules, Andy, Leanne and Jennifer, who, in particular, read a little about Franny's isolationist policies and immediately said, 'You know I'd never let you do that, don't you?' To Kez and Maz, for Phone Bar. To Cindy, for 'brown drinks' and lending your name to a Staffie. To Simon, for trying to get me to a red carpet somewhere. To the Mrs Underhill Book Club, for the good food, good talk and good insights. And to Andy H. for keeping me employed.

Thanks to my many teachers and classmates over the years, in workshops and writing events too numerous to mention. Special thanks to Antoni and the Masterclass clan for elevating my thinking from hobbyist writer to potential professional, and making it feel okay to be obsessive. To my first readers, Andrea and Susan, a gigantic thankyou for your time, respect and honesty. It was momentous.

Some angels swoop on down in the final act. Marion W., you're one of these. Thanks for making me feel like the real deal and providing insights into being a grandparent. Thanks also to the Lazy Writer's Lock-in crew: your humility, good humour and work ethic buoys me more than you know.

To my treasured mum, Mary (Maureen) Byron née Mangan, for pretending everything I do is brilliant; I know you would be out hand-selling this book at your local Readings if your dicky hip allowed it.

Thank you, Jason, for tolerating 'the book' coming before all else at times, and for keeping up the supply of martinis and wisecracks; you're not quite Frank but then he's not quite real.

We're blessed with a wonderful writing community in Australia, and I must thank the Australian Society of Authors whose 'Speed Pitching' program catapulted *Happy Hour* from Word document to novel. Thanks also to Coco at Affirm, whose initial interest got the ball rolling; I look forward to your brilliant literary career evolving, as you clearly have great taste (wink, wink).

Thanks to my publisher-angel, Kelly Fagan, and the entire Allen & Unwin team. Each of you has been a pleasure to deal with, helping me to produce the best book possible and making it feel easy along the way. (Special thanks to Emma Rafferty, who flatters even when slicing and dicing: a delightfully cunning skill.) Finally—crucially—thanks to my agent, Grace Heifetz, for your outrageous work ethic and super-wattage smile: from our first conversation you knew Franny better than I did and that enthusiasm changed my life.